NO WAY BACK-

The Underworlds

Also in the series:

Taken With a Dark Desire: The Underworlds

Rejecting Destiny: The Underworlds

DENNIS SCHEEL

NO
WAY
BACK

THE UNDERWORLDS

Dedicated to Yuki, the treasured cat I did everything to protect.

Thanks to Nina for the invaluable inspiration, Katherine's dear feedback, and my sister Winnie.

Also, thanks to the edit by Diane.

Table of Contents

Chapter 1- A Strange New World

Winter, a new beginning for the Underworld, a season that would change everything forever. Dan, a scientist, had been experimenting on a mysterious Gate in the Underworld. When his close friend Denida had first discovered the structure, following the war with the Dark Angels, Dan didn't think much of it. "It's just some ancient construction," he had said. *Who would've thought it was made of an unknown alloy?* Dan now smiled down at all the chemicals he had used to try to stain the material to identify it. *None of them even reacted with it, but it's cold, like metal.* He eyed the towering, two-story Gate. *There's something special about it; I just know it.*

Today, after his logbook's twentieth recorded try, Dan flipped a switch, and the Gate lit up. Dan danced in excitement while his assistants laughed. *I can't wait to call Denida!* He eyed the myriad power cords connected to the Gate with a chuckle. *Three near electrocutions, and one downed power grid...* He laughed. *- but now, it's finally perfect.*

***

Denida stopped at the door of Dynasty, his mansion, as his cell phone vibrated.

"Denida?" Dan asked as Denida picked up the phone. "I made progress!"

"How so?" Denida glanced at his watch.

"I made a new discovery. You'll want to see this."

Last time he called me about the Gate, it was to tell me that he found a way to connect it to a power source. Denida rolled his eyes. *An hour later, they still had no idea how to turn it on.*

"It's important this time; I swear," Dan spoke with that voice he only used when he was begging on his hands and knees, usually for additional funding.

Sounds like it's worth checking out this time. Denida bit his lip and sighed heavily. "Alright, I'll stop by before I head into the office." Denida hung up the phone, his heart beating a little faster with excitement. *Maybe it's something cool about the alloy. Dan told me it could have some amazing potential as an energy source.*

Denida pocketed his phone, ready to hurry off, but Nina sat at the dining room table with slumped shoulders.

"Nina?" Denida sat down beside her.

She faced him with a furrowed brow.

Denida's heart sank. *This must be serious; Nina's always in control.*

"Daniel," she replied shortly, her bitter tone betraying a bit of frustration.

"What's wrong? Where is he?"

Denida wanted to brush him off, but if Dan really had made a breakthrough with the Gate, it was too tempting to pass up.

"I don't know, Denny. He's always running around, up to no good." Nina sighed and peered down at her tea. "This morning, he tried sneaking into the military headquarters and the Colonel called me to send the butler to pick him up."

Denida's jaw tensed. *Not good.* "I will have a word with him after work. Dan insisted he has something imperative to show me now, before I head to headquarters. I must tend to that, now." Denida kissed Nina goodbye. *The grounds are huge, and Daniel knows every hiding place around Dynasty.* Denida grunted. *I'll talk to him tonight.*

***

Dan has something to show Dad? Daniel stood just outside of the room where his parents were talking, his back pressed up against the wall. *Dad always tells Mom about Dan's secret lab and some old Gate the height of the stables! I wonder if that's what he wants to show Dad...*

Daniel sniffed. *It does sounds interesting. Why should my dad have all the fun, again?* He slowly tiptoed past the door, as his parents' conversation continued.

Outside, he spotted his dad's car in front of Dynasty. He peeked around to make sure he was alone and ran over to the vehicle. He opened the trunk, smiling upon finding it unlocked. He climbed in and held the lid down, making sure it didn't click shut. *Maybe I can finally go on an adventure like the ones Dad always describes!*

He heard countless stories about Dan, his dad's scientist friend, who had a secret lab and some ancient Gate. Daniel's dad would always talk about that Gate when he didn't think Daniel was around.

Denida approached the car within a few minutes. *This is going to be so cool!* Daniel trembled with excitement. His dad quickly set the car in drive. Daniel covered his mouth to suppress his giggles. They drove for so long that Daniel almost regretted hiding in the trunk. His elbows were becoming sore and red from the bumps in the road. Maybe they weren't going anywhere interesting after all. *That'd be such a bummer.* The car finally halted briefly, drove a short distance farther, then stopped again. This time, the engine stopped humming. His dad stepped out and the vibration of his door slamming shut rattled the car. Daniel could hear his dad's muffled voice. *He's talking to someone. What are they saying?*

Finally, two distinct sets of footsteps crunched away on the asphalt parking lot. Daniel climbed out of the trunk just in time to see his dad disappear into the building next to the car. Daniel ran toward it and jiggled the doorhandle, but it responded with unwavering resistance. *Probably for the best.* Daniel crossed his arms, rethinking his efforts. He would've most certainly been caught if he had used the common entrance. Daniel sighed. *Maybe I missed the chance to explore this-* He noticed a small window he could fit through, a short distance from the door.

When Daniel climbed through the window, he crouched and listened. Staying low to the ground, he followed his father's voice around the corner, and saw his dad talking to Dan.

"It's powered up, I see."

"Yes." Dan nodded excitedly. "We can finally see what's on the other side, but I'm not sure if it's safe." Dan scratched his head. "I mean, it's been on for half an hour, and nothing's come through, but we have no idea what's on the other side."

The Gate's flickering lights and sparkling sheen looked so inviting that Daniel couldn't help but sneak forward.

Daniel could see his dad and Dan, through the Gate. They rippled as if he were viewing them through water.

Enough hiding! Daniel clenched his fists, ready to let his dad know he had tagged along. *Maybe I can help somehow.* Daniel jumped up and ran to his dad, taking the shortest route, which led right through the Gate. His Dad became increasingly clearer as he approached the Gate, but as soon as he ran through, a bright silvery light engulfed his vision.

***

"Dad!" a voice rang from across the room.

Denida turned to the Gate, just in time to see Daniel run into its portal. *What's Daniel doing here?* The Gate buzzed loudly, and Daniel vanished.

"Daniel!" Denida shouted.

The Gate fell silent, and its lights dimmed. Denida's heart sank, as cold terror filled him from the inside out. The shock of seeing Daniel vanish froze him in place, leaving him itchy all over with anxiety. Dan's team ran to the Gate and tried to power it back on, but despite their best efforts, the Gate remained dark and quiet, like a massive monster that consumed its fill just before hibernation.

Denida opened his mouth, and the only words he could think of tumbled out. "We need…" He knew deep down what he wanted to say, but he couldn't finish his sentence. His jaw clenched in defiance.

The tense atmosphere in the lab birthed an air of discomfort and silence. Nina had arrived in no time, following a call from Denida. If looks could kill, both Denida and Dan would have been dead on the floor.

The assistants kept nervously peeking over at Nina's face, in between failed attempts to restore power to the Gate.

Nina bared her teeth, appearing even more furious than Denida, despite the rage in his eyes. "How could you let this happen?" Nina pointed at Dan. "This is your lab. And you!" She whipped around to Denida. "- you were so eager to play with your new toy that you couldn't even check to make sure that your son was safe!"

"Look." Dan raised his hands to fend off Nina. "I've got a device that should be able to control the Gate from the other side." He handed Nina the device. It was about the size of a cell phone and had the same mysterious alloy as the Gate at its center.

"Why can't you control it from this end?" Nina's fingers curled into claws. "You should never have had it on, especially without a contingency plan."

"The controller isn't technically ready, yet." Dan backed away from Nina. "We found it with the Gate, but haven't had much time to test it." He trembled, as though still prepared to retreat.

"Who knows where Daniel is now, or with whom. He is just twelve years old, a child!" Tears prickled Nina's eyes, so she turned away and wiped her face on her sleeve.

"I will get him back; I promise." Denida hugged Nina to try and calm her worries, but it did little to ease his own concerns.

Nina turned back and nodded. The couple gazed deep into each other's eyes, as they held a deep conversation without words.

"This is purely experimental. We don't know what's on the other side, or if you can even get back through from the other side." Dan stepped in between them and the Gate.

Denida frowned, ignoring him. *Of course, it's risky, but Daniel's my son. What am I supposed to do, forget about him?* The mental image of Daniel cold and scared pierced Denida's mind and his body began to shake with concern.

The Gate buzzed, and all the lights flickered back on.

"It's back!" a lab assistant yelled.

"Showtime." Denida darted over to the Gate.

"I think we should send troops, too, just in case there are demons or militant forces on the other side." Dan ran in front of Denida.

Denida paused midstride, listening to Dan, only to shake his head.

"No, we don't have time to prepare the troops for a mission." He hugged and kissed Nina tenderly. "I will bring Daniel back. You'll see." He smiled at her and took the controller from Nina.

"Wait." Dan pointed to the controller. "That device is sensitive, so don't touch it, unless you intend to use it. It has a cooldown period in between uses, so it's important you don't use it by accident."

Denida paused, imagining being stuck in an unknown area with a faulty controller. "Dan, maybe you should call the Colonel," Denida admitted. "I'll be going on this adventure alone but having our colonel's advice on standby could be helpful." He smiled in Nin's direction. "Watch over her, Dan." Denida strode through the Gate. As soon as he vanished, it powered down, like it had after Daniel used it.

Denida found himself in a forested area on the other side of the Gate. He had almost expected to find green aliens chasing Daniel through a wasteland, but the aliens were a figment of his imagination, and the ground was so covered in leaves that it was impossible to see his son's footsteps. *Where could he be? The smartest decision would've been to stay right here.* Denida scratched his head. *Maybe he did stay a while, but gave up on waiting, after several hours passed.*

Denida decided to search the area. *Have I been here before? This forest feels familiar.* "Daniel!" he hollered repeatedly as he marched through the dense forest. "Where are you, Son?"

Denida stood still to collect his thoughts and realized that he could hear the distinct "whoosh" of cars passing by. He walked in the direction of the sound until he discovered a road. *Maybe he approached the road to seek help?*

When Denida reached the road, he stopped dead in his tracks. He saw a familiar symbol on a building across the highway.

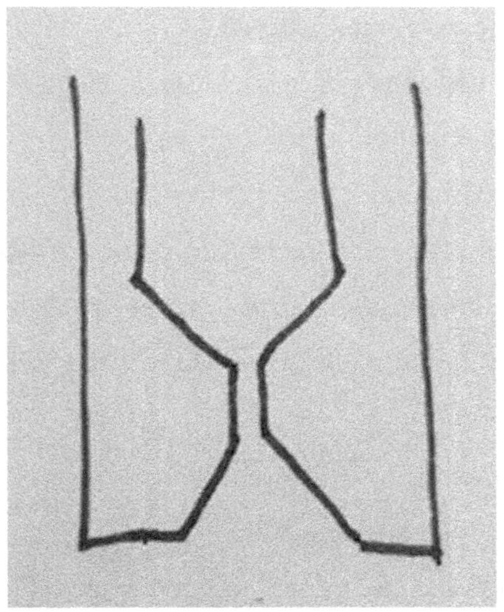

Denida knelt behind a bush, staring at the insignia. He eyed the building for any clues that would justify the symbol's existence. *What is it doing here? I designed it myself after the war with the Dark Angels.* He was sure he'd never seen it before the moment he drew it for Dan, yet this building proudly boasted the emblem.

A troop of soldiers marched around the building, clearly on patrol. The symbol decorated their uniforms, but other than that, their gray getups only confused Denida more. *Where am I?* He sauntered down the slope, trying not to draw the soldiers' attention to his presence. He circled the building, scoping it out. Having seen nothing significant, he approached a soldier, who seemed to be on a smoke break. The soldier leaned up against the front wall of the building. *Maybe he can tell me about this building.*

"Hey." Denida pointed to the building. "Tall building, here. I really like the insignia engraved above the door."

"Get out of here, bum. This is a military installation." The soldier pushed Denida.

Military installation? Denida backed away. *Very interesting, seeing as the soldiers are wearing a gear with the symbol decorating it.* As he turned to leave, he noticed movement out of the corner of his eye, which caused him to halt.

The door had opened and Denida could see a ring of soldiers inside, with Daniel standing in the middle.

"I said move it!" The soldier yelled at Denida.

Denida's jaw trembled. *I can't leave without Daniel, but if I try to fight this guy, the rest of the soldiers will attack me.* "That's my boy in there, but why?"

The soldier's eyes followed Denida's finger to the building and the soldiers inside.

"Well?" Denida trembled with impatience.

The soldier pushed him into the building.

"This guy says he's the boy's dad," the soldier announced.

"Oh? This kid said he's the president's son. This is the guy he was referring to?" Another soldier snickered.

The rest of the soldiers laughed.

Denida looked at the unfamiliar soldiers, still with a sinking sensation in his chest. *They have the UW symbol here, but they don't know who we are?*

A decorated sergeant stepped into the room, commanding attention. "From what I've heard, this boy claims he's our colonel's son, and the man says he's the kid's dad. Something's wrong, here." The sergeant raised his gun, taking aim at Denida.

"I just want to take my son and leave." Denida raised his hands in surrender.

"We could just kill you here, instead." The clicks of arms sounded as the rest of the soldiers cocked their guns. Before the situation escalated, another man ran over from behind the troop.

"Stop! The colonel wants to see both prisoners." *The colonel? It can't be our colonel, can it? Come to think of it, that would explain the UW symbol's prevalence here.* Denida nodded in acquiescence, relief hastening his stride, on his way to their colonel.

The soldiers led Denida and Daniel up endless stairs to the top floor of the building. Each landing they passed had guards patrolling each door onto their respective floors. *How strange...* Denida bit his lip. The military presence sure seemed prevalent, and he really hoped they were taking him to see his own colonel. At least then, he'd be able to get some answers about this strange place.

When they reached the leader's office, two the guards frisked Denida and Daniel with a pat down. After turning to one another, the guards nodded and knocked on the grand, mahogany door behind them.

"Enter!" a voice called from within.

The guards opened the door, so Denida and Daniel could step inside, then closed it behind them with a loud bang.

The man at the desk resembled Denida's colonel, right down to his stern smile. *Is it really you?*

"I am this world's colonel, and the president of this underworld."

Denida's mouth hung agape. This man looked and sounded so much like his friend, but how did he become the president, here?

"What the..." *I'm in a different underworld?*

"You claim to be President Denida's son?" the colonel asked.

Daniel's eyes were as wide as Denida's, as he glanced over at his dad.

Whoever this man is, he isn't the colonel I know. Or, perhaps this is what my world would've been like if I had never become president? But that couldn't be the case, given the prominence of the UW emblem in this world.

Denida stepped over to the desk and leaned against it. He drew in a deep breath. "How is it possible that you don't know me?"

The colonel stared into Denida's eyes as if he could hear Denida's heart thumping in his chest. After a moment, he chuckled and leaned back in his chair. "Guards!"

Several men stormed into the room.

"I'm sorry, Mister, but I've never seen you before." The colonel gestured for his troops to act. "They're crazy. Get them out of my sight and remove them from the compound."

Before Denida could object, the guards had grabbed him and Daniel and escorted them out of the building. *How can this be?* Denida knew his colonel very well, especially following their shared history fighting against the Dark Angels. *Is that colonel in the office just a doppelgänger of my colonel?* It seemed like the only explanation for the lack of recognition.

"I want to go home," Daniel whispered.

They ventured through the forest, heading back to the Gate. One thing seemed evident; they had to leave this strange place, wherever they were.

Denida peeked down at his son and a tinge of annoyance drew Denida's lips into a snarl. If only his son hadn't followed him to the lab, if only he hadn't gone through the Gate, none of this would be happening. But that wasn't important anymore. Denida managed to find his son. As they approached the Gate, Denida froze. *Somebody's here!* He pulled Daniel down with him, just in time to hide.

Chapter 2: The Colonel vs Denida

Several soldiers stood between Denida and Daniel, and the Gate. The emblem on their uniforms still perplexed Denida.

"This Gate is just like the other one; it doesn't work!" one guard moaned.

The other one? Intriguing! Maybe our underworld has two, as well... I'll have to explore when we get home.

Denida and Daniel snuck past the guards, who remained focused on their conversation. Denida and his son neared the Gate, relieved to be heading home, and away from this odd world. Denida withdrew the Gate's controller, which Dan had given him from his pocket. He followed Dan's instructions, but the Gate remained inert. He stepped closer and tried to activate the Gate again, but it refused to turn on. He held the device at different angles, but the result remained the same.

"Why isn't it working?" Daniel asked, worry in his wide eyes.

Denida shook his head and pocketed the controller. He sat down next to the Gate, giving up. *Maybe Dan was wrong about the device. He never had a Gate to test it on, after all.* He heaved in a deep breath. *Wait; the guards mentioned another Gate.* "Stay here; I'll be back!" He hurried over to the two guards.

"Why are we even here?" one of the guards groaned.

"The colonel wants us to move this Gate closer to the other one."

"*Snap!*" The guards clammed up when Denida stepped on a branch. They spun with their guns raised, peering into the bushes, before splitting up to approach from two directions.

Just as I hoped. Denida's wartime instincts always tended to reemerge when his life was on the line. He ambushed the first guard from behind, grabbing him, and breaking his neck. *Daniel won't understand, will he?* A twinge of regret stabbed Denida's heart. He bit his lip, as he imagined Daniel killing a man to follow in his footsteps. To his relief, Daniel wrinkled his nose and turned away. *Good... he hates it.*

"Anything?" The second guard called for his friend's status update, but barren stillness responded. His face twitched, and his finger stroked his firearm's trigger, as he carefully approached Denida's hiding spot.

Denida shuddered as he crouched over the first guard's corpse. *I'll need to keep the second guard alive so that he can tell me where to find the second Gate.*

"Show yourself!" A loud "*click!*" rang out as the soldier cocked his gun.

Daniel stepped out of the bush with his arms up.

The guard shifted and raised his gun, but Denida snuck up behind the guard and sucker punched him before he could fire.

"Daniel!" Denida hollered. "I told you to stay put." He sat the guard up and smacked him across his face to wake him.

"Ngh…" The soldier's eyes closed tighter for a moment as he started to come to his senses.

"Hello, you mentioned a second Gate?" Denida smirked.

The soldier glanced around. "Where's my friend?"

"Gone, like you'll be, if you don't answer me." Denida snatched the first guard's gun to emphasize his threat.

The guard drew in a deep breath. "The colonel has the second Gate in his office, in the UW building!"

"We were already there, and I didn't see a Gate!" Denida's hands tightened on the firearm. Daniel's disgusted gaze was the only deterrent preventing Denida from striking the man again.

"It's in the back of his private chamber!" The guard jeered. "But you'll be dead before you reach it."

"Daniel, can you fetch the other guard's cap?"

Daniel sped back to retrieve it.

Denida smiled at the second guard. "Don't count on it; we've survived this long, haven't we?" He pistol-whipped the guard, rendering him unconscious.

Denida sighed, tapping his fingers on his wrist in thought. They had no choice but to return to the facility that they had just escaped from. It was the closest thing he had to a means of getting home, seeing as the other Gate seemed to be out of commission, now.

It's settled, then. Denida sighed and his eyes settled on Daniel. He could not be as forceful as he wanted to be, not with Daniel beside him. After all, Daniel lacked the military training that Denida had acquired throughout the war against the Dark Angels. *We need another day.* Denida tied the guard up, as he let his mind wander to viable solutions.

Daniel returned with the cap and froze, watching his dad. "Why not just let him go?"

Denida faced Daniel. "Because it would be open season on us." He slipped into the guard's uniform and grabbed the cap from his son.

Daniel furrowed his brow. "Why are you dressing up as the guard?"

"To get access to the building. You'll have to act like I'm escorting you in as a prisoner." Denida straightened his beret and lapels. *Not a great plan, but it will have to do.*

Daniel sighed and began following his father back to the compound.

Denida stopped as they reached the road and faced Daniel.

"I know this is going to be hard, but you need to remain silent, no matter what!"

Daniel nodded and held a finger to his lips, as if to acknowledge his father. After a second, he rolled his eyes. "I'm not five, you know. It's not hard to stay quiet."

Denida squinted at the building with the symbol, from his hiding spot on the edge of the forest.

Within an hour, the guards changed shift, leaving a new patrol squad out front, men Denida didn't recognize.

After a half an hour, to the second, Denida dragged Daniel up to the front door with a hand wrapped firmly around his arm.

"I found this boy near the Gate!"

"So?" A guard shrugged.

"He had this with him." Denida lifted the Gate's controller in his free hand.

The guard's eyes widened with intrigue.

"Come with me." The soldier hurried inside the building, waving his arm as an indication for them to follow him. He led them back to the top floor, approaching the colonel's office.

That's where their lucky streak ran out; the same guards from earlier stood at attention outside the colonel's door.

"You!" one of the guards shouted and aimed his gun at Daniel.

Denida charged and pushed him to the floor, then used the soldier that had escorted them as a shield while gunfire rang out in the hall. The guard's body shook in Denida's grasp as the bullets pulverized him. As soon as the shots ceased, Denida threw the corpse at the guards.

Denida drew and fired his pistol, shooting the guards, who slumped to the floor, dead. He knelt and listened for anyone else who might be around. Despite the eerie silence, Denida was certain that the colonel knew a threat was looming on the other side of his door.

They ventured into the colonel's office, finding the room to be vacant. Denida steadied his gun with his free palm. "Stay behind me," he whispered to Daniel before clearing his throat. "Colonel? I know you're here!" Denida yelled. "I don't want to hurt you; I just want to use the Gate."

***

This is bad. Daniel crouched in the hallway, where his dad had pushed him. *Why is Dad stupidly declaring that he's here?*

The colonel started shooting, and Daniel could see his dad crouching behind the desk.

"You made a mistake by coming back here!" The colonel's gunfire ceased, and the *"click!"* of him reloading his weapon echoed throughout the room. "You'd better leave, before my troop hears the gunshots."

That colonel has a point. Daniel peeked at the elevator, noting its open doors. He ran down the hall and dragged one of the soldier's legs between the doors, just in time for them to close on the fabric of his pants. The other guard slumped against the door, from whatever Daniel's father did to him.

Daniel's heart pounded with stress as he watched the guards. *This isn't the adventure I wanted. Is this the sort of thing Dad went through with the Colonel?* Daniel bit his lip. *I thought "legendary" was a good thing, that he was an indisputable hero, so he became the president after the war...* Daniel's heart pounded a little harder. - *but he's acting like a monster.*

"We can't!" His dad yelled back at the colonel.

The colonel's only reply came in the form of loud, popping gunfire.

Every cracking sound made Daniel wince. *If he's like the colonel in our world, he's in charge of his world's security. This can't end well...* Daniel stepped closer to his dad. He'd been told never ever to touch a gun, but one of the guards had a nightstick on his belt...

***

The shooting lasted less than a minute before Denida's magazine clicked, empty. The colonel cursed from where he hid.

"You're out, too, huh?" Denida asked after a few minutes of silence.

"You too?" the colonel replied.

They both chuckled.

Denida tossed the gun out into the room and stood up with his arms raised.

"You said you want to use the Gate? You'll have to go through me. I want that controller my soldiers told me about." The colonel stood and faced Denida, who nodded back at him.

A split second later, Denida rushed colonel. Denida was an equal match for his brute force and knew his techniques well from his time on the battlefield. But the colonel seemed to counter all of Denida's strikes just as effectively, with the same fighting style that Denida's own colonel favoured. However, this colonel was so much stronger and faster, that he deflected all of Denida's blows with ease and Denida found it increasingly harder to shift quickly enough to block this colonel's assault.

Denida panted, growing tired, as the colonel fired more blows, which breached Denida's defenses.

With a few precise strikes, the colonel forced Denida into a corner. Denida breathed heavily. *I don't think I can escape this guy a second time.* Denida's exhaustion became obvious when the colonel managed to shove his arms aside to land a kick, forcing Denida to rely on waiting and dodging to conserve energy.

Denida closed his eyes for just a moment. "I'm sorry, Daniel; I've failed you."

"Yes, you have." The colonel grinned, still punching and kicking Denida with increasing ferocity.

Suddenly the colonel stumbled, revealing Daniel behind him, with a nightstick. Daniel struck the colonel again, and the colonel collapsed.

Daniel screamed like a banshee and continued beating the colonel until Denida grabbed the club.

"Enough!" Denida eyed the man on the floor.

Denida knelt beside the colonel and checked his pulse with two fingers on his neck. He had some serious bruises, courtesy of Daniel, poking out from under his now untucked shirt, but his breathing and heartbeat seemed steady.

Denida led Daniel into the colonel's private chamber beyond the office. Just as the soldier had stated, a gigantic Gate stood against the far wall of the colonel's room. Denida withdrew the controller again, took a deep breath, and clicked a button on the controller. The Gate buzzed and lit up.

Denida smiled at his son. "Thank heavens, we can finally go home!" Denida took Daniel's hand, and they stepped through the Gate.

Chapter 3- The Last Dark Angel

Home! Daniel smiled as he and his dad stepped out from the Gate.

"Where the hell are we, now?" Daniel surveyed the dark world they'd arrived in.

His dad pointed the controller at the Gate. "It isn't working here, either. There must be a second Gate here, too." He sighed as he stowed the controller before glancing up and scoping out their surroundings for the first time since they'd arrived.

"Something about this place reminds me of home, but it isn't home," Daniel whispered.

Denida nodded. "It feels familiar." He frowned. "Wait; no, it can't be!" He rushed forward.

Daniel scrambled up the hill.

"It can't be," Denida pleaded again.

"What can't?"

"You'd think that it was bad being in a world where our emblem inexplicably exists, and where a colonel who didn't recognize us reigns supreme. But that pales in comparison to this!"

"What?" Daniel grabbed his dad's hand, still confused. *Sure, the place looks gloomy, but how can it be that bad?*

Denida fell to his knees. "I'm not the president here; I'd be willing to bet this place doesn't have a president," He whispered. "Say hello to the Dark Ages, Daniel. The old, ruthless, and vicious control this world!"

Daniel's heart pounded. *Why is he acting this way?*

"The Dark Angels used to rule our world. They are back and they are here." Denida pushed himself to his feet.

"We have to find the second Gate, and we must avoid the Dark Angels." He started to creep down the hill.

Daniel followed close behind, seeing monsters in every shadow. His father had mentioned the Dark Angels before, in horror stories about the history of their world. *It took my father, and an entire army, to fight them. That's why Dad's name is in our school's history books.*

"The rebel force is our only hope; we need to find them."

"There's a rebel force?" Daniel squinted.

Denida nodded. "Yep, and the colonel will lead us right to them!" He clenched his fist and pointed dead ahead.

***

Morning came with a faint stream of light, even in this shadowy world. Denida stretched the kinks out of his joints, then sauntered to a field to reacquaint himself with the close quarters combat techniques his colonel had taught him years ago. Daniel tried to follow along, but his movements lagged behind Denida's, due to his beginner status. Denida watched his son out of the corner of his eye but pursed his lips to suppress a comment. *Daniel seems like he's having fun. That's important at a time like this. Besides, the basics might come in handy someday.*

When they'd finished, Denida's stomach growled. If he was hungry, Daniel must have been famished.

"Come, Daniel, we can't stay here. I have an idea of where we are and where we need to go."

"Dad, is finding the colonel really such a good idea? He's going to be mad at us for what we just did to him in the other world."

If it's anything like the other world, he won't know who we are. Denida sighed. "He will be the colonel, but probably not the same one."

Daniel's face scrunched up in thought.

"Remember?" Denida probed. "The last colonel looked like our colonel, but he didn't know me. So, maybe this one won't know us either. He probably won't even know about what we just did."

Daniel shrugged, but there was still some uncertainty in his tense expression.

Denida's head started to ache with confusion, so he could only imagine what his son must've been feeling. Still, they crept through the woods until they arrived on the outskirts of a town.

The people here walked with their heads down. An uncomfortable sensation tingled in the back of Denida's thoughts, until he realized why; the absence of laughter, smiles, and idle chatter seemed all too prevalent. Denida rubbed his eyes. Even though he lacked vision in his left eye, it still ached occasionally. Seeing the fear prevalent on these peoples' faces triggered memories of his home world all those years ago, which sent a bout of pain knifing through his heart. He'd sworn to himself that no one would ever have to feel this way again.

"We'll follow the village's perimeter." Denida led Daniel down a path that forked to the right. "I know where we are, now."

"You've been here before?"

"No." Denida exhaled a heartfelt sigh. "I just know how the Dark Angels operate."

One house, farther from the town than the others, appeared deserted, with its drooping shudders and overgrown yard.

"Stay here." Denida stood Daniel up against a tree, while he crouched next to a bush. "Don't wander off. The soldiers here won't be as nice as the ones in the last world."

Daniel wrinkled his nose. "They were jerks."

Why does he always try to correct me? Denida closed his eyes tightly before responding. "Yes, and these soldiers will be worse."

Daniel's eyes widened, and he nodded.

Good. Denida crept toward the house, sneaking from bush to a tree, to another tree, until he could peek into a window, confirming his worst suspicions with a sinking sensation in his stomach. *It really is vacant. Just like in my world, the Dark Angels must have demanded its inhabitants' loyalty and sent them on a deadly errand.*

Denida slipped through the door and ransacked the kitchen. He snatched food from the cabinets and refrigerator, tossing it into a bag he found in a cabinet under the kitchen counter. With the heavy sack full of food, he hastily returned to Daniel's hiding spot. With every moment Denida had left his son unattended, his concern had only grown until it burnt like a fire around his chest. Under the Dark Angel's control, dark soldiers had roamed his world. If they were here, too, Daniel's life depended on his ability to stay hidden.

Denida stumbled over his feet on his last sprint back to Daniel's tree, and he exhaled a sigh of relief at the sight of his son. *Thank God.* After they had eaten, Denida led Daniel toward a training ground, which Denida remembered from his world. It had been his colonel's favorite sparring terrain. Denida made sure they stayed as quiet and unassuming as possible, keeping their heads down like the rest of this world's residents, to avoid drawing attention to themselves.

It was still morning when they arrived at the training grounds. Denida and Daniel stopped on a cliff, where they could clearly see anyone sneaking up on them from any direction. He could've been wrong about the colonel, but if this world, and the people living in it, were similar to the world and people he knew, he didn't think he had much to fear.

The colonel finally marched onto the grounds. Daniel and his dad exchanged a glance. Denida's suspicions had been right; the colonel had come to train at his preferred spot.

"Remember; yell if there is any danger! And stay hidden." Denida bit his lip with concern for his son, but he needed the colonel's help. He rose and approached the training grounds.

The colonel copped an offensive stance, facing dead ahead, and began to practice his knife forms. Denida slowly ambled up to him. This wasn't the best time, if he remembered correctly.

"Colonel?" Denida asked cautiously.

The colonel spun around, lowering his knife to his side. "You talking to me, Mister?"

Denida released a heavy sigh, as this colonel clearly didn't recognize him. *Not my colonel, unfortunately.*

"Yes, I am a part of the resistance! We heard talk of a huge structure that kind of looks like a gate?"

The colonel stopped and stared at Denida.

A cold sensation filled Denida. *Does he recognize me?* That's when he noticed the colonel's furrowed brow, indicating his puzzlement.

"I've heard rumors about a Gate in the Dark Angel's fortress."

It just has to be in their house, didn't it! "Don't you want to overthrow them?" Denida's jaw tensed as soon as the words tumbled out. *But I know we can do it.*

"Overthrow them? Are you nuts?" The colonel paled.

With the suggestion out in the open, this was the only path forward. "Why not? The time is ripe!"

"The time is ripe," the colonel muttered to himself.

Denida could see the fire in the colonel's eyes. He knew he had him, just from that remark. *Exactly the same as the colonel I know.* Denida turned and waved for Daniel to join him. Once Daniel trotted up to them, the colonel led them back to the resistance's hideout.

Once again, Denida found himself at the center of the uprising, with Daniel listening intently to his strategy, as if intending to mirror his father's exploits. If the colonel helped, Denida and Daniel could reach the Gate, and a successful rebellion would be a by-product of their trek through the world.

"We need to plan our strategy." Denida cleared his throat, hoping he could take the lead, despite his uncertainties about what unfamiliar factors he may encounter in this world. Still, he steeled himself with a deep breath. *We'll make history, no matter what.* The colonel, the troops, and Daniel stared at Denida with wide, desperate eyes.

"This is what we must do." Denida outlined the strategy that had been successful in his world.

"That's nice, except you are forgetting the most important part." The colonel examined the tactical wargame Denida had laid out.

"And that is?" Denida tilted his head.

The colonel laughed and shook his head. "You mentioned seven Dark Angels, but there's only one."

What? Denida furrowed his brow. *How could one angel be behind all this madness? Who could claim to be…. wait!* "Who!" He grabbed the colonel and pushed him up against the wall as his heart thundered in his chest.

A minute that passed like an eternity elapsed before the colonel spoke. "Danyel."

Denida released the colonel, his heart freezing over at the answer he had expected, and feared, more than any other.

"Me?" Daniel squeaked.

Denida kept his eyes on a point straight ahead as he responded in a defeated voice. "I named you after my old friend but spelled your name differently." He sighed. "Danyel led the Dark Angels and he was the only one escaped our world before he could be brought to justice. We knew him as the most brutal among their ranks."

Daniel bit his lip.

Denida turned around to face Daniel and the colonel. "It seems that Danyel is here now, representing the Darkness." He clenched his fists. "Let's put an end to the Dark Angels, once and for all!"

The troop and the colonel murmured quietly. Their voices filled with excitement as their conversation wore on.

However, as their confidence increased, Denida's confusion only developed. Back in his world, there had been a whole group of Dark Angels, but not here. *Was the Danyel terrorizing this world a different Danyel from the one he knew, perhaps one from this world? How could that be, when Denida was the one who started calling them the Dark Angels in the first place, but there didn't seem to be a version of Denida here to have coined that phrase?* As much as Denida wanted answers, he knew that questions could create distrust and if he wanted to reach the Gate, he needed the colonel to trust him.

"How exactly do you know Danyel?" the colonel asked.

Denida peeked up at Daniel, verifying that he was out of earshot. "I come from a world, where Danyel led seven Dark Angels. I had dealings with him, and we became friends."

"And you overthrew them?"

"Yes." Denida frowned, wondering if the colonel was becoming suspicious, but his expression remained steady, eyes narrow with curiosity.

The colonel fell back into his seat as stress weighed heavily on the corners of his lips.

Denida could no longer put returning home at the top of his priority list, not with Danyel oppressing this world. *We're going to rise up. And he won't escape this time.*

"Dad, if we only just got that Gate working, how did Danyel get here before us?"

Denida opened his mouth to respond, only for words to remain just out of reach. *That's a good question. Were the Dark Angels using the Gates, too?*

Denida's throat tensed. Maybe it wasn't going to be the Danyel he knew, after all. "I don't know. We should ask him, if it is him."

"Ask him?" Daniel demanded.

It does sound insane. Denida scratched his head. Danyel would've needed to cross worlds to get here, provided that it was the same Danyel, who had terrorized Denida's world. With no other choice, Denida formulated a plan. *At least Danyel won't be anticipating it.*

Denida's idea involved creating a diversion to draw Danyel's attention to one front, while some of the colonel's forces snuck in to take the world back.

Daniel straightened his posture. "Dad, I'm coming. I'm going to help, too."

Denida shook his head and responded on raw instinct alone. "It's too dangerous."

Daniel smirked, developing an arrogant glow. "The Gate is there, so I have to come."

Damn... Denida couldn't argue with that point. He glanced around the room at the colonel and his soldiers, and Daniel standing beside them. *He looks so mature...* Denida couldn't seem to find words to speak as he watched Daniel preparing right along with the colonel's troops.

Daniel turned back to the colonel, fists clenched. "Let's go!"

They all gathered outside of Danyel's fortress.

The colonel deployed most of his soldiers to the other end of the castle with careful instructions. As they departed, he turned to Denida. "They will start a riot, soon. All we can do now, is wait."

Denida sighed and nodded back the colonel.

"So, you fought this friend of yours before?" the colonel asked.

"Yes, in my world, he was the leader of the seven Dark Angels. Unfortunately, he vanished after we overthrew them."

A huge explosion rumbled in the distance. The dark soldiers guarding the fortress ran to investigate it.

"It's time!" Denida jumped up and led his allies to the fortress.

Once inside, the colonel sent the rest of his soldiers down a hallway with instructions to create a second rally.

Within moments, gunfire echoed throughout the castle.

With the firefight intensifying, the colonel, Denida, and Daniel didn't have much time. The three of them quickly, but carefully, climbed the stairs, heading to the top floor.

Luckily, rather than encountering Danyel immediately, they only came across, and swiftly defeated, several dark soldiers on their ascent.

Satanic relics filled Danyel's chamber, and the Dark Angel stood at a desk near the side of the room. As Denida's forces entered the room, Danyel's eyes turned to them and widened in shock. Within a moment, Danyel recovered from his stupor and snatched up a gun to open fire.

Denida jumped to the side and hid behind the statue of a demon, and his allies followed suit.

The colonel had to crouch, as his statue was smaller than Denida's. Daniel's was even more stout, but Danyel's stood tall and wide, the perfect shield.

Denida glanced back to make sure, his son was out of harm's way.

"Welcome to my world, Denida!" the Dark Angel yelled, as if they weren't engaged in a shootout.

It is the Danyel I know! Red spots tainted the edges of Denida's vision. Danyel really had gotten away from him, before. *But that won't happen again.*

"Did you miss me?" The Dark Angel batted his eyelids.

"No! You recreated the Dark Angels here, by yourself? How did you manage that? And how did you even get here?"

Danyel chuckled. "Yeah, how did I get here? I bet you'd love to know all about that, Denny!"

Denida twitched at the nickname uttered in Danyel's voice. It struck something deep down inside of him. After all, Nina called him Denny, but Danyel communicated something different from Nina's affection. The nickname came from further back in time, predating Denida's relationship with Nina, from a time Denida couldn't remember. Danyel seemed to know that.

"What's wrong, cat got your tongue?" Danyel mocked.

Denida yanked himself back to the moment, rather than being sucked further into the void of memories that he could not recall. He couldn't afford to lose himself; stopping Danyel was more important.

One of Denida's guns clicked, empty.

The colonel across the way cursed, as he dropped one gun and readied a second one.

Denida caught his eye and holstered his gun with his last clip, relying on the colonel, for now. "Stay here," he hissed at his son. "We surrender!" Denida threw his first gun out, followed by the colonel's.

The Colonel nodded at him, as Denida stepped out from behind a statue with his hands up.

"Good boy." The Dark Angel levelled his gun at Denida. "You never were very good at preserving ammo."

Denida stood perfectly still as his eyes scanned Danyel, watching for any small indication of aggression. "Want to tell me how you got here?"

"The boss wouldn't like it if I did." The Dark Angel sneered. "You'll have to die without answers."

Denida's jaw clenched. "The boss?"

"My boss is the one who brought me here to finish the Dark Angels' work, of course." Danyel shrugged. "But that's enough small talk."

"Wait!" Denida shouted.

Danyel raised his gun. "Nice seeing you again!"

Before Danyel could fire, the colonel pushed Denida aside and grabbed the gun from Denida's holster. He emptied the clip into the Dark Angel, until the click of Denida's gun echoed throughout the room.

Danyel froze, then dropped his gun. After what seemed like an endless second, he collapsed, dead.

Denida ran to his side. Danyel couldn't die, not yet, not with the answers Denida desperately needed. But it was too late; the chance had passed.

"I found the Gate!" Daniel yelled.

Denida sighed and stood up straight. He turned to the colonel.

Denida rested a hand on the colonel's shoulder. "Thank you for saving us." With a smile, he followed his son to the Gate.

Denida withdrew the controller from his pocket and turned it on.

The Gate lit up.

"Guess we can't go back through the Gates that we come through," Denida mused.

The colonel removed his beret in a respectful gesture. "Where are you going?"

"Home." Relief brought a grin to Denida's lips. "I wish you all the best as you rebuild your world. It was a lot of work for us back home, but it was well worth the struggle."

Denida and Daniel exchanged a glance and took each other's hand before stepping through the Gate. To home, they hoped.

Denida left this world with more questions than ever before, and no one left to answer them. That knowledge created an icy lump in his gut.

Daniel squeezed Denida's hand, bringing him back to his senses.

The third time they stepped through a Gate, a warm comfort settled in Denida's chest, now that he knew what to expect, but the world they stepped into stunned him so much that his warmth froze over immediately.

This world had a high-tech atmosphere with robots sweeping the roads and people snapping photographs of them completing their functions, like tourists at an exhibit. This clearly wasn't home, after all.

Denida tried the controller, just in case, but the Gate remained inert.

Denida and Daniel smiled at some cameras beside the Gate, then set off in search of its counterpart.

"Hey." Denida stopped one of the tourists. "Do you know where the other Gate is?"

The man shrugged and muttered something in a different language.

Figures. "Daniel, let's go!" Denida yelled, but as he turned, his son appeared to have vanished into thin air, leaving Denida all alone with the tourists.

Chapter 4- Nina

Nina paced back and forth, eyes flitting to the Gate every few moments. It had been days since Denida had followed their son through the Gate, but neither of them had returned, yet. *Has something gone wrong? Are Daniel and Denny okay? Are they even together?* Nina's heart sank, as she considered the horrific possibility that Denida hadn't found their son, yet. Nina knew Denida would be too ashamed to come back without him.

Our bond is usually strong. Nina rested her hand over her heart. Denny and Nina had a special kind of bond, an unbreakable one. Normally, she could feel pain in her chest if something was wrong with Denida, but today, she couldn't feel anything. *I don't like this hollowness; it's making me restless. I'm certain that something must be wrong.*

"Dan!" she called, as she saw her husband's friend cutting through the lab.

"As soon as we hear something, you'll be the first to know. Right now, we're just trying to find a way to turn the Gate on."

The Gate buzzed as soon as Dan finished speaking, and all the lights turned back on.

"Daniel, Denny!" Nina sprinted to the Gate, expecting them to step through at any moment.

However, after a long moment of inaction, Dan rested a hand on Nina's shoulder. "I'm sorry." He sighed and resumed trudging up to the Gate to check its power supply.

Nina stared at Dan in disbelief. *How can he be so calm about this?* "I'm going through!" Nina stomped over to the Gate.

"No!" Dan grabbed her arm, pulling her back. "We need to be sure it's safe, first. We have no idea what's on the other side."

"My son and husband are on the other side!"

Dan heaved a deep breath. "Nina…"

Nina sighed. "You're right; it won't do any good if I disappear, too." *And he's right; Denny probably has our son, so I have to stay optimistic.*

"We can still find Denny." Dan stepped over to a desk and picked up a gray object that he could hold comfortably in both hands.

"What's that?" Nina tilted her head to the side.

"We spent the last few years trying to turn the Gate on, but we didn't know what would happen when it finally worked, so I made a robot to examine it up close." Dan cradled a robot in his hands. "When the Gate turned on, we realized that it was a portal and I called Denida here to watch the robot go through the Gate to explore for us." He scratched his head. "… Daniel went through, first."

Nina's jaw tensed as Dan mentioned her son's name and his disappearance. "You're sure this is going to work?" Nina's tone carried a severe edge.

"We'll see." Dan tried to smile, but he wasn't very successful. Dan's assistants helped him prepare the robot. No one knew what it might encounter on the other side. It could be anything, so they had to make sure it was durable.

Dan's assistants gathered around a table to help Dan prepare the robot. They attached a camera to it and tested its remote-control steering. The controller spun the robot around, and made it move forwards and backwards. With a click of a button on the controller, the camera's red, "recording" button lit up.

An assistant turned on a large monitor mounted on the lab's wall next to the Gate. With a few keypresses on a computer, the feed from the robot's camera appeared on the screen.

Dan took the controller from his assistant and drove the robot up to the Gate. He heaved in a deep breath and slowly drove the robot through the Gate.

The screen showed the surface of the Gate, and its bright lights growing and becoming more detailed as the robot neared them. The feed flickered as the robot rolled through the Gate, and the Gate shut down, just as it had before.

For the briefest moment, Nina's heartbeat rose into her throat. *Did Denida and Daniel die the second they went through the Gate?*

All eyes stared at the monitor to see if the signal was strong enough to reach them from wherever the other side was, if the robot and camera even survived their maiden voyage. The room contained an eerie, frightening silence.

As the black screen persisted, Nina's jaw trembled. Some of the scientists in the lab peeked at her with sympathetic expressions, until her eyes met theirs, at which point they'd avert their gazes. After the longest thirty seconds of Nina's life, the feed returned.

An abnormally large troop of soldiers wearing the familiar UW insignia appeared on the feed. A colonel's very bruised face filled the screen, as he examined the robot.

"Is that our colonel?" Nina pointed at the screen.

"What is this thing?" The colonel stroked his chin and turned the robot over in his hands, just before the feed went black.

"No!" Nina dropped to her knees. Her gut twisted. Seeing the colonel and the UW emblems only contributed to her despair. The number of soldiers and the state of the colonel's face told her that something was definitely wrong.

And worse, now they needed to wait for the Gate to power on again. Her gaze flitted to Dan. *He won't let anyone go through there after something happened to his precious robot. How will we find out what became of my family?*

Dan turned to Nina, pursing his lips with stress.

"I know!" Nina snapped.

Dan shook his head. "I was just going to say that I sent a message to our colonel. He's coming here to oversee our operations."

Nina smiled slightly. "Good." She nodded. "We should hang tight until he gets here. He can help advise us on our next course of action."

The Colonel arrived within twenty minutes. His tense jaw trembled like it always did when he was deep in thought. "I understand that we have an issue?"

His face looks fine. How is that possible? "Yes, we sure do!" Nina led the Colonel to the monitors, so that he could rewatch the recorded footage himself.

The Colonel's eyes widened when he saw someone with the same face and voice as his own.

"Denida and Daniel went there and never came back?" The Colonel asked after Nina explained the details surrounding Denida and Daniel's disappearance.

The Colonel's expression remained unexpectedly stoic. "We found this Gate when the Dark Angels fell, but there were rumors surrounding another Gate."

Dan's jaw dropped.

"Where?" Nina demanded, recovering from her shock much more quickly than Dan did.

"We haven't found it yet, but when we captured the Dark Angels' sympathizers, some of them hinted that it was utilized to travel somewhere in the past. Some of my soldiers have been searching for it for years." The Colonel grinned at Nina reassuringly. "Maybe Denida will come back through that one, if it's true."

Some of the tension left Nina's chest at that possibility. Being near Denny's longtime friend and hearing this new information about the Gate allowed a sense of tranquillity to cushion her heart. After just a moment, she felt her connection to Denny starting to return. She held her hand over her heart. *From what I'm feeling, they have to be all right.*

"I don't like this!" Dan complained. "He left through this Gate, but we're thinking he'll return through another one, just because someone said a second Gate might exist? That seems like a farfetched theory."

Nina shook her head. "There's nothing normal about giant Gates that teleport you across worlds! The colonel in that world destroyed the robot, for God's sake!" Nina stormed out.

Nina leaned up against the building and fumbled in her pocket for a cigarette and her lighter, only to pause with the cigarette hanging from her mouth, ready to be lit. *Wait… if anything's wrong with Denny, his human form on Earth would be acting strange.* She slipped the cigarette back in its pack and pocketed everything. *Besides, this is something the guys in the lab can't do, seeing as their souls were made in the Underworlds.*

Nina arrived on Earth, appearing next to two lakes. She sighed heavily. The trek to her human form always seemed so frustrating, but today it just filled her with suspense. By the time she saw Den, Denida's human counterpart, her stomach was a massive knot. But he stood before her with his trademark smile as he chatted with his friends, like always. *Good, nothing's amiss, here.* Nina sat down on a rock outside the schoolyard and watched for a while, hoping this temporary getaway would be enough to make her relax.

***

The Colonel and Denida had forged a strong bond during the war. The Colonel smiled at the warm memories of the years since he started overseeing every aspect of the Underworld's security.

I remember the whispers regarding a second Gate, which had some sort of connection to the Dark Angels, but where could it be, and why haven't we found it? The Colonel inhaled deeply and released a heavy sigh, when a thought stuck him. *We need a way to learn more about that world.* He just couldn't explain his doppelgänger or the presence of the UW emblem in a world that didn't seem connected to his own. Even so, the similarities, such as his counterpart's age and status as a military leader, filled the Colonel with optimism. After all, he could understand why that colonel destroyed the robot. *I would have done the same thing, given my focus on security. But where, or what, was that place? Is it even possible to come back from there?* Clearly, sending anyone else through the Gate would be too dangerous, but he had to do something.

They needed to get someone, or something, past the other version of himself if they wanted to find Denida. Would his counterpart really be that bad? *Maybe we've gone about this the wrong way.*

Of course! The answer had been staring the Colonel in the face. With a sudden realization, he headed to the Underworld's headquarters, where Claus, Denida's vice president, carried out the arduous task of running their world in Denida's absence.

The Colonel had never met the man in-person, seeing as Claus hadn't fought in the rebellion, and didn't carve out time to mingle with the military like Denida did.

As the Colonel stepped into Claus's office, he took off his beret and saluted. "We have a problem, Vice President Claus, Sir. Denida is missing," the Colonel announced. "The council has been informed, and by law, you are now in charge."

Claus's face wrinkled with concern.

"He'll be back!" The Colonel raised his hands defensively. "He's just gone through the Gate in the HQ laboratory. We're currently trying to find a way to bring him and Daniel back to our world," the Colonel explained reassuringly. "You are to handle his duties until he returns."

Claus nodded in agreement. "Understood."

The Colonel was glad to know the world's leadership would stay intact, despite Denida's absence. He smiled at Claus and spun around to leave.

"Wait; I'll walk with you. I should go to Denida's office to retrieve his current files and pending paperwork." Claus stood.

I'd better inform his secretary, too… The Colonel tailed him to the office.

"Sir," The secretary sitting at a desk near Denida's office door greeted them with a friendly smile.

"Yes, Claus is to handle day-to-day operations for the time being."

"Hello." Claus stepped up to the secretary and shook her hand, but his eyes remained locked on the door behind her. "That's…"

"You could lead…" the Colonel began.

Claus stepped past them, heading into the office, and circled Denida's desk with a gigantic smile. He slowly sat down behind it.

A peculiar sight! The Colonel shook his head. "We shouldn't need long, hopefully only a week, tops."

"Those Gates have always been intriguing…" Claus ran his fingers over the mahogany desk.

The Colonel headed straight back to the lab, discovering tension now filling the lab, weighing down the air in the room. Everyone seemed to be avoiding Nina and Dan, as they argued next to the Gate's control panel.

"I spent some time on Earth and was feeling calm and ready to face this, only to come back to discover that you've gotten absolutely nowhere!" Nina pointed a finger at Dan's chest as she chastised him.

"I have an idea!" The Colonel grinned, pleased with his plan.

Dan exhaled a sigh, seeming relieved with the diversion.

"What is it?" Nina raised an eyebrow.

"You sent a robot after Denida and Daniel, but someone identical to me destroyed it. We need to get his attention with the next robot we send, so that he doesn't destroy it."

Dan's heart sank. "How? And why would I send another one through after the first one was destroyed?"

"We're going to send another robot, but it'll have a screen on it, showing my face."

***

Denida was at a loss, struggling to figure out where Daniel could have gone. He asked a few tourists if they'd seen his son, but none of them even admitted to having seen Daniel in the first place. Denida ran through the surrounding area, yelling his son's name repeatedly but the only response he received was sideways glances from tourists and townsfolk. In fact, some of the tourists snapped photographs of him running around, as if he were a lowly street performer. An uneasy feeling squeezed Denida's heart. Daniel had disappeared in a strange, unknown world. *Where did he go? How can I find him?*

What happened? It had been only a few minutes, and Daniel had just vanished into thin air. Denida was just about to give up when he noticed something out of the corner of his eye. Across the road, which had cars hovering above it, Denida spotted a building with a sign, "Police." He hurried across the road and flung open the door.

The building appeared normal on the inside, *no robots or anything. I guess police work remains a human task.* He glanced around the room, sighing contentedly at the empty nature of the building. The marked absence of a queue generated unease for Denida. *Why can't my world be crimefree, too?*

"Hello." Denida trotted up to the front desk. "I have a problem. My son, Daniel, is missing!"

The officer turned his chair to face his computer, which had a transparent, crystalline screen.

"His ID?" the officer inquired.

"ID?" Denida frowned in confusion.

"You know, the universal ID that we can use to track him," the officer's voice rang out, laden with mockery, as if Denida were an especially inept citizen.

How was he going to answer this? How could he even acquire an ID, and how would he get one for Daniel?

This really is a strange world. "Um, I…"

The officer rolled his eyes, clearly disgruntled.

"I can tell you where I last saw Daniel, if it helps?"

"Where's that?" the officer asked.

"We were by the Gate, near the tourist spot with robots cleaning the streets," Denida explained.

The officer glanced at his computer, while Denida watched over the officer's shoulder to see what he was doing.

The officer deftly controlled his computer with efficient typing patterns and mouse clicks, until a map appeared on the computer's screen, showing footage from surveillance cameras in the area. The officer logged Denida's facial features in a database, using footage from a surveillance camera in the police station, and a path of his movements appeared with a timetable. The officer finally managed to backtrack to the last point of time when Denida and Daniel were still together. The officer tried to highlight Daniel. After several failed attempts to find Daniel's whereabouts in the database, he frowned at Denida.

"He doesn't have a chip?" The officer peered from the monitor to Denida, trying to highlight Denida on the screen instead. The only option that appeared on the screen was for facial tracking, because the officer had added Denida's information manually.

Only the most influential people in Denida's world had GPS chips, as an additional security measure, but this system didn't seem to recognize his. Strikingly, his world had a tough time setting up that system, and for less than ten people, at that. *Is every citizen in this world really microchipped? How did they manage that?*

The officer grabbed his gun and pointed it at Denida. "Freeze! You're under arrest for child endangerment and refusal to comply with safety protocols. Down on your knees!"

Even if Denida had been armed, there was nothing he could do without prolonging his sentence. He allowed the officer to handcuff him without resistance.

"What did I do? Why am I under arrest?" Denida's head spun around in confusion.

The officer yanked Denida to his feet.

"Neither you nor your son have the required ID chip, which is required by law, for safety purposes."

The officer led Denida to an interrogation room, which resembled every interrogation room Denida had ever been in. It stood dark, empty, and boring, to try to make prisoners confess as soon as possible. *Does that really work?*

The door opened and a detective stepped inside. Denida had been expecting to see another version of his colonel, but his eyes widened at the sight of Claus's doppelgänger.

"Hello," this version of Claus greeted him with a bit of a wave.

Should I? Denida couldn't believe his eye; this had to be the luckiest turn of events possible! He leaned forward in his seat. "Do you happen to go by Claus?"

Detective Claus's eyes widened. "Yes, you may call me Claus." He smiled and put down a tablet he had been typing on. "What's your name, Sir?"

Denida knew this tactic after all, a good rapport was everything. "I'm Denida, and my son is missing."

Claus jotted down the name in his digital notepad. "I heard about your son; we'll find him, soon. Just explain why it is that you don't have an identification chip, Mr. Denida."

Denida's patience was wearing thin. This officer dared to treat him like a common criminal when Daniel could be in serious danger? All these officers wanted to talk about was a stupid ID! They weren't going to look for Daniel at all; *it's just another trick.* Denida eyed Claus. He could tell the officer what he wanted to hear. This was a new place for Denida, after all; no one knew him here. but to say he came from another world? That would be too much for anyone to believe; Denida hardly believed it himself. *A lie might be easier.*

"I am a special agent in the UWS. That's why I'm not chipped, security reasons."

Claus tapped his notepad with his pen. "UWS? Special Agent?"

Denida could see it would not be enough, so he gambled. "Yes, I answer directly to the colonel." He maintained steady eye contact with Claus.

"Sorry." Claus stood and uncuffed Denida.

Guess it worked. Denida rubbed his wrists. "Daniel is really my protégée, a special agent in training, so I need to know his whereabouts."

Claus nodded and picked up his notebook. He found the surveillance footage showcasing Denida's first few moments in this world, while Daniel was still with him.

They watched as Denida talked to the tourists. Daniel turned to follow a blonde girl, who was around his own age.

Denida's heart sank. *Why?*

"He followed that girl." Claus clicked on her, and her photo and biography appeared on the screen.

A pretty… "Oh God!" Denida blurted out.

The detective furrowed his brow.

"That's Nina." Denida's heart raced. *But she's so young! Did Daniel recognize her somehow?* Denida's jaw trembled as he perplexed about this situation. *How could she be so young, here? Claus appears to be the right age.*

Claus handed Denida a notepad. "You can follow this."

"Using her ID?" Denida clarified, examining the notepad. While his world had its own GPS tracking system, it paled in comparison.

Claus hummed in agreement, as if Denida had stated the obvious.

Denida couldn't help but wonder what else in this world was obvious to its citizens, but fantastical to him.

Claus led him out to his car, which Denida still found to be fascinating. It hovered a few feet above the ground.

Denida needed to act familiar with this world's technological exploits, so he just stepped into the car as if it was normal. "You're a detective?"

Claus shot him a sideways glance. "Of course, A-Rank."

"A-Rank?"

"We are all ranked according to our skill." Claus cast Denida a strange glance.

I have to be careful; I need him so I can find Daniel. "We've been watching your unit, Detective Claus," Denida replied calmly. "And we are not sure if that rank suits you!"

Claus's hands tightened on the steering wheel. "I assure you-"

Denida motioned for Claus to stop. "Your actions will show us where you really belong."

Claus stopped the car at the girl's supposed location. They were in the middle of nowhere, with only a few lacklustre buildings nearby.

Another pang of fear shot through Denida's chest as he worried, once again, about Claus becoming suspicious of him. His prevalent concern for Daniel's situation only made it that much worse.

"After you." Claus waved him forward. "I'll cover your back." Claus smiled and handed him a gun. "Just take this for self-defense."

Denida treaded carefully, following the notepad's guide like a beacon. They walked through a café. A few coffee drinkers glanced up briefly at the pair, then resumed their conversations. The notepad showed Nina at the back of the shop.

"Pick up a couple of coffees." Denida nodded at the counter. "I'll meet you in the back." He slowly followed the dot on the map until he saw someone familiar.

"Daniel!" Denida ran to greet his son, relieved to see him safe. He examined Daniel up and down to be sure that no harm had befallen him, before pulling him into a tight hug. *What a day!*

"You must be Daniel's dad," a feminine voice mused.

Denida glanced up and gasped at the sight of Nina's spitting image. *Except she's so young, probably still a teenager, just like that profile picture associated with her tracker!* He turned back to Daniel, then again to the young Nina, who seemed unreal to him.

"Nina." Denida warmed at the sight of her face. It wasn't the version of Nina that he had wanted, but she was better than nothing.

"You found him." Claus finally joined them.

"Yes," Denida replied with his gaze still locked on Daniel, as if afraid he'd vanish again if Denida turned away for even a second. "Where did you go?"

Daniel sighed. "I saw her and so I had to follow her."

Denida understood exactly what Daniel meant; he felt drawn to this younger version of Nina, too. While he also found it strange in a heart-warming way, he knew he had to stay guarded. He still needed to pretend he belonged here to ward off Claus's suspicions. As Claus came to mind, Denida glanced around and spotted Claus drinking coffee in front of the shop.

"Thank you for watching Daniel, but we must go, now." Denida started leading Daniel away with a hand on his shoulder.

"Wait!" Nina jumped up. "He promised! We need his help."

What has Daniel gotten us into, now? Denida turned around and smiled. "What do you need help with?"

Nina mirrored his grin. "We must stop the time machine!"

There's a time machine, here? Denida clasped his hands, wondering if that could justify this Nina's age. Then again, he found this world befuddling, even with a time machine. Just like the other worlds, familiar faces didn't recognize him, and he lacked a counterpart, despite other significant people from his world having one. Certainly, this world's current state wasn't just the result of time travel. "Does this time machine resemble a Gate?" Denida asked.

Nina quirked one eyebrow.

Denida's heart pounded. She looked so much like his wife, and resembled her mannerisms so thoroughly, that it made him positively yearn for his sweet Nina's embrace.

"I haven't seen it; it's new." Nina shrugged.

If it's new, it can't be a Gate that they've mistaken for a time machine. Denida bit his lip. "We'll help." Still, he had to make sure the time machine wasn't the Gate, possibly on a different setting. Besides, he couldn't resist spending a little more time with this young version of Nina. Being around her took the edge off his loneliness.

"I bet I know a way to get us in to see it." Denida winked and sauntered up to Claus, who was still sipping coffee in front of the shop. "Would you like to demonstrate your worth, Claus?"

Claus stood and smiled. "Yes, most definitely! What can I do?"

Denida and Nina briefly explained their need to access the time machine.

As they spoke, Claus nodded along, and as soon as they finished, he nearly trembled with pent-up energy. "I'll take you there." He followed Nina's directions, transporting them from the coffee shop to the laboratory in his police car.

"The president here erected this building," Nina whispered as they pulled up to the laboratory, as if suddenly concerned she might be overheard. "Will that be a problem?"

Claus laughed. He led them to the laboratory doors, decorated with a sign saying, "No Entry." He suddenly shifted his focus to Denida. "Why does the UWS want the machine, anyway?" Claus folded his arms.

Denida cursed himself. *I should've known he'd ask.*

Nina whirled to face him, eyes gleaming with distrust. "Wait, you're with the UWS?"

Claus reached for his gun, and Nina pulled Daniel away.

Denida faced Daniel, who hid behind Nina. "Sorry." Denida struck Claus hard, sending the detective tumbling to the floor. "I had to say something to convince him to help us."

Nina and Daniel exchanged a glance.

Denida knelt and pilfered Claus's badge for the clearance that he hoped it would grant and tied him up with his own shoelace. He stuffed a sock in the man's mouth and fastened it with the other lace.

Claus woke up and rolled about, trying to break the laces.

"I'm really sorry, Claus, but your badge will help immensely, thanks!" Denida flashed the A-Class Detective badge.

***

Back in Denida's underworld, Claus was enjoying filling in for the president. He'd dreamed of this day, imagined sitting behind the esteemed desk, making important decisions, and having all the power he could ever want. Now, he had trouble imagining relinquishing control one day, like he'd need to if Denida managed to return. Claus's heart pounded a little harder with contempt. *Can I prevent him from coming back?*

Claus hurried out of the office, stopping only to tell Denida's secretary that he would not be available to meet anyone for the rest of the day.

Claus sauntered to the world's second Gate, the one the Colonel's troops had yet to discover. Claus had stumbled across it while relaxing in a nearby cottage with Denida. Claus laughed, proud that he was the only one who knew the location of the rumored second Gate. Like the first Gate, the Dark Angels had controlled it. Now, however, Claus had been waiting for the right time to make this historic reveal.

Now, he just had one thing to do before its grand debut. He traced his finger along the Gate's alloy, and found a removable chunk of the Gate tucked away in a little nook. *The Gate's power unit.* Claus smirked and ripped the chunk off the Gate with a *"click."* He smiled down at the device in his hand. *That should be enough to disable the Gate.* He grinned and slipped the part under a nearby rock, very pleased with himself.

Claus returned to his office, where he picked up his phone to call the Colonel. "I heard you are looking for a second Gate?"

"Yes, do you happen to know where it is?" The Colonel's voice rang with hope.

Claus described the location of the second Gate. He was practically drowning in his excitement, feeling so thrilled that it actually hurt a little. If he wanted to maintain full control of the Underworld, he had made sure Denida would never be able to return. Yet, if he somehow managed to make it back, it would only be possible because Claus decided to reactivate the Gate for him. He'd be a hero; no one would suspect the acting president. *My future is guaranteed!*

***

Denida glanced around at the machines and people in the huge laboratory. The time machine stood in the center of the room. Idle chatter and the time machine's buzzing struck Denida, Nina, and Daniel, as they sauntered into the lab with Claus's badge prominently affixed to Denida's jacket. The time machine glistened and shone like new, but the world's second Gate, also in the laboratory, stood filthy and decrepit, forgotten. What can we do with a time machine? *It sure seems like it would have required hundreds of manhours to complete this project.*

As they approached, a man who acted like he was in charge directed a question at Denida. "How's the security?"

Must be the badge. Denida opened his mouth to respond.

Nina whispered to Denida before he could speak. "That's our president."

Denida scanned him. *Another president, huh?* "The security is up to our highest standards. How is the time machine? Does it work yet, Mr. President?" Denida nearly tripped over the question, not used to addressing someone else as "president."

The president smiled excitedly. "Yes, it's a wonder; I tell you!"

The president and the crowd's attention made Daniel tremble nervously, so he spoke without thinking. "But does it work?"

Everybody in the lab stopped and glared at Daniel.

This is bad. Denida realized he should have stayed in the back.

"Why do you have a kid with you?" The president asked.

"He's my son. He was just curious; I'm sorry if it was unprofessional to bring him." Denida peeked at the president to see if he was convinced.

The president chuckled. "Of course, the time machine works," the president said light-heartedly.

Denida glanced around the room, spotting the decrepit second Gate. *But how do we disable the time machine?*

"That old relic proved useful! Destroying it was the best thing we could ever have done."

Denida bit his lip. *Relic, what could he mean? Not...* "Relic?" he asked.

"Yes." The president led them to the machine, where a familiar chunk of a strange alloy rested at its center.

Denida knew the only other thing he'd seen that was made from the alloy was the controller Dan had given him. Now, he needed access to the Gate. Maybe they could repair it? He didn't know why Nina wanted the time machine destroyed, but she was right; they needed to figure out how to dismantle it.

***

Claus accompanied the Colonel and Dan to the second Gate. They circled it, wide-eyed.

"Can we get this back to the lab?" Dan's hands twitched, as if he couldn't wait to start experimenting on this new Gate.

"Too big." The Colonel glared at the Gate. He'd had teams of soldiers lugging generators and power cables out here to hook it up to a power supply.

Claus had to force his face into a concerned expression.

"Claus." The Colonel marched over and eyed him sternly. "Was something removed from this Gate?"

"Removed?" Claus really exerted effort to appear confused.

The Colonel's militaristic composure slipped as he sighed resignedly. "We searched far and wide for this Gate, but something doesn't feel right. I can't quite explain it."

"No, sorry, nothing out of the ordinary, as far as I know." Claus chuckled on the inside. Keeping a secret from the Colonel imbued him with a warm, giddy sensation.

The Colonel and Dan exchanged a suspicious, yet disheartened glance.

"There's nothing we can do, here. It's not going to work." The Colonel's phone rang, interrupting him.

Claus could see the hope fading from Dan's face. *Heh, if only he knew.*

The Colonel hung up his call and turned to Dan. "We just got our lucky break. Your new robot, and the first Gate, are ready to go. We're ready to go see me."

The Colonel pocketed his phone. Standing straight again, he led Dan to their ride back to the lab, as if the broken Gate no longer mattered.

Wait, the other Gate is operational? I thought this Gate was their only hope... Claus ran after them. "I'm coming, too!"

Chapter 5- Thirty Years Ago

If they destroyed the Gate to build that stupid time machine, we're stuck here. Denida clenched his fist. "Why use the Gate's parts for this?"

"The Gate was made of some material we'd never seen before!" The president grinned like a child in a candy store. "The power it contained was unparalleled, so we put it to good use: time travel!"

The president's attitude struck a nerve with Denida, causing him to grit his teeth in frustration. *They never realized it's powerful as part of the Gate?* Sure, the material was strange, but how could a world this advanced not deduce the Gate's intended purpose?

The door flew open behind them, and Detective Claus stormed through, followed by a group of guards.

"Those intruders are here to destroy the time machine!" Claus yelled.

Before anyone could move, Denida drew his gun and held the president at gunpoint. "Sorry," Denida whispered, as if the president would believe him.

Claus and the guards ran up to them.

"No closer!" Denida pointed Daniel toward the Gate.

"You won't get away with this." Claus seethed.

Denida pointed his gun at the president.

Claus motioned for the guards to lower their arms. He raised his hands. "Relax; we won't shoot. Just let the president go."

Denida watched them relinquish their weapons, but he still pointed his firearm at Claus, as he knew Claus in his own world always had a backup plan. *If he's similar to my world's counterpart, like Nina is to hers, and the colonel is to his, we need to tread carefully.*

"Lower your gun." The tremble in Claus's voice indicated uncertainty.

Denida pointed his gun at Claus's leg and stroked the trigger.

"Wait!" Claus yelled and discarded a gun he'd kept hidden on the floor.

"Still the same Claus." Denida chuckled and turned his attention back to the president.

"When did you destroy the Gate?"

The president's eyes widened.

"When?" Denida nudged the president with his gun.

"Christmas, thirty years ago," the president blurted out.

This was all Denida needed to know. He pushed the president toward the time machine. "Set it for thirty years ago!"

The president hastily complied with Denida's command but glanced at his guards worriedly in between keypad presses. "Just don't hurt me. You won't be able to get back without my device."

Denida clenched his jaw. "Where were you thirty years ago?"

"Where?" the president sputtered. "The hospital."

"Thanks." Denida snatched the president's remote from his belt. Denida used his gun to gesture for Daniel to come closer.

The young Nina started running in their direction, but Claus caught her before she could reach them.

"Look who's here!" Claus smiled and held her in a chokehold. He glared at Denida, who sighed, glanced at Daniel, then shoved the president toward them.

Denida and Daniel ran through the time machine, hoping that he could change the events in the past to prevent everything that happened here. When Denida stepped through the time machine with Daniel, they were surrounded by a blizzard unlike any. *Wow, what a storm!* Denida shielded his face with his hand to try to see Daniel through the whiteout. Denida led Daniel to a building to seek shelter from the snowstorm. *This place seems strange.*

"It's Christmas!" Daniel smiled at the lights in the houses, clearly visible from the road.

Yes, guess the time machine worked, then... "We need to keep moving, in case they're following us." Denida pulled Daniel with him. Christmas or not, the president could still send someone to stop them.

They trudged through the Christmas Eve blizzard, needing to find the president before he could destroy the Gate.

Denida and Daniel endured the frigid gusts and heavy snowfall, which raged on as they plodded to the hospital. They knew that making any direct contact with someone from the past could disrupt the flow of time, so Denida and Daniel kept their heads low and their jackets tight around their shaking bodies.

The president sat in the hospital's lobby, quietly talking to another person. Denida had never seen the other man before, but the president clearly thought him to be an important figure, judging by the undivided focus the president offered him. The president kept his eyes on the man and nodded along respectfully whenever he spoke.

Denida's heart thundered, and his instincts screamed at him. This person had the answers to all his questions. "Follow the president," he whispered.

"Why?" Daniel scrunched his nose, and his eyes had a classic deer-in-the-headlights expression.

"I need to follow his friend; I'll catch up soon."

The president's quiet conversation with the man ended. As the president started to saunter away, Daniel sighed and stood to follow him.

Denida tailed the mysterious man as he rose, too.

The man suddenly stopped at the end of a hallway and froze for a moment. "Why have you been following me?" He turned around to face Denida's hiding spot in a doorway.

Busted, and so quickly, too. The Colonel would be disappointed. "How did you know I was there?"

"I've honed my ability to sense what's going on around me. Do I know you?" The mysterious man winked and scanned Denida's face. "Denida?"

Denida twitched. *How does he know my name?* Here he was, in a foreign world, thirty years in the past. He didn't know this man; *yet this man knows me.*

***

Daniel crept along the hallway, watching the president's back. In his dad's stories, you were supposed to give the impression that you had a reason to be wherever you are when you're stalking someone, thus granting yourself an ability. *But who'd believe a healthy kid belongs in a hospital?* The president turned a corner, and Daniel ran to catch up.

Soldiers grabbed Daniel, as he rounded the bend. The president continued down the hallway as if nothing had happened.

"Let me go!" Daniel writhed against the soldiers. "You have no-"

Claus smirked and sauntered closer. "His father must be nearby. Search the hospital!"

"Wait!" Daniel panicked. "How did you get here?"

Claus turned back with a smile. "The president sent me back to stop you."

"How did you find us?"

"Nina!" Claus grinned. "Did you forget that we nabbed her? We know what you're after."

Claus led his soldiers deeper into the hospital, leaving just two soldiers with Daniel.

***

Denida and the mysterious man stared at each other. *How the heck does this man know me? I certainly don't know him. Or do I?* A long blackout had settled into Denida's memory at some point, creating a number of lost years. Perhaps he met that man during those forgotten years. *We are in the past, now. Wait a second, thirty years ago... Christmas Eve? This is the morning I was born!*

"You can't possibly know me!" Denida shook his head in disbelief.

The man smiled as he neared Denida. "You do not belong in this time."

How can he possibly know that? Maybe I shouldn't be so surprised, as he seems to know me. "I um…" Denida stuttered. "- need the Gate."

"To continue through the Underworlds?"

Again, the man shocked Denida. *The… Underworlds?* The realization that he was in another world entirely crashed into Denida, making his legs shake. "Who are you!"

The man shook his head and handed Denida a piece of paper. "This map will guide you to the Gate."

Denida peered at the note, then slipped it in his pocket. "Why are you helping me?"

"I am here to help you, in this time, and the present." The man removed a ring from his finger and handed it to Denida. It had the UW symbol engraved into it.

Denida examined the ring. *What is this?*

The man took it back from him. "This ring is for you, but not yet. You will find it where your true self feels most at home. And it will *only* work for you."

Denida found that statement a little strange. "Why me? I'm nothing special." His eyes remained locked on the ring as the man slipped it back on his own finger.

"Oh, but that's where you're wrong! Many legends speak of you, singing your praises, Denida. You are here, after all, so it has already begun."

Denida spotted Claus out of the corner of his eye, pointing him out to some soldiers. *This is bad.* He had so many questions, even more than before, but Claus's soldiers aimed their guns at him.

"First Daniel, now you. Aren't I lucky?" Claus clapped.

Was this really another version of Claus, Denida's dear old friend, back home?

The mysterious man stroked his ring. "I'll handle this; you go get your son."

Claus frowned and lifted his handgun, pointing it at the man. "You want to try me, old man?"

The man smiled as if he found Claus's antics funny. "Do you feel strong? You won't after this!" He raised the same hand that he wore the ring on.

Denida snuck away as the soldiers' attention focused on the man but paused in a doorway to peek back, to make sure the old guy would be alright.

The man swept his hand through the room, and Claus, along with all his soldiers, were thrown backward like ragdolls.

"Told you." The man proceeded to the maternity ward as if nothing had happened. "Time to play my role."

Claus locked eyes with Denida.

Denida sped down the corridor, before Claus even managed to stand, and bolted through the hospital, searing for his son. "Daniel!" he called his son's name despairingly. Anything Denida could do that would mess with the past seemed inconsequential, after all the mayhem with the soldiers. He sprinted outside, where there would be fewer people.

He found two soldiers restraining Daniel, as his son shivered in the cold winter morning. *I have to get Daniel away from them, but they might know my face, so I have to be careful.* He hurried back inside and approached a guard. "There are guys with guns outside. They're trying to hurt a kid!"

The guard lit up and charged outside with his own gun raised.

Denida slipped through the snow, arching his way closer to Daniel.

"Hey, leave him alone!" the guard commanded.

One of the soldiers raised his gun.

"Bang!" The guard fired his gun, wounding the soldier.

The other soldier released Daniel. "You!" He fired at the guard in retaliation.

Denida smiled and ran to Daniel. "Miss me? I know where to find the Gate; let's go." He patted Daniel on the back, and sped away with Daniel's hand in his, as they approached the Gate, at last.

It was their final stop before they would leave this cold day in history. *If the Gate doesn't lead us home, it will at least bring us closer.*

Denida's heart lightened with hope. *That conversation with that man was so strange.* He slipped into the lab through a conveniently unlocked door and listened. He could hear the president talking to his technicians.

"The Gate must be destroyed!" The president pointed at the Gate. "I've received direct orders to forbid travel between the Underworlds."

That man must have commanded the president to destroy it, but why? And why would he send me here to use it after having given an order like that? Denida had to reach the president before they destroyed the Gate. It was now or never.

***

The Colonel had affixed the next robot with a camera, speaker, and a monitor so it could send and receive video and audio. He really wanted it to work this time. The Colonel didn't want to risk another robot, but the other Gate wouldn't turn on, so what other option did they have?

"Is this really a good idea?" Dan crossed his arms.

"Maybe not, but it's the only way, so we're doing it." The Colonel turned away from Dan.

Claus danced on the edge of the crowd of technicians.

Poor guy must really want his boss back. The Colonel raised the robot above his head. "It's ready! You know what's at stake, people. We need answers, so stay sharp."

Dan fussed with the Gate, while the Colonel checked the robot one last time.

Claus meandered over to Nina, whose eyes seemed glued to the robot. "Not worried about what we may find?"

Nina frowned at Claus.

Claus tilted his head at the Colonel. "The Colonel should take you through the Gate, so both of you can escort the robot..."

The Colonel saw Nina's face fall. *What's Claus saying to her?* He stood up to go find out.

"We have to try something." Nina's voice quavered.

The Gate lit up, snatching everyone's attention.

The Colonel would just have to talk to Claus later. He adjusted the robot's position.

"This has to work." Nina clasped her hands.

"Stand back!" Dan yelled, and everyone backed away from the Gate.

The Colonel drove the robot through the Gate.

Just as before, the Gate powered down as the robot passed through, and all eyes turned to the monitor on the wall.

"It's not..." Claus began to speak, but everyone shushed him.

An image finally appeared on the screen, but unlike before, only low-ranking soldiers appeared in the robot's line of sight.

One pointed his gun at the robot but stopped short. "What the..." He lowered his gun. "Sarge, you may want to see this."

An older soldier stepped forward to investigate the robot, then the first soldier joined him.

***

The bruised colonel didn't appreciate the soldier's interruption. *What could be so important that my sergeant interrupted my duties?* It couldn't be anything vital, but whatever it was could be over and done with in a second.

The colonel followed his sergeant to the Gate in the woods, where a crowd of chattering soldiers surrounded a robot. *What could be so interesting about that robot? They should have destroyed it like I did the other one.*

"The colonel's here," the sergeant announced.

The soldiers stepped aside.

The colonel examined the robot and froze. A screen affixed to the robot displayed a lab with people the colonel didn't recognize, all except for one figure, a man identical to himself.

"Hello," the Colonel on the robot's screen greeted him in a voice exactly like his voice.

"Who are you?"

"I am you," the Colonel on the robot's monitor replied.

The other colonel brought the robot to his chamber, where he could talk to himself in peace. He pointed to his bruises. "Your friend did this… most of it, at least. His son had a go at me with a nightstick, too."

The Colonel in the robot chuckled. "Must want to be just like his father." His face turned stoic. "So, he went through a second Gate?"

"The Gates only teleport you in one direction, so yes." The colonel leaned back in his chair. "Didn't you know about that? A long time ago, the Gates were used to travel between the Underworlds."

Chapter 6- A Doubt in Time

Denida's and Daniel's lives depended on stopping the president from destroying the Gate, but technicians surrounded the president.

Denida surveyed the lab, formulating plans in his head.

Daniel tugged on his sleeve.

"Dad, we're in the past." Daniel's forehead wrinkled. "If we prevent them from destroying the Gate, won't it mean that the time machine we used to come here would never be built?"

My, my, Daniel has a point. How could I have missed that? Denida hadn't been paying enough attention to his son to recognize his cleverness. "You're right." Denida focused on the president. "We have to find some other way to keep the Gate in one piece, and still have them build the time machine." He bit his lip and turned to Daniel, only to see his son staring at him.

"Who are you? Why are you here?" a masculine voice asked from behind them.

Denida whirled around, his stomach sinking, as he expected to see a soldier with a gun. Instead, a lab tech stood in front of them.

An idea came to Denida, making him smile. "Sorry, we came in to get warm, but we got all turned around and can't find the exit." Denida sensed Daniel's questioning eyes on him, so he squeezed his shoulder reassuringly.

"Okay, this way." The lab tech led them to a door. "Here it is. You're lucky I'm the one who found you, and not a soldier." He opened the door with a smile.

No kidding. "Thank you." Denida extended his hand to shake the tech's. When the tech took his hand, Denida twisted his arm and forced the tech up against a wall.

"What are you doing?" Daniel shouted.

"We need answers!" Denida glowered at the trembling tech.

"Please, just answer his questions." Daniel pleaded with the tech.

The man slumped forward and nodded. "What do you want to know?"

"How can I reach the president undetected?"

"You can't!" The tech's eyes filled with dread. "The only way you could reach him alone would be to approach him in his private chambers."

"Perfect, where are they?"

The tech drew in a deep breath. "In the back of the lab."

Denida nodded and bound the lab tech, despite him not putting up much of a struggle. Daniel and Denida left the lab tech in the locker room before ransacking it to find extra coats to wear as disguises. They followed the tech's instructions and crept through the lab undetected.

The lab held the giant Gate, still intact, for now. *We must make sure they leave it that way for thirty years.* Denida glanced over at the Gate as he passed it. In a short time, they carefully reached what the tech had described as the president's office.

Denida knocked on the door. "Hello?" Silence filled the air, so he opened it. The office was empty. He scoped the room to be sure no one was around, but also to state his curiosity.

"This is a bad idea! What are we gonna do to him?"

"I don't know, maybe explain why he shouldn't destroy the Gate?" Denida turned to face Daniel.

"That's all you'll do?"

What does he mean by that?

Denida and Daniel hid as they heard a rustle at the door.

The president appeared, sitting down at his desk.

"Sir." Denida approached, startling the president. "We are here about the Gate. Who told you to destroy it?"

The president frowned. "The president of the Underworlds commanded me to dismantle it."

The what? Denida turned his head to Daniel, who shrugged. "Aren't you the president?"

The president shook his head. "No, I'm talking about the president of all the Underworlds, not just mine."

Denida, a president of one underworld, had never even heard of a president above him. *Would that president be even higher than the Dark Angels?* Did he help Danyel, the Dark Angel, get to his new world?

"The mysterious man with the UW ring," Denida muttered under his breath. "The guy you met at the hospital, was that the president of the Underworlds?"

"Yes." The president's gaze interlocked with Denida's. "He said everything will change now," his voice had a solemn, defeated edge to it.

"What's going to change now?" Denida raised an eyebrow.

The president shook his head. "It's always been common for souls to travel between the Underworlds at will."

If it had always been common practice, why was it suddenly important to change it, now? Denida leaned over the table, close to the president. "I am from the future, and I need the Gate. You cannot destroy it!"

The president retreated a few steps.

"You destroyed the Gate to make a time machine, which we used it to get here. We need both the time machine and the Gate in order to get home."

The president plopped back down to his seat. "That's impossible. The Gate can only be disassembled and recycled. The material cannot be destroyed or replicated."

Hope set Denida's heart racing. Was that true? Did the Gate still exist in this world? Had it been there all along?

"The only thing that can be removed is the circuit."

The piece that made the time machine work... Denida remembered Dan pointing that out with the Gate back home.

"We have to return to the present, Daniel!" Denida grabbed Daniel and headed for the door.

"Wait!" the president yelled.

Denida turned back to him.

The president stepped closer and peered at Denida. "Who are you?"

Denida winked at him. "You'll see in thirty years." He clicked a button on the device to return himself and Daniel to the present. He was certain the president would remember that experience, even for the next thirty years.

As Denida and Daniel returned to the present, the world's atmosphere seemed different, given the marked lack of soldiers and lab technicians. He scoped the room for the younger version of Nina and Claus, only to find the room to have an eerie silence to it. The lab was empty, except for one person, the president, sleeping at a desk.

The president suddenly woke up. "You're here!" He rushed over to them. "I have been waiting here for you."

How could he afford to wait for so long? Wasn't he busy with his presidential duties? *Wait, we didn't...* "Aren't you the president here?" Denida's heart pounded in fear of the answer he might receive.

"No, Claus is the president."

"Detective Claus?"

The ex-president glanced at his feet. "He overthrew me a few years after I met you. I am under house arrest, but I have the Gate all ready for you."

"Overthrew you? How?"

"Claus is very strict. Anyone who doesn't do what he wants..." The ex-president lifted his hands in despair. "He still runs this world that way, no exceptions."

Denida snuck to the window to peek out at the guards surrounding the building and marching through the streets. Denida couldn't leave without fixing this mess. It was his fault that Claus had found the opportunity to seize power in the first place, a mistake he needed to rectify.

"Watch Daniel; I'll be back." Denida slunk past two guards, who surveilled the house. A photo on a newsstand caught his eye. It showed President Claus standing beside his wife, Susan. *What the hell?* Susan wasn't someone to be pushed around in the world he was from, and based on what he'd seen in the other underworlds, that should be true here, too. *Was she happy with Claus, or had he found a way to control her?*

***

Daniel sat, watching the ex-president. He had nothing to say to the man. *Why did Dad have to leave me here like some little kid?* To make matters worse, Daniel was afraid of what his father might do to people. After everything he had seen, he didn't feel like he knew his dad anymore. That Dark Angel, Danyel, knew his father quite well, after all. Maybe his dad wasn't the good person Daniel always thought him to be. Over the course of this adventure, he had started to see a dark side to his father, which he never could have expected. Maybe his dad didn't expect it, either. *I should have gone with him.*

"So…" The ex-president smiled at Daniel like they were suddenly best friends. "You travelled through time with your dad?"

Daniel was surprised the president wanted to talk to him, but his mom taught him to be polite.

"We're from an underworld where my dad is the president. I went through a Gate and Dad came looking for me. When we came here, we had to travel through time to make sure the Gate would be intact for us to leave," he explained proudly.

"Tell me about your father," the ex-president requested.

Why does he want that? Oh well… Daniel told him how his parents met, how his father fought against the Dark Angels and was considered a hero for his role in the resistance, which led to him being elected president. Daniel concluded by describing the last Dark Angel, who had escaped, only for them to encounter him from the previous Underworld.

"And you said your father doesn't remember his youth?" the ex-president asked with a quivering voice.

Daniel shrugged. His parents' whispers echoed in his mind. "We can't let Daniel know that you don't remember, so just pretend…" Daniel bit his lip and sighed heavily at the memory. All his dad's attempts to impart wisdom since then felt like soulless platitudes and generic advice, nothing grounded in reality. *Sometimes I wish he didn't even bother.* "No, he can't remember it. No one knows what he used to do or the sort of person he used to be."

The ex-president leaned back in his seat, a little pale. "Could he be the one?" he muttered.

***

Denida didn't have a plan to get into the presidential palace. He had abandoned the lab coat and still found himself wearing Claus's uniform, so his getup resembled the soldiers'. Probably due to Denida's attire, the guards let him pass like any other member of the security detail. *Logically, Susan is the key to finding Claus.* A maid in the servant's quarters told him where Susan was and he headed for her room. *Does Claus have some dirt on her? Is that how he's getting her to comply?*

As he'd been trained, Denida strolled onward as if he belonged there, and no one stopped to question him. When he reached Susan's room, he knocked on the door.

"Come in!" a woman's voice called.

Denida grabbed the handle and stepped into the room.

Susan sat in front of a mirror, carefully applying some makeup.

"*What!*" Susan snapped at Denida, as he entered the room. "What does he want now? I have done everything Claus asked me to."

Did Claus blackmail her into marrying him? "Will you excuse us?" Denida smiled to her aides and showed them to the door.

Susan rose from the chair, and her brow creased with worry… or fear.

Denida smiled at her. "Claus didn't send me."

Susan rolled her eyes. "Sure, just tell me what he wants."

Denida would need something more convincing. "Susan Marie… that is your name, right?"

The tension left Susan, and she leaned forward, taking a deep breath.

Good. Denida watched her and nodded. "I'm with the real president's resistance."

Susan sighed heavily and returned to her seat. "I cannot help you; Claus has my family." She combed her long silvery hair.

"I don't need you to do anything, except tell me how to get to him. I'll handle the rest." Denida knelt beside her, trying hard to make eye contact with her, but she just kept combing her hair.

After a moment of awkward proximity, Susan smashed the comb on the table and stared straight into Denida's eyes with a defiant gaze that Denida knew extremely well. "You don't know who you're dealing with, or what he's capable of."

"I do." Denida broke in before she could continue. "But he does not know what I'm capable of, either." *Will this be enough to convince her?*

In truth, Susan was right; Denida didn't know what Claus was capable of, but Denida was certain that Claus was a man who would never dare cross him. *Or would he?* He desperately needed Susan's help. She was the only one who could get him close enough to Claus.

Susan finally sighed. "Fine, I will help you, if you promise me that no harm will come to my family. Swear it!"

"I promise," Denida vowed, because without her, this mission would be impossible.

***

Back in Denida's underworld, Claus 1 listened while the bruised colonel explained what had happened to his counterpart. They hadn't made any progress with finding Denida or Daniel, despite knowing they went through that world's second Gate. It was clear now; they had to send the robot through that Gate to find out what was on the other side. Was Denida there, or had he already ventured farther? There was only one way to find out, but how would they turn on the Gate? Denida had used the controller, but they didn't have one. The colonel's counterpart didn't know how to work the Gates at all, so Dan had to explain them to him.

Claus left during the explanation. *I'm not interested in how the Gates work.* He'd been concerned when he'd seen the other colonel for the first time, but since Denida had already left that world, they were no closer to Denida than before. *Thank heavens.*

Claus returned to the presidential office and plopped down on Denida's chair, kicking his feet up on his desk. *I could get used to this.* He might never have needed to sabotage the second Gate, after all. *Oh well, better safe than sorry.* He leaned his head back with a contented sigh. *This really is my time to shine.*

Claus's moment of peace shattered the second Susan burst through the door. The secretary followed, apologizing profusely.

"It's okay." Claus waved his hand at his secretary, dismissing her.

"You have no right to this office, Claus." Susan gritted her teeth.

"I'm doing his-" Claus tried to protest.

"I'm watching you until Denida gets back. Don't you dare get out of line!"

"You don't need to worry about that."

"Oh, yes, I do. You are too comfortable sitting in Denida's chair." She stormed out, leaving Claus's good mood ruined.

Susan might be headstrong, and she never liked him, but she wasn't stupid. *I need to be careful. Good thing he'd broken the Gate before she started watching his every move.*

***

On Denida's end, he and Susan discussed how they would get to Claus in private. Even for Susan, his wife, finding him alone wouldn't be an easy feat. Claus kept himself busy and surrounded himself with security around the clock.

"I'm not sure it's possible," Susan muttered. "Claus will always have four guards watching him, even at the gala. But if there's a time when he might relax, it would be then." She finished with her hair and makeup. "You interrupted my preparations, so you should have little trouble getting in. You are dressed kind of like security already."

If all went well, Susan and Claus would gather with the aristocrats of this world. Denida wouldn't make an appearance until later, when most of the partygoers would be half-intoxicated. Susan would have to toe a fine line between softening Claus and not making him suspicious by being too friendly with him.

Night dawned and it came time for Denida to make his entry. He almost forgot his purpose, as he saw a room full of people he knew from his own world. It made him flinch as this underworld instilled a nostalgic warmth in his heart. *They must all be connected, yet like in the other worlds, I still haven't seen another version of myself, yet...*

He spotted Dan and couldn't resist. "Dan, long time, no see!"

Dan frowned. "Do I know you?"

Even Dan didn't know him. How come Danyel, the Dark Angel, and the mysterious president over all the worlds, both knew Denida, but those he knew and cherished didn't? *None of them have.* "No sorry, guess not! Wrong person."

Denida wandered back into the crowd, leaving Dan peering at him, puzzled. He eventually returned to the conversation that Denida had interrupted. *So many of my friends here, yet no one knows me. Will Claus remember me?* History had changed, but did Claus know that? Denida would find out soon enough. He made eye contact with Susan and nodded.

Susan waltzed into the crowd to find Claus. "Claus, I have something to show you," Susan spoke suggestively.

Claus, half-intoxicated, leered at her but followed willingly, waving off his security detail.

Susan led him out of the ballroom, in the direction of her room.

Denida tailed them.

When Susan left Claus leaning against the wall to fiddle with the lock on her door, Denida stepped up. "Hi again, Claus." Denida struck him, knocking him out, before dragging him into Susan's room.

Chapter 7- Claus

Denida and Susan stood before a middle-aged Claus, who was now tied to a chair. Denida smiled grimly.

Susan smacked Claus across the face to wake him up.

Claus's face soured.

Denida smirked. *She isn't any milder in this world.* The Susan he knew from his own world would do exactly the same thing.

"How could you do this to me?" Claus eyed Susan. His leer shifted to Denida, and a hint of recognition settled on his features.

Denida smiled. "You remember me? That will make this easier."

"I do, from thirty years ago. What do you want with me?" Claus asked.

Denida sat down opposite him. He smiled deviously at Claus, gazing deep into his eyes. "You're not supposed to be the president. I'm here to correct that!"

"So, you don't want money? How can I help you, then?"

Just as predicted. "I need you to sign over control of the Underworld to the former president." Knowing what this Claus was doing to Susan, he'd probably try to get out of relinquishing power. Denida had to make sure he didn't have that opportunity.

Claus raised an eyebrow. "And you'll let me go?"

Denida nodded, but Susan grunted in protest. Despite her unspoken dissent, Denida set to untying Claus, before handing him a resignation letter and a pen.

Claus examined the letter for a second before taking it. He signed it, and handed the letter back to Denida as if this proceeding was merely business as usual.

As Denida reached for the paper, Claus jabbed the tip of the pen to Denida's neck, holding it against his skin. *Dammit, I let my guard down!*

Claus's hand shook as raw excitement shone in his eyes. "You should never trust a former soldier." Claus pressed the pen against Denida's neck with a little more force.

"Claus, you don't want to do this." Denida tried to buy some time to think of another plan.

Claus applied more pressure.

The warm sensation of blood flowing down Denida's neck, and feeling his pulse in his veins, made him twitch.

Claus pulled Denida out of the room, the pen never budging from his neck.

Denida saw the worry on Susan's face. "Don't worry, Susan." He hoped he sounded calm, even as Claus dragged him from the room.

Out in the hall, a servant stepped into the room, dropping the tray she carried. The clatter made Claus jump and his grip on Denida loosened.

Denida twisted out of Claus's grasp.

"Guards!" Claus darted down the hall.

Denida dashed back to the first room, where he'd left Susan.

Within moments, an alarm rang out.

Denida and Susan knew the guards would check that room first, so they ran to hide in another part of the castle, while the deafening alarm sounded all around them.

Denida had achieved what he came here to accomplish; Claus had signed the document, relinquishing control of the Underworld. *If I can get it to the right people, his reign is over.*

"You promised that my family wouldn't be hurt!" Susan's eyes narrowed with determination.

"They won't. We'll escape before Claus can do anything to your family."

"How? They must be sweeping the rooms to find us."

That's the question of the hour. Denida licked his lips. He knew they were lucky, given the castle's expansive layout, with tens of rooms and long corridors. It brimmed with potential hiding spots, but that was a double-edged sword; while it gave them plenty of places to lie low, it also increased their odds of crossing guards unexpectedly. Denida jotted down an address on a piece of paper, and handed it to Susan, along with Claus's signed resignation letter. "Deliver these papers to this address. The former president is waiting there with my son. He'll know what to do." Denida rested his hand on Susan's shoulder. "You'll find the ex-president and my son, Daniel, at the address I wrote down. Bring them the letter. I believe in you!"

Susan studied the documents for a second. "What will you do?"

Denida tried to return the warm expression, but his gut warned him that this might not work after all, so it was hard to force himself to grin. "I'll create a diversion."

As Susan crept one way, Denida hurried in the opposite direction to create a distraction. He knew exactly how to grab their attention and keep their minds solely on him: *Time to surrender!*

"Looking for me?" Denida called out.

***

Susan darted as fast as she could to the castle exit. As she neared the door, she encountered the first guard, surveilling the building's threshold. She broke into a cold sweat as the guard turned toward her. *I'm done for!*

To her relief, another guard called out. "They caught the intruder; leave her be!"

Just like that, Susan was free. Still carrying the resignation letter that Claus desperately wanted back, she bolted to the ex-president's address. She knew Denida had been caught, but he'd want her to continue; she was sure of it.

Susan ran down dark streets under a starlit sky in silence, finding everyone else to be quiet as well, as if they were aware of the unrest in their underworld. After all, trouble for Claus meant danger for everybody.

When Susan arrived at the president's address, she found two guards patrolling the premises. *How am I going to get past them undetected?* She'd just escaped the palace and the guards, only to come to another heavily surveilled building. *Is it worth it?* She swallowed hard, reminding herself that Claus had her family, who would pay for her crimes against him. Susan had no choice but to see this through, if she wanted to rescue them.

"Hold it!" one of the soldiers yelled as she approached.

Susan acted entitled to be there and flashed Claus's signature, but moved the paper so fast that the guard couldn't see that it was his resignation letter. "I'm here with President Claus's signed consent; open the door!" she commanded.

The soldiers saluted and stepped aside.

Inside, Susan spotted an old man hunched over a table, staring up at her. A little boy stood next to him.

The boy's eyes widened. "Susan?" he asked.

Susan's heart pounded faster in surprise, but on the other hand, Denida had seemed to have inexplicably recognized her too. "Yes, you must be the ex-president and Daniel. Denida sent me."

That announcement eased some of the tension in the room, as both the ex-president and Daniel seemed to nod and draw in deep breaths of relief.

Susan stepped closer and handed Claus's resignation letter to the ex-president. "Denida said you would know what to do with this."

The president picked it up, peeked at it, and jumped to his feet. "He actually did it!"

"Yes, but we must hurry; Claus caught him."

***

Words could not describe how happy Claus felt to confront Denida, who'd humiliated him and escaped his clutches.

"Who's the winner, now?" Claus gloated.

"Do you even know why you came after us thirty years ago?" Denida seemed awfully level-headed, for a man who was tied to a chair.

"All I remember is that I had to capture you, which I have achieved, now." Claus shrugged. "Nothing beyond that matters."

Denida smirked. "You never knew why, did you?"

The question bothered Claus. A bout of discomfort settled in his gut at the idea that he could be missing something. "You want to tell me why I had been ordered to chase you, then?" Claus sat down opposite Denida, grinning wickedly. "Do tell." *Hopefully he'll tell me, for my own sanity.*

"I had the time machine's controller. You were supposed to retrieve it, not get stuck thirty years in the past. The president never cared about you," Denida mocked him.

"Really?" Claus rose from his chair with disbelief tainting his tone. "No, I know you're lying. Tell me the truth now, or I will punish Susan's family. You can't win against me."

"You can't be this far gone," Denida muttered under his breath.

"What? Speak up!"

"You're forgetting about Susan."

Claus tilted his head, not understanding.

Denida snickered. "She's not here, is she? I wonder where she went… and where your signature might be too, seeing as I sure don't have the resignation letter on me!"

Nobody had bothered searching for Susan, since they caught Denida. *Wait; they didn't even capture him because he surrendered willingly! Could that mean...* Sweat dripped down Claus's back. He had lots of enemies who'd be happy to use that resignation against him. Claus rushed to a phone across the room and called the ex-president's estate, but nobody answered it. *Are they already gone?*

"Not getting through?" Denida taunted him.

Claus paced throughout the room, trying to conceal his jittery nerves. He dialed again after a few moments and tried contacting the soldier guarding the ex-president.

"Worried about something, Claus?" Denida chuckled.

If only Claus's eyes could kill, Denida would be dead.

"Seal the door!" he ordered the guards, not taking his gaze off Denida.

The last guard left and closed the door.

Claus locked the door behind him and sat down again. He knew what he needed to do but still had to organize his thoughts.

"What now?" Denida asked.

Claus smiled. "It is not over, yet; they're coming here."

"That doesn't worry you?" Denida blinked.

Claus drew his gun and checked that it was loaded. "Daniel wants you, and Susan wants her family, badly enough that they're willing to risk everything."

"Clever," Denida mumbled.

***

The ex-president stared out the car window as soldiers from his estate drove him, Daniel, and Susan to the palace.

"Where's Claus?" the ex-president asked the soldiers at the palace's door.

A guard crossed his arms. "He boarded himself up in the interrogation room."

"Where's that?"

"Doesn't matter, there is no way in from this side of the building."

The president stepped out of the vehicle. "Take us there!"

The soldiers led him deep below the palace, with their chief of security beside the ex-president. "Claus tried to call your estate, probably to lure you here. You should know that he's still armed."

The ex-president nodded. *Claus must be getting desperate, but he must have known we'd come.* When they reached the door, it was clear they couldn't get through, given a blockade around it. *We have to get Claus to come out.*

"Hello again!" Claus yelled from within.

How does he know we're here? There were neither windows into the room nor cameras in the hallway. *Did someone tip him off?* "Claus, why don't you come out here, so we can talk?" The ex-president called back.

"You would like that, wouldn't you?"

***

"You know this will never work. I should have just killed you when I had the chance." But Denida knew why he hadn't killed Claus. Back home, Claus was his friend. Now, Daniel, and Susan's family might suffer for his weakness.

"Too late, now." Claus sauntered back to the door.

"How did you know they were here?"

Claus sneered at Denida. "Magic."

"Magic?" Denida raised an eyebrow.

"Yes, you remember thirty years ago? There was a man at the hospital. He used some sort of enchanted ring against us. It was more powerful than anything I'd ever experienced before, knocked us all out cold with a single blast!"

Denida shook his head. It hadn't been that long ago for him.

"I searched for information about what he might've done to us. I dug through every bit of knowledge I could find to learn about it. Eventually, I discovered the truth: magic is real. I spent the last thirty years learning as much as I could, but nothing compares to what that man could do with his ring!" Claus stared past Denida. "Mind reading has been my most notable, perhaps most advanced, exploit. You'd understand if you'd stuck around with me, but not everyone has a talent for the arts."

Denida sat stunned.

Claus faced the door. "Sorry for the delay, my old friend. I have Denida here, but Susan's family is also at my mercy. How about we make a trade?"

Denida tried to gaze into Claus's mind, but he lacked the necessary talent and knowledge to see his thoughts. *How foolish of me… he's probably just making it up!* But what if he wasn't? Denida shook himself, and stared at Claus, redoubling his efforts.

"Yes!" Daniel yelled from outside of the room, breaking Denida's focus.

Denida's heart sank. This would not end well. *Claus might just kill us all.* There'd be no stopping him without Denida and his allies, especially if Claus's resignation letter never managed to find its way into the right hands.

"We don't have your letter with us! We'll get it and call you when it's here," the ex-president announced from outside.

***

Daniel rushed back to the ex-president and Susan. "It's ready!"

The ex-president nodded in acknowledgement. "We're ready, Claus." He smirked. and then muttered under his breath, "This had better work."

The door opened slowly, and Claus stepped out into the hall. "What had better work?" he snapped.

"What?" The ex-president's eyes widened, both shocked and terrified.

"You said, 'this had better work.' What is 'this?'"

"He can read your mind!" Denida shouted from inside the room.

Claus started retreating.

The president sighed, grounding himself.

"My plan, then!" Daniel rushed forward.

"What's that, Squirt?" Claus snapped.

"Dad taught me to always have a backup plan, so here it is." Daniel slowly removed a gun, pointing it at Claus. "Let Dad go!" he commanded.

Claus smirked, drawing his own gun. "You think I wasn't a step ahead of you?" He advanced, watching Daniel step back. "Get rid of your gun, and we'll negotiate."

Daniel grimaced and threw his weapon on the floor near Claus's feet.

"Okay, then. You, Boy, bring me the resignation letter!" Claus pointed his gun at Daniel, who took the document from the ex-president and handed it to Claus.

Daniel backtracked and raised his hands innocently.

Claus examined the paper. "Yes, that's what I signed, so I've won!"

"Happy, now? Give us Denida," the ex-president demanded.

Claus waved his gun, gesturing at Denida. "Take him."

Daniel ran to his dad and untied him.

The ex-president smiled. "Thank you."

Claus frowned as if he knew something was wrong. "You are nothing. All of you will die tonight!" Claus threatened. "Shoot them!" He ripped the letter in half.

The soldiers stood perfectly still.

Claus arched his neck, glancing around.

"Did you think it would be that easy?" The ex-president nodded at the soldiers, who aimed their guns at Claus. "Arrest him."

"Yes, Mr. President." The soldiers closed in and grabbed Claus.

Daniel followed his dad, sauntering to the Gate,

The reinstated president and his bodyguards accompanied them.

"Um…" Denida stopped short. "I have to know…"

What's Dad doing? Daniel tapped his thigh impatiently.

The President smiled at Denida. "Your brilliant son came up with everything." He chuckled. "We didn't know what to do, but he suggested that since we had the contract that would turn the presidency back over to me, we might as well use it, so we submitted it to the powers that be." The president ruffled Daniel's hair. "Once they recognized it, the letter itself became useless."

Following the president's explanation, Daniel turned his eyes to his father, seeing the broad smile on Denida's face. *Finally, he can see that I'm not a little kid anymore!*

Denida clapped Daniel on the back. "Good work!"

It felt surreal, after all that happened in this world, to finally be here, at a Gate that had been destroyed, but now stood intact. *Finally, I can see Mom, again!* Daniel smiled gleefully.

Denida cleared his throat. "What happened to the man at the hospital thirty years ago?"

"He was the last president of all the Underworlds."

"The last?"

"He said it was time to fulfill the legend, even if it would cost him his life, which might have come to pass. I haven't seen him since that night." The president peered over at Daniel. "I don't know what the legend is, but it seemed very important to him."

Denida sighed and nodded. "Very well. Good luck, Mr. President."

"Will you be okay?" the president asked.

"Yes, I just need to get home. I am the president of my own underworld, after all." Denida winked.

Denida took Daniel's hand and stepped through the Gate.

Chapter 8- World of Magic

In Denida's underworld, everyone's morale seemed to be on the rise. The Colonel and his counterpart had been talking for a while, explaining the nuances in their respective worlds. The conversation had been educational for both of them, resulting in plenty of nods and laughter. When the conversation ceased, Dan stepped forward. He provided instructions, detailing how to power on the second Gate in the other colonel's world.

The two colonels said their final goodbyes, both unsure if they'd ever see each other again.

Dan took the controller from the Colonel and drove the robot through the Gate.

Once again, everyone in the lab held in their breath, waiting for the signal to return to the feed. To everyone's relief, the feed resumed after a moment. A dark world appeared on the monitor.

Dan slowly maneuvered the robot through this new world, while continually adjusting the camera.

The Colonel had an uncomfortable sensation, like a pain in his gut, which he couldn't shake. He'd seen this place before. *Maybe in my past?* The Colonel steeled himself and pointed to a man, who stepped out of the woods. "Ask that man what's going on here." The Colonel slammed his hand down next to a computer's keyboard and lowered his mouth to a microphone. "Hello!" he called through the robot.

The man jerked around when the robot spoke to him. His features settled as he peered down at the screen. "Oh! You're from the resistance."

Resistance, like the one we had during our civil war? "Why do you say that?" the Colonel asked through the robot.

The man gazed intently into the robot's camera. "You look exactly like our colonel, who ordered us to watch this Gate, in case anyone else came through."

There are multiple worlds with different versions of me? The Colonel wasn't sure what to make of it. He lowered his face in front of the camera again. "Where is the colonel who looks like me, then?"

"The Dark Angel's palace, of course." The man pointed in the direction of a massive fortress.

"The Dark Angels?" *It really is like our world, in the past.* The Colonel turned to Dan. "Head to the palace. Their colonel is our best bet to find their second Gate."

It will be interesting to see yet another version of myself. On the way to the palace, the houses resembled those in their own underworld right after the war against the Dark Angels. Discarded memorabilia and propaganda littered the streets, as people distanced themselves from their oppressor. As the robot drove, it passed several posters and news clippings mentioning "the Dark Angel." *This world must have had one Dark Angel, unlike the seven we fought.*

Dan drove carefully, avoiding the worst piles of debris.

The Colonel shifted in his seat with his gut as tight as a guitar string.

Soldiers swarmed the palace's entrance.

Dan stopped the robot and used the camera to scope out the area.

"Jesus Christ… enough already!" The Colonel yanked the controls out of Dan's hands and drove up to the nearest soldier. "Where's your colonel?"

The soldier's mouth hung agape for a second, then it snapped. "You're in the palace, Sir, with the stranger and his son."

He's still here? The Colonel's heart pounded with excitement, as he hoped that Denida had stayed put.

Nina gripped the Colonel's shoulder with an ironclad grasp, as she stared at the screen.

"Bring your colonel here, Soldier!" the Colonel commanded.

The soldier stumbled back. "Stay here." He turned and fled into the palace.

The Colonel growled, then maneuvered the robot behind the soldier. He simply couldn't wait any longer. The robot followed the soldier around piles of rubble, which several soldiers had started cleaning up. The soldier leading the Colonel peered back, paled, and sprinted faster.

In the Colonel's haste, the robot knocked over piles of debris, but Dan had built the robot for all kinds of terrain, so it merely rolled over everything in its path.

The Colonel grinned ferociously, as he almost caught up to the panting soldier, just before the soldier spun and staggered into a room.

The robot arrived in time for the Colonel to see the soldier hide behind his own colonel.

"Sir, it won't leave me alone!" The soldier pointed at the robot.

Everyone in the room turned to the robot and a couple of soldiers raised their guns, before freezing.

Yet again, the Colonel faced himself. He turned the robot's camera from side to side and frowned. "Where is Denida?"

The colonel in charge of the world cleared his throat. "He left after I shot Danyel."

Nina's entire body tensed. "You shot my Daniel, and Denida just left after you killed his son?" Nina dropped to her knees, weeping.

The other world's colonel waved his hands. "No, no! Not the boy, the Dark Angel. His name was Danyel, too."

The Colonel's heart thundered in his chest. The thought that the Dark Angels might have made their way to other worlds was an alarming consideration. The Colonel remembered that Danyel had been their leader, and the worst of them.

Denida still occasionally told the Colonel that he had to capture and kill Danyel, once and for all.

With deep breaths, Nina pulled herself together and stood, waving Dan's hand away. "Where's Denny… I mean, Denida?"

"Denida and Daniel left through the Gate. They were heading home." The other colonel frowned. "Didn't they make it?"

****

Denida stood with Daniel and scoped out their surroundings. This wasn't home. In fact, it wasn't like any place he'd ever seen before. *Where are we, now?*

They stepped away from the Gate, examining their surroundings. Two boys were fighting in a field, shooting magic beams at each other, and deflecting them with invisible shields. Daniel clenched his fist.

Denida understood Daniel's reaction; he was stunned, too. After all, Claus had mentioned magic, but nothing like this. *This is surreal.*

"With enough practice, they will be quite strong!" a man beaming with pride spoke from behind Denida.

"Everyone uses magic, here?" Daniel asked cautiously.

The man frowned. "Yes, of course! Everyone can use at least a little."

Interesting, everyone here knows some magic. Denida smiled and nodded at the man. He jerked Daniel away from their spot beside the Gate. In a world where everyone could use magic except for them, they were at a disadvantage and had to exercise caution on their trek to the second Gate. *But how?* Denida didn't see anyone he recognized in this world, unlike in the others. Who was he supposed to ask for help? He had to be careful not to raise suspicion, especially when it was possible that some of these residents could read minds, like the last world's Claus learned to do.

Denida and Daniel meandered down the streets, not seeing anyone they recognized. The houses didn't look as automated as they had been in the last world, but there was evidence of magic all around them. Levitating carts without horses or engines ran down the roads instead of cars, and magical energy filled the air, travelling between the houses, instead of wires.

"I'm tired and hungry, Dad." Daniel clutched his stomach.

Denida bit his lip. Finding the second Gate would be a challenge. Maybe there was someone around the first Gate who could point them in the right direction. *It's worth a shot and better than wandering aimlessly.*

They headed back to the first Gate. When they arrived, the proud father and his dueling children were gone, but Denida saw a person he recognized. *Dan!*

Dan peered at the Gate, examining it from all angles, just like the Dan in Denida's home world. Denida smiled at the similarity, happy to see that trend manifesting in this world as well, but his face fell almost immediately as an unsettling realization set in. *Is it possible that the Claus in my world is secretly devious and power-hungry?* Denida pushed that thought away and approached Dan.

"We don't know magic!" Daniel reminded his father.

Denida nodded and sighed quietly, strolling up the hill to the Gate. He had to risk this. He hadn't recognized anyone else in this world and hoped this Dan was just as trustworthy as his friend back home. Denida approached this version of his old friend, crossing his fingers that it wouldn't turn out like his encounter with the last world's Claus. "Dan?"

"Yes, do I know you?" Dan raised his eyebrows at Denida, then tilted his head at Daniel.

Now Denida hoped this Dan was as curious as the one back home. "Sort of." Denida pointed at the Gate. "We came through your Gate."

Dan stood up straighter, as if lightning had struck him. "You have my full attention."

Daniel rolled his eyes and kicked a loose stone on the path.

Denida glanced at Daniel, then turned his attention to Dan. He smiled, trying to appear open and honest. "I'm from a world far from this one. Magic doesn't exist there, but you do."

Dan crossed his arms.

"I will tell you everything, but not here. It's not safe."

Dan turned to Daniel. "Both of you?"

Denida nodded. "Read my mind, if you can." Denida's mind conjured up a memory of his world's Dan, immersed in the mystery of the Gate.

Dan surveyed Denida and Daniel again. "So, there is something special about you two."

***

Dan led the strange pair to his home, where the man called Denida told him an unbelievable tale of alternate worlds beyond the Gates.

"I'm not usually one for drinking in the afternoon." Dan set a couple of bottles of beer on the table and poured Daniel a glass of milk. "But your story has convinced me to make an exception."

"Do you know where the second Gate is?" Denida sipped his beer, while his son shrugged and chugged his entire glass of milk.

"I've got good news and bad news." Dan gulped down half his beer. He'd better be careful; he'd find himself quite drunk, soon. He pushed the bottle away. "The good news is that the Gate's in the city." He watched Denida light up and knew he had to raise his finger and continue immediately. "But it's sealed away behind a magic barrier, which only the strongest magicians can pass."

Denida sighed.

"Our leaders hold a magical championship every year to choose a worthy adventurer who can pass through the Gate. No one knows anything else about the Gate, seeing as it's on what many consider to be holy ground." Dan raised his hands, as Denida straightened. "I'm not saying that I don't believe you. Just, try to imagine yourself in my shoes."

Denida nodded and sipped more of his beer. "When is this championship held?"

"In two weeks."

"Not long from now, then."

"As I was saying, if that Gate leads to other worlds, I can see why they keep it behind a barrier."

Denida and the kid sat with glum faces. The kid fiddled with his glass, so Dan refilled it and put a plate of fruit on the table.

"What if we offer to help the magicians?" Denida smiled at Dan with childlike optimism.

"They'd realize right away that you don't have any abilities to speak of, and they'd never let the kid in."

"My name's Daniel." The kid lifted his head from an apple he was devouring.

"Right; I should be able to remember that." Dan took another swig of beer and stared at the ceiling.

Daniel, stood and wandered about the kitchen, munching on his second apple.

Dan picked up the newspaper and started skimming it.

The crinkling sound of pages turning kept the silence at bay. Funnily enough, Dan really did want to help these people, as if they were friends, whom he'd known for years.

Denida jumped to his feet and pointed at his son. "Teach Daniel magic."

Dan stared at him in disbelief. "If only it were that easy." He stared at their long faces and sighed. "Fine, I guess we can try."

Dan led them out to his garden. Anyone who saw them would just see them practicing magic, which was normal, here. "Parents start teaching their kids different kinds of magic when they're quite young. It's all a matter of imagining what you want and believing it to be real. Kids have strong imaginations, so a lot of the time, parents are teaching them to control their magic, rather than explaining how to use it."

Daniel stood with fierce concentration on his face and waved his hands. A faint beam of light shot across the yard. He grinned and tried again. The beam shone more vibrantly, but not nearly potent enough to compete with this world's residents' aptitude. "Dad, you try."

"Why not?" Denida squeezed Daniel's shoulder. "Can't hurt."

He strolled a short distance away and copped a sturdy stance, which gave Dan the impression that he was more prepared to throw a punch than launch a magical blast.

"Alright, let's start with the basics. Create a fireball," Dan suggested.

"How?" Denida glanced at him.

If he's asking, I doubt he'll be able to win that championship, let alone use magic. "Just picture it in your mind."

Denida moved like he was fighting invisible enemies, throwing punches and kicks, ducking and weaving.

Dan would have been fascinated if he weren't trying to teach magic. He stepped forward to intercept him, when Denida spun and shouted. Denida threw his hand out, as if to punch, but with his palm open like he was pushing the air. A fireball bloomed and Dan threw himself to the side to avoid the blast.

"You can use magic?" Dan rolled to his feet and dusted himself off.

"I guess so." Denida stared at his hands.

"That was too powerful a blast for someone who's never used magic before." *Something about this guy is very strange.*

Over the next few days, the three of them practiced magic. As Dan watched Denida absorb whatever Dan could tell him about magic, and apply it immediately, Dan had the distinct sensation that he wasn't teaching Denida, but rather, helping him to remember lessons he had already learned. Dan's distinct feeling that he possessed a connection to Denida grew stronger over the days, and he began to believe Denida had a real chance of winning the championship and advancing through the Gate.

Over the course of their training, Dan couldn't help but wonder if Denida knew stronger spells. Dan had never learned anything beyond the basics, so he had no way to teach Denida more advanced magic. *Where did he originally learn magic, anyhow?* From what Denida had told him, his world lacked magic. *What could he have forgotten about his past?* They would need to strengthen his magic as much as possible before the championship, so they had to seek help from a warlock in this world, who knew more advanced magic than Dan.

One day, after training, Dan sat beside Denida. "You will need to see someone who can teach you more than I can. I know someone, too."

Daniel tensed. "Dad has to leave?"

Dan nodded. "The Warlock is one of the proficient users of magical arts."

Denida approached Dan. "I will need to leave Daniel here, then."

"Yes, you'll need to see her alone, if you want her to train you."

***

The Warlock was a being of myth. *Is she even real?* Denida knew that myths had a tendency to be half-truths, at best, but they were generally inspired by something real. The question was: how much reality was there behind the legend of the Warlock? According to the myth, the Warlock lived far away, isolated from civilization. With nothing else in sight, Denida ventured onto a small island, situated in the middle of an expansive lake. Dan had said that he knew the Warlock personally, so he had told Denida where to meet her.

Denida shook with concern about this whole thing. *Is this really the only way?* He had traveled through towns inland, toward a region of mountains, where this lake was situated, and he had to charter a boat to reach the island. He stepped off the boat, wading to the shore.

"Good luck, you'll need it." The captain of the boat waved and sailed away, seemingly in a great hurry to put distance between himself and the island.

Needless to say, Denida found the comment less than reassuring. Had others fallen here? Regardless, he hadn't come all this way to turn back.

A house perched on a bare spot on a hill, well inland, the only sign of inhabitants.

Aside from the house, beautiful foliage graced the island, creating a strange serenity, despite the heat from the afternoon sun. Denida wouldn't mind finding a different warlock, in a colder climate, but Dan had told him that this was the only warlock who could teach him.

Denida hiked up to the house, listening to birds chirping, and watching squirrels scurrying about. The heat parched him. *I need rain.*

Finally, he made it to the estate, and as soon as he stepped through a picket fence around the property, everything in the vicinity changed. The beautiful island he had admired, with all the birds and wildlife, vanished. Even the heat evaporated.

"It was a mirage?" Denida turned to examine his new surroundings, as if to convince himself to acknowledge the change.

"Well noticed," a woman's voice praised him.

Denida spun around to find an old woman leaning on a cane, peering at him with intense eyes, as if she could see right into his soul.

She stood still, as if she'd always been there, despite Denida's certainty that he had not passed her. "Welcome, shall we get started?"

Chapter 9- Training

Daniel, having a little bit of magical aptitude, was now confident running errands in town, and never accrued much attention.

Dan spent most of his time focusing on his research, so his version of babysitting Daniel was telling him to stay close, only to ignore him in favor of his work.

Daniel had far too much time to think about his dad, which always made his chest sting with concern, so he took an interest in distracting himself with Dan's projects. Today, Dan returned to the Gate for further investigation. Daniel had been back here several times, watching the boys he had seen before honing their magic abilities. He had joined them once or twice to get some training in, too, but he never told Dan, out of fear of worrying him. He had grown so used to Dan's nervousness that it felt like they'd known each other forever.

Worse still, it had been weeks since Daniel had been home with his mom, and he found himself more jaded, more grown up, missing her for sure, but not yearning for her affection like he had at first. In fact, he missed being a kid without a care in the world and he longed for the old days when his only fear was getting caught acting up. Daniel wished he could tell his mother how much he appreciated the life she had given him. *It will be different when we're back, if we ever get there.*

"Hm." Dan poked the Gate's metallic material. "No recognizable controls. There might be a few modular elements, however …" He peered at the Gate so closely that he almost left a nose print on it.

Why bother… haven't we told him enough about it? "Like I told you, Dad has a controller, but this Gate only lets you come into this world. You need the other Gate to leave." Daniel rolled his eyes.

The Gate emitted a loud buzzing sound, and Daniel's heart started pounding.

"Someone's coming through!" He dragged Dan behind a bush and peeked back at the Gate.

Dan stood, brushing himself off. "If someone's coming through, don't we want to greet them?"

"Not until we know who they are." Daniel pulled Dan down. "There are some bad people out there."

The last world's middle-aged Claus stepped through the Gate, followed by twenty soldiers.

"Weird place…" Claus scoped the area.

Daniel shook with fear.

Dan leaned over to whisper. "Who's he? And what are those things they're carrying?"

"Claus was the president of the last world, before we overthrew him. Now he's here. This is bad." Daniel bit his lip. "Those things are guns. They'll kill you before you can even think of a spell to cast. We've got to get out of here!"

Neither Dan nor Daniel knew an invisibility spell, so Daniel pulled Dan along, crawling behind more bushes, while Claus and the soldiers admired the new world.

How did Claus manage to follow us? We needed a controller to turn the Gate on. Once they were far enough away to stay out of sight, Daniel's head filled with questions. *What has happened to the reinstated president… and what is Claus going to do here?*

Dan twiddled his thumbs in thought. "Maybe if we made a distraction?"

"Follow me!" Daniel commanded and began to sneak away, unnoticed.

The soldiers checked their gear, as Claus surveyed their surroundings.

"What if that Claus fellow finds us? If he's as bad as you say, we have to get away, maybe even go find Denida."

"No, Dad needs to train to get us through the second Gate, or we're stuck here for a full year. If anyone can stop Claus, it'll be Dad, but he'll need magic to beat him!"

"You said those things would kill us?" Dan gestured toward the soldiers, clearly indicating their guns. "What exactly do they do?"

"They shoot bullets. Those men just need to pull a trigger."

"Oh, any decent magician could stop them. Magic is stronger than weaponry."

Daniel rolled his eyes. "So, you think, but what about this world's kids and the civilians who aren't as magically gifted?"

"Our military can stop them with ease. No one else would need to fight."

Daniel, now outside the house, turned back, almost expecting Claus and the soldiers to march up behind them. Claus wouldn't be easily beaten. Twice, his dad had stopped him, and here he was, showing up again. Dan stepped inside. "I'll stay hidden until my dad gets back."

"That might be a good idea." Dan closed the door and sat at the table with his fingers drumming nervously.

***

Claus noticed the two kids using magic. *Truly fascinating!* He approached slowly, as if in a trance. *What is this power?* He had not seen anything like it since that man had knocked him and his team over with a magical blast thirty years ago.

"Admiring my son's talent?" The proud father nudged Claus.

Claus grabbed his arm. "Who can teach me that power? Who's the strongest, meanest fighter in your world?"

"What the hell?" The man tried to pull away but couldn't break Claus's ironclad grip. That's when Claus saw the answer to his question in the man's mind. He released the man, allowing him to stumble over to his children and whisk them away.

Claus grinned. *The time has come.* He whistled to get his soldiers' attention. "We're going to meet someone."

They collected their gear and followed Claus.

Claus knew exactly who could teach him what he wanted, but first, he and his soldiers would need to break him out of prison.

***

Nina frowned. She had been so close to seeing her son, only to have missed him again. *Is he okay? Is Denny?* She shook with anxious energy and glanced over at the Colonel, who was contentedly talking to yet another version of himself. Were there other versions of Nina, too? What would it feel like to talk to another version of herself? But while the Colonel's idle conversations made Nina want to crawl out of her skin with impatience, he was the one trying the hardest to get her boys back, so how could she object?

The colonels had been talking for hours, and her colonel had learned more about Danyel, the Dark Angel, who seemed to know Denny. How that Dark Angel had arrived in that world was a mystery, but that world's colonel had shot him before he could harm Denida or answer any questions. All they had learned was that he'd been brought there by a mysterious individual he'd called "the boss."

None of the colonels' discussion gave them any insight into this boss's identity, plans, or abilities. Had he moved the Dark Angel between the worlds? If so, how could he, when Denida had just discovered the ability to travel through the Gates? No one had mentioned other worlds during the war, but if there was another way to travel between them, maybe they could use it to get Denida and Daniel back more quickly.

The other colonel showed them the Gate, which was identical to theirs, but as with the others, it needed power. The people in the other world had already started working on powering up the second Gate.

"We fought the Dark Angels here, and if what you say is true, your Dark Angel was the same one that escaped our world after our war." The Colonel in Nina's world shifted on his feet. "I'm more than a bit worried about someone who not only has the power to move people between worlds, but can also chose to bring a Dark Angel there, of all places."

Nina rubbed her eyes. It was too weird watching the Colonel talk with himself, but at least they knew Denida and Daniel left that world alive and well. *That's all that matters.*

***

Susan peered up from her seat in the waiting room outside Denida's office. She'd been following Claus like a bad smell.

The door to Denida's office finally opened and Claus exited with a stack of papers in his arms. He set them down on the secretary's desk.

The secretary smiled as she picked up one page to examine it. "How were the reports?"

Claus grunted. "The reports about the latest development are worrisome. I should really head back to the lab and make sure-"

"I'll join you." Susan rose from her seat.

"Hi Susan, nice to see you." Claus smiled at her through gritted teeth. "I'm just going to see the Colonel and Lady Nina, but of course, you may join me."

"You know, on second thought, someone should stay here, in case of an emergency." Susan nodded to him with a smile as fake as his.

"Okay, you can stay here, and I'll be back in an hour or so." Claus sauntered away.

Susan still suspected him of something. Claus just gave off this vibe that made her uneasy. Now she had a chance to investigate, hoping to either find some real evidence against him, or quell her suspicions. *Finally, that snake left*

Denida's office! Denida and his son could be in jeopardy, and Susan had to save them.

Denida's secretary resumed typing, focused on her work, so Susan slipped into Denida's office. Claus had made it his own, decorating the desk with his own pictures and nameplate. It only reinforced Susan's belief he was committing treachery. He kept acting like he knew Denida wasn't coming back. *Why does he seem so sure?*

Maybe she could find a clue here to put her on the right track. Susan examined the drawers and cabinets, whatever she could think of, but everything seemed normal. *Either I'm wrong about him, or he's just that good at covering his tracks.*

Susan slumped down in the chair behind the desk. She had broken into Denida's office, searched through it without permission, and despite finding nothing, still had a sinking feeling in her gut. *Maybe I should just give up, even if everything still feels off.* She dropped her head on the desk, almost at the point of tears.

When Susan raised her head, preparing to leave before someone found her, she accidentally nudged the mouse with her hand and the computer's monitor lit up.

Of course. She clicked on a recently opened folder. Denida had secured all his files with a password. *He's always been careful.*

Claus had some files password-protected too, but not all of them. One folder, which was still open, contained files named after each high-profile individual in the Underworld, including Susan. She remembered hearing a little about this. Each file contained a detailed map, which stored the hour-to-hour movements of the individual it was named after. Susan remembered the Colonel giving all the important residents of the Underworld GPS trackers to set up their maps, due to residual fear and paranoia from the old days, when the Dark Angels occupied this world.

Claus's file revealed that he had been at the second Gate for half an hour before he left and called the Colonel to tell him about the Gate. *Why would he take that long before contacting someone? He must have been up to something.*

Susan shut the computer down and examined the office, closing a drawer that stood ajar so that no one could tell she had gone through it. *I'm going to check out that second Gate.*

***

Claus arrived at the lab to find the Colonel talking to another version of himself, discussing how to power up the other world's Gate. From what Claus saw, turning on the Gate proved to be a real challenge. The Dark Angel had left things scattered and some power supplies had shorted out. *Thanks, Danyel.*

As Claus sauntered up to the Colonel, his phone beeped. *What now?* He had to answer it. With Susan at headquarters, only God knew what she might get up to if he didn't check the incoming message.

The text on the phone alerted him to a data breach on the computer in Denida's office. *I have to get back there as soon as possible.* Internally, he envisioned folding his hands in a silent, thankful prayer to Denida for putting that security system in place. *And I'd thought it unnecessary.* He suppressed a chuckle but couldn't hide his smirk.

Back at headquarters, Claus turned to Denida's secretary. "Has anyone been in here?" He jabbed his finger in the direction of the office.

"Nobody has been here since you left, Sir."

"We'll see about that." Claus stormed into the office. If Susan had done anything, he'd have a record, thanks to another gift from Denida: security cameras. He rewound the footage to the timestamp on his phone's message and played the tape.

As an image of Susan hunched over his computer appeared on the screen, a knot formed in Claus's stomach. *Crap.*

Claus plopped into his chair. *What was Susan after?* He opened the computer's usage log to find that his GPS record had been opened while Susan was in the office. That record showed his trip to sabotage the Gate.

A bead of sweat ran down Claus's back. If Susan told anyone, he could lose everything. He almost ran out of the office, but instead, he sat back down at the computer. *Two can play at this game.*

Claus opened the log, hoping to see what Susan would have accessed. She spent most of her time exploring the GPS tracker right around the time he had wrecked the Gate. *Where is she, now? Don't tell me…*

Claus arrived near the second Gate and plodded through the forest. He usually hated how quiet it was, but today, it was a good thing. He could hear Susan poking around by the Gate. If she found the chunk of the Gate that Claus had hidden, he could face serious jailtime.

Claus peeked at his phone. Sure enough, Susan had downloaded a local copy of the GPS tracker and was using it to track his location. He'd be sure to erase those files when he got back so that nobody else could use that data against him. Suddenly, he heard Susan's triumphant, "Found it!" resound from near the rock, under which Claus had hidden the piece of the Gate. Claus picked up a hefty stick and charged at Susan.

Susan's phone beeped, warning her to Claus's proximity. Her eyes widened. "Claus is here?" Susan spun around with her phone in one hand, the Gate's main unit in the other.

Claus appeared behind Susan and swung the branch.

Susan collapsed, dropping the phone and Gate piece on the grass with a muffled thud.

Claus peered down at her unconscious form lying in front of him and wrinkled his nose in disgust.

Now I have to deal with her, too. "You found the main unit. Are you happy, now?" Claus nudged her with his toe. The woman could never keep her nose out of things, but what was he going to do, now? She was Denida's friend. If he managed to return, she could be valuable leverage. *There's an abandoned cabin near here…*

Claus sat in the cabin, twiddling his thumbs, until Susan started to come to with a grunt. He sat in front of her and waited for her to fully wake up.

Susan's eyes snapped open, and she tried to shift her position, but restraints Claus had wrapped around her arms and legs kept her fastened to a chair. "You…. I knew you were a snake, but this? This is low, even for you."

Her panic made Claus smile and he laughed at her. He placed the Gate's main unit and Susan's phone out of her reach. "You caught me, but I could have killed you." Claus patted her cheek. "You should feel lucky; if Denida ever manages to come back, you're going to be my insurance." He could practically see the emotions swimming through her head. Despair, fear, defiance, hope, all in an endless power-struggle.

"You've forgotten about the GPS system. Someone will find out what you've done, or find me."

Claus stuck out his tongue. "I locked those files down before I left. I'm now the only one who can access the GPS files, and I'll be sure to erase all traces of our excursions."

Susan tried to writhe against the chains.

"I see you'll be occupied for a while. I'll leave you to think." Claus sneered. "I'll come by and feed you when I can, but you could really stand to lose a little weight." He closed the cabin door behind him and made sure it was locked from the outside, before heading to his car, whistling happily.

***

Denida stood in front of the Warlock, ready to prove himself worthy of her coaching. *But am I really?* Maybe his skill was just pure luck. Everyone in this world knew magic, so why would his aptitude matter? There might just be something in the air in this world that made everyone naturally adept at learning magic effortlessly. But on the other hand, Daniel's skills had been weak at best, and Dan's were only slightly better, so just maybe Denida's ability to learn magic so quickly had merit. He interlocked his thumbs, palms out, prepared to shoot a beam of magic at the Warlock.

"No!" the warlock interrupted him, as knowing what was on his mind.

Of course, she does; she read my mind. Denida kept his hands poised, but turned his focus to her.

"Everyone who comes here shoots magic beams and fireballs. Show me something I haven't seen." The Warlock smirked.

Easier said than done. What he was here for, after all? Why would he have come, if he already knew what he was doing? He had no choice but to try, or he'd fail before the test even began. He racked his brain, but nothing Dan had taught him seemed sufficient. *Wait; that man at the hospital used magic. Maybe I should try that spell.* Denida stood still, drawing in a deep breath, and focused until his head ached.

The Warlock stood up and started to wave dismissively when Denida released the spell with a prayer that it would work.

A heavy gust of wind blew across the island, almost knocking over a tree in the distance.

"Impressive." The Warlock turned away from him and took several steps. "You have talent." She peeked back at Denida with a faint smile. "You coming?"

Denida released a sigh and hurried after the Warlock. He'd passed the first test.

"That man used the ring's power to do that." the Warlock explained calmly, still heading forward.

In the days that followed, the Warlock taught Denida a great deal of magic, awakening even more of the talent buried deep inside of him.

Denida soon learned that reading minds was child's play.

On a lunch break one afternoon, the Warlock sat across from Denida. "Have you gotten any closer to figuring out where you first learned magic?"

Denida set the apple he had been eating down and shook his head. *That has been weighing on her mind for a while.*

The Warlock sighed. "There's a black aura around your memories, as if they've been sealed by a dark spell." The Warlock rested her hand on her shoulder. "The good news is that you're relearning magic. The bad news is that I can't lift the seal. Maybe a group of us could remove it, but I certainly can't do it alone."

Denida frowned. "I've lived with it this long. Regardless of whether or not you can give me answers, I need to get back to my own underworld."

The Warlock nodded, and brushed a hand through her hair in thought. "Yes, your world needs you, and magic won't get you there without the Gates." She tapped her lip. "Although the president of all our Underworlds had a ring of legendary power that allowed him to travel freely throughout the underworlds in a heartbeat."

Denida's mouth hung agape. "It's not just for offensive spells?"

The warlock chuckled. "Of course not!" She smiled softly, but there was sadness under it. "I would actually be afraid to wield his ring, with all its power. I don't know if I'd be able to control it."

"Where is it from?" Denida asked, curiosity making him a bit antsy.

"I wish I knew." The Warlock sat in silence for so long, that Denida was surprised when the old woman continued. "What I do know is this: it is made from the same material as the Gates."

That alloy, again? Neither Dan nor anyone else who manipulated the material could learn anything about it. Its composition, origin, and properties remained a mystery, despite everyone's continued attempts to understand it. However, it contained the power to travel between worlds, and even throughout time. How had it ended up in these worlds?

As much as the ring was a puzzle, the spell sealing Denida's memories was even worse. His mind returned to that, despite his best efforts to prioritize finding his way home.

"You're still thinking about the seal," the Warlock stated.

Denida sighed and nodded, ashamed to admit it when he knew he had more important goals to achieve.

"You understand," the Warlock began. "- there is no guarantee that we will succeed, and it could be dangerous. Would you be willing to try, anyway?"

"Yes." Denida struggled to maintain his composure. He wanted to go home to Nina but he needed to know about his past. How did Danyel know him, and the president of the Underworlds, as well? *My past must be important.* Why would anyone spend so much energy creating such a strong sealing spell, if not to hide something earthshattering? *It's time to find out what I've forgotten.*

Chapter 10- The Magic Competition

Claus and his soldiers assembled outside a high-security prison, where the magic world held its most dangerous criminals. A strong seal surrounding the prison negated magical aptitude. *This is perfect.* Claus chuckled down at his gun. The prison guards were also armed with non-magical weapons, but they paled in comparison to the rifles Claus's soldiers carried.

The soldiers charged through the front gate, guns blazing. The assault became a bloodbath, as they gunned down everyone in their way. Some guards tried to return fire, but the troop killed them before they could wound anyone. Claus strolled down the halls, stepping over bloody corpses. Occasionally, a downed guard would shift or grunt, and Claus would point his gun and fire until they fell still.

The magic users didn't have computers, so after flipping through folders in a filing cabinet, Claus found the location of the person he came here for.

Some of the inmates cowered in the corners of their cells, while others yelled for Claus and his men to release them, but he just ignored them. He was here for one specific person, so his shoulders shot the prisoners who became too rowdy. Soon, many more prisoners huddled in the backs of their cells, and only the stupidest men remained shouting. How Claus enjoyed their fear.

When Claus finally reached his target's cell, he found his man, this world's infamous Dark Wizard, reading a book. "Hello," Claus asked cautiously, suddenly unsure of himself.

The Dark Wizard raised his hand to stop him.

Claus fell silent, watching the wizard finish his chapter. He put a bookmark in his book, closed it and peered up at Claus. "I know what you want, and my answer is no." The wizard returned to his book.

"But…" Claus attempted.

The wizard merely shook his head and turned a page.

Claus's commander approached. "The prison's secure, Sir. Is that the man who's supposed to help you finish off Denida?"

The wizard set his book aside, and his eyes glowed. "Yes." He stood up and approached the cell door.

Claus stared at the wizard, trying to piece together what had just happened. "Excuse me?"

"You want my help to defeat Denida, don't you?"

Claus licked his lips. "Well yes-"

"Good, you have it." The wizard crossed his arms. "Let's go!"

"Release the wizard," Claus commanded with a shaky voice.

Claus's commander opened the cell door.

The wizard patted Claus on the shoulder and strolled down the hall, leaving Claus and his commander to catch up.

Claus's head swarmed with questions, but he pushed them aside. If the Dark Wizard would help him defeat Denida, everything would be fine.

As Claus marched out of the prison, the wizard turned to him. "Blow up the prison."

Claus's heart sank. "What about the other prisoners? Aren't they your friends?" He saw the smirk on the Dark Wizard's face, and felt his heart drop lower. "Perhaps your inmates could be useful?"

The wizard smiled at Claus with gleaming eyes. "No, blow them up with it!" He turned and sauntered to the road.

"Destroy it!" Claus waved his arm and followed the wizard.

"Yes, Sir." Claus's commander saluted, then gathered the soldiers, rattling off orders.

The soldiers ran through the prison, laying explosives, then filed out one by one, standing in formation. When all the soldiers were accounted for, the commander handed Claus the detonator.

With a push of a button, a loud bang filled the air, followed by a billow of flames and smoke, reducing the prison to rubble.

"That was for you," the wizard murmured under his breath, as he watched the building fall.

When the dust finally settled, the wizard grinned at Claus. "So, you need training? Shall we begin?"

Claus had a hard time believing he'd met someone colder and more callous than he was, but he needed the wizard's help, no matter the consequences. "Yes." Claus swallowed hard.

"Good." The wizard smiled brightly. "You've proved your worth." He patted Claus on the shoulder again, but this time, Claus was certain the touch burned through the back of his coat.

Claus needed this wizard but couldn't shake the pervasive feeling that he would come to regret this. His singular goal to defeat Denida gave Claus severe tunnel vision, so he hadn't thought to check the reason behind the wizard's imprisonment. *But he wanted us to blow up the prison with hundreds of inmates still inside. Is this a bad omen, or am I just overthinking things?* It was too late, now. If the wizard got out of control, they would just have to kill him.

***

The Warlock had contacted several of her fellow warlocks. The most powerful ones agreed to help, but they were scattered throughout the world, so it would take some time for them to arrive. The results, however, would be worth the wait. They were all to gather on the Warlock's island to try to remove the spell that sealed Denida's memories. The Warlock stayed optimistic, maintaining her soft smile with ease. She wished Denida could assist with their mission, as he had surprised her with his strength, but magic users could not remove self-afflictions.

Deep down, the Warlock still puzzled over who might have cast the spell in the first place, and why they would want to seal Denida's memories in the first place. *What could've happened in Denida's past that was so important that it needed to be hidden, even from Denida himself?*

In the interim, the Warlock continued training Denida. He needed to be as strong as possible to endure what they were going to do to him, as well as for the magic competition to follow. Denida's strength continued to grow, as did the Warlock's curiosity.

The appointed day arrived, and the warlocks arrived. As members of an elite group, all six of the warlocks were already acquainted, so they greeted each other with friendly smiles, affectionate hugs, and basic spells to bolster each other's magic.

"Are you sure about this?" One of the visitors frowned.

"Yes, but I can sense a powerful force behind it, so we need to protect our space." The Warlock gestured around them with a sweeping gesture.

"We will set up a spell to prevent anyone from intruding. But will we need-"

"No!" The Warlock raised her hand to stop him.

She had set up a room with shelves full of relics, which could strengthen and focus their magic. She had already shielded the room to prevent external interference.

The warlocks formed a circle around a pentagram drawn on the floor. Candles burned at each intersection and the Warlock had salted the circle around the pentagram to prevent outside forces from entering. Denida lied down in the center of the pentagram.

Denida was naked, as unnatural objects inside the circle could interfere with the spell. Without his shirt, a mysterious scar on his side was clearly visible, and would serve as the target for the warlocks' spell.

The Warlock closed the door. "We must work together with confidence and unity." She stared at each of her visitors in turn. "We've had our differences, but they must be set aside for this spell to be successful."

"We could use the Spell of Lys," one suggested.

The other warlocks muttered and glared at him, wide-eyed.

"It is forbidden," another stated. "You know that."

The speaker nodded with a frown.

In the absolute silence, the Warlock initiated a chant, allowing the others to join in.

The power of their spell became a visible stream, which wrapped around the pentagram. It seeped into the circle around Denida, growing until it filled the circle and pushed against the barriers chalked on the floor. Red magic wafted from the scar on Denida's side, forming a shield around him. They focused the stream on the shield, trying to shatter it, but the red screen remained intact. Despite their best efforts, the warlocks' magic couldn't even dent the barrier.

The Warlock fell silent, and the chanting faded out. "We must try the Spell of Lys."

The others stirred, but the room's silence persisted.

The Warlock nodded at Denida, and they began a different chant.

This time, rather than the power slowly building up, a hard blow immediately slammed into the seal. Denida twitched in the center of the pentagram but stayed silent. This time, they attempted to transform the shield into something else, seeing as their efforts to brute force their way through it had failed before.

As the seal weakened, a shadowy face appeared above Denida. "You will not break my seal."

A tremendous gust blew the door off the hinges and scattered the salt. The candles fell over, birthing a fire, which raged throughout the room.

The warlocks continued chanting, ignoring the flames. Windows exploded and the flames licked the rock walls and ceiling, making molten rock drip like candlewax. Still, the warlocks persisted. Wolves approached rapidly with foreboding howls drawing ever closer to the Warlock's house. Several of the warlocks had beads of sweat on their faces but maintained their chant.

The wolves leapt through the flames and attacked the warlocks. One turned away from the spell to defend himself.

As soon as the circle broke, the power vanished, along with the wolves, the fire, and the rest of the damage, as if none of it had ever even been there.

Denida still remained in the center of the pentagram. The warlocks had tried the strongest magic they knew, to no avail.

***

Claus hadn't expected the Dark Wizard to train him in the dark arts, yet that seemed to be the wizard's plan. "I'm not ready to learn advanced dark magic." Claus protested, after the wizard described a powerful, destructive spell. "Don't I need the basics to do something that advanced?"

The wizard waved his hand dismissively. "We don't have much time, so just follow along with my teachings." The Dark Wizard cleared his throat. "We'll start off with black fireballs." He pointed to a target. "Find the darkness in your heart, the rage, the hate, and focus it into a huge ball." The wizard smirked. "Then throw it at your target."

Claus imagined the physical target as Denida and had no trouble demolishing it with black fire.

The wizard made him practice the same spell over and over until he could summon the dark fire without envisioning anything.

"Now, you are ready-"

"Great! Time to take care of Denida." Claus rubbed his hands together.

"As I was saying, you're ready to give your soul to the master."

"The master?"

"Lucifer!"

Claus blinked in shock. "The Devil?"

"Yes, you cannot hope to master the dark arts without him." The wizard stepped into a room, wherein a dark aura flitted about, nearly filling the room. A pentagram was drawn in blood on the floor. Black candles burned but barely lit the room.

"What do I need to do?" Claus carefully stepped into the room. He sauntered to the middle of the pentagram to stand beside the wizard.

"Simple." The wizard unsheathed a dagger and slashed Claus's palm.

"Ouch!" Claus yanked his hand back. "What the hell did you do that for?"

"You'll see." The wizard grabbed Claus's hand again and shook it, making blood drizzle down on the pentagram.

With a sickly feeling forming in his stomach, Claus withdrew his hand from the wizard's grasp.

"You're ready." The wizard chanted and held his hands in front of his face. When he lifted his hands, a different face appeared.

Wow! Claus gasped. "That is some spell."

***

"The opening ceremony for this year's wizardry championship has finally arrived!" The world's High Sorcerer announced. "The winner gets to choose any prize in the land that he or she desires!" The sorcerer smiled at the crowd.

"You're laying your lives on the line, so we expect nothing less than your best. If you die, it's because you were too weak. However, duels do not need to be fought to the death," the sorcerer grunted.

The Dark Wizard had modified his appearance to that of a young man. Claus could tell he enjoyed his new disguise. "You heard the rule. You must win at any cost; don't be too weak to kill."

Claus nodded and approached a desk to sign up for the competition.

This will be interesting. The wizard had told Claus that dark magic was frowned upon, but not officially banned, so Claus would have an edge for his first duel, as his opponents wouldn't expect his black spells.

Claus locked eyes with his opponent.

Claus's opponent shot a fireball at him as soon as the starting bell chimed.

Claus waved the fireball away, all the while maintaining a bored expression. He thought about toying with the man a bit more but caught the fierce glare on his mentor's face out of his peripheral vision.

As Claus's opponent readied another attack, Claus blasted him with a black fireball. It burned clean through the man's shield and sent him flying across the room.

Claus's opponent twitched a couple of times, then laid still.

The Dark Wizard nodded.

Claus examined the crowd of combatants for one face. When he spotted his target, he grinned and pointed at Denida.

***

When the Warlock brought Denida to the competition, the High Sorcerer greeted her warmly. The sorcerer pulled her aside for a private discussion.

Denida watched them curiously, then turned away to focus on the fights. His sole concern was attaining access to the Gate. Everything else would have to wait.

As Denida prepared for his first match, he saw that all seven of the warlocks were in attendance. Given his status as the Warlock's pupil, the competition's judges slated him to start competing come the semi-finals.

Denida surveyed the holy arena. Only competitors were allowed to be here. He wondered if Dan and Daniel could see him through their feed at Dan's house.

As Denida prepared to take his place, he noticed concern on the Warlock's face, and she sighed. "What name should we use to introduce you?"

Denida scrunched up his nose at the question *Do people here really use stage names for these fights?* "Just call me Denida. It is my name, after all."

"The Warlock's pupil, Denida!" the announcer's voice rang out.

Guess the teacher matters more than the student. Whatever... His name had been called. Denida inhaled slowly and stepped into the arena.

Denida felt as nervous as his trembling opponent looked, but as the bell rang, Denida clenched his fist to build his confidence. A gust of wind struck him, preventing him from concentrating on counterattacks. The gale pushed Denida back, tearing his breath away. He had almost reached the arena's boundaries. If his foot crossed the perimeter, he'd lose automatically. Denida turned his back to the wind, ignoring the triumphant shout of his opponent, and chanted a spell to conjure a wall between himself and his opponent. Free of the wind's assault, Denida flung a ball of energy at his opponent, who continued showboating as if he'd already won. His opponent collapsed without even having an opportunity to react to the attack.

"Denida is the winner!" the announcer declared, when the other man failed to rise.

Denida smiled at the Warlock. This was the first step to winning the whole competition.

Has Claus been watching, too? Denida scanned the crowd until he spotted him. Their eyes met for just a moment.

"You will die in this building," Claus spoke to Denida in his mind.

"I told you he would be strong. You'd better be stronger!" The Dark Wizard peered intently at Claus, who nodded and clapped. "You won't be so happy if you fail me," the wizard growled.

Claus ceased his clapping. "Come on; haven't I learned enough to beat Denida?"

"Yes."

"Okay." Claus smirked.

"Long time, no see." The Dark Wizard smiled at the Warlock.

Claus watched the wizard's smirk broaden with the Warlock's confusion.

The Dark Wizard let his disguise slip for a moment, revealing his face to the Warlock.

The Warlock frowned. "So, it's true that you escaped…"

The wizard chuckled. "My pupil set me free and blew up the whole prison."

"Why are you here?"

"Claus wants to kill Denida."

***

The Warlock sighed heavily as the Dark Wizard sauntered away. She'd hoped she would never see that man again, not after she'd helped the police capture and imprison him. Like the Dark Angels, who had ruled over Denida's world, the wizard had oppressed this world with dark arts, killing countless civilians. The man had even bragged about serving the Devil himself.

That same wizard was mentoring Claus. *This might not end as well as I'd hoped.*

***

Denida watched the Warlock's face drop and immediately knew that something was wrong. "What's the matter? Is there a problem with the competition?" Denida's gut twisted.

The Warlock shook her head and sat down opposite him. "Of course not." She drew in a deep breath. "I should tell you the truth."

Denida prepared himself for a long story.

"I guess it was a long time ago." The Warlock stared at Denida. "There's a wizard in this world who is a renowned Satan worshipper. While your world lacks magic, Satan and his worshippers throughout the Underworlds have magic."

Denida struggled with the idea of Satan, and someone worshipping him with real intent. "Demons are real? This… wizard you're talking about is one?"

"Yes, they're real, but they're much worse than you can fathom." The Warlock motioned with her hand, as if to push the idea away. "We don't know quite what the wizard is. What is important, is that he is the Dark Wizard who has been training Claus. He was a man with great power and promise, but he vowed to serve Satan blindly."

Denida's stomach knotted again. *A Satanist has been training Claus? Claus is already bad enough on his own!*

The Warlock glanced at the floor. "He tried to seize power here, but I led all the warlocks to fight him. Many of the warlocks died to imprison the Dark Wizard, so that he could never harm another soul."

"Why not just kill him?" Denida gazed at his mentor.

The Warlock sighed. "If he's a demon, he cannot die, as he'd just be sent back to Hell. He could return anytime, anywhere."

Denida stood and paced across the room. *What have I gotten myself into?*

"Claus cannot win!" The Warlock grabbed Denida's shoulders.

Denida shivered. *That wizard must have taught Claus black magic. How am I supposed to fight against black magic?* "I don't want him to win, but I don't know how to counter dark magic!"

"Dark magic only differs in intent. You fight it the same way you fight any other attack. Keep your mind free of fear and anger, as those feelings will only strengthen your opponent's dark attacks."

As the competition continued, Denida kept an eye on Claus, finding himself under the impression that Claus was pulling his punches, avoiding using his full capabilities in order to hide his true strength. And just like Denida, Claus moved up the ranks until he was due to face Denida in the finals.

***

Daniel watched the competition intently. He was proud of how strong his dad had become, and his smile showed it.

"No!" Dan yelled, startling Daniel.

Dan reversed the program and paused it, glaring at something on the edge of the screen. The Warlock was talking to a young man, who only appeared as a dark figure. Dan gasped and sped out of the room.

What's up with him? Daniel watched Dan snatch up the phone and make a call. He seemed increasingly upset.

"Got it!" Dan hung up the phone and stormed back into the room, joining Daniel again.

Dan tossed Daniel's jacket to him. "Come; we need to get to your father immediately." Dan led Daniel through the crowd surrounding the arena.

Daniel followed Dan, keeping as close as possible, despite Dan's quick pace.

"What's so urgent that we have to run like this?" Daniel yelled from behind Dan, who stopped to wait for Daniel.

"Claus's mentor is an escaped convict, who's an expert in the dark arts. We need to meet with someone who can stop him!"

"What? Is my father okay?" Daniel tugged Dan's sleeve.

Dan sighed. "I really hope so."

They pushed through the mob to one of the arena's gates, encountering scowling, uniformed guards.

Daniel froze in shock, staring at one of the guards. "Susan?"

"Yes," Dan said. "Let me guess, there's another Susan in your world, too?" Dan chuckled as he ran up to Susan.

"There's no way to get you in." Susan pointed at the guards. "The shield is up, so there's nothing to do but wait for the wizard to come out. We'll grab him when he leaves."

Daniel's face filled with evident concern.

"Who's that?" Susan gestured at Daniel.

"Denida's son, Daniel."

Susan nodded. "We won't need any military force to detain him this time, Dan. We've got it under control!"

***

"Will dark magic triumph over the light?" the announcer asked.

"It is a show, after all," Denida whispered to the Warlock before stepping out onto the floor.

Claus strolled out from across the arena.

"You really want to do this?" Denida spoke into Claus's mind.

"I'll have my revenge," Claus replied in Denida's thoughts.

Claus fired a stream of black fireballs at Denida as soon as the battle began, which Denida deflected with a flick of his wrist. Denida hurled a spear of energy back at Claus, who sneered as he pushed it aside.

Denida increased the power of his strikes, trying to think of a way to breach Claus's defenses.

Claus demonstrated his passion to win and his hatred for Denida as he assaulted Denida with a barrage of strong, dark spells.

Denida frowned in concentration and started to sweat from exertion.

Claus stood with a broad smile on his face. He quickly drew his hand back, and a powerful blow struck Denida in the back of his head.

Denida collapsed in the sand, still blocking Claus's attacks, but Denida's head ached so severely from the blow that it compromised his focus. He was in serious trouble.

Claus sauntered closer, building up a spear of dark magic above him.

"Time to die." Claus's grin widened. He slammed the spear against the weak magic shield that Denida struggled to hold in place.

Sorry, Daniel. The arena darkened until all Denida could see was Claus's twisted face.

The Dark Wizard appeared behind Claus and stabbed him with a long dagger. As he twisted the dagger with a vicious sneer, his face changed back to his original face.

Claus's magic faded, as he stared at the blade impaling his chest. "Wh…"

"Thank you… you brought me exactly what I needed." The Dark Wizard yanked the blade out, watching Claus's corpse collapse in the arena.

"You!" Denida pushed himself to his feet, but the wizard was already plodding away. Denida spared a glance at Claus's body, still with surprise on his face. *You're not coming back from this one.*

"Well, we haven't seen that before!" The announcer interrupted Denida's train of thought. "The judges have conferred, and because Denida is the only combatant left standing, he is the winner!"

Denida ignored the applause, focusing on the Dark Wizard's back.

Why did he sacrifice his own student? Didn't he train Claus to kill me?

Chapter 11- Treason

Denida had recovered from the battle and annoyed the announcer by ignoring his demands for an interview. Instead, he searched for the Warlock and found her talking to Dan.

"Susan's guards are scouring the building," Dan explained. "No one has left, aside from one of the warlocks."

"The Dark Wizard in disguise." The Warlock frowned.

Susan approached, shaking her head.

"Dad, you won, so we can get to the Gate!" Daniel hugged Denida.

Denida could see the fear and anxiety on his son's face. *This world has taken a toll on him, but...* "No, I'm sorry, but the Warlock and I have to find the Dark Wizard. You'll have to stay with Dan for just a little while longer."

Denida didn't like the last world's Claus, but the Dark Wizard had used him for something, and for a reason Denida still couldn't fathom, which was a troubling consideration. Not even his enemies should die to a literal knife in their back.

"I have an idea of where he might be going." The Warlock frowned. "There's one place in this world where dark magic is at its strongest."

Denida and the Warlock traveled by horseback to the location with prominent dark magic. Meanwhile, the Warlock contacted the others and informed them that they were heading into dangerous territory.

The foreboding atmosphere made Denida's skin crawl. They dismounted their horses to walk the rest of the way to where the air was at its densest. With a sense of foreboding, they saw the Dark Wizard standing in the center of a black pentagram, ready to summon his master.

"All of this has been for you, my master!" The Dark Wizard raised his hands over his head.

"Enough!" the Warlock shouted.

The Dark Wizard turned and smiled at them. "Perfect, you're just in time."

"You won't get away." Denida focused to accumulate magic around his hands, ready to attack on his mentor's behalf.

"Really?" The Dark Wizard laughed. "You couldn't beat Claus, but you expect to defeat his master?"

Denida let the magic subside.

"I thought so." The wizard turned back, ready to continue his dealings.

"I'm here, too." The Warlock strolled around the perimeter of the pentagram to face the wizard. "And more of us are on the way. It's over!"

The wizard glared at the Warlock, then Denida. "Fine, then." He mumbled something under his breath and extended his hand while spinning in a circle. A black cone sprang up from the ground, creating a wide perimeter around the pentagram, and shielding the three of them from the rest of the world. "Nobody will interrupt us, now."

Light magic won't work. Maybe we should just kill him.

"No," the Warlock responded to Denida's thoughts in his mind. "That wouldn't help, remember? His master will just send him back with demons assisting him."

They faced the wizard, who still stood in his circle.

"Why did you kill Claus?" The question surprised Denida, even as he asked it.

The Dark Wizard's gaze remained on his preparations. "Because it was what my lord wanted from me."

"Why?"

The Dark Wizard ignored his question.

Denida leaned closer to the Warlock. "How do we stop him?"

"I don't think we can in here. This is the one place where the dark arts are at their strongest, so much so, that nothing else compares."

"Problem?" The wizard jeered.

"You don't want to do this!" Denida yelled in desperation.

"Oh, no? Why not, oh, not-so-great one?"

At least he's slowed down his incantations. "I suppose you expect the Dark Lord to be impressed? You killed a pupil from another world, who might have carried worship of the Dark Lord to even more worlds."

The Dark Wizard opened his mouth, but Denida didn't give him a chance to respond. "Sure, offer him this world, when he could have had many."

The Dark Wizard hesitated, the smile slipping from his face. "I suppose you like your light magic?" the wizard put as much scorn on "light" as he could.

"I have a gift." Denida crossed his arms.

"Are you sure about that, when you've never even tried black magic?" The Dark Wizard raised an eyebrow.

"Light magic is stronger," Denida stated.

"Ha! Ask that warlock beside you why she needed six additional warlocks to defeat me before, if light magic is so powerful."

The Warlock hurled a blast of magic at the Dark Wizard, who shifted to block it. Their hands wove spells faster than Denida's eye could follow, firing magic from their fingertips faster than bullets from a gun. Even with his strong aptitude for magic, he'd never stand a chance against either of them.

Denida shielded himself to protect against stray blasts and crept around the pentagram, extinguishing candles, and blurring the satanic drawings wherever he encountered them.

The Warlock stumbled to the side.

The Dark Wizard resumed his incantation. He frowned, and the Warlock peered from where she stood, holding her ribs to nod at Denida.

The Dark Wizard reached out with magic and yanked Denida into the pentagram. "I guess you're going to need to help me."

"I'm no black magician!" Denida writhed.

"Is that so? Or do you just need to remember?"

Does he know about my sealed memories? Did Claus tell him?

"You have the Darkness in you." The wizard shook him. "You'll help me, or I'll find Daniel and we'll learn just how much Darkness is buried in your soul."

"How?" Denida relented, his heart pounding. *Anything to protect Daniel from this madman.*

"Your right eye is the key." The Dark Wizard pointed at it.

"My blind eye?"

"Yes, it's a passageway to the Darkness inside of you."

How is my eye the key? Denida closed his eyes, digging deep into himself. He'd go to Hell to save his son. At the edge of his attention, the Warlock shouted something and waved at him from the edge of the pentagram. The cone had thinned out, now resembling frosted glass. Susan and the other warlocks stood on the far side of the room, outside the cone, attacking the magical barrier with an onslaught of energy strikes.

The Dark Wizard's mind snatched Denida and tore through him, reaching deep. The candles flared up and the pentagram blazed with a dazzling red flame.

A dark cloud covered the pentagram, but the cone dissipated under the six warlocks' combined might. They erected a shield between Denida and the Dark Wizard.

"Too late!" the wizard shouted.

Evil filled the air, suffocating Denida by thickening the atmosphere to the texture of paste. The Dark Lord had arrived.

Yet, as suddenly as the menacing force appeared, the ordeal ended. The cloud vanished, taking the Dark Wizard with it.

"What happened?" Denida gaped at the spot where the wizard had been standing. The entire pentagram had disappeared.

The Warlock eyed the ground instead of answering Denida.

"This is what you feared." Denida turned to the Warlock.

The warlocks maintained their silence, but glum expressions weighed heavily on their features.

"The Dark Wizard escaped," the Warlock reported to the High Sorcerer. She looked old for the first time since Denida had met her. "It appears that his master was pleased with his efforts, after all."

"We have no way of knowing where he'll show up next or what he'll bring with him," another warlock added.

"I need to see the Gate," Denida broke in. "If it weren't for Daniel…"

The Warlock nodded. "We understand."

At the Gate, Daniel stood at Dan's side.

"Thank you for everything. You've done more good for this world than you know." The Warlock rested her hand on Denida's shoulder and squeezed it.

"Perhaps, but it's unfortunate how everything ended." Denida held the controller and powered up the Gate. He held his hand out to Daniel. "Ready?"

Daniel took his hand. "Let's go home." He led his dad through the Gate.

***

"We need to prepare," Dan said to the Warlock, who continued to gaze at the Gate.

"You didn't tell him," Susan asked accusingly.

"No, it's best that he doesn't know. He'll find out himself soon enough," the Warlock's voice brimmed with confidence, but her expression appeared unsure.

Dan shook his head. "I hope so."

***

The Colonel sat stunned, listening to the other version of himself describe the rebellion. With Denida's help, in a matter of mere days, the other world had achieved what had taken years in this world.

Danyel mentioned his boss? They should send more assistance: soldiers, maybe even another robot. Claus had to agree to it, given the circumstances. *Right?*

But when the Colonel spoke to him about it, Claus shook his head in response.

"Why not? If a Dark Angel managed to get there, one could come here, too. Surely you must realize this?" The Colonel cringed at the sensation that he was begging. "We can at least learn from their experiences to prepare ourselves."

"Our mission is to find Denida. I'm not authorizing you to send anything, or anyone else through the Gate. That's final!"

The Colonel's eyes narrowed in confusion at Claus's rejection, then anger burned inside of him. *Is this really the guy who's standing in for Denida?* There was no logic to it, but the Colonel was powerless to change it. *Denida would've sent assistance immediately.*

The Colonel paced restlessly after Claus left. "How could he?" the Colonel muttered under his breath.

"I have an idea." Dan approached the Colonel.

"What?" The Colonel stopped and glared at Dan.

"Dan, we need to talk!" Nina rushed Dan away from the Colonel before he could say anything else.

Maybe it wasn't important. The Colonel returned to the other him. *Perhaps he can tell me something useful that can help us, even if we don't send anyone to learn from them.*

Nina reentered the room.

The Colonel lifted his head. He could snarl at Dan, but not Nina. He cocked an eyebrow.

"Dan's had considerable time to study the Gates, and he thinks he can build a second controller, based on his new knowledge."

"You want to build a second device?"

"We could reach them faster if we didn't have to wait for each world's leader to figure out how to power up their Gate. Dan's idea is not to send soldiers, but rather a second robot, with a controller attached to it." Nina peered at the Colonel, her eyes pleading with him.

"No, Claus already rejected our request to send additional reinforcements through the Gate…"

"But we must try, for Denida and Daniel."

The Colonel sighed and closed his eyes. He could never refuse Nina.

The Colonel talked to Claus, while Dan prepared another robot.

Denida's secretary escorted the Colonel into Claus's office. The Colonel clenched his teeth at how Claus had taken over, but that wasn't the purpose for his visit.

"Something wrong?" Claus frowned. "Why couldn't you just call me?"

"Dan has an idea to speed up our journey through the Gates."

"I told you: nobody is traveling through them; it is not safe!"

The Colonel shook his head. "He wants to send a robot, rather than people."

Claus rose from his chair. "I addressed that the last time we spoke too, didn't I? The other worlds don't have controllers for their Gates. We can't endanger our technology. Imagine what could happen if a Dark Angel were to steal it?"

The Colonel straightened up. "Without this measure, we could wait forever!"

Claus returned to his seat. "Sorry, my decision is final."

***

Susan sat in the cottage with her shoulders screaming in pain from being restrained in one position for so long. She had put all her military training to the test to try to break the ropes, but Claus had been thorough. Neither her physical aptitude, nor any objects in the room, provided the leverage she needed to break free.

He might get away with this after all.

The door flew open, and Susan's heartbeat sped up, but when Claus stepped through the door, she had a hard time holding back tears. *He's just here to check on me, and maybe feed me.*

"Nobody misses you. Funny, isn't it?" Claus set food down in front of her. "I have plans to make sure it stays that way, too."

Susan gritted her teeth. "How do you plan to do that?"

"Easy, I'll just say you're searching for a third Gate!"

Is he serious? Why would anyone believe such a ludicrous tale? Then again, this was Claus, and everything he had done so far had worked in his favor.

"You will sign this request to search for it." Claus untied her and began ensnaring her with chains he'd brought with him, leaving her arm free, for now. He handed her a pen and a piece of paper.

Susan glared daggers at the paper and Claus. "You've gotta be kidding me!" she yelled.

"You will sign it, if you want to live long enough to see Denida's return!"

Susan recoiled from Claus. He'd always been a bit of a snake, but now, he terrified her. *I'd better not make him angry...* She heaved in a deep breath and willed her hand not to shake as she signed the paper. She'd be no help to Denida if she died.

Claus took the paper and examined her signature before pocketing the request.

"You really think this is going to work?" Susan asked while she ate.

"Yes." Claus checked his pockets, preparing to leave.

"And no one will question this?" Susan asked before he left.

Claus peeked back at her. "If they do, I will take care of them, like I took care of you." He slammed the door, leaving her all alone, yet again. But in chains now, so she could use the toilet, and move around the cabin a little, but she still couldn't reach the door or her phone.

***

Despite the chaos following a successful coup, the other colonel managed to secure enough power to use the second Gate.

The Colonel disagreed with Claus but couldn't defy his boss. "Where's Dan?" he asked a lab technician, as he returned from Claus's office.

"At the Gate."

Why would he be at the Gate? No, they wouldn't dare... The Colonel sprinted to the Gate, and as he had feared, it was on.

Dan stood beside Nina, showing her how to control a robot.

"No!" The Colonel rushed in front of the Gate to block the new robot's path. "This is treason!"

Nina yanked the controller from Dan's hand. "If Claus wants to court martial the First Lady of the Underworld, so be it!"

"I agree that we might need to send it, but defying Claus's direct orders is going too far."

"I am the president's wife. Claus isn't here, so I am your superior. Step aside!"

"That's not how the governmental chain of command operates." The Colonel held Nina's gaze for a long moment. As a military man, this violated all his training. But clearly, Nina intended to stand by her decision. The Colonel stepped aside with a sigh. "We're all going to regret this."

"I won't!" Nina returned to the monitor and handed the controller back to Dan.

The Colonel sauntered back to the monitor to update the other colonel. "We're not ready to go, yet."

"Why?" The other colonel scratched his temple.

The Colonel scoped the lab, finding himself unable to admit the truth.

"We just deployed another robot with a device that can control the Gates!" Nina announced.

The Colonel rubbed his forehead in distress. And so, the act of treason was spoken, given life and validation, revealed like public knowledge. The seconds that passed were agonizing.

Loud clapping broke the silence.

Turning his head, the Colonel saw everyone in the lab applauding in support of Nina's decision.

"Good, Claus is out of his mind!" one lab tech exclaimed.

Nina nodded in agreement.

The Colonel appeared to be alone in his worry, finding some solace in the rest of the room's support. But when Claus found out, which he was bound to do, *will he charge Nina with treason?*

Dan drove the robot through the forest in the first world and into the massive building boasting the UW symbol. Knowing where he needed to go, he drove past all the bystanders, who watched the little robot, as if it were the most natural thing in the world.

The little robot knocked on the colonel's door, as any normal person would do.

"Enter!" a voice called from within.

Dan drove the robot into the room.

"You're back?" the second colonel asked.

They explained only briefly, as Nina insisted that they continued to the next world, much to the Colonel's distress. It was her show, now.

"We have a controller to use the Gate, which will make the journey easier," Nina explained.

The other colonel helped activate the Gate, then Dan drove the robot through.

The robot drove through this now familiar next world, in search of yet another colonel. Most of the debris in the streets had been cleared, making the trek easier on the robot. They reached the palace and headed to the other colonel's command center.

"What exactly are you doing?" Claus's voice spoke from behind them.

"I have some papers I need to review with you, Sir." The Colonel led Claus to an office with stacks of requisition forms.

I don't like this. The Colonel fiddled with the papers. In his perspective, Claus had delayed their search for Denida. *No, it's worse than that.* He glanced back at the monitor, just as the other robot appeared on the screen.

"What the..." Claus muttered. "Colonel, why are there two robots?" The Colonel had violated his direct orders, committing treason. Claus had every excuse to court martial the only leader who had fought alongside Denida in the war. Claus turned to the Colonel. "Explain yourself."

"I did it." Nina's face tensed, hard and determined.

"You?" A bead of sweat ran down the back of Claus's neck. Nina was the last person he could challenge.

Silence filled the lab, as Nina and Claus engaged in a staring contest. "I don't support your decision, Lady Nina. But it's there now, so let's see if it helps." Claus relented. "Maybe I was wrong; we do want to find Denida, after all." He forced a smile and turned to the monitor. "Well? Let's keep moving."

Confusion spread across Nina's face.

Claus chuckled then peered at the soldiers, who stared at him with distrustful expressions.

The Gate had been powered on, so they didn't need the second robot and the controller, yet.

Maybe they wouldn't find Denida in the next world, either. From their faces, nobody expected to find him. The colonels said their final goodbyes and both robots drove through the Gate.

The room remained silent until a feed appeared on the screen. With a tap on the controller, the second robot's feed synced up with the first one's and its camera stopped transmitting its own data.

The image on the screen was nothing anyone could have expected. A crowd of people laughed and pointed at the robots, taking pictures of them. Camera flashes whited out the feed.

Are they tourists?

"How are we going to get anywhere with this nonsense?" Claus hissed.

The crowd only grew.

The Colonel pointed to something on the screen that appeared between whiteouts and leaned closer to the monitor. "I'll be damned."

"What?" Dan peered at the screen.

"Denida?" The Colonel asked, commanding everyone's attention.

Claus's eyes darted across the monitor. "Where?" He grabbed one of the robot's controllers, desynced the feed, and drove it to where the Colonel had pointed, revealing the object that had captured the Colonel's attention. A tourist wore a pin with Denida's face on it.

"Maybe it's a different form of Denida, like all the versions of myself?" the Colonel asked.

Claus's smile faltered.

"Hello, nice pin you have," the Colonel complimented the tourist.

The tourist blinked as the robot addressed him, of all people. "Uh… thanks. It's Denida. He helped reinstate our president!"

"Where can we find this president of yours?"

The tourist shook his head, appearing a little surprised by that question. "You can't. He's busy with the colonel because Claus escaped, again."

The Colonel dragged Claus in front of the monitor. "Does your Claus look like this guy?"

"Yes, but a lot older."

Claus wrenched himself free from the Colonel's grip. "Interesting, there must be doubles of all of us in the other worlds." Everyone's eyes shifted to Claus as he spoke. "Time's ticking." He redirected everyone's attention back to their mission with a wave of his hand.

"You look like our colonel," a voice came from someone behind the man with the pin.

Claus rolled his eyes.

"I'd like to meet my double, where would he be?" The Colonel leaned forward.

"The palace." The man with the pin gestured down a road.

As the robots followed the man's directions to the palace, the Colonel leaned over to Dan. "It seems that both doubles of people and buildings appear in every world."

This world had one too, the Dynasty estate. Denida had constructed the huge building by himself.

The palace turned out to be quite far away, but this world lacked old historic relics, unlike the last world. A normal security detail stood out front with a little girl, a teenager at the oldest. She played while the guards watching the building.

There's something about that girl. The Colonel leaned even closer to the screen.

"What?" Dan asked the Colonel, who had paled, staring at the young woman.

"Nina?" The Colonel gaped.

Nina lifted her head at the sound of her name.

"Look at this girl. Do you see what I do?" The Colonel gestured to the screen.

"Oh, my god… that's me!" Nina couldn't tear her eyes away from the monitor.

Dan drove over to her to get a better look.

Is it really her, or just a close resemblance? The closer they drew, the clearer it became this was indeed a younger version of Nina. A time abnormality could also explain that man's insistence that there had been an older Claus here, too.

The younger Nina stared at the robot approaching her and backed up cautiously.

"Don't be afraid!" Nina stepped up to the monitor.

"Who are you?" the younger Nina asked.

"I am you." Nina smiled nervously.

The girl appeared scared, but also very intrigued. The sight of Nina had commanded her focus. "Your name is Nina, then?" the girl inquired.

Nina nodded.

"Thought so." The girl grinned. "Daniel and Denida mentioned you."

"What?" Nina turned to the Colonel with a panicked expression.

Soldiers interrupted them, surrounding the robots with their guns drawn. One pulled the young Nina away from the robot.

"Freeze!" a distinctly familiar voice called out.

"Why is there another colonel everywhere we go?" Claus threw up his arms. "What makes the Colonel so important?" He grunted quietly, only to glance around quickly as if he'd made a mistake.

"What?" the Colonel whipped around.

"Why are you everywhere, but the rest of us aren't?" Claus rested his hands on the table in front of him.

"Interesting point." The Colonel returned his attention to the screen, where his other self marched into view.

"Who are you?" the other colonel asked.

The Colonel prepared to give a long explanation. "I'm in another dimension."

The other colonel waved the troops away. "You need to see the president."

"I guess that was enough?" The Colonel bit his lip.

Claus's eyes narrowed at the Colonel.

The Colonel led them to the palace, with the younger Nina in tow. The other colonel escorted them to the president, who stood inside.

The president welcomed them, as if he had been expecting them. His charisma spoke for itself, as he knelt in front of the robot. "Hello."

The Colonel didn't recognize the president. Judging from the faces of everyone else in the lab, they didn't recognize him, either. *Interesting, the first leader without a counterpart in our world.*

The president smiled. "You must be Nina, Denida's wife… and Daniel's mother?"

"Yes," Nina's voice quavered.

"I think I need to explain." The president sat down on the floor.

"Please do." The Colonel leaned back in his chair.

The president told them the full story of what Denida had accomplished in their world.

The Colonel peered over at Claus, as the president described the part about Claus's reign. *So that world's Claus snatched power from the president, huh? Kind of reminds me of what Claus has done to Denida's office, but... no. I'm just paranoid.*

"A time machine?" Claus interrupted the president when he reached that part of the story.

Both colonels glared at him.

"Yes, we used the central unit of the second Gate to power it." The president glanced at him briefly.

"How fascinating." Claus rubbed his palms together and stared at his watch, before jumping up. "I have a meeting," he announced. "Let me know what you find out."

Chapter 12- What Happened?

Claus raced back to the cottage to retrieve the Gate's main unit.

"My, my, have you come to free me?" Susan asked sarcastically.

Claus spotted the main unit next to the door, right where he had left it. *I have to tell someone about my plan; it's too good to keep to myself.* "This can be used for some powerful stuff!" Claus laughed and ran out the door before she could respond.

Claus returned to the city, but not to Denida's office. He had a secret apartment above a shoe store, where he would often stow things that might be useful someday but would cause him trouble if others knew about them. He dug through a stack of papers until he found a scrap of a napkin with a phone number scribbled on it. The Dark Angels had sent a man to recruit Claus during the war, but when Claus saw that the rebels were going to win, he stayed on their side instead. *Losers have no power.*

With shaking hands, he used an untraceable phone to dial the number. The phone rang until Claus had almost given up hope.

"Talk." The voice that answered the phone sounded distorted.

Claus grinned. "I have a proposition for you." He smiled, hearing the voice of his recruiter, whom he only knew as the Scientist. "Meet me at the abandoned lab the Dark Angels used to use. Come alone."

"Two hours." The call terminated.

Can an acting president commit treason? The Colonel would probably say so, given all his pesky morals, but the Colonel would never find out.

Claus arrived early and entered the building. When the Dark Angels fell, the citizens of the Underworld left their stronghold to rot, choosing to forget about it like a nasty blemish.

The Scientist could kill Claus, and no one would know about it. After all, Claus hid his intentions and snuck out here alone. *It's worth the risk, if it means ridding myself of Denida.*

The Scientist stepped out of the shadows.

"Glad you came." Claus smiled tranquilly.

The man didn't respond, but he'd been famous for his apathy.

"Denida vanished, leaving me in charge." Claus leaned against a pile of debris. He thought he saw a glint of interest in the Scientist's cold eyes. "I have a method to ensure that he never returns. If you help me, I'll see your name removed from the most-wanted list."

"Freedom for my work, and I want the Colonel's head, too."

Lovely, I'll get my time machine and get rid of that nuisance. "Deal. What can I call you instead of Scientist? That name is too high-profile."

The Scientist glared at him. "If you insist, then call me Doc."

"Doc, then, do we have a deal?" Claus extended his hand.

Doc stared at him for a long moment before grabbing it in a crushing grip. "I'll be in touch."

***

"I'll warn you," the president said. "Another version of me allegedly trusted Claus enough to send him back in time to stop Denida."

"Another version of you?" the Colonel interrupted him. His head was spinning. "Like a soul version?"

The president shook his head. "It's complicated." He shrugged. "When Denida got to this world, the second Gate had been dismantled to build a time machine, so he took Daniel back in time to stop the president from destroying the

Gate. Claus followed them with a troop of soldiers. What they didn't know was that I'd been meeting with the president, who reigned over all the Underworlds, and he ordered me to shut down the Gate."

"A president of all of the Underworlds?" the Colonel asked shakily.

"Yes," the president confirmed. "Thirty years ago, all of the Underworlds were connected by Gates, and travel between them was quite the common occurrence."

The Colonel's mouth hung agape.

"That president wanted me to disable the Gate before a legendary child was born."

The Colonel gripped his chair's arms. The Gates had existed before the Dark Angels, and had been used? And who the heck was this legendary child?

"Legendary child?" Dan asked, beating the Colonel to the punch.

"Yes, it was an old legend; that's all I know, but it sure meant a lot to the president. Unfortunately, that was the last time I saw him, so I never had an opportunity to ask him for an explanation.," the president mused.

The Dark Angels had been in power thirty years ago, which would explain why they'd neither heard of the president of all the Underworlds, nor received the order to shut down their Gates.

The president cleared his throat. "Denida met me thirty years ago and we learned that we only needed one component of the Gate to power the time machine, so I promised to keep the Gate intact, and he returned to the present day."

"Good." The Colonel tried to imagine what it would be like if Denida and Daniel were thirty years older when they found them. He glanced at Nina, knowing she would've been furious.

"The timeline changed, however. Claus stayed in the past, using his soldiers with their modern weaponry to overthrow me so that he would become president in my place."

The Colonel scratched his nose. *I hope our Claus's reign here is only temporary…*

"When Denida reappeared in the present day, he saw how this world's timeline had changed, and he insisted on setting things right." The president clasped his hands.

"That sounds like my Denny." Nina smiled fondly.

I'm the same in all the worlds. If Claus is too, he could be trying a similar trick, here.

The president frowned, and Nina rested a hand on the Colonel's shoulder. The Colonel drew in a breath and nodded at the president.

"Denida and Susan, Claus's wife, forced Claus to sign a resignation letter. Certain people in the council were more than ready to be rid of Claus, so we locked him up and I took over again."

"Susan?" Nina asked. "Where is she, anyway? I haven't seen her in a while."

"Ahem." The president cleared his throat and finished his tale with a quick summary of his return to power and a description of the jail holding Claus.

"Everything's as it should be, then." The Colonel relaxed a little.

"Not quite," the other colonel said from off-camera. "I came here because some soldiers maintained their loyalty to Claus. They broke him out of jail."

The Colonel's stomach curdled. Everything he learned about this other Claus filled him with unsettling dread.

"He wanted to seize power again…" the president resumed his story. "- but I was too well-guarded, and my colonel was ready for him. Instead of attacking me, he did the only other thing he could."

"Why do I have a bad feeling about this?" The Colonel rubbed his face.

"Because, like me, you have good instincts." The other colonel winked. "The Gate hadn't been disabled, yet due to the chaos following the coup." A note of embarrassment entered the other colonel's voice. "Claus escaped through the Gate with his armed troops."

"Wait!" Nina yelled. "Didn't Denida and my little Daniel go through there, too?"

"Yes," the president spoke almost too quietly to be heard. "I understand your concern, but you need to hear the rest of our story first."

"Well? What is it then?"

"Denida told us that he doesn't remember where he came from or anything about his youth." The president tapped his fingers on his desk.

"Why does that matter?" Nina asked.

"Did he always live in your world?" the president asked.

"Yes... no, he might not have. I really don't know," Nina's voice shook.

The Colonel rested his hand on hers.

"So what?" Nina wrinkled her nose.

"He could be the legendary child." Excitement filled the president's face. "The one the ultimate president spoke of."

"No." Nina raised her hands to block the screen. "He couldn't have been born in another world. He's human!"

"Yes, Nina's right," the Colonel interjected. "This underworld is Earth's soul world. For those of us with a physical form, that form lives on Earth. Denida has a human form, so his soul must belong here!"

"That doesn't necessarily mean he's always been in your underworld." The president rubbed his chin.

"Hold on; I've never even heard of this legend." Nina crossed her arms.

"The Dark Angels could have known something about it, but they wouldn't have told us." The Colonel rubbed his eyes. "It wouldn't have been to their advantage."

"Whatever." Nina waved her hand. "We've gotten off-topic, haven't we? Claus brought a bunch of soldiers through the Gate to follow Denny. We need to follow them, now!"

The president nodded and pushed himself to his feet.

"Bye!" The young Nina waved before standing gracefully with her hands clasped in front of her.

The other colonel led them to the other Gate. The controller on the second robot worked perfectly, lighting up the Gate as it turned on.

"Go!" Nina snatched the controller for one robot and Dan held the other.

Together, they drove their robots through the Gate.

***

mhg

"We have to be extra careful, here." Denida squeezed Daniel's hand. "Stay close."

Children standing around the Gate turned to him with cold eyes.

What are we doing wrong? Denida's heart pounded.

A boy with a gun stopped them and glanced at Denida with the same glare one would give a tarantula. "You do know adults aren't allowed outside, right?" The boy turned to Daniel.

Did I hear that right? Why aren't they? Denida attempted to read the boy's mind, but it was blocked. *Why don't I know that trick? It would be useful.* While he'd been watching the boy, a part of him figured out what was wrong; powerful magic clouded the world.

"I'm sorry; I needed to bring him, but I will bring him inside ASAP," Daniel said.

The boy nodded and left, sneering at Denida as he passed.

Daniel turned to his dad. "So, you feel it, too? We need to get inside."

Denida nodded, and Daniel led him away from the kids. Denida kept an eye open for a place to hide.

The kids watched them intently.

"Can you believe what was on his mind?" Daniel shuddered as they settled down in an abandoned building.

"What? You could read his mind?"

"You couldn't?" Daniel frowned.

Denida tried to peer into Daniel's mind, but even his son's mind, which should have been easy to read, yielded a white, staticky blur.

"Adults are considered bad, here," Daniel said.

"Our magic is sealed, too?" Denida asked half-questioningly, as he still had trouble believing it himself.

Daniel nodded. "His mind showed that adults disgust him."

That's not very helpful. Denida was too flustered to monitor his thoughts around Daniel. *This mindreading thing can take some getting used to.* More importantly, how would they ever learn anything about this world if Denida wasn't allowed to move about? *Aside from Daniel, I don't know any children, and Nina would kill me if I put Daniel in harm's way. Wait; Nina...* Nina had been young in the last world. Maybe all his friends from back home were all children here, or was that too much to hope for? At least if it were the case, Denida could try to reason with them, given his familiarity with them.

"You stay here; I'll go look for them!" Daniel ran off before his dad could say anything.

Denida was about to hurry after him, but Daniel had already disappeared. Besides, Denida would draw too much attention in a world where adults weren't allowed outside. He'd have to lie low and wait. *Can Daniel really handle this himself? Will he be alright?*

Denida paced around the house for a while. He wanted to stay and wait for Daniel, but he was too worried about his son to sit still any longer. He scribbled "Went looking for you!" into a layer of dust on the wall. Denida crept out of the building, hoping to find Daniel before he got into trouble. He'd need to be careful not to be seen.

Denida crept about five paces, becoming more confident with every step. As he quickened his stride, a twig snapped under his foot with a loud crack.

"You!" A boy spun to face Denida and fired his weapon, but instead of killing him, the shot froze Denida like a statue. "Take him to the others," the boy ordered.

This kid must be some sort of officer.

The children locked Denida in a dark room full of unfamiliar adults. *What's going on with this world?*

"You almost got away, huh?" A man approached.

Denida peered at the others, hoping to see a familiar face, but nobody stood out.

When the spell from the gunshot vaporized, and he could move again, Denida paced throughout the room. All the adults bore huge frowns and sad eyes. *It would take a very powerful warlock to conjure the magical seal afflicting this world.* "Who could have done this?" Denida muttered.

"Claus," a familiar voice sounded from behind him.

Claus is here, too? Denida sought out the man who'd spoken, but almost didn't recognize him. He trembled as he knelt beside the shadow of a man he knew as the Colonel. "Colonel?" Denida asked, almost afraid of the answer.

"No, I was a general once, but Claus is too strong. Only children can use magic now, and they never age!"

So, this is what Daniel has to look forward to? On top of that, this was the second version of Claus Denida had run into, and he seemed to be bad news here, too. *But the Claus in my world is good, right?* For a moment, his fear for Nina and his world created a stabbing pain deep in his gut.

The Colonel's counterpart had been a general here, before Claus took over. *Interesting.* And still, Claus managed to overpower him. *How can we hope to beat Claus?* Daniel had a little weak magic, and Denida's powers were useless here. "We need to get out of here!" Denida exclaimed.

A bell chimed, and the others scurried to stand in line.

"Good luck with that," the general muttered.

The door flew open, and the adults shifted nervously. Children marched into the room, followed by a child version of Claus. He marched up and down the line, purposefully glaring at each adult in turn, as if examining them with a goal in mind. "I heard that one of you tried to escape." Claus announced to the crowd and stopped in front of Denida. "Hi!" He smiled at him. "So, you thought you could escape from me?" he yelled, spitting on Denida's face.

"I was wrong." Denida hung his head to hide his anger. *Have I been that wrong about him?*

"Yes, you were!" Claus sneered and stepped back. "Don't you know what happens to adults who try to get away?"

The children surrounded Denida with eager faces.

Now what? Without magic, Denida stood helplessly at everyone's mercy. "What are you up to now, Claus?"

"You dare to talk back to me?" Claus smirked. "Hang him up in the yard!"

***

It feels strange, but good, to be out and about by myself. Dad is counting on me. Daniel had to learn more about this place, but he was alone among all these unfamiliar children.

Some of them darted past him, as if heading somewhere important.

Maybe if Daniel followed them, they would lead him to something useful. He pursued them into a grand building filled with even more children. They sat at tables in an expansive dining hall with adults carrying trays of food to them. *Adults are our servants?*

"Yes, they are," a voice said from behind him.

The kid stared at Daniel cautiously. *Adults serving children has a certain appeal, but it doesn't feel right. Something is very wrong with this world.* Even children having a magical aptitude, while adults couldn't conjure even the most basic spell, seemed ludicrous.

Daniel hung around the dining hall, but the kids ate and chattered about kid nonsense, instead of speaking about this world's peculiarities. Even Daniel's efforts to steer their conversations in a more favorable direction ended in vain, so he headed back for his dad. He didn't want his father to worry, but when he returned, he saw the note Denida had left for him in the dust. "Frack!" Daniel muttered under his breath and surveyed the room.

Distant shouting pierced the silence, growing louder by the second.

Daniel ran to the window and peered outside, only to see a crowd of kids marching past the building. He slipped outside, following the mob to the middle of the town's square. He gasped as his eyes settled on his dad, hung by his hands, as the children took turns beating him with sticks and clubs.

Even as children, they caused some serious damage, covering his dad with lacerations and bruises. Blood seeped from his father's wounds. Denida peeked up and smiled at Daniel, which only enraged the children more.

"Your turn." The boy with the gun pointed it at Daniel's dad. "He escaped from you, didn't he?" The boy smirked at Daniel.

"Yes." Daniel sauntered over to his injured dad. The other children glared at him suspiciously.

Denida stared Daniel in the eye and nodded faintly.

Daniel gritted his teeth and smacked his father across the face with all his might. "Serves you right!"

Chapter 13- World of Youth

Claus watched as Doc turned the main unit over in his hands, peering closely at it. He'd done a lot of tests that Claus didn't understand.

"What?" Claus frowned with a curious expression on his face.

"You want me to make a time machine from this? It took them thirty years, but you want me to do it in a matter of days." Doc let out an irritable grunt.

Claus could see his point, but Doc continued before he could speak.

"We have no idea what this material is, and you know nothing about that time machine, aside from the fact that it existed."

Claus couldn't tell his full plan to Doc; he was just a pawn, but he knew he could satisfy him for the time being. "I'll go find out what they know." Claus left Doc, still turning the device over in his hands.

When Claus returned to the lab, Nina and Dan were about to send the robots through the next Gate. The techs glanced at him with narrow, suspicious eyes.

"Back so soon?" The Colonel stepped in front of the others.

"Yes," Claus began. "I realized that Denida will want a full report on the time machine when he returns."

"Wrong!" The president on the feed clenched his fists. "He opposed its very existence. He made sure it was destroyed, after all."

"Oh." Claus bit his lip. *This won't work.*

"Where is Susan, by the way?" The Colonel raised his eyebrows.

Uh oh. Claus stared at the Colonel. This could be the end of his plans, if he wasn't careful. That president must have really poisoned them against him. *Even the Colonel seems suspicious of me, now!* "She volunteered to search for a third Gate." Good thing Claus thought to have a backup plan.

"Susan did what? She never told me that she had an interest in that sort of mission." The Colonel's tone had a cautious edge to it. "And no one we've seen in any of the other worlds have mentioned a third Gate. That seems like intel she should've been given before taking on this sort of mission."

The others stared over at Claus, frowning.

"Well…" Claus scratched the back of his head. *He has a point.*

"Why would Susan volunteer to do something like that for you, anyway? She doesn't seem very fond of you." The Colonel crossed his arms.

"I am the acting president." Claus lifted his chin. *Why does the Colonel have to be so tall?*

The Colonel poked Claus's chest. "Just remember that you're only a temporary installment. I'd like to see that request Susan made."

Claus nodded.

"Ahem." The president from the other side of the feed coughed. "Shall we send the robots after Denida?"

Everyone turned back to the monitor.

The time machine was becoming more of a necessity with each passing second. If the Colonel didn't trust Claus, there would be others who'd join him in his suspicions. *That would make luring him away for Doc that much harder.* Claus needed to stay to try to undo some of the damage inflicted upon his reputation in his absence. At least with the robots moving on, the president couldn't keep filling their heads with doubts about Claus's true intentions.

The two robots proceeded through the Gate. When the image returned to the screen, it depicted a barren field. Unlike the other worlds, this world appeared desolate. *Has everyone here died? Denida and Daniel, too?*

Nina's eyes filled with unshed tears, as she began to tremble.

Everyone else in the lab wore glum frowns.

Claus turned his head, surveying the lab techs. *At least this world's atmosphere is distracting them from their suspicions. That should buy me some time.*

Dan slowly maneuvered the robots around the area, but the world appeared lifeless. As they explored farther, a town appeared.

"Life, at last." Dan pushed the robots to speed up.

The town had been abandoned. Doors swung open, as if people had deserted their homes in a hurry. Unfinished meals sat on kitchen tables.

Claus hoped that some horrible destruction had taken the world by storm. The thought almost made him laugh. Maybe his wish had been granted, after all.

Suddenly, darkness covered the town, making it impossible to see anything on the feed. Then a figure appeared, not far from the first robot.

Finally, a sign of life.

"Hello?" the Colonel greeted the figure cautiously.

The person, if that's what it was, fired a black ball toward the robot, terminating the transmission.

Dan flinched.

"Jesus! What was that?" The Colonel had recoiled, as well.

Silence filled the room.

With any luck the second robot will be destroyed too, and Denida will never return, assuming he's still alive. Claus had to leave before his smirk gave him away.

"Hey!" The Colonel strode to catch up to Claus. "I still want to see that form."

"Sure." Claus led the way to his car. The more he worked with this man, the more he loathed him. Too bad he needed the Colonel's trust, for now.

After a painfully silent car ride, Claus escorted the Colonel up to his office. He stepped aside, ushering the Colonel inside, praying that he hadn't left anything suspicious out in the open. He handed the Colonel a piece of paper on his desk. "Here it is. As you can see, everything is in order." Claus raised an eyebrow as the Colonel examined it.

"Maybe I was wrong, after all. This checks out." The Colonel handed the form back to Claus. He paced around the room, inspecting it. "Nice office."

Claus tapped his foot impatiently, poorly concealing his concerns.

"I haven't been here much, seeing as Denida rarely used his office for anything more than to keep up appearances." The Colonel nodded at Claus and departed from the office. "I should get back to the lab. Sorry to bother you."

"Where did you usually meet with Denida?" Claus spoke up, before the Colonel departed from the office.

"At Dynasty, of course." With that, the Colonel left.

Dynasty- Susan might know something about that! Claus sat down in his chair and finished his paperwork to mitigate suspicions. When he finished, Claus hurried for the cottage, and burst inside, glowering at Susan.

"If the office I'm using is a front, where's the real office?" Claus slammed his hands down on a table, leaning forward with undisguised intrigue.

"The hell if I know," Susan said calmly, but the slight widening of her eyes gave her away.

"You're lying." Claus pushed her into a chair. "I don't have to bring you food, you know. Everyone thinks you're searching for another Gate. If you never returned, they'd be sad, but they'd still never suspect a thing. Decide now if protecting Denida's secrets is worth your life!"

Susan hung her head for so long that Claus worried she might defy him. He clenched his fists in preparation.

"It's in Dynasty's basement, but you can't enter it. Denida's the only one who can," Susan whispered without meeting Claus's eyes.

"You'll take me there." Claus drew his gun and held it in between her eyes.

Susan shook her head. "You aren't listening to me. It's impossible for anyone to enter, except for Denida."

"Let me worry about that." Claus tossed her his car keys. "Any tricks and you're dead. If you're telling the truth, I don't lose anything by killing you."

***

Outside the cabin, Susan lifted her face to the sun and inhaled deeply. Freedom felt sweet, even if it was only temporary.

"Don't get used to it." Claus nudged her with the gun. "You're driving."

The drive was long with Claus scowling and keeping his gun trained on Susan. He seemed to be guarding her carefully. *Oh well... even if he finds the chamber, he'll never get in.*

The security guard at Dynasty's front gate saw Susan and Claus and waved them through. Though Claus craned his neck to peer around Susan, his gun never wavered.

Susan parked and led Claus to the front door.

The butler opened the door. "Everyone's out at the moment."

"Nina asked us to bring a sweater to her at the lab. We just need to grab it; we won't be long." Claus's gun might've been concealed under his coat, but it was still deadly.

I can't let him cause any more pain. Susan gritted her teeth.

The butler stepped back and ushered them in.

Susan guided Claus toward the family's rooms, but after checking to see no one was watching, she opened a door and led Claus down a long flight of stairs to a door with an iris scanner and a keypad next to it.

"Ta-da!" Susan gestured to the door with a grand gesture. "You'll never get in."

Claus rested his palm against the door. "What is Denida hiding behind such heavy security? What's really behind this door?"

Susan smirked. "The Underworld's real command center."

***

Apparently, Daniel had proved himself to the boy with the gun. The others treated that kid like a soldier. Daniel swallowed hard to keep his nausea from expressing itself on his face.

"Your property will be in working order again soon; don't worry!" The boy held out a bag of nuts he had been munching on. Children had been selling them like popcorn at a movie.

Daniel helped himself to a handful. The idea of viewing his dad as property bothered him, but it was a relief to hear that he'd be okay. "Thank you… what can I call you?"

"Mark!"

Daniel nodded. "Mark, when do you think he will work again?" Daniel eyed Mark, hoping for good news.

Mark shrugged. "Depends."

That isn't very helpful. But wait, there was something he might know. Daniel tried to keep his tone casual. "I heard there are two Gates. Mark, you wouldn't happen to know where I can find the second one, would you?" Daniel smiled.

Mark peeked around to see who might have heard his question.

"The Gates need to be patrolled, especially the working one. Stop asking questions, or you'll get in worse trouble than your servant just did." Mark walked off, cradling his gun as if it were a toy.

The working one? That's why not many kids were around the first Gate when we arrived! They consider the other one to be the working Gate.

"You're the escapee's master?" a voice asked.

Daniel turned to see an adult cleaning a desk while talking to him.

"Don't look at me!" the man hissed.

"They beat him," Daniel whispered to him as he averted his eyes.

"Hmm." The man started to stack some plates. "Claus came and he got mad."

"What? Claus is here, too?" Daniel's voice cracked as his stomach twisted. *Will he follow us everywhere we go?*

"He's the kid in charge around here, and he's powerful." As the man strolled past Daniel, he dropped a piece of paper in Daniel's lap. "Even our general couldn't beat him!"

Who's their general? Daniel scanned the paper, which depicted a hand-drawn map with an "x" marking something. Daniel had no idea what he'd find there, but this was the only clue he had, and his gut implored him to trust the man. Clenching the note tightly in his hand, he set off to find whatever the man wanted him to see.

Daniel meandered through the town. The adults worked in shops or on the streets as slaves. Older kids patrolled the town with their guns, predominantly surveilling the adults. Two children broke out into a fight over something, leaving one adult frozen in the street. *Strange, the buildings and everything on the streets are built to be adult-sized, so they must've been in charge at some point, right?*

Daniel examined the map and roamed, free of suspicion. His journey ended at an abandoned building. He stood outside, considering whether it was safe to go inside, but he hadn't come this far to run away.

The door creaked a little when Daniel pushed it open. A mouse scurried through the filth and gloom in front of him. Despite cobwebs and dust littering the interior, Daniel's magic alerted him to the fact that people were inside.

Before he could try to sense anything specific, someone tossed a cloth over his head, blacking out his vision.

"Make sure no one followed him!" a voice ordered.

How many people are in this room? A bead of sweat ran down Daniel's neck.

Someone snatched Daniel, carrying him away from the foyer.

What are they going to do to me? The only way Daniel would find out his fate would be to comply. *At least they didn't knock me out... or kill me.* Soon he was set down on his feet and the cloth was ripped away from his face.

The man who'd given him directions stood before Daniel, eyeing him warily. "He wants to meet you." The man stepped back, revealing the mysterious "he" in the shadows.

Though dirty and bearded, Daniel recognized him immediately. "Colonel!"

The two men glared at each other. The man who resembled the Colonel grunted at Daniel. "I'm a general, not a colonel. That new guy called me 'colonel' too. You really like kicking a man when he's down, don't you? Demoting me like that…"

"Dad!" Daniel blurted out.

The men exchanged a glance.

The general nodded. "I see. Well, don't worry; he'll be alright."

Daniel relaxed. No matter what world he might be in, he'd trust the colonel, no… the general, here. *The general will know how things work.*

"How did you get here? You aren't like the others." The general leaned forward to examine Daniel.

"We came through the Gate from another world, where adults aren't oppressed."

The men's eyes widened. "My dad is president in my world, and a guy just like you is his colonel, our highest, most trusted soldier."

"Hm, but not a general!" The general chuckled and whispered something to the other man, who nodded and left. On the man's departure, the general sauntered over to Daniel. "We need to get your dad. I have a good feeling about you two. You might be the answer we've been waiting for."

Daniel approached a kid, who appeared to oversee an infirmary. "I'm here to get my slave! I brought another one along to carry it for me."

The children waved their hands and left.

Denida woke up in the adult ward of the infirmary. "Guess they don't want to let their servants die," Denida jested.

The doctors, all adults performing first aid under the watchful eyes of armed children, gave Denida the minimum treatment required for his injuries. It was just enough for him to recover, but nothing to help mitigate his pain. "Your item will survive." The doctor nodded to Daniel.

The general approached Denida and helped him out of bed. He could have used another day or so to heal. The doctors had wandered off, so Daniel grabbed some clothes for his dad, and they marched him to the abandoned building, inside of which Daniel had met the general.

"You look a bit better in this light." As soon as the door closed behind him, Daniel stepped up to help his dad. "There's a bed over here."

Denida lied down on the bed with a groan but smiled at Daniel.

"He needs time," the general mused.

Daniel nodded in agreement. "The kids are guarding the Gate. They said that it's the one that works. Do you know where it is? We need to check it out." He turned to the general.

The general's face fell, indicating that he understood.

"We have to," Daniel insisted.

"No, Daniel." Denida shook his head lethargically. "Do not go to the Gate. Claus is probably there and he's way too powerful." Denida tried to sit up in the bed. When he couldn't, Daniel and the general rushed to help him. Denida grabbed the general's arm. "Don't take him to the Gate! We can't leave this world in this state, anyway."

"I won't." The general squeezed Denida's arm. "We couldn't beat Claus before the magical seal, so we don't even stand a chance, now!"

Denida sipped some water and pointed at Daniel. "Yes, we do. children can use magic, here. Daniel knows some, and his magic is stronger in this world, it seems."

Daniel hung his head as he stood beside his dad. "Dad, I'm so sorry."

"You needed to do it; I know that. Sometimes life presents us with very hard choices." Denida rested his hand on Daniel's shoulder. "I'm proud of you."

"I should have stayed behind the crowd." Daniel peered at Denida.

"Then you wouldn't have found the general."

Daniel smiled at his dad.

When the general and his dad started talking, Daniel found a corner to sit and think. His dad didn't want him helping with the Gate, and the general had promised not to tell Daniel anything.

Yet, Dad just said I'm the answer to this world's problems. Daniel needed more information, so he slipped out, searching for the Gate.

Asking children for help wouldn't work; Mark had warned him of the dangers associated with that approach, so Daniel wandered about until he noticed an area that the kids appeared to be giving a wide berth. Daniel conjured up a cloaking spell for the first time ever, then walked in front of a kid to test it. When it worked, Daniel crept just far enough to see the Gate. It stood, bright and buzzing, as children with guns patrolled it with harsh eyes.

Daniel snuck far enough away, then released the cloaking spell before strolling back to the adults' building.

The general had returned to his master with a promise to return when he could sneak away again. Daniel waited with his dad, enjoying being near him, even in their silence.

At dusk, the general returned.

Daniel opened his eyes from where he sat beside his dad's bed.

"You know magic?" The general crept over to Daniel.

"Yes, Sir."

"We need to disable whatever force is preventing the adults from using magic."

"Yeah, but how?"

The general smirked and laid his hand on Daniel's shoulder. "You wanted to see that Gate, didn't you?"

"But my dad said…"

"We're at war, Daniel. We need to take some risks. Your dad would agree, if he felt better." He pulled Daniel to his feet. "We need to cut the Gate's power to disrupt the seal."

Daniel had seen the Gate lit up, understanding now that it was responsible for sealing the adults' magic. "Alright." He rose to his feet.

Daniel handed the general an empty box to carry for him and led him out of the house. He crept through the town without regretting his decision. When they were close enough to the Gate, Daniel slipped into a shed to hide.

The general followed him inside.

A window had a perfect view of the Gate. Its glow illuminated its surroundings, revealing the armed kids patrolling it.

"They're kids; their only defense is magic. Once we remove that advantage, we can easily deal with them."

"What about their guns?" Daniel's stomach churned as nervous anticipation filled him.

"Don't worry; all those guns can do is cast a paralyzing spell."

"We aren't going to accomplish anything from here." Daniel glanced at the general. "I'll take some of them on with my magic, maybe even try to get one of those guns away from them. With their attention on me, you'll be able to get close to them."

"Good plan, Daniel." The general gave him half a salute, before they inched out of the shed.

Daniel didn't want to waste magic on a cloaking spell, so he snuck through the bushes until he was only a few feet from the first guard. He whispered a drowsy spell, and the kid fell to the ground. Daniel crawled forward and grabbed the kid's gun. He took out two more guards before someone noticed they were missing.

"We're under attack!" a kid shouted.

Daniel shot the kid with his gun, leaving the next two to the general, and made a shield. He felt like he was in one of those espionage movies his dad watched, as he ran from one hiding place to the next, either shooting the guards, or incapacitating them with sleep spells.

The general, savvy in combat, used his fists and gun to knock out any of the guards Daniel missed.

The Gate stood in the center of the guarded area, glowing brilliantly. Daniel could see visible magic being sucked out of its main unit. *Unreal, one world built a time machine from a part of the Gate, but it's actually strong enough to control all the magic in a world?*

"How long have kids been in charge, here?" Daniel asked as the general stepped up beside him, breathing easily and sweat-free, clearly still ready for more action. "Has the seal always been this strong?"

The general peered down at Daniel for a moment, as if waiting for another question. Eventually, he shrugged. "It's been like this for seventy years or so. Nobody's aged in all that time."

Daniel scoped out the Gate, a bit freaked out by what they were about to do.

"This is going to change everything." Daniel waved, gesturing to the town. "You sure you want this?" He met the general's gaze.

"Yes, we must." The general's face hardened. They walked closer to the Gate.

This close to the machine, Daniel saw an element connected to the main unit, keeping the Gate on. He gathered his thoughts, thinking of the children who beat up his dad, and him needing to slap his dad to satisfy them. He shouted and threw a fireball at the weakest part of the connection.

The magic field exploded, and Daniel expected to be thrown back through the air, but it passed right through them, as if they weren't there, and flew out into the night. *So, this was how it must've felt to work with Dad's colonel.* Daniel smiled and turned his focus down to his hands. *I can feel that the magic balance has already changed. If I can feel it, Claus can, too.* Daniel pointed to the main unit. "Remove that."

The general obeyed and put it into the empty box he had brought for Daniel. "We can't destroy the Gate, but we can make sure Claus can't use it again."

Chapter 14- Nina's Suspicion

Kid Claus woke up with a pit of dread in his stomach, as he felt the magical energy shift in the world. *Am I powerful enough to maintain control without the amplified magic? Do any grown-ups rival me, now?* He couldn't remember their skill level before implementing the seal.

Claus grabbed a couple of guards and sprinted to the Gate. *I hope my fear is misplaced.* He had to fix it before it was too late.

All the guards around the Gate had been knocked unconscious or shot with a paralyzer gun. The main unit of the Gate had vanished. The machine that had been extracting magic from the Gate to create the shield had been blown up by a powerful fireball, judging by the ash around the element. *Who could've done this?*

Claus grabbed one of the sleeping guards, and used mindreading to see what had transpired. A vision of a child and an adult wreaking havoc on his guards flickered. They stayed in the dark and moved too fast for Claus to identify them. He checked the rest of his guards' memories, but none of them had seen any notable details about their attackers. They'd wake with headaches, but that was the least they deserved for their failure.

That child and adult had broken the magical seal, then left with the Gate's main unit, preventing Claus from rebuilding a functional inhibitor.

People will notice the change soon, especially the adults. His problems were about to multiply.

***

Denida was still in bed when Daniel and the general returned, clearly in a good mood. The general laid his hand on Denida's chest, healing his injuries with magic.

"How did you do that?" Denida sat up in bed.

"We disabled the magic seal." The general smirked. "Daniel said you know strong magic?"

"Claus." Denida jumped off the bed and paced throughout the room. "You want my help to beat Claus, correct?"

The general nodded, taken aback. "Even without the machine, Claus is strong, but most of the kids are not. I don't know how many adults will remember their magic quickly enough to help. We need you, or Claus's reign will continue, even without the machine."

Denida stopped and faced the general. "Let's get started then." He stumbled over to a table for some breakfast.

Echoes of chaos reached Denida in the house where he, the general, and Daniel waited for an opportune time to strike. Adults had discovered their magic again, and children ran screaming from the rage of those who, just the day before, had been slaves.

"Stay low." Denida signaled Daniel. "Don't make the same mistake I did."

The general had adults reporting to him, but none of them had seen Claus, the real culprit behind the world's horrors.

A crowd stormed down the streets, enacting revenge.

The general stepped outside to reason with them. "We can't do this; they're just children."

"They stopped being children when they enslaved and beat us!" someone yelled.

"Wait; this is wrong!" Denida yelled over the mob's hollers.

The general nodded in concurrence, but most of the crowd kept shouting.

Some of the adults screamed that they didn't know Denida, and that he couldn't be trusted, since he had missed most of the children's tyrannical reign.

Denida peeked back at his son to make sure he was far enough away that the crowd couldn't get at him. With a relieved sigh, he turned back to the mob, watching the general's attempts to quell their madness.

Denida raised his hand and started to mumble something. The sky turned dark, and a pentagram appeared around him.

The mob fell silent and stepped back, eyes wide.

"Do I have your attention, now?" Denida shouted loudly enough to be heard over the wind howling around them. He lowered his arm, and the spell subsided. "Claus manipulated those kids. He needs to be punished, not them."

The crowd edged away before splitting up to avoid Denida.

"That was some show." The general stood beside Denida, still watching the adults with a worried frown. "You might be even stronger than Claus."

"It's just a dark spell I learned in the last world. It's the only one I know," Denida whispered.

"They might be worried now, seeing as Claus is the only one they've ever known with magic as strong as that."

What Denida didn't mention was that, while using that spell, a strange power rose within him. It had been like a fire, hotter and stronger than any strength he'd ever felt before. *Was the Dark Wizard right about me? Do I have an implicit talent for dark arts?* Regardless, the question of what to do with Claus remained. *Where is he?*

"You've given us our magic back." The general handed Denida the unit he'd taken from the Gate. "You press on; the other adults and I will clean up this mess."

"I want Claus." Denida's knuckles whitened as he gripped the main unit. "I can't leave until we've dealt with him! If there is one thing I've learned, it's that Claus will find a way to seize power at any given opportunity."

Mark walked in. "You want Claus? I know where he is!"

Denida glanced at the general, who shrugged and nodded. "We sure do." He approached the boy.

"I have one condition." The boy stared between them.

"What's that?"

Mark tilted his head at them, then his feet. "Claus ran this world for seventy years. We did bad stuff, too. The adults want revenge. I'll help you if you promise to exonerate us."

Denida was about to ask why he was suddenly offering to help but caught himself with his mouth open. *This boy must have seen me use that spell. Word of my might will spread quickly. People talk, after all.* "Alright, you have my word." Denida extended his hand to shake Mark's.

The general gaped but kept his mouth shut.

Having secured Denida's promise, the boy's defiant façade faltered. "Claus will be at the fortress deep in the forest, near the mountains. It takes ages to get there, so it's sensible that he'd go there to feel safe."

Denida pried a few more details out of Mark, then rested his hand on Daniel's shoulder. "General, I'm putting Daniel in your care." He stalked outside and vanished.

***

Claus returned Susan to the cabin. He pushed her inside and refastened her chains.

With a time machine, I can go back to when Denida built the command center and see what he's hiding there. "I will discover Denida's secret." Claus faced Susan with his arms crossed.

Susan frowned. "What are you talking about? Denida doesn't have any secrets."

"If he isn't hiding anything, why does he have that room and all that security?" Claus's blood boiled. He'd have shot Suan right then and there if part of him didn't believe he still needed a hostage. He had to build that time machine. Time was running out, and the net was tightening around him.

Claus met Doc, knowing he was exactly the person Claus needed to bypass the door's security measures. Claus bit his lip, trying to think of a good way to redirect Doc away from the time machine for the time being.

"Dynasty has a secret door in the basement with an iris scanner and a keypad. It may hold the key to building our time machine." Claus hoped it would be enough to convince Doc.

Doc glared at Claus from across a table that was covered with unrecognizable tools.

"We have nothing to work with, now," Claus reinforced his point. "We're stuck, but the chamber may hold the secrets that we need."

"No!" Doc's scowl deepened as he began work with his equipment. "You want me to crack a password and an iris scanner? Do you know how hard that is? And worse, we'll only get one shot at it."

I don't care how hard it is, I need it. "But–"

"What part of 'no' are you struggling with?" Doc's face reminded Claus of just how dangerous this man was.

Claus gulped. *One more try.* "All of his personal files are there, including his records on the Dark Angels, and you."

Doc's shoulders hunched, and Claus's hand slipped toward his gun. The man relaxed and dropped into his chair, staring at the ceiling.

Got you. Claus patted him on the shoulder. "Let me know when you're ready."

***

Nina paced back and forth in the lab, awaiting the Colonel's return. He had to have discovered something about Susan's whereabouts.

"Susan?" She rushed over to the Colonel, right as he entered the room.

"It was her signature; she requested it, after all. She will be back soon." The Colonel rested his hands on Nina's shoulders comfortingly.

"No, I don't believe it." Nina turned away from the Colonel. "Something's wrong; I can feel it. It's not like Susan to volunteer to search for a third Gate without reason to believe there is one. She's too logical for that."

The Colonel's eyes narrowed. "I'd know her signature anywhere, so I'm convinced that she did sign up for this mission. What more can I say?" He approached Dan and stood behind him, watching the monitor from over his shoulder.

Nina glared at his back. As the First Lady of the Underworld, she had certain privileges that she could take advantage of. She'd investigate Susan's disappearance herself with all the means available to her. *I just need a plan.* Claus had been picked and trained by Denny to be his vice president, so it would be hard to convince the others that something seemed off about Claus. *What would Claus do to Susan, and why? If the Colonel won't investigate further, I'll do it myself.*

Nina left the lab and ordered her driver to take her to the Underworld's headquarters. She swept past Denida's secretary, heading into his office.

Susan's request rested on Claus's desk, and Claus sat in Denida's chair. Nina quickly glanced at the form. Sure enough, she recognized Susan's distinctive signature.

"You've really made yourself at home, here." Nina turned around, hardly recognizing the room with its marked lack of Denida's belongings. She glared at Claus, and he paled.

"Until Denida returns." Claus leaned forward in his chair. "I'd hate to be court-martialed."

With that response Nina knew for sure that something was off, but nothing here would help her. Even so, she wouldn't give up, no matter what Claus implied. *Let him try to win this game.*

"Sorry to have bothered you." Nina smiled at him and left.

Claus grunted as she closed the door behind her.

***

The Colonel stared into the new town's darkness. Whatever had destroyed the first robot seemed to have vanished as soon as it appeared, never encountering the second robot.

What's going on? The Colonel had too many questions to not have a single answer.

The darkness finally lifted just enough for him to see that the people who had destroyed the first robot had left. *Where is everybody, and who were those weird people? And what's with that darkness? Something's off about this place.*

With nobody around, they had no other choice but to continue. They were down to their last robot, creating and deploying another one would take far too long, now. After all, no one knew how much time Denida and Daniel might spend in this place, and they wanted to catch up to them. As the robot drove through the ghost town, everyone in the lab wore discouraged expressions. The place was quieter than an old Western movie's abandoned village.

"Maybe we should try to find whoever destroyed the robot?" Dan turned to the Colonel.

The Colonel clenched his fist to withhold his anger. Maybe Dan had a point. *That was the only living thing we've seen so far.*

"Maybe, but it's too late, now. Besides, it's possible that those people caused all this mayhem. There's no way to know if they'd make good allies."

As the robot reached the town square, a broadcast began on a wide monitor. An old woman warned this world's residents of new dangers they could expect to face. He advised them to stay well-hidden and informed the public of a shield on the Holy Lands, which would keep the Dark Wizard and his people off those grounds.

A woman's face in the background seized the Colonel's attention. *Susan!* If he knew one thing about this world, it was that he wanted to be on Susan's side. Besides, this broadcast was the first sign of life, other than the dark beings who had destroyed the first robot.

"Let me guess… we should try to find the Holy Lands?" Dan's fists clenched. He hadn't left the lab for more than a few minutes since Denida had gone through the Gate.

The Colonel worried that the stress would break him. "Dan-"

Dan smacked his own head. "Library… we need to find a library! If this is the main square, there should be one nearby." Dan picked up the controller again and drove off, in search of a library.

The trek proved simple, given the desolate streets. Maneuvering the robot through crowds always took so much extra effort, making this a welcome change. The Colonel peeked at Dan worriedly, but Dan just continued, until the robot stood outside a building with "Library" above its door.

Pamphlets on the door highlighted famous landmarks and tourist locations.

"You really think the Holy Lands will be on that list?" The Colonel's heart sank.

"Of course!" Dan searched through the pamphlets, turning each page more hastily than the last. He sighed loudly, and turned to the last page, where he finally found one with a listing entitled, "The Holy Lands." Dan smiled at the Colonel.

"Good, you found it. According to this, it's due south. Take us there, Dan!"

The robot trundled through the vacant town. Dan stopped and turned to a poster advertising the world's annual magic championship.

The Colonel shrugged. He'd worry about details later. For the first time since entering this blasted world, it seemed like they could finally find Denida and Daniel.

Up ahead, they could see the building, but an invisible barrier prevented the robot from getting any closer to it.

The Colonel gritted his teeth. This place was too weird for him, and it only became stranger with every new development. "Drive around the building; check for an opening."

"No gap." Dan sighed, after checking the perimeter.

The Colonel saw a person pacing outside. He tried to yell through the robot to get their attention.

"It's a robot," Dan said.

"Your point?"

"Well…" Dan fiddled with the controls. "- it can do a lot of things that we can't, like emitting a very loud, high-pitched noise." Dan pushed a button, and an agonizing, technological buzz filled the lab before Dan cut the audio feed.

The person ran into the building and came out a few seconds later, followed by Susan and a squad of soldiers, all with their hands covering their ears.

"I think we have their attention," the Colonel said.

Dan hit the button and the sound stopped. He turned the feed on again and faced the Colonel. "You're up."

The Colonel stepped in front of the monitor. "Hello."

Susan jumped and a soldier pointed at the robot. "Who are you?"

Guess they don't have a version of me here, seeing as they don't recognize me. "We come in peace." The Colonel held out his empty hands. "We're searching for Denida."

"Denida?" Susan waved at the soldiers, who relaxed at the gesture. "He already left through the Gate." She pointed to the building. "I think you need to talk to Dan and the Warlock."

Chapter 15- Final Attempt

Nina watched as Susan and the soldiers escorted the robot inside the building. People packed the arena-style establishment, filling every corner. From the fear on their faces, cynicism gripped this world's residents.

At least Denny and Daniel are okay. Those dark creatures seem more menacing than the Dark Angels, given the fear on these peoples' faces.

Susan escorted them to the old woman they had seen on the broadcast. That world's Dan stood next to her. Everyone in the lab leaned forward in anticipation.

"Is… that a version of me?" Dan's eyes widened and he smiled excitedly.

"What's going on here?" Nina's voice cracked with worry.

The old woman stood calmly, barely sparing the robot a glance. "You're from Denida's world, I presume?" The Colonel and Nina glanced at each other, but before they could reply, the old woman continued. "I am the Warlock. I taught Denida how to use magic."

Magic? How can she teach him that?

"Magic exists?" Skepticism laced the Colonel's tone, and he crossed his arms. Nina couldn't blame him, but it would explain some of what they'd seen here.

"I know it's hard to believe," the Warlock said. "But Denida is naturally gifted."

"But he left with Daniel, right?" Nina interrupted, asking the question she needed answered. Magic didn't matter as much as her boys.

"Yes, but the Gate is no longer accessible."

"What do you mean?" Nina's hope faded into numbness.

The Warlock stepped back and conjured an image of the Gate. She zoomed out to reveal some black creatures, identical to the ones that had destroyed the first robot, standing around the Gate.

Ugh. They only had one robot left and couldn't afford to lose it, too.

"What are they? And how do we get rid of them?" The Colonel asked.

"They're demons from Hell, controlled by the Dark Wizard. I'm not sure if we can get rid of them, so we're hiding from them."

"What's going on here? Magic? Demons? What was Denida involved in this time?" the Colonel muttered.

"I have things I need to do." Nina stood up and waved vaguely at everyone. "Let me know when you get to the next world."

"You're leaving, now?" The Colonel gasped.

Since Denida and Daniel had already moved on from that world, Nina lost interest in that world's discouraging situation. Someone else would have to help them. *This world's magic is nothing compared to what's really out there. I'll let them learn all about it, but I have to save Susan, now!*

For now, Nina had time to deal with Claus. She had a clear starting place in mind, too: *the computer in Claus's office.* It was the most logical first place to look. She didn't even need to risk going to his office. Dynasty's command center could access any computer on the Underworld's HQ and laboratory network. *Claus won't see me, and the process is totally discreet.*

The butler greeted her when she arrived at Dynasty. "Welcome back, Lady Nina. Did Susan bring you the sweater you requested?"

Susan's been here? She shook the thought from her head as she hurried to the secret room in the basement to access the computer network. She checked the security footage first, to confirm her fears. She rewound until the monitor showed Susan marching through the door with Claus. *Of course.* Nina had been right. *Claus lied.* He didn't just know of her whereabouts, but he had brought her here.

What's Claus up to? The question remained. *How much trouble will he cause me, and more importantly, Susan?* One thing was certain; Nina had to show this footage to the Colonel. She made a copy on her flash drive and headed off to the lab. When she left the chamber, she ran into the butler again.

"Did you forget something in the command center, like Susan did?" the butler asked.

"No." Nina dismissed the idea, not thinking anything of it.

***

Denida quickly traveled into the mountains, aided by his magic. Mark had assured him that Claus would be hiding up in the desolate region with some child soldiers, who served as Claus's security detail. Claus would not escape, not this time. The wilderness remained untouched, without so much as an eroded path snaking through the terrain, but lingering traces of magic betrayed the fact that people were nearby.

Children guarded a building in a tiny valley from high up on a mountain, like snipers monitoring a rendezvous point. Denida noted each of them, but only for the sake of gathering intelligence. *Claus is my only target.*

Several versions of Claus had been causing problems across the worlds. Denida would need to watch his own Claus carefully when he returned home.

Denida cast a cloaking spell around himself but couldn't think of a way to stop his footsteps from crunching on the dry grass. He walked until one child lifted his head, then he froze in place, until the kid resumed his standard patrol duties. By the time Denida reached the door, most of the children seemed to be glancing up quite frequently.

As Denida expected, the door was locked. He hunkered down next to the entrance to wait. To amuse himself, he rolled pinecones across the ground, sending the guards darting this and that way, chasing the pinecones, thinking someone was kicking them. *It's good to distract them.*

Finally, one of the guards radioed for help to find out what was going on. More children poured out the door.

Denida swept the house's door for magical traps, setting off one, which only stung his hand. He slipped into the house after the last kid exited and locked the door with magic to avoid distractions.

Inside, Denida strode silently as he checked each room for Claus. Denida found Claus sitting in the center of a room with a window looking out into the forest. Rugs covered the wooden floor. A fireplace sat empty behind Claus. From what Denida had learned of the house's layout, the door he'd entered the house through was the only exit.

Claus turned to face him. "Who are you?" he asked as if he knew Denida was there.

"You know why I'm here." Denida dropped his cloaking spell.

Claus chuckled a little. "You came alone to bring me back? Being an adult doesn't make you stronger than me." He rose and circled Denida, as if sizing him up.

"None of your guards know anything more advanced than basic magic."

"Few people do. You're not from here. What's your name?"

"Denida. We met before; you had those children assault me."

Claus smirked and stepped away from Denida. "As much as I'd love to find out just how much you know…"

Child soldiers burst in through the door, waving paralyzing guns.

Claus laughed as Denida spun around and thrust a wave of magic at the children, throwing them against the wall and pinning them in place. When he turned back to Claus, the boy had vanished, abandoning his guards and the building.

Denida stepped up to one of the children and used a spell to read his mind. The child had no idea where Claus might have gone. None of them did.

Denida did not intend to return empty-handed. Claus had to be stopped before he could use his magic to reassert his control. Denida closed his eyes, focusing to discover traces of magic, and saw a clear trail leading north, away from the cabin. He let the children drop to the floor and pursued Claus into the woods.

Denida followed Claus's trail through the mountains. *Is Claus leading me into a trap? Even if he is, what else can I do? There's nobody else around to help me, and nothing to do but to follow him myself.* Denida had to play into Claus's hands, for now. He stared up at the moon briefly. *I hope Daniel and Nina are okay.*

It had been a long time since Denida had left his own world. He knew Nina couldn't be sitting around doing nothing, but he hoped she didn't get into any trouble in his absence. The fact that she had the Colonel with her provided a small sense of comfort, but Nina was always the go-getter type. Sometimes, it seemed like she was raring for a conflict. Up ahead, Denida spotted Claus, and pushed his homesickness aside.

Claus stood in the middle of a clearing, which appeared black and white under the moonlight.

He has some nasty surprise planned. Kid or not, this is still Claus! Denida approached the clearing, fully prepared to take him on. "Hello, Claus."

"Hello, Denida," Claus replied in a low voice with his back to Denida.

"It ends here!" Denida carefully neared his combatant.

Claus suddenly spun to face him. "I know who you are. I know everything that you don't remember." Claus stood with his hands in his pockets, smirking. "If you want to know everything that I do, all you have to do is let me go."

Denida studied Claus suspiciously. The boy seemed certain that he had answers to the questions that Denida hadn't even asked. *But I'd have to let him go? What kind of damage would he do? He's bluffing.*

"It's not a bluff, Denida." Claus tapped his head. "Answers to everything you've been wondering are all right up here."

Denida cleared his mind.

"Don't you want to know why you can use dark arts so easily?" Claus started to sound desperate.

"Yes." Denida covered his eyes with his hand and chanted, striking Claus with a powerful sleep spell.

Claus slumped to the ground.

Denida sighed and shook his head. *But this is what I have to do.* He'd find his answers another way.

When Denida returned with the unconscious Claus, he helped the general prepare a cell, which sealed magic inside and around the cell, such that Claus couldn't escape, and his allies couldn't assist him.

"Claus needs to be tried." Denida stretched and suppressed a yawn. "Watch for sympathizers trying to break him out."

"I'm a general." The general winked. "I know a thing or two."

The Gate stood ready for Denida and Daniel to leave, but Denida paid one last visit to Claus's cell.

"Hello, Claus." Denida leaned against the wall.

"Do you expect me to tell you anything about your past, now? You wasted your golden opportunity!" Claus sauntered over to the bars of his cell. "You'll find out in time, *my lord*." Claus sneered at him and turned away.

"Come." The general escorted Denida and Daniel to the Gate and reinserted the main unit.

"Don't be too hard on him." Denida peeked back in the direction of the town where they were holding Claus.

The general rolled his eyes. "I'll try, but it's not just up to me."

Denida sighed and shook the general's hand. "Take care, General. I may have to give my own colonel a promotion." He took Daniel's hand and stepped through the Gate.

***

Nina rushed back to the lab, so she could show the Colonel what she'd found. At least she had proof, now. *Claus is lying about Susan, and I'll show everyone.* The man always gave Nina chills. She didn't understand it for the longest time and had pushed it aside, but now, she knew that her concerns were valid. The Colonel would have to deal with him.

Wait... what will happen to Susan? Claus had Susan. If she gave the Colonel this evidence, he wouldn't sit still. Nina pulled the car over and sat in the driver's seat, eyeing the flash drive. "I'm sorry, Denny. I have to do this, for Susan." *I wish there was another way, but...* Nina stowed the flash drive in her glove compartment and resumed her drive.

Back at the lab, the Colonel was explaining their recent findings to Vice President Claus.

"I'm back. Hello, Claus." Nina had to fight not to attack him. First, she'd find Susan. Then, she'd show the Colonel the damning footage on her flash drive. It was the only way; she was sure of it.

Claus glanced at her, and their eyes met for a second. A shadow passed through Claus's eyes.

He doesn't trust me any more than I trust him. If only he knew... Nina smiled her most gracious smile.

"Hello, Lady Nina." Claus's entire face seemed tense.

The robot sat in front of the old woman, known as the Warlock, and the others behind her.

"They're strong, aren't they?" Nina pointed at a group of men behind the Warlock.

The Warlock glanced back at them. "Yes, they are the other warlocks. How did you know?"

"I can feel it," Nina murmured.

"Hm. You are sensitive. Like Denida, you have a gift."

"Our world doesn't have magic." Nina folded her arms.

"You can feel Denida and Daniel, can't you?" the Warlock asked after a while.

Nina's heart skipped a beat. How did she know? Nina had always felt connected to Denida, and still did, even now.

"I can sense it in you," the Warlock spoke in Nina's thoughts.

"Enough of this! Can we get to the Gate or not?" Claus interrupted and stepped in front of the monitor.

"Claus?" The Warlock furrowed her brow. "How are you there?"

The Colonel stepped between Claus and the monitor.

Nina's eyes widened. *Why is the Warlock so suspicious of Claus?*

"Claus almost killed Denida. He set the Dark Wizard free and torched the prison with all the inmates still inside." The Warlock scowled, as the air around her crackled. "I know souls, and his is rotten to the core!"

The Colonel peered at Claus. "I will send you a report, but we'd better not anger them! We need their help to find Denida."

"That Claus is another soul, not me." Claus laid his hand over his heart, like he was hurt.

If Nina didn't know any better, she would have felt sorry for him.

The Colonel frowned. "That warlock doesn't trust you, Claus." He sighed. "I am fine with you, but we're trying to work with the Warlock, here, so could you please respect their caution so we can figure out how to get to the Gate?"

"Of course, I only want to get Denida back." Claus smiled and departed from the lab. "Let me know if there's anything I can do to help."

Nina watched him leave. She might not need the flash drive after all.

The Warlock studied her with intrigued eyes, and then spoke to her mind only. "You must tell me what's going on, there."

Nina scoped out the room, worried that the others had heard it, but no one else reacted. She gazed at the monitor, into the Warlock's eyes, and thought the words that she wished she could say aloud. *I know Claus has taken Susan hostage!*

Chapter 16- The Secret Chamber

Susan jumped when Claus burst into the cottage. His overjoyed smile only made her heart pound faster.

Another man followed Claus inside, and Susan stepped back. "Why are you so happy? Who's he?"

Claus tilted his head at Doc and his grin turned into a smirk. "His name's Doc. He found a way into Denida's chamber." Claus chuckled. "And you said it was impossible." He unlocked Susan's chains.

Something about Doc bothered Susan. *What is it that's so wrong with him?* Before she could assert her suspicions, they forced Susan outside.

A different car from earlier idled next to the cabin. Susan glared at Doc, trying to deduce anything she could about him. *That must be his car.* At least it was a start.

Claus sat in the driver's seat while the other man rode in the back with Susan.

Why would anyone want to work with Claus? Susan couldn't imagine Doc would find anything of value in Dynasty's command center.

Still, the longer she stared at Doc, the more shivers she got. She couldn't shake a feeling in her gut that there was something awfully familiar about him. Then it clicked, and her heart sank. "Wait! I've seen your face on Denida's wanted list. You're the Scientist!"

Doc scowled at Susan. "You can call me Doc, and I won't be wanted for long. Denida will be done hunting the Dark Angels soon enough."

They must think Denida's files on the Dark Angels and their supporters are in that chamber. Susan's heart raced. If they accessed Denida's hidden room, the entire Underworld would be in danger.

They arrived at Dynasty's checkpoint, and Susan had to worry more about not throwing up on Doc than alerting the guard with a stray glance.

"Hey, Miss Susan, you alright?"

Susan nodded without raising her head.

"She's fine, just a little carsick." Claus smiled.

The guard waved them through, and Claus drove to Dynasty.

Claus dragged Susan out of the car and inside, passing the butler with Doc following close behind.

"Sorry, Susan is sick. Where's the washroom?"

The butler pointed down the hall. "Do you need anything?"

"No, just rest." Susan gulped. "Upset stomach."

Claus dragged her down to the door to the secret passage and pushed her into a corner.

"You're up." Claus gestured for Doc to approach the door.

Doc put his equipment up against the security pad.

"Worried?" Claus smirked at Susan.

Susan bit her lip.

"Here we go." Doc pressed a button, but nothing happened.

"What's going on?" Claus frowned at Doc's tools.

"It's spoofing the code by throwing millions of combinations at it. As for the iris scanner, I managed to swipe an image of Denida's eye from his optician."

Within minutes, heavy bars clanked as they shifted in the wall, then a repetitive beeping sound emanated from a speaker near the door.

Susan turned her head to see a security camera pivoting to face them.

"Emergency Power Shutdown" scrolled across the keypad's screen while the beeping continued.

Susan heaved in a sigh of relief. *I should have known Denida would have an extra layer of security.*

"It won't work!" Claus yanked Susan to her feet.

Doc snatched his device off the door. The three of them bolted up the stairs. The perpetual beeping chased them away from the door.

Susan wanted to laugh as her worries lifted. *That's one nightmare averted.*

"Leaving so soon?" the butler asked when they stepped into Dynasty's foyer. "You and Lady Nina always seem to be rushing about lately."

Claus glared at Susan and turned back at the butler in surprise. "Nina has been here?"

"Yes, is something wrong?" The butler frowned.

"I will need to talk to her." Claus sauntered to Doc's car.

Claus's words echoed in Susan's mind. With each repetition, her nausea returned and worsened, as she knew what Claus meant by needing to 'talk' to her." *At least we got away before the alarm caught us.*

***

Nina, Dan, the Warlock, and the Colonel were devising to plan a way to get to the Gate when an alarm on the Colonel's phone wailed.

The Colonel snatched his phone out of his pocket. "There's a security breach at Dynasty. Everything's on lockdown." He snarled questions into the phone. "Who would try to break into Dynasty?"

"Oh no," Nina groaned. *The system will need to be reset to access the video feed. I bet Claus triggered the lockdown.*

"What?" The Colonel glared at her.

"I may know something," Nina said.

"Something?" The Colonel's face tensed, his expression frozen somewhere between rage and confusion.

Nina knew she might have to tell him about the flash drive, but that would put Susan's wellbeing in jeopardy. She could see from the Colonel's confusion that she had no choice but to tell him. *But is now the right time?* "I put a tracker on

Claus," Nina admitted. "Remember when the Warlock said I had a gift for sensing evil? There's evil in Claus. The Warlock feels it, too."

The Colonel's frown remained intact. "And how exactly do you plan to explain the tracker when he finds it? You can't do these things without telling me."

Nina raised her finger to force the Colonel to pause. "If he finds it!"

The Colonel's stoic expression remained just as prevalent.

"If I'm right, Claus was at Dynasty, and I can prove it!" Nina tapped a command into the computer and brought up her tracker.

The Colonel watched over Nina's shoulder.

The tracker showed Claus's position at the Underworld's headquarters, and he appeared to have been there all day, based on the GPS records.

"So, he didn't trigger the alarm." The Colonel turned to her. "Are you satisfied, now?"

Nina's mouth hung agape. She had been certain that Claus had attempted to break in, but the tracker hadn't moved. "It must be broken!" Nina hissed.

The Colonel raised an eyebrow.

"Okay," Nina muttered. "I was wrong." The admission sent a spike of pain through her stomach. She had proof but she couldn't use it. *Not until Susan is safe.* If Nina gave it to the Colonel, and he arrested Claus, they'd never find Susan.

The Colonel spun on his heel and returned to the monitor to talk to the Warlock.

"What's going on?" Dan rested his hand on Nina's shoulder.

Nina blinked at him. Dan was Denida's closest friend, second only to the Colonel, as Denida knew both of them since the war. Judging from the suspicion on his face, he knew Nina was hiding something. As she was about to brush him off, she changed her mind, but words continued to escape her.

"What is it?" Dan's focus seemed sharper than the Colonel's, and his tone sounded genuinely concerned.

Maybe he can help. It would be nice to share her secret. Nina pulled Dan aside. She was about to act innocent, but as she smiled at Dan, she realized he would not buy it. She surveyed their surroundings to ensure that no one would overhear her. "Claus has Susan somewhere."

Dan rolled his eyes, just as doubtfully as the Colonel.

"Come on." Nina took Dan's hand and dragged him along. "I'll show you." She led Dan out to her car and showed him the flash drive. Nina connected it to her phone to play the video of Claus outside of Dynasty.

"Why haven't you shown this to the Colonel?" Dan started back toward the lab.

"I can't." Nina grabbed his arm. "He'll knab Claus, and we'll never get Susan back. We have to find her first."

"Do you have any idea why Claus went to Dynasty with Susan?"

"I don't know." Nina stood, lost in thought. It hadn't even occurred to her to figure out his motive.

"Could he have been trying to frame her for the intrusion at Dynasty?"

"Maybe," Nina muttered. She hid the flash drive in the glove compartment again before they returned to the lab.

***

Doc watched Nina and Dan from around the corner beside a garage. When Claus first instructed him to keep an eye on Nina, Doc had rolled his eyes. Now, it was becoming exhausting. *To think I could be working, now.*

Once Nina and Dan headed inside, Doc allotted a few minutes to make sure they wouldn't come back outside before pacing over to Nina's car. Its lock didn't stand a chance against the man who cracked Denida's security measures. He attached the flash drive to his phone and played the video with a smirk. *Always good to have dirt on Claus.* He dialed Claus's number.

"Hello?" Claus's voice interrupted the third ring.

"Hey, Claus, all's quiet here. Make sure you remember to clear the data on the Underworld's servers." Doc chuckled as he pocketed his phone. *Claus sounds relieved.* He flipped the flash drive in his hand. *Nina's the least of his worries, now.* Doc left the garage, plotting to turn everything to his favor.

***

The Colonel was speaking to the Warlock when Nina returned to the lab with Dan. They'd learned everything about the Dark Wizard, except for how to defeat him. Pushing himself away from the monitor, the Colonel almost knocked Nina over. "Sorry, I need coffee."

Nina sat in the Colonel's chair to talk to the Warlock in his absence. "He's not used to being helpless. Magic's prominence in your world has diminished his confidence."

"And what about your confidence?" The Warlock tilted her head.

"I need to learn magic, specifically how to read minds. It may be the only way to save a friend."

"The friend you told me about? Sure, you have an affinity for magic, but it will still take a lot of work for me to teach someone magic to someone who has never used magic before." The Warlock's smile hardened.

Nina rubbed her forehead while glancing around. "I know how magic works. I've seen it once…"

"Intriguing. We'd better get started, then. Firstly, clear your mind."

Nina and the Warlock worked for several hours. Her mind felt as shaky as her legs would after a long run. Once again, Nina reached out into the room to try to hear another mind. "Why did she have to tell me? I don't need this stress. Now that warlock is teaching Nina magic. How does that even work?" Nina giggled, eyeing Dan, but her smile froze quickly as Dan's thoughts resumed. "Claus has Susan; I can't waste time with these games. Who knows what Claus is doing to her!"

The Colonel pushed himself between Nina and the monitor, breaking her concentration. "You said the wizard cannot die, so he needs to be locked up, right?"

"Yes, correct." The Warlock's brow wrinkled.

Nina stepped away to give the Colonel more room. *Did I really read Dan's mind?*

"Then call me your solution." The Colonel bared his teeth.

Nina guessed that the Colonel's expression was supposed to be a smile. The techs had stopped pretending to work, now clearly eavesdropping.

"How?" The Warlock leaned back. "We've been over everything."

"They use magic, so we shouldn't use magic to catch them. We have to use the opposite of magic!"

"I'm not sure I follow." The other warlocks gathered around to join the conversation.

"There must be something that doesn't react to magic. We can use that to set a trap that they can't see or affect. We'll lure them into it. Once they spring the trap, they're ours."

The Warlock scratched her cheek. "I can see why Denida trusts you to be his colonel. That plan might work."

The Colonel paced in front of the monitor. "Once this works, we can get to the Gate." He laid his hand on Nina's shoulder. "At last."

Nina stood stunned, as the Colonel ran back to the table where he had papers and plans strewn about. *Can the Dark Wizard and the demons really be that stupid?*

"Yes," the Warlock's voice spoke in her mind. "He wants vengeance, and his demons are driven by their hatred."

Nina blinked rapidly. *But Denny wasn't there when the demons were. This is the first time you'll face them head on.*

The Warlock exhaled heavily.

"Denida and Daniel are gone, but it will be alright. We can fight, too; we know more than just magic."

Nina raised her eyebrows. "Everyone I see around you uses magic. Does anyone there know how to fight without it?"

The Warlock pointed back into the crowd, where Nina could just barely see Susan and Dan in close quarters. "Dan and Susan lead our military. I'd imagine your military practices unarmed combat. Similarly, ours trains in non-magical combat. One of the warlocks has also suggested a material, which will work well for the Colonel's proposed trap."

"I hope so." Nina sighed.

The Dan in the lab fiddled with some equipment on a table, putting things together and pulling them apart.

Nina nodded to the Warlock and headed over to Dan. "You okay?"

"How can I be? How can you be?" Dan hissed, clearly at the edge of his mental capacity. "Claus has Susan, but we don't know where, or even if she's still alive. No, I'm not okay!" He dropped what he was holding, letting it clatter on the table. "I won't be okay until we find Susan." Dan stalked off.

Nina watched him. *Maybe I shouldn't have told him, after all. Can he keep it together?* She clenched her fist. Unfortunately for Dan, he had no choice in the matter, as far as Nina was concerned. She'd told him, and now, he'd have to suck it up.

Nina ran to catch up to Dan. "The Warlock has been teaching me how to read minds with magic. I'm going to try it on Claus." Nina rested her hand on his sleeve. "Just relax; we'll get Susan back soon."

"You might want to hurry, before Claus does something to mitigate our chances of getting Denida back."

Nina shrugged. "There's time; he's not-"

"Claus already tried to prevent us from sending a robot through the Gates and seemed especially furious when we deployed it without his consent. To make matters worse, the Colonel told me that Claus has taken over Denida's office and made it his own!" Dan's eyes flared red.

Nina's heart sank. "You're right; Claus doesn't want Denny to return."

Chapter 17- The Trap

Six times, Denida and Daniel had walked through a Gate without arriving back home. Denida's faith that this Gate would lead them home had dwindled significantly, as memories of the various worlds flooded his mind. Needless to say, he wasn't surprised to step into yet another unfamiliar world. "Alright, Daniel, let's be careful. You know the drill; we need to find the second Gate."

They followed a path leading away from the Gate. Denida immediately detected magic around him. He froze in place, trying to locate the source, when Daniel pointed out powerlines running along the side of the path up ahead. *They have technology and magic?*

"Dad, all the worlds we've seen have had magic, except the first two."

"Strange." *That makes this the first world to have both, aside from the one where Claus learned magic by getting stuck in the past.* "We know what Claus did when he introduced magic to a technologically advanced world. We'll have to stay extra vigilant in a world that's always had both magic and technology. We don't know what we'll encounter."

Denida stood with Daniel on a hill, from which they could see a town below. Cars drove all over the civilization's roads, honking at each other. Some veered off the roads to escape traffic jams, leaving tire tracks through people's lawns. Denida held his breath, waiting for an inevitable head-on collision. Children ran through the town, ducking into stores, coming out with arms full of goods. Clerks chased them down the streets.

"Good grief." Denida rubbed his temples. "This is even worse than that world run by children. This is pure lawlessness."

Daniel shrugged and led the way to town, eventually stopping outside a café. "Let's try asking around, here." He ducked into the building with Denida in tow. Daniel sat at a table.

Denida joined him, glancing around the establishment. Advanced androids served customers, but magic hung heavily in the air.

Daniel traced his fingertip along a pattern on the tablecloth. "We don't know much about the Underworlds, do we?"

"I guess not." Denida twisted in his chair to survey the room. "I don't know if we should ask anyone here about this world. This whole world feels intrinsically unsafe."

"You might be right," Daniel admitted.

"Give me your money!" A stranger stood in front of Denida, hand outstretched expectantly.

"This isn't going to go well." Daniel leaned back in his seat, as if to make room for a fight.

Denida frowned at the man, who had disheveled hair, but tidy clothes, an average joe. Given the way his aggressive façade continually faltered and reasserted itself, he appeared to be exerting a lot of effort to make himself seem intimidating.

A man resembling the Colonel rushed over to them.

"Get out of here!" He glared at the man, who raised his hands and hurried out the door. The Colonel's counterpart turned to Denida and Daniel, scratching the back of his head. "Sorry about that."

"Colonel, or General, I presume?" Denida attempted, delighted to meet his friend in this world, too.

The man raised his eyebrows. "Sorry, but you have the wrong man. I'm not a colonel or a general."

He's important in all the other worlds, so why not here? This place keeps getting stranger by the second. Denida cleared his throat. "My mistake. What do you do, then?"

"I run this store, of course." The man who wasn't a soldier stepped behind the counter.

"Of course," Denida muttered. *A shopkeeper is still an authority, especially given how crowded this café is, but it's still nothing compared to his high-profile role in the other worlds.*

"I do have an Inn on the second floor, too," the shopkeeper hollered as Denida turned away from the counter.

Denida and Daniel left the establishment. Denida's head spun. The colonel's counterpart didn't help lead this world, which brought another concern to his mind. *If he's not in charge, who is?*

"The castle!" Denida snapped his fingers.

Daniel tilted his head up at him. "What?"

"There's been a significant building in all the other worlds, so there must be one here, too." Denida marched down the street with Daniel in tow.

Their eyes darted back and forth as they journeyed through the world, taking in every person, every car, and every potential threat. The residents continued driving like lunatics without repercussions, due to the lack of a police presence. After a while, Denida spotted a building that could only be this world's castle. "See? Told you!" He ruffled Daniel's hair. "We have to have faith in what we've seen."

Daniel licked his lips. "This world's version of the Colonel isn't in charge here, so who do you think is in there? What if it's Claus?"

The smile faded from Denida's face. The idea of meeting Claus again knotted his stomach. "Dan, maybe?" Denida tried to convince himself, but he couldn't bring himself to believe it.

Daniel frowned, letting out a sarcastic little snort, as if he didn't believe it, either.

"There's only one way to find out." Denida grabbed Daniel's hand. "We have no choice but to check it out." *No way I'm leaving him alone in this crazy world.* He escorted Daniel to the castle.

***

The warlocks in the other world had been in a frenzy, preparing to lay the Colonel's trap. For the trap to work, they needed to act as calmly as possible to ward off suspicion.

At the Colonel's advice, the warlock cast a multitude of strong spells to make it feel like the room oozed magic to create a bait-and-switch.

The Colonel paced in the lab, his nerves getting to him. He hated this part, when they'd planned as much as they could, and could only wait, now. There would be surprises, and everything depended on how the other world's Susan and her soldiers reacted to the unexpected.

One warlock stepped out of the building for a few moments, pretending to go check on something. When they returned, they ran back inside, as if responding to something so urgent that they had forgotten to close the door behind them.

"We need a lure." The Colonel sat in front of the monitor, rubbing his temples. "We don't have time to sit and wait."

"I'll go." The other world's Dan volunteered.

"You just need to go far enough to get their attention. No heroics."

"Hey, if we go with him…" one of Susan's squad leaders began. "- it will look like a recon mission."

In dawn's light, they began. Dan and the soldiers marched out with straight backs and wandering eyes, appearing alert, as they collected food and supplies in an abandoned shopping center that the wizard had reportedly been at the day before.

The Dark Wizard appeared with a shout, and his demons charged at them from all directions.

Dan's eyes widened as he and the soldiers dashed back to the building where the trap awaited its victims.

The wizard and the demons chased Dan and the soldiers into the building, right on their heels.

Susan's soldiers jumped out with metal nets. They overpowered the demons, who'd followed the Dark Wizard inside.

The Dark Wizard frantically cast spells and cussed in frustration as his magic bounced into magical shields in the room, which absorbed each blow's power, before the spells could strike any of his targets.

"It's over!" The Warlock stepped out with Susan and her troops.

The wizard disarmed a soldier, who was moving in to capture him, then fired spells at the others. In the chaos, he broke through a door leading farther into the building, where magic would be more effective.

"Crap," Susan hissed. "At least we captured his demons."

The Warlock stared despairingly at Susan. "Even all that planning wasn't enough to stop him."

"No!" Dan ran up to the Warlock. "We can't let him get away. Pursue him!"

"The Dark Wizard knows powerful magic. He almost beat all of us warlocks before."

"Maybe so, but we've got him cornered, now. Do you want to give him the chance to come back with more reinforcements?"

"I guess not." The Warlock raised her hand, summoning the other six warlocks, and they headed into the building, tailing the Dark Wizard.

Dan crept along behind them, while Susan and her soldiers spread out to create a barrier behind them, so that the Dark Wizard couldn't double-back.

A miasma of fear seemed to hang in the hallways, given the caution with which Dan and the soldiers walked, always glancing around, their steps appearing slow and uneven. Even over the monitor, the Colonel was certain he could see black whisps flitting through the air.

"The Dark Wizard is creating your fear; don't give in." The Warlock summoned a light in her hand, which illuminated the room, dispelling some of the black energy.

Beads of sweat shone on Dan's face and dampened the back of his shirt. His hands trembled at his sides.

The Dark Wizard waited for them in an atrium, where four walkways convened. He summoned a fistful of darkness, which spread to envelop the hall. "Are you ready?" the wizard called out from the blackness.

One of the warlocks groaned and fell to the floor.

"You're jealous of my power. You can't stop me. Step aside, and I might spare you."

The Warlock focused hard on one spot in the inky haze, and her gaze shifted with purpose, as if she could see the wizard through the miasma. "Like you spared Claus? No thanks!" The Warlock shot a beam of light magic into the haze, but the darkness devoured the beam.

"You're too weak. Would you like to reconsider my offer?"

"Go to Hell." The Warlock raised her hands.

The six remaining warlocks combined all their energy into an attack, which illuminated the room for a moment, weakening the darkness. It created a weak light, allowing everyone to make out each other's nervous faces.

The Warlock stood in front of the others. "We cannot let you die. You'll just return to Hell, and then return with a vengeance."

As soon as the Warlock spoke, Dan drew his gun and shot the Dark Wizard in the thigh.

All seven warlocks gathered their energy again, suspending the Dark Wizard between life and death.

The Warlock smirked. "You cannot return to Hell if you're in a coma!"

The Colonel grinned, pleased that they'd contained the Dark Wizard, but the demons still required explanation. He turned the robot to face one of them.

"Who are you? How did you get here?" The Colonel cut himself off, waiting for an answer from the indistinct dark figure on the screen.

"I am a demon from Hell. We do as the Dark Lord instructs. The Dark Lord sent us to reward the wizard for destroying Claus before he could kill Denida."

The Warlock stepped in front of the robot. "Susan needs to take the demons to a secure prison, now."

The Colonel leaned forward. "Wait! I want to know more about what he said regarding Denida."

"The Gate is clear. You can move on, now."

What's she hiding? Did the demon's words upset the Warlock, somehow?

"You know something." Nina rested her palms on the counter.

"Sorry, but you'll be taken to the Gate, now." The Warlock left and placed the robot inside a truck to send it to the Gate.

"She is preventing me from reading that demon's mind." Nina gritted her teeth and paced behind the Colonel, as the screen was now black, due to it being dark inside the truck.

Eventually, light streamed inside, and the Warlock placed the robot on the grass in front of the Gate.

"Why won't you answer us?" Nina asked again.

The Warlock sighed and closed her eyes for a moment. "All I can say is that you all have a challenge ahead of you. You likely will meet more demons, and even worse foes than them, but I wish you luck with your Claus."

"If that's all she's going to tell us, let's go." The Colonel nodded at Dan, signaling him to maneuver the robot through the Gate.

Nina frowned. "But…"

So far, each world had been worse than the one before, so the Colonel had a prevalent sense of concern tightening inside his chest. "The demon mentioned Denida, and the Warlock interrupted them. How does the Devil know about Denida?" The Colonel muttered under his breath.

***

Nina left the lab to visit Claus, hoping to escape the oppressive mood in the lab. Claus welcomed her in with a broad smile, apparently forgetting the animosity of their last meeting.

Nina sat across from Claus and tried to read his mind, but it was like staring at a white screen; something was blocking her.

"So, what brings you here?" Claus leaned forward.

Nina's mind went blank. She had expected to be in and out by now, but the mindreading she had learned wasn't working. *Maybe I don't have talent for this, after all.* Nina pursed her lips. *Then again, I read Dan's mind quite easily.* She took a compact mirror out of her purse and checked her face to buy time.

"After spending all that time at the lab, I must look a mess," she muttered. *Maybe the Dark Angels used magic to create a permanent barrier, here? Or did something else shield this room?* Nina had to get Claus somewhere else.

"There was a break-in at Dynasty. I think the person running the Underworld in Denny's absence should investigate it, No?" Nina watched Claus's face, but he only gasped.

"No, I'll gather reports, but I'm not qualified to investigate the incident myself. I'd only get in the way."

"Okay, then." Nina stood up and continued to the door. *Can I give up just like that? Denny wouldn't.* An idea struck her. She turned in the doorway. "We found demons in that last world, the one with the Warlock."

"Really?" Claus peeked up, as if he suspected she was kidding.

"Yes, it would seem the Devil is rewarding people who are protecting Denny, for some reason."

"Good God, I'll have to look into that." Claus hurried out of the office, leaving Nina to make her way back to the lab.

Denny's on that man's mind, for one reason or another. Nina climbed into her car and drove back to the lab, where she knew she could read minds with magic.

Chapter 18- Susan

Doc watched Claus and Nina speed off in different cars. *Something got them excited.* Whatever, he'd find out the catalyst later. Right now, he had more important work to take care of. He stepped out of hiding and sauntered into the headquarters for the first time since the Dark Angels had been defeated. He stepped through the front doors, casually nodding at the man sitting behind a security desk. Even during the war, Doc's face hadn't been well-known. There were advantages to supporting the Dark Angels from a lab. He rode the elevator up two floors and stepped out onto a floor of offices for the bureaucrats who ran the Underworld on a day-to-day basis. At the end of a long hallway, he encountered a large conference room used for internal meetings.

Nobody so much as glanced up from their work as he passed them.

Doc strolled into the conference room and sauntered to a far corner. He ran his hand over the wall. Within seconds, he found a secret panel, dusty and undisturbed since the days of the Dark Angels' reign.

"Hey," a voice greeted him from behind.

Doc grabbed what he needed, closed the compartment with a swift motion, and turned around slowly with a smile pasted on his face. *No one expects anything bad from a guy who's smiling.*

"Is there a meeting today? I thought so but I left my planner at home." A thin, balding man with a crooked tie stood in the doorway, wringing his hands.

"Not that I know of," Doc said. "The boss got mad at me, so I came in here to cool off."

"Yeah, she's a tyrant. If she asks, you didn't see me here." The man winked in solidarity.

"Sure thing." Doc sauntered away after giving the man ample time to return to his office.

Leaving the building was as easy as entering. He strolled to his car, then drove to where he'd set up his research.

Once there, he checked the GPS on his phone and found the cabin where Claus was holding that woman. The unit from the Gate lay in a testing box in Doc's lab. *That thing intrigues me.* He stowed the unit in a bag he'd lifted from the HQ. *Claus has been very useful.* Doc scoped the room once more. He had already taken every other object of interest and stowed them in his car. His plan seemed to be moving along well, just as he'd planned.

At the cabin, Doc withdrew a tranquilizer gun and a pair of bolt cutters from the trunk without unlocking the car doors.

"I'm in here!" the woman yelled from within the cabin.

She's in for a disappointment. Doc kicked the door in and walked into the cabin.

"What are you doing here?" Susan's expression froze between caution and curiosity.

"I'm here to take Claus's ace in the hole." Doc shot Susan with the tranquilizer gun and watched as she slowly slipped unconscious, despite her pathetic attempts to drag herself closer to Doc.

Once she collapsed, Doc examined the chains. The most efficient maneuver would be to snap them where they were fastened to the floor. *They might prove useful, so I shouldn't do too much damage to them.* He cut through the chains.

Now, Doc had both the woman and the Gate's main unit. *Claus will have to listen to me, now.* Doc couldn't possibly invent the time machine within a few days, like Claus had requested. Besides, the noose around Claus's neck was starting to tighten. Soon, he would be discovered, and Doc wanted to ensure that no one could connect him to Claus when the witch hunt began. He carefully loaded Susan into his car.

Doc drove off, smiling as he imagined Claus's face when he discovered that he'd been double-crossed. Doc sure enjoyed a solid treachery masterwork. *It brings me back to the good old days.*

Doc peered at Susan's reflection in the rearview mirror. *So, she's the mighty soldier that I've heard so much about. They say that the only soldier who outranks her is the legendary Colonel.* He scratched his chin. *She doesn't look all that special to me.* Claus had captured her, after all, and he was hardly more capable than that guy with the crooked tie back at HQ. *Yet, she never escaped from Claus's clutches, so can she really be a concern?* He shook his head after a moment. *Nah, not to me.* She had not been a part of the rebellion against the Dark Angels, but here she was.

***

Claus was in a rush to get back to the lab. The Devil, if he was even real, was a terrifying consideration. *Someone protected Denida, and that person was granted a position of power. If the Devil really rewarded that guy for protecting Denida, should I be worried about being discovered? Will the Devil help Denida return, and punish me for what I've done?* The horrific consequences of his actions raged in Claus's head as he drove to the lab.

Claus drove as fast as he dared. He needed answers, and he'd find them at the lab. Claus darted into the building with a dignified swagger.

The Colonel faced Claus and approached him with his most recent report.

Claus's patient persona grew increasingly agitated as he listened. According to the Colonel, The Dark Wizard killed the futuristic world's Claus, and had been rewarded with an almost endless supply of demons. *Can we really meet the Devil himself?*

"I need to talk to you alone!" Nina spoke from behind, making Claus jump.

What could possibly be so important? Claus faced her, trying to devise an excuse.

Nina rested her hands on her hips.

I'd better go along with it. Claus followed Nina outside, where she turned and met his eyes with a piercing glare.

"The cabin?" Nina asked after a few seconds.

"Cabin?" Claus's stomach sank. *This is bad.*

"Yes, where you have Susan!" Nina smirked.

Claus twitched. *How does she know about that?*

Nina hurried to her car.

Claus's legs planted themselves like roots, as heavy as lead bricks, as his gaze tracked Nina's movements. *How?*

"Because I can read your mind." Nina rolled up her window and sped off.

Claus shook himself. He'd deal with his questions later. He had to stop Nina, or it would be all over for him. He sprinted to his own car and took off after her.

Claus ran stop signs and red lights, trying to catch up to Nina, leaving a trail of angry, cussing drivers behind him. Once Claus reached a country road, he could floor it and drive as fast as his car could go. Every time he crept up on her, Nina pulled away as if he'd been standing still. Obviously, the First Lady of the Underworld could afford a much nicer car than the vice president.

Claus pulled into the cabin's gravel driveway behind Nina, breathing hard, as if he'd been running rather than driving.

Nina stood in front of the door, which hung open, only attached to one hinge.

Did she help Susan escape?

Nina scowled at Claus. "Yes, maybe she escaped from you."

This mindreading thing is creepy. Claus drew his gun for protection.

"You do realize that shooting me will land you in even more trouble than abducting Susan?" Nina smirked and sauntered into the cabin, inspecting the floor. Her gaze lingered on the bolts, which had held Susan's chains.

Claus raked his eyes through the cabin, trying to keep his mind calm, despite being on the verge of a panic attack. He drew in a deep breath to ground himself.

Nina rummaged through Susan's belongings.

She's gone! Claus deliberately held that single thought in his mind in case Nina reread it. Judging from the focus on Nina's face, she seemed to be trying hard to pry some ideas from the far reaches of his mind, as he had expected, but he didn't know where Susan was, so he had nothing to hide from her.

"Susan couldn't have escaped by herself, right?" Nina asked.

"I don't know. She might have never even been here at all." Claus smiled convincingly.

"Oh, she was! That's why you keep thinking 'she's gone.'" Nina stepped closer to Claus, with an accusing finger raised. "And someday, everyone will see you for the snake you are." Nina rushed out to her car and sped away before Claus could react.

As he heard her tires screech away, Claus sighed, glancing around the cabin once more. He knelt next to the rings on the floor, which had held the chains, seeing that they were still intact. *Whoever helped Susan must've used bolt cutters to break through her chains, which means they came prepared to free her. But who...* Cold sweat manifested on his brow. The only person who knew she was here was Doc. *Don't tell me...* With his heart pounding away in his chest, Claus began to pace. Did he take her to try to get the upper hand? *I'll have him hunted down for this!*

Suddenly, he froze in place with a wicked smirk appearing on his features. Nina could accuse Claus all she wanted, but without Susan, she couldn't prove anything. Perhaps this was a blessing in disguise. It would keep Nina from interfering while Claus tracked Doc down for a little payback.

Claus drove to the hidden research center, using the drive to plan his accusation. He considered the exact words he'd say to Doc when he saw him. With his confidence at an all-time high, Claus marched straight up to where Doc had been trying to analyze the main unit, finding some equipment on the table, but the Gate's main unit had vanished. *Doc must've taken it and Susan and made a run for it!* Claus needed to erase all evidence of Doc's existence, and their connection, to get Susan and the main unit back.

"Denida can't return to the Underworld!" Claus hurled a piece of equipment against the wall, then sent Doc a text.

"You win. I will keep Denida from returning, and your files will be inaccessible."

But how? An idea came to Claus, and he drove back to the cabin, where he parked his car. He stepped out of the vehicle and turned his head in the direction of the second Gate, only to hesitate.

Claus withdrew his phone and called a contact, Donaldson, who'd been on the right side of the war, but Denida had discharged him for committing gratuitous killing sprees, evidently for the fun of it. The man had become something of a mercenary since then, operating under the radar.

"Meet me at the cabin near the unused Gate," Claus instructed Donaldson, making sure to hang up rather quickly. *If worse comes to worse, Nina and her cronies will check my phone records and suspect that Donaldson abducted Susan for revenge on the Underworld. I'll be off the hook.*

Claus smirked, pacing back and forth outside the cabin until two cars pulled up, parking beside his own. Donaldson stepped out of the first car, and several of his cohorts stepped out of the second.

Claus shook Donaldson's hand before leading him and his team to the second Gate. "It's highly unlikely that Denida can use the Gate, but if he ever returns, you need to kill him. I'll become the president and can pay your usual fees, plus a bonus." Claus was certain this measure wouldn't be required, but he had to take every precaution, now that Doc had gone rogue.

***

Dan watched the Colonel on the phone. He seemed upset but didn't say a single word. The very short call concluded with the Colonel's persistent, stony silence. When it ended, the Colonel turned, recoiling a bit at everyone's focused gazes.

"That was Claus." The Colonel announced. "He wants to be sure that we'll tell him if we find Denida, even if we find him dead."

Some idle chatter in the room died down. Magic, demons, and who knew what else awaited them in the Underworlds… *Can Denida really survive all that?* Dan didn't like the odds.

"He'll be fine. He knows magic, now." Despite the certainty in her tone, Nina's face appeared pale and strained. "I know a little, too."

Everyone's eyes shifted to Nina. Judging from their faces, Dan didn't think they believed her.

"It sounds like Claus isn't expecting Denida to return." Nina stood in front of the Colonel with her hands on her hips.

"That doesn't mean anything; he's just being cautious." The Colonel faced the monitor.

Nina peered over at Dan and sent a thought into his mind. "Susan is gone! Someone took her, and Claus doesn't even know who could've abducted her."

"You could read his mind?" Dan asked Nina, who simply nodded.

"So, we cannot prove that Claus is rotten. And Susan may be…" Nina couldn't finish the sentence.

Dan understood how she felt; he was worried, too. The concern was creating a knot in his stomach. "I'm sure whoever has her won't hurt her!" Dan tried to console her but didn't even believe it himself.

***

Denida and Daniel approached the castle. The exterior appeared old and overgrown. From the rustic, forgotten atmosphere around it, no one had been there for a long time, which only added credence to Denida's belief that there was something very strange afoot in this world.

"What now?" Daniel stopped and stared at the castle, pursing his lips. "This is a dead end."

Denida turned to his son and opened his mouth to speak but didn't know what to say. He sat on the curb in front of the derelict castle, while Daniel kicked rocks across the road.

"The Colonel's doppelganger." Denida jumped and turned to march back to the café.

"He said he was only a shopkeeper, here." Daniel ran to catch up.

"But he might know where the Gate is."

After two hours of backtracking, they arrived at the café. The owner still stood at the counter, guarding the cash register, and glancing around at the rowdy patrons every few seconds.

"Hello." Denida smiled as he approached the counter.

"You again?" The man's eyes drifted up from wiping the counter down with a rag. "What can I do for you?"

Denida glanced at Daniel, who hadn't lifted his eyes from the floor. His discouraged frown spoke a million words.

"This world must have two Gates," Denida said. "I know where one of them is but can't find the other. You can help me, can't you?"

"No!" the man hissed. "I know of them, but I cannot help you."

"Why the hell not?" Denida punched the counter and stepped right up in the man's face, straightening his posture to appear more intimidating.

"You're going to fight him again, aren't you?" Daniel murmured.

The question shattered the tension. Denida relented, retreating a step, and drew in a shaky breath.

The man at the counter knitted his brows. "When did we fight?" the man asked. "I've only just met you both."

Denida and Daniel locked eyes, and Daniel shrugged.

Denida decided to gamble. "We met you before, just not in this world. We came through the first Gate, which is why we need to know where the second one is." He sighed, leaning his head back. "We're trying to get home to our own world."

"And that's how you know me?" The man's eyes trailed from Denida to Daniel and back, as his frown deepened. "- as a colonel?"

"Yes." Denida nodded slowly.

"I understand but I still can't help you."

"Please, we really need to get home!" Denida yelled, frustrated that his plea had failed.

Daniel rushed between them, but the man raised his hands.

"The second Gate won't bring you back home." He stared intently at Denida. "Many have traveled through it, but no one ever returns."

"That's because the Gates are one-way. They'd have to travel through all the Underworlds to come back here again, like we've been doing." Daniel stuck his jaw out stubbornly.

"That makes it sound even more dangerous." The man crossed his arms and glared at Daniel before turning his focus to Denida. "If what the kid says is true, I don't know how you intend to get home by going through these blasted Gates."

"We have to try," Denida insisted.

The shopkeeper pinched the bridge of his nose. "Fine, I'll tell you where it is, but there's no guarantee that you'll survive your trip through it!"

"Why not?" Daniel asked.

The man sighed. "Allegedly, it leads to a dark world." He gazed straight at them. "… or so our magicians claim."

Denida rubbed his chin. "Like Daniel said, no one can come back through that Gate," he mused. "Maybe that is why those rumors started?"

"Maybe." The man shrugged. "But it's on the other side of our world, where the lawlessness puts our town's lack of authority to shame. Darkness reigns that half of our world." He drew in a deep breath. "Light and pure magic simply don't exist there, just the darkness."

"And we have to trek through that to reach the second Gate?" Denida asked.

The man nodded. "The Gate you claim to have come through is the light Gate. The second is the dark one."

"The Dark Wizard used dark magic and he almost killed you." Daniel's face tensed, and he grabbed his dad's hand. "But I guess we've got no choice. Let's go."

Daniel and his dad set out on their long journey to the other side of the world, marching to the second Gate. They had no idea what to expect. According to what the shopkeeper had implied, the only people who ever ventured there were shady characters.

As they travelled, the sky, and even the air around them, became darker, as did the people. Violence and dark magic surrounded them like an aura. Constant shouting and cussing echoed all around them.

"I don't like this; it reminds me of the people who wanted to hurt us before." Daniel leaned closer to his dad, shifting his hand up to grab higher on his sleeve.

"Magic is magic." Denida shrugged. "All that matters is how you use it, and we're using it to get home."

As they ventured deeper into the darkness, they started attracting attention. People muttered and pointed at them as they passed.

Entering the darkness was bad enough, but to bring a kid with me? I'm just asking for trouble but what choice do I have? Denida bit his lip, trekking farther. Everything grew darker until Denida felt Daniel's grip tightening on his shirt. "Don't worry, Daniel, it will be okay."

"Maybe staying here won't be so bad." Daniel's voice shook.

"No, we can't. We have to get home to our own world, to your mother." Denida squeezed Daniel's hand, and they meandered through a wilderness of evil people and other beings, who appeared to flit about in the deepest shadows.

Denida's legs started to ache from their hours of walking today. He could only imagine what his son must be feeling. "We can't ask anyone here about the Gate," Denida whispered. "These people can't be trusted, but we need a safe place to rest for the night. We'll find the Gate tomorrow."

Everyone's eyes fixed on them as they wandered, despite Denida's best efforts to give their stride a purposefulness.

We need to find somewhere safe to rest or these people will mug us or worse. Denida's eyes fell on a stranger among the chaos, whose eyes didn't seem to have the same evil gleam as everyone else's. Denida bit his lip, watching the man for a moment, noticing that he didn't seem to engage with the rest of the strangers in their whispering and plotting. Denida approached him cautiously, tightening his grip on Daniel's hand, just in case. "Hello."

The man's eyes widened, as if he had seen a ghost.

Denida squeezed Daniel's hand. *Maybe I was wrong about this guy.*

"No, you weren't," the stranger said. "I will keep you safe, and you need to learn how to shield your thoughts from prying ears!"

"Sounds perfect!" Daniel nodded.

"That requires advanced magic, however. Denida knows it; he just needs to remember." The stranger smiled.

He knows my name… does that mean he knows me?

"I do," the man spoke directly into Denida's thoughts before continuing aloud, "Follow me; I'll take you somewhere safe. The dark creatures won't attack you while you're with me." He began leading them to a shack up ahead.

Denida shot a glance at the creatures, noticing them avoiding the house.

Chapter 19- A Stranger's Help

Denida sat beside the stranger, fighting the confusion in his head. "So how do you know me?"

The stranger waved at Denida and Daniel and smiled at Denida's question. "How can I not know the almighty Denida?"

Almighty Denida? Those words rang deep in his head, but Denida couldn't let them distract him. "You know how to shield your thoughts from others?"

The man's face lit up "Yes, of course, I do! I'll show you." He stepped over and sat in front of Denida. "I'm going to try to read your mind. I want you to think a thought, any thought, but imagine a metal barrier around it."

Like this? Denida conjured up the question in his mind but delegated some additional focus to generating a barrier around it. Just like his prior training, Denida picked up the technique as if he'd always known it.

"Are you thinking something? I can't see it," the stranger mused with a confidence that implied that he already knew the answer.

The affirmation made Denida smile, but it faded in a second. "Why didn't the Warlock know how to do that? She knew very powerful magic, too," Denida whispered.

The man smiled with a sparkle in his eyes. "Probably because shielding one's thoughts requires dark magic."

"I see." Denida glanced over at Daniel, knowing his son didn't like the dark arts. Yet to Denida, the dark arts were just the same as the light, provided that they weren't abused for evil. *Who taught me advanced magic? Was it the same person who sealed my memories with dark magic?* Denida pushed his questions aside. "We need to find the second Gate. Do you know where it is?"

The man tilted his head, staring at Denida, eyes wide with intrigue. "You want to go through the Gate? And go home?"

"Yes." *How much does this man know about me?* Sitting with a man who knew more about him than he knew about himself made Denida's stomach crawl with discomfort.

"Well then, I know where the Gate is," the man responded. "But Claus only lets people through if he deems them worthy."

Claus is here, too? Of course, he'd be the one controlling access to the Gate that Denida and Daniel needed to use. "How can we convince Claus to let us through?"

"I will get you an audience with him. Wait here!" The man left the shack.

Denida sauntered over to Daniel. "All we can do now is wait for him to return." His heart ached as he saw his son trembling and glancing around with wide, alert eyes.

"Maybe we'll get to the Gate after all." Daniel yawned and leaned against Denida.

As the night progressed without the stranger's return, Denida lied down beside Daniel and slept, content to have found a safe place to spend the night.

Denida woke to see the stranger sitting in the corner, waiting for them. "You're awake! Morning," the stranger exclaimed.

"You're back!" Denida jumped up, disrupting Daniel, who let out a little groan of dissent.

"Of course," the man replied. "I prepared breakfast for you both. You'll need your energy." The man smiled, but Denida couldn't shake his unease with everything involving Claus. *And what is with all this guy's smiles?*

"Don't worry," the man said. "My name precedes me."

What a strange thing to say. "Who are you, anyway? How exactly do you know me?" Denida's heart raced at the possibility of finally getting some answers.

The man's calm disposition remained pertinent. "You will understand soon enough."

First Danyel, now this guy! The fact that no one wanted to tell Denida what they knew about his past was starting to get annoying. Clearly, the man wasn't going to answer, and Denida couldn't push the issue because this man was going to escort them to the Gate, so Denida woke Daniel up, and they ate their breakfast before heading out to see Claus.

"Claus controls both the Gate and the entire dark side of this world," the stranger explained as they neared the rendezvous point. Crowds parted for them to pass, shooting them nervous glances.

Denida kept an eye open for anything that could pose a danger to Daniel or himself, and kept his son close to his side, but aside from that, he barely paid any attention to their surroundings. His mind was on his own world, and what his Claus might be doing in his absence.

They reached a castle, which resembled the one on the light side, but this one bustled with activity.

The stranger moseyed past the guards, leading Denida and Daniel right to Claus's chambers. The stranger hardly slowed before a guard pulled the door open and waved them in.

"So, you're here to use the Gate?" Claus's voice resonated from the far side of the room. This Claus was in the position of authority that his former counterparts had craved.

Denida tried to make out Claus's face, but the shadows in the dim room concealed his features all too well. "Hello, Claus! Yes, we do."

"Out!" Claus yelled at his guards.

The other men in the room escorted the stranger out, and the door shut behind them with a bang.

As soon as Denida and Daniel were alone in the room, Claus raised his hands and a cone of magical energy formed over them, eventually surrounding Daniel, Denida, and Claus.

Denida frowned, clearing his mind for a moment to focus. He sensed the magic in the cone and understood it to be a shield to inhibit magic. As they stood trapped within the cone, a man stepped out of the shadows. He seemed familiar, but Denida needed a moment to place him. *Wait! That's the Scientist, who assisted the Dark Angels.* Claus stepped forward too, with his eyes as black as coal, and his body covered in scars. He looked as though he could've been the Dark Lord himself.

"You know my name, so you can't use the Gate. And now that you've seen me, it's time to die!" Claus nodded to the Scientist and turned away.

Daniel's eyes widened, and he whipped around, throwing himself up against the door behind them, but it held tight.

"Wait! I only know of your name from the other Underworlds I've passed through," Denida explained quickly.

Claus stopped for a moment. "Lock them up! I need to decide what to do with them." Claus vanished into the shadows, and the cone dissipated.

"You're lucky," the Scientist hissed.

The other guards poured into the room and surrounded Denida and Daniel, escorting them to a cell with a strong magic shield around it.

"How do we get out?" Daniel crouched in the corner of the cell. "What if Claus decides to kill us, after all?"

***

Daniel slowly woke up, finding his dad still asleep. The stranger who'd brought them to Claus sat across the cell from Daniel.

"Morning!" the stranger greeted him. "Your father won't wake up yet, but don't worry. I think we need to have a little chat."

Daniel's stomach ached. *Why does he want to talk to me? How did he even get into this cell?*

The man casually waved his hand in Denida's direction. "Don't worry about how I got here. I will not harm Denida's son." He turned back to Daniel with piercing eyes. "But you need to know that I knew your dad at a time when he was evil. So, I've come to implore you to exercise caution around him!"

Daniel's heart pounded in his chest. "He was evil?" His jaw trembled. *Wait...* "He doesn't remember those days-"

The man raised his finger. "I know he doesn't, but deep down, your dad has a part of him worth fearing. I just wanted to warn you!"

Denida rolled over in his bed.

Daniel glanced over to verify that his dad was still sleeping. He turned back to address the man, but he'd vanished. Daniel spun around. *Where did he go?* He sat against the wall and stared at his dad. For the first time in his life, Daniel was afraid of Denida. His dad had beaten the Dark Angels. He'd led the rebel force to free the Underworld. Maybe he hadn't been a good person before that, but he was different, now. *He has to be...*

As his eyes stayed locked on his dad, a strange light leaked out from under the covers. Daniel crept over to the bed and pulled back the covers. The scar on his dad's side pulsed with an eerie, black light. Daniel dropped the blankets and scuttled back. *Maybe it's because there is so much dark magic around us. Yes, that must be it.* He bit his lip, finding himself unconvinced. *Could that man have been right? Is Dad's darkness coming back to him?*

***

Denida woke up and stretched the kinks out of his back. Daniel sat in the corner, wide-eyed.

Poor kid is scared. I don't blame him. Denida sat up, trying to organize his thoughts.

The guards opened the door, leaving only a few bars between Denida and Daniel, and freedom. The guards glared at their prisoners, then left.

Why would the guards...

Claus materialized in the doorway, answering Denida's unspoken question.

Denida approached the bars. "I was expecting you, Claus."

"Do you know why I'm here?" Claus asked.

Denida shook his head. "I don't even know why we're locked up!"

"You escaped Hell and now, you're back!" Claus scowled at Denida. "On top of that, you addressed me by my name."

"Escaped from Hell?" Denida asked shakily.

Daniel whimpered behind him.

"Yes!" Claus exclaimed. "You are Denny, or Denida, to be precise, aren't you?"

Denny… the nickname from before my earliest memories. "Yes, but they started calling me that in my underworld, not Hell!"

Claus approached the bars. "But you don't remember where that nickname came from, right? Just feels right to call yourself Denida, instead…"

"No, I didn't choose my nickname; the resistance did! You must be mistaking me for someone else."

Claus stared at Denida, who knew what he was fishing for. Denida didn't conceal his thoughts, allowing Claus access to his memories, wherein people in his underworld started calling him Denny without any prompting.

After a short time, Claus turned away. "You will not get out of here; I assure you!" Claus clenched his fist and vanished as fast as he had appeared.

Denida turned to talk to Daniel, who was biting his lip so hard that it appeared to be starting to bleed.

"Don't worry; he wasn't talking about me."

"That stranger was right! You are dangerous. You're from Hell." Daniel's eyes narrowed accusingly. "Stay away from me!" He raised his arms defensively.

"I'm not!" Denida tried to reassure him, but Daniel didn't seem to be listening.

Daniel's frigid glare persisted.

But I'm not, am I? Denny is just an old nickname. There's no significance to it; it's just what others started calling me. But how would this Claus know that nickname? Perhaps something about the spell on my memories tipped him off, but that doesn't explain why I can perform dark magic so easily. Claus knows something!

Denida's anger flared up, and he grabbed the cell's bars. The hinges flew off the cell's door, and when he let go of the bars, the door clattered to the ground with a thunderous clang. Denida stopped a moment in shock, facing Daniel. "Stay here; I'm going to get some answers from Claus." Denida stomped down the hall.

***

Daniel's iciness faltered as soon as his dad left the cell, and his legs began to shake.

How could he use magic, when it was supposedly inhibited inside the jail? Daniel didn't feel safe around his dad anymore, fully believing he'd do something terrible.

One thought echoed in Daniel's mind: *I have to get out of here!* He scampered to his feet and ran out of the cell and down the hall, away from his dad. Tears streamed down his face as he sobbed, whether in terror or grief, Daniel didn't know.

***

Denida strode toward the castle. *Getting to Claus might be hard but not impossible.*

"Wondering how to get in?" a familiar voice asked.

Denida turned to see the stranger who had brought them to Claus earlier. "You?" Denida scoffed and spun back around to examine Claus's domain.

"Wait!" The man stepped around Denida to face him again. "I can get you into Claus's chambers again."

"Who are you, anyway? Why are you so interested in me facing Claus, here?"

"My friends call me Luci, and I promised, didn't I?"

"Yeah, and that worked so well the first time." Denida rolled his eye.

"It will be different this time!"

"No." Denida walked past him, entering the building.

Luci looked after him with a smirk. "Just as I expected, Denida. Still as stubborn as a mule! We will meet again, soon," he mused.

Inside, the heavy, dark atmosphere reigned. Dark magic surrounded Denida. It didn't bother him, like it had Daniel. In fact, it put Denida at ease, giving him the same serenity that one might experience in a lush meadow.

The guards ignored Denida as he strolled through the building. Any of them who stood in Denida's path stepped away so he could pass them.

Self-preservation over loyalty, an advantage if you're on the wrong side. Denida reached the door to Claus's private chamber.

The guards jumped to attention. "He has been expecting you. Here you go, Lord Denida." The guards opened the door for him.

Is this a trap? Denida surveyed the room, finding it odd that the guards at Claus's door, the leader's last line of security, paid him the same meager attention as the guards patrolling the halls. Inside, Denida stepped slowly and cautiously, not knowing what to expect. *Is he really expecting me? Why would he be?*

"Welcome." The darkness in the room faded to reveal Claus, who sat on a throne.

"You knew I was coming?" Denida asked cautiously.

"Yes." Claus nodded. "The master wants you to speak to me."

"The master?" Denida didn't like where this was going. *Is Claus somebody's pawn?*

"Heh." Claus rose. "Sorry, but that's not for me to say!" He strolled up to Denida, stopping right in front of him, still gloating. "I am truly honored, but you don't know why, do you?" Claus raised his eyebrows.

Denida wasn't here for games. His temper had been on the rise, thanks to all the people in this world keeping secrets from him. "I want answers!"

"I know why you're here, but you need to understand, I cannot help you."

Denida grabbed Claus's head and used all his power to try to read his mind, but Claus's block was too strong for Denida to penetrate.

Claus shoved Denida back and pinned him to the floor with the strongest magic Denida had ever experienced. A devious sparkle danced in Claus's eyes. "As I said, sorry."

From where Denida squirmed on the floor, Claus didn't sound sorry at all.

"If certain people weren't protecting you, you'd be dead already! I hope you know that." Claus leaned over Denida. "I can't kill you, either; I'm not allowed to, you see."

Denida struggled to stand, ignoring Claus.

"But what can I do? Your own son thinks you are dangerous now, so he ran away. Did you know that?" Claus winked. "Nobody said I couldn't hurt him." Claus sneered, then moseyed to the door. "Maybe it's time to end him!"

Fury burned in Denida's chest. *No one is going to hurt Daniel!* He waved his hand and shattered Claus's restraint spell. Denida's eyes flickered red. Everything turned crimson and black. Denida yanked his hand back, and the door slammed shut in front of Claus.

"Yes?" Claus raised an eyebrow.

Denida stepped between Claus and the door with his fury burning deep into Claus's eyes.

"You won't hurt Daniel," Denida snarled.

Before Claus could react, Denida struck him with a spell, which had clawed its way out from deep inside of him, and Claus disappeared. Denida smirked. Claus might come back from Hell, but not before Denida managed to rescue his son.

***

This world of dark magic terrified Daniel. *And here I thought I was ready for anything after helping the last world's general start a coup.* He wandered through the jail's halls, finding it even more disquieting with everyone ignoring him, until he spotted the stranger who had helped them earlier. "Mister?"

Luci faced Daniel. "You made the right choice, my child. It's unsafe around Denida." He extended his hand. "My name is Luci. Please come with me."

"But my dad…" Daniel's heart sank.

"Don't worry; your dad won't even know you're gone."

Daniel felt strangely at ease with this man. He was comforting, safe. So, when they arrived at Luci's house, Daniel laid down and dozed off.

***

Luci watched the boy sleep.

Claus entered the room.

"Denida succumbed to his anger?" Luci's eyes lingered on Daniel, even as he addressed Claus.

"Yes, Master. Everything is ready, just as you planned."

Luci picked Daniel up and handed him to Claus. "Good, take the boy to my world."

Claus nodded and left with Daniel in his arms.

Luci glared at where Daniel had been sleeping. "It's time for us to meet again, *Denny.*"

Chapter 20- Luci's Offer

The Colonel and Nina waited for the video feed to resume. The Colonel tried to look hopeful for Nina's sake, but lacked the conviction to believe this world would yield results.

After the last world's mayhem, the Colonel let out a sigh of relief at the sight of a green forest in front of them. "Let's investigate, Dan, but be careful; we don't have any backup, now."

Dan nodded and drove the robot along a faint path.

Nina breathed over the Colonel's shoulder, so he stepped aside to let her have his seat.

"Maybe we'll get lucky this time." Nina's eyes locked on the screen.

"What are you?" a voice asked, as they drove around slowly. The camera swiveled to reveal a child eyeing them with a mixture of curiosity and suspicion. "Are you magic? We banned magic after arresting Claus!"

The Colonel sighed loudly and stepped up to talk through the other monitor. *Not another Claus...* "We come from another underworld. We're looking for Denida and Daniel." He peeked at Nina. "We don't know any magic; I assure you! This is technology."

When the child saw the Colonel's face on the monitor, his eyes widened. "Oh… my… god! Come with me; you need to meet someone." He darted off, occasionally stopping to glance back at the robot. The boy led them to the town square, where a barrier that shimmered like a soap bubble surrounded a child version of Claus.

"Magic." The Colonel stared up at the ceiling.

"He must've caused trouble here, too." Nina groaned.

The boy ran past Claus to a man talking to a cluster of children and adults. The boy said something to the man, who turned around.

The Colonel knew what he would see. *Another version of me.* He eyed the man's rank on his lapel. *And a general, this time!*

"Interesting." The general studied the robot. "Who might you be?"

"I'm a colonel."

The general held up his hand and grinned. "I know who you are, then! You're in Denida's world, aren't you? He and Daniel kept demoting me by calling me a 'colonel.'"

Nina laughed for a second at the general's comment.

I wouldn't mind being a general. The Colonel smiled, daydreaming for a moment.

"I'm sorry to say it, but if you are searching for Denida and Daniel, they've already gone through the Gate." The general removed his beret in solidarity.

"Of course, they did." The Colonel rubbed his forehead.

"Before they left, Daniel helped me shut down a machine that prevented adults from using magic, here. Claus took over the world and the kids enslaved us, but Denida managed to capture him."

Nina gasped and covered her mouth. "Daniel helped you?"

The general nodded. "He's a clever young man, just like his father." He pointed at Claus. "I've been trying to get information from Claus about the machine that Daniel helped me destroy."

"You can just give up; I won't tell you anything!" Claus stuck his tongue out at the general.

"Has anyone else noticed that Claus has been evil in every world we've visited?" Nina remarked coyly.

"I'm a product of the Underworlds, unlike Denida, who's from Earth," kid Claus bragged.

"It's like that president said, then." Nina turned away from the general. "You like power?" She asked without facing him.

Claus smirked and walked up to the edge of the bubble. His eyes shone greedily. "Like it? I belong in power. Power begets me!"

"Why do you care?" The Colonel asked Nina.

"Because." Nina whirled around to face the Colonel. "If every version of Claus believes he belongs in power, maybe our Claus thinks so, too!"

Not this again. "Those Clauses aren't our Claus."

Nina pointed at the general. "He's not you, but he'll be as much like you as all the others we've met."

The Colonel licked his lips. *But still...*

"I'm going to tell our Claus about this new world." Nina jumped to her feet. "Denny has already moved on, so nothing you find out about it matters to me, right now." She smiled brightly and waltzed out of the lab.

"I really hope she doesn't cause any trouble." The Colonel turned his attention back to the general.

***

Claus worked at his computer, moving money between several accounts. If Denida miraculously survived his journey, Claus would need a contingency plan. *These funds should be enough for the mercenaries.*

Nina burst into the office with the secretary flapping her arms apologetically behind her.

Claus closed his tabs and focused on Nina. *Nina isn't reading any more of my thoughts.* "Nina, what a pleasure." Claus delighted in the frustration on her face.

"Stop faking it; we've met yet another evil version of you. Soon, everyone will understand just how bad you are."

Claus's gut twisted, but he kept his thoughts on Susan's disappearance.

"So, you haven't found Susan, yet." Nina's eyes narrowed.

"Sorry." Claus couldn't resist smirking, just to piss Nina off. "Anything else I can help you with?"

Nina glared at him. "You're up to something."

"No." Claus rested his hand on his chest, as if he were wounded by her words. "I just want to get to the lab and learn about this new, awful Claus." He watched Nina struggle with her anger, reveling in her helplessness.

"I'll take you." Nina glared at him. "We both know my car's faster."

Claus spent the drive focusing on the prospect of speaking to another wicked version of himself while he gazed out the window, watching the scenery fly by.

When Nina parked at the lab, Claus unbuckled his seatbelt. "Thanks for the drive." He smirked and stepped out of the car.

Nina stayed put with all her muscles tense, visibly seething.

Claus thought he caught a glimpse of doubt in her eyes but couldn't be certain it wasn't just his imagination. He whistled an upbeat, little tune as he marched into the lab.

***

Susan watched Doc, hoping to learn something about his goals. He kept her close at hand and her chains short.

"So, what do you hope to gain?" Susan was bored enough to try engaging him in conversation.

"That's simple. I want to see Denida and his colonel destroyed so that I can attain freedom after all these years of being a wanted man." Doc leaned over the Gate's main unit, studying it more closely. "Claus cannot reveal his role in your abduction, and he needs this piece from the Gate to achieve his master plan. He thought it wise to use me, but I have turned the tables on him."

"You're both nasty." Susan grunted.

Doc shrugged and resumed ignoring her.

Susan's voice filled with disdain. "Denida will not be defeated so easily."

Doc slammed the meter in his hand down on the table and towered over her.

"Denida's human; he's only gotten as far as he has because he's had luck on his side, but his good fortune has run out." Doc turned to focus on his work, but Susan hooked her foot around his ankle. He skipped free and smirked at her. "Nice try; I'll make sure to tighten those chains."

***

Magic radiated from Denida's hand, guiding his search for Daniel. Dark thoughts concerning Daniel's fate raged in his head. *Why did he leave, anyway? It doesn't make sense. He knows I'm not a bad guy!*

The magical trail led Denida back to Luci's house. He pushed the door open.

Inside, he found Luci sitting behind a table, sipping coffee. "Hello, Denida. I've been expecting you," Luci greeted him warmly.

Denida peered around the room, but there was no sign of Daniel.

"Daniel isn't here! He's gone somewhere that you can't find with light magic." Luci gestured for Denida to sit down. "Won't you join me?"

Denida grabbed a chair and banged in on the floor, still in a huff as he sat down in it. "What do you mean that I can't use light magic to follow his trail? Where's my son?"

"Is this how you were with poor Danyel, the Dark Angel?" Luci asked, catching Denida off-guard.

"How do you know about the Dark Angels?" Denida swallowed hard.

Luci sipped his coffee. "You don't need to worry about that. I have Daniel, and you want him back, so I have a task for you, Denny!"

"What?" Denida furrowed his brow. *What could he possibly want from me?*

"You took care of Claus, so he brought Daniel to the next world." Luci held up his finger to keep Denida from interrupting. "But." He smiled at Denida over the rim of his mug, before carefully setting it back down on the table. "This time…" Luci ran his finger around the rim of the mug. "I want you to kill Claus and take his soul!"

"How? That's impossible!"

"A demon who dies will always return to Hell." Luci chuckled.

"I know; the Warlock couldn't think of a way to permanently kill the demons in her world because of that."

"That doesn't make killing one impossible!" Luci hunched over the table. "The method is very graphic, though. You have to rip out one's heart, while it's still beating."

Denida gaped at Luci with disgust. "You want me to do that to Claus?"

Luci leaned back. "Only if you want to get Daniel back." He took another sip.

"Of course, I do!"

"Then, the time has come at long last!" Luci grinned and swallowed the rest of his coffee in a single gulp.

"Just keep up your end of the bargain!" Denida stood and stormed out of the shack. Now knowing that Claus abducted Daniel, Denida tracked Claus's magical signature back to the building he had used to control access to the second Gate.

More guards stood watch at the door than there had been earlier.

Denida scoped out the premises, then stomped up to the guards. "I have a message for Claus." He stood at ease in front of the guards, who encircled him. "It's from Luci, so Claus will want to hear it; trust me."

The guards stopped and peeked at each other.

"Well?" Denida urged.

"Let him in." The Scientist trudged up behind them and waved his hands.

"You sure?" one of the guards asked.

The Scientist glared at him. "Don't make me repeat myself."

"You should take him," the guard said. "We need to stay here and keep watch."

"Right." The Scientist pushed the door open and shoved Denida inside.

"Do what Luci asked, or else."

Denida raised an eyebrow. "So, you can succeed Claus when he's gone?"

"Aren't you perceptive?" The Scientist nudged Denida forward again, then stepped back out the door.

Inside, Denida yelled into the darkness, "Claus, I'm back! Luci sent me."

"So, you've come to kill me," Claus mused.

"I have to; it's the only way I'll get my son back!"

"Heh." Claus chuckled. "We'll see."

"I guess so." Denida clenched his fists. "You should just tell me what I want to know. Your master can't punish you after you're dead."

"No." Claus glanced around the room as if Luci were watching. "You don't betray the master, no matter what!"

Is this necessary? Denida locked eyes with Claus, waiting for one of them to accumulate the courage to make the first move. *This is the calm before the storm.*

Suddenly Claus raised his hands, mumbling a chant, and a black gust of wind tore toward Denida, who dodged it by jumping behind a pillar.

Claus shot black fireballs at Denida in rapid succession.

Denida stepped out of hiding, hurling his own balls of light energy at Claus.

Claus ducked, avoiding one energy ball right in the nick of time. "You won't win!" He stood tall and sent another gale tearing through the air, bustling in Denida's direction. It shoved him up against the wall.

With his back to the wall, Denida shifted his position, squirming to the side, just before Claus's fireballs smashed into him.

The room turned so black that Denida couldn't even see his own hands. Denida chanted a spell and his hands glowed. The magic on his hand spread, rending the darkness.

"Got you!" Claus shot a beam of darkness at Denida with as much force as he could muster.

Denida sensed the dark beam nearing him, so he spun and fired a beam of light directly at the impending dark wave.

"You cannot beat me!" Claus yelled, gasping, as most of his energy had been concentrated in his spell.

"Yes, I can! You don't know how strong I am," Denida bluffed, his heart sinking. *I'm losing.*

Claus's magic slowly inched closer, so Denida fired another beam from his other hand, but this one used dark magic. With light magic emanating from one hand, and dark magic around the other, Denida discovered that his dark magic was definitively more potent.

"I… do…" Claus stuttered as Denida's beams grew stronger. Claus tried to mimic Denida's trick, now using both hands to strengthen his blast. With Denida's beams almost at the tip of his nose, sweat dripped down Claus's face. Claus shouted and a burst of magic strengthened his beam, but Denida's magic cut right through it, striking him, sending him flying across the room.

Claus tried to move but could barely writhe. "Heh, guess you are strong again, Denny!" Claus muttered as Denida approached him.

"How do you know that nickname?" Denida growled.

"Everyone does. Your name precedes you!" Claus scratched his arm. "Say hello to the master when you see him."

"I won't see-"

"Yes, you will." Claus smiled sadly. He staggered to his feet. "You know what you must do." Claus handed him a knife. "Don't prolong the inevitable!"

Denida took the blade, feeling the weight of it in his hand. "You won't fight me?"

"I won't oppose my master's will. This match has already been decided!"

Denida did not like this, but he had no choice; it was the only way to save Daniel. He stiffened, and before his courage failed, he cut Claus open with the knife, as if fileting a fish. Denida reached into the gash he'd created, and seized Claus's still-beating heart, then met Claus's eyes.

"Thank you," Claus murmured.

Denida stood with the heart pulsating in his hand. *What have I done?*

"Good work." The Scientist strolled in.

"Is it really?" Denida let the heart slip out of his grasp, the blood making it slick, and it rolled on the floor.

"I presume you want to use the Gate?" the Scientist asked.

"This may be normal to you, but it's not for me!" Denida breathed heavily, staring at Claus's body. *Daniel's in the next world...* he reminded himself from the far reaches of his mind. "Yes, the Gate… take me to my son!" Denida peeked at his bloody hand. *How can I ever get used to this? Was I ever used to it?* He sighed and followed the Scientist, who led him to the Gate.

"Here!" the Scientist exclaimed. "You did very well, Denny; I assure you."

There it is again. Everyone here seems to know my nickname, but most people back home don't use it. Denida never used that name publicly, but he now lacked the energy to ask. He withdrew the device from his pocket, ready to use it.

The Scientist ripped it out of his hand and chucked it onto the ground, smashing it to smithereens.

"What the hell!" Denida stared at the pieces on the floor, his heart pounding heavily in his chest.

"You won't need that anymore." The Scientist smiled. "Rest easy; you will get to the next world."

The Gate turned on by itself.

"He's ready for you!" The Scientist gestured to the Gate.

Denida felt uneasy as his stomach knotted. He feared whatever was to come next but he had to continue this journey to find Daniel and bring him home. He inhaled a deep breath, then stepped through the Gate.

"Finally, you're home again, Master Denny!" the Scientist said to himself, as Denida passed through the Gate.

Denida shot a shocked, confused glare back at the Scientist, but it was too late; the Gate sucked him in.

Chapter 21- The Young Claus

Nina watched Claus stroll into the lab. *Susan is gone, and he allegedly doesn't know where she went.* Her eyes dropped to her car's dashboard. *Maybe it's time to show the Colonel after all!* She opened the glovebox and reached inside for the flash drive. *Where is it?* Nina leaned over and peeked inside, seeing only the car's driver's manual and her vehicle registration. *It's gone.*

"Where's Nina?" The Colonel asked Claus, who shrugged.

"I'm right here! Is something wrong?" Nina strode into the lab behind Claus.

"No, but you both need to hear this!" The Colonel returned his focus to the general and the imprisoned young Claus.

It's true. There really is another version of me, and he's a child, at that, Nina read Claus's mind, and glared at him.

"What could possibly be so important? Denny and Daniel already left, no?" Nina asked.

"Yes," the general affirmed. "Claus had a seventy-year reign, during which he had extracted magic from the Gate's main unit with some sort of machine. Denida and Daniel left right after bringing him to justice."

"Wait, seventy years?" Claus asked.

"Is that part of the Gate really that powerful?" Nina heard the thought in Claus's mind and squinted at him again.

"Yes." The general nodded. "What's worse; our Claus knows something about Denida, but he won't tell us what it is!"

"Really?" Claus stepped in front of the camera. "I'm curious, too; what do you know about Denida?" Claus asked the other version of himself. "I really need to know!"

The child version of Claus startled when he saw this world's Claus. "You are me?" the young Claus asked, his confident façade faltering for the first time.

"He won't answer you; I've tried-"

"I will tell you, but you may not believe me." The young Claus smirked.

The general grunted but waited for the child to speak.

"I know of Denida but not from here, and not from your world either, but from Hell," the child quipped in a singsong voice.

"Hell?" The general frowned, shaking his head.

"I knew you wouldn't believe me, but it's true. He escaped from Hell," the young Claus explained. "That's all I know, aside from the fact that his memories were sealed away by the Dark Lord himself!"

"No, that can't be true!" Nina's heart hammered in her chest. "He's never even been to Hell." *This is too much.* She could see all the eyes in the room gathering on her like lasers. "I know him; he doesn't have any darkness whatsoever in him!" Nina yelled, more to convince herself than them.

The Colonel raised his gaze, as if reminiscing.

Nina peered into the Colonel's mind for just a moment, realizing he was recalling the days he fought alongside Denida, searching his memories for any instances of Denida harboring darkness inside of him. Nina's jaw trembled. She couldn't help but wonder, *what if...* Denida couldn't remember his early years, after all. "I am not staying here and listening to this drivel!" Nina fled the room. She needed air and to be somewhere that she wouldn't have to hear anyone's doubts, or worse, listen to her own.

***

"Well... ahem!" The Colonel tried to break the tension in the room. "Shall we continue? You caught Claus after his reign?"

"Like I said, Denida captured him, all by himself. I watched Daniel while Denida pursued Claus," the general explained.

The young Claus broke in. "I offered to tell him who he was, in exchange for my freedom."

The Colonel shook his head, despite finding it amusing. "Denida would never take a deal like that!"

"Maybe the deal wasn't right!" The young Claus's smirk darkened. "Everyone has a price, even the mighty Denida!"

The Colonel still pushed the consideration away. To change the subject, he focused on the general. "We need to continue our journey. Can we use the Gate?"

"It's off."

"That's okay." The Colonel allowed himself to smile. "The robot is equipped with a device for that!"

"Alright," the general conceded. "I'll take you to the Gate after we sentence Claus."

"Good, you are staying for the show. Rejoice!" the young Claus cheered.

The Colonel couldn't help but wonder how similar his world's Claus was to this evil child. "How do you like the young you, Claus?"

Claus turned to face him. "A nasty child." Claus waved his hand dismissively.

The Colonel didn't know what to think. He knew what Nina thought, but Denida had trusted Claus enough to make him his vice president. *Has Denida been wrong all this time?* "I see." *A lot of good that does me.*

***

Young Claus's trial was well underway. This world's Claus listened intently to everyone's accusations against the kid Claus, and all the evil deeds he had been responsible for over the last seventy years. Claus watched his younger self with intrigue throughout the trial. *At least he reigned supreme for seventy years.*

Nina returned to the lab with a quick glance at the monitors.

What will happen to me if Denida returns? This feels oddly foreboding. Claus bit his lip, staring at the monitor. *I will never end up like that.* With the thought, he startled and turned to Nina. Their eyes interlocked for a second. *Stop reading my mind.*

After a brief recess, the trial resumed with testimonies from the adults. They described how Claus empowered the children and encouraged them to physically beat the adults in the public square.

"Denida couldn't be trusted," the young Claus rebutted. "He had strong dark magic because he came from Hell."

Nina rushed to the monitor to object. "No, he has done nothing but good for all the worlds he's passed through. He is our president, the father of my son, and a former leader of our world's rebellion against the Dark Angels. He's a hero!"

"Sure, when he didn't remember who he was," the young Claus countered her argument. "He's not the same man, anymore."

Nina trembled.

"I'm sure he's wrong." Dan rested a hand on Nina's back. "Denida's going to come back with Daniel, and he'll be the same reputable man we've always known."

Maybe. Claus shot Nina a devious smirk with that thought.

"I have something to do!" Nina and Claus exclaimed in unison, well-aware of each other's goals.

"You haven't heard the worst of it, yet." The young Claus smirked. "Denida abandoned Daniel, leaving him with the general, just to chase after me, at a time when kids were in the adults' crosshairs. He knocked out my troops and left them to die in the freezing cold mountains! They were mere children, just like innocent, little Daniel." He frowned.

"Enough." The general stepped forward. "Daniel and I had just destroyed the machine that allowed Claus to oppress all the adults in our world." The general turned to the monitor. "He wanted Daniel to be safe, and he trusted me to watch him because of my status among this world's adults."

Nina smiled faintly. "That does sound like Denny."

The younger Claus started to appear more desperate. When he spoke, his words came out fast and shaky. "You won't achieve anything by killing me. I only brought out the feelings every child carries right under the surface: the frustration, the rage, and the prevalent sense of injustice."

The jury deliberated briefly before declaring Claus guilty.

The general wore a wide smirk as he approached the young Claus. "That didn't end like you expected it to, did it? Do you have anything to say before I decide your punishment?"

"The legend." Claus pushed his hands up against the barrier. "I will tell you why Denida is so important to the Devil, in exchange for my life."

The general frowned. "A little desperate, now?"

"No, really!" Young Claus clasped his hands, almost pleadingly.

The general turned to the robot, and Nina shook her head at the Colonel.

"You attempted this garbage with Denida," the General stated. "It didn't work with him, and it won't work with me, either."

***

Denida stepped through the Gate on high alert. Whatever waited for him could only be awful. He wasn't surprised to find himself surrounded by demons but he hadn't expected to see Luci standing in the middle of them. The sight made him jump.

"Welcome home, Denny!" Luci exclaimed ecstatically. "I've missed you."

"Luci?" *How did he get here?* The uncertainty made Denida's gut twist.

"Luci… fer. Lucifer is the name you're searching for. Luci is just one of my many nicknames." Luci sneered at him.

"You're the Devil?"

Luci wrinkled his nose. "That's such a nasty name. Deep down, you knew it was me, didn't you, Denny?" Luci patted Denida's back. "Take him to my castle!"

The demons surrounded Denida. "Sorry, Lord Denida! You have my deepest admiration," a demon said just before he cast a drowsy spell on Denida.

Denida came to himself slowly. Somehow, despite everything, he knew Lucifer wouldn't hurt him. *Is it true? Did a part of me really know that Luci was Lucifer this whole time?*

"Hello." Lucifer appeared out of nowhere, as if Denida waking up had summoned him.

"You must really want to talk to me! Where's Daniel?" Denida clenched his fists.

"I can grant you everything you want. Daniel is safe; don't worry." Lucifer smiled.

"And you will give me everything I want, in exchange for my soul, I presume?" Denida rolled his eyes.

"Heh! I don't want your soul, Denny. You are far too valuable for a mere soul!" Luci still grinned deviously, which started to make Denida very uncomfortable.

What's so important about me? Why doesn't he want my soul? Lucifer is the Prince of Darkness, after all. Is that not what the Devil wants? "What do you want from me, then?" Denida stood up.

"Don't worry about that; you're home again." Lucifer waved his arm dismissively.

Denida glanced around the dark room, fully feeling the oppressive atmosphere. The darkness was so thick that it was hard to breathe. "I've really been here before?"

"Of course!" Lucifer nodded. "And you have finally come back home to us."

Denida started to pace throughout the room, searching his soul for any sign of hope, but his heart ached. "I know this place," Denida muttered after a few steps.

"You will remember everything soon, now that you've returned."

"How do I get Daniel back? Claus is dead, just as you requested!" Denida's anger burned away his confusion.

"That's right; you've served me well! Welcome the anger inside of you." Lucifer outstretched his arms and breathed in deeply, as if absorbing warm, wonderful sunlight, but Hell didn't have anything bright to revel in. "You will see your son, soon." Lucifer vanished, leaving Denida no closer to Daniel, but a lot more confused.

"Enough!" Denida muttered to himself. He strode to the door and yanked it open, finding his arm swinging back far more than he had expected it to. It hadn't been locked, like he'd anticipated. *Probably because Lucifer knows I won't leave without Daniel.*

Darkness coated everything outside, and despair thickened the muggy air. A flickering light emanated from Denida, or more specifically, from his scar, as it pulsated from all the dark energy.

God, how can I really be from Hell? And more importantly, how did I leave? Denida's gut told him that wandering around outside was a bad idea, so, he returned to the building. If he wanted to get Daniel back, he'd have to play the Devil's game, for now. *Is this the Devil's mansion?* With nobody surveilling him, Denida explored the house, finding that most of the doors had been sealed with powerful dark arts.

When Lucifer returned to the room, Denida played ignorant.

"Luci!" Denida smiled. "Welcome back. Nice mansion you have, here. Won't you take me on a tour?"

"That won't work on me!" Lucifer chuckled.

"What is it that you want with me, then?" Denida asked. "I have a lot of money in my world from some shady business I conducted before I became president."

Lucifer's eyes sparkled. "I don't want your money, Denny. It's nice to know you still embrace your dark side, though. I want you to remember who you really are!"

"Well, I'm home, aren't I? Back at your home, Luci." Denida stared straight at Luci with a blank expression. "But you won't get what you want from me so long as you keep Daniel away from me! You know what I can do."

"Sure, Denny. Follow me." Lucifer led Denida to a sealed room and lifted the spell on the door.

As Denida stepped through the door, a tingling sensation shot through his body, not unlike the one he experienced when he passed through the Gates, tipping him off to the fact that the door teleported him somewhere.

"There you go!" The glint in Lucifer's eyes returned as he grinned. "I will let you get reacquainted." He left, closing the doors behind him.

Denida checked the door, but it was sealed with the same strong magic he'd found throughout the mansion. Turning back, his eyes widened at the sight of his son sitting against a wall across the room, chin tucked. "Why did you leave me?" Denida fought the anger that manifested with his fear. "You have no idea what kind of trouble we're in now, do you?"

Daniel quickly lifted his gaze to his father. "But Luci said-"

"Luci cannot be trusted. He is the Devil himself, not some mere Luci, but Lucifer!" Denida sat down next to Daniel. "Danyel, the Dark Angel, answered to him!"

"But..." Daniel objected.

"You were played," Denida stated.

Daniel frowned.

"Is he really the Dark Master we've heard so much about? Can that really be him?" Denida listened to Daniel's thoughts and nodded exasperatedly. "Yes!" he exclaimed.

"But he knows you!" Daniel countered.

Denida sighed and ran his hand through his hair. "No, he only thinks he does, but I will handle it." He smiled at Daniel and rested his hand on his son's shoulder, only for Daniel to pull away.

"He knew stuff about you that no one should know!" Daniel snarled.

Denida paced across the room, fighting his anger. The kid was so pigheaded that he couldn't even see Lucifer's clear attempts to manipulate him. Denida stopped and sighed. *Daniel got his stubbornness from me.*

"Where's the proof?" Denida turned to face his son. "If he knows me so well, he would have a picture of us together, no? Where's that?" Daniel's expression was unreadable, so Denida continued, hoping to make his point home. "I haven't seen any pictures of Luci and me. I presume you haven't, either!" He attempted to rest his hand on Daniel's shoulder again. "He's bluffing; this is the first time either of us have ever been here."

A heavy silence filled the room. Daniel eventually rolled his eyes. "He doesn't have any pictures with anyone," Daniel grunted sarcastically, not meeting Denida's eye. "It's more likely that he just doesn't like being photographed."

Denida groaned. *He's too perceptive for his own good.* "You've got me there." He sighed, realizing he needed to change his tactic. "Look, Daniel, I just need you to trust me. Have I ever hurt you or given you any reason not to trust me?"

Daniel pursed his lips.

Denida drew in a deep breath. When he spoke again, his voice had a soft, genuineness to it. "Honestly, Son. this journey has been extremely difficult. I've been scared, angry, and homesick… and I think you've felt that way, too."

Daniel raised his eyes, finally looking at Denida.

"I just want to get us both home safely. After everything we've been through, I'm sure you can see that that's all I've wanted since I found you in the world just beyond our Gate." Denida finished speaking with a meek, vulnerable smile.

Daniel sighed and nodded. "Yes, you're right." He closed his eyes for a long moment. "I just want to get home."

Denida's chest tightened. *He's become so mature, and I didn't even notice it until now.*

"Can we really beat the Devil?" Daniel's voice shook.

"Don't worry," Denida commented reassuringly. "I've already outsmarted him."

Chapter 22- Lucifer

Once again, Denida examined the room. *Nothing.* He sat down at the table with Daniel but couldn't think of anything to say.

Daniel ran his hand across the table.

Suddenly, Lucifer appeared in the center of the room. "What a somber reunion you two are having!"

"Hello, Luci." Denida greeted him, finding it hard to act polite with his annoyance peaking. "You cannot gain anything by keeping us in here!"

"Of course not. Come." Lucifer waved his hand, gesturing at the door.

Denida rose, smiling, and reached for Daniel's hand. "Come on; we can go!"

"Wrong!" Lucifer corrected him.

Denida could feel despair turning his insides cold.

Daniel's face creased with worry.

"You're coming with me, but Daniel stays here, for now." The room faded, leaving Lucifer and Denida outside, alone in the darkness.

Denida's stomach knotted as he glanced around.

"You need to accept the fact that you won't get him back until you've done what I want you to do."

Denida tried to read Lucifer's thoughts, but the Devil shielded them from mindreading. "And what is it that you want me to do, Luci?"

"You will understand in time," Lucifer replied. "And you will call me Lucifer, not Luci."

"Lucifer, it is." Denida conceded, determined to keep Lucifer happy, while he devised a plan. *Soon, I hope.*

"I want to show you something, Denny!" Lucifer led Denida to a small pool of water on a pedestal.

"This is the Well of Memory. I've stored all my memories, here."

An image formed in the water, revealing a young boy, seemingly familiar, resembling Daniel, just a bit. A shock ran through Denida, as he recognized the image of himself with Lucifer. *I really have been to Hell before.* "How did I leave?" Denida asked shakily, unable to tear his eyes away from the image.

"You left after Hell's original Dark Angels were destroyed. Where to, I have no idea."

The image shifted, now showing the young Denida torturing a soul before ripping its heart out and devouring it.

"To gain his soul's power," Denida mumbled to himself.

"Yes," Lucifer agreed gleefully. "You're finally coming back to me!"

Denida hardly listened; his head spun at the fiendish grin on his younger self's face.

"I was training you to be my successor." Lucifer laid his hand on Denida's shoulder. "Everyone knows who you are because of your importance to me. Now it's time to reclaim your place at my side, as my heir."

Denida shook his head in disbelief.

"I understand that it's a lot to take in, but you are back for a reason. Destiny has ordained this, my son." Lucifer lifted his hands. "It will all come back to you, and everything will be forgiven!"

"What will be forgiven?"

"You led Hell's Dark Angels, trying to help souls escape from Hell…" Lucifer's eyes burned with anger. "- then, you left Hell, after I had been preparing you to take my place for years. All the work I put into you, wasted!"

Denida recoiled from the Devil's glare.

"All the magic you had been taught, lost! Thankfully, I sealed your memories to punish you for abandoning me." Lucifer inhaled deeply and smiled. The fire left his eyes. "But that's all history, now."

"Danyel, the Dark Angel, was part of my effort?"

"Yes, you two are the last traitors from that era," Lucifer gloated. "He's a demon, so he is back here in Hell, following your little… conflict. Would you like to see your old friend?"

"Yes!" Denida clenched his fist. He had unfinished business with the Dark Angel.

Lucifer teleported them to his throne room, where Danyel spun to face them.

"Danyel." Rage and hate churned in Denida's gut.

"Denida!" Danyel nodded but couldn't hide the tremble in his hands.

A flashback crossed Denida's mind. He twitched a little, as he recalled the memory. "You betrayed us, sold us out to Lucifer. You killed the original Dark Angels!"

Visions of blood and violence flashed through Denida's head. The fire in him burned hotter.

Danyel turned to Lucifer, who sat on his throne.

"I won't help you. This is between you two." Lucifer smiled.

"I… I…" Danyel stuttered.

"No!" Denida shouted into the Dark Angel's head. "It's over."

Danyel retreated, his fear feeding the fire in Denida.

Denida liked the feeling of control. He licked his lips, and his eyes glowed red, making Danyel's face look bloody, and a malevolent smile twisted Denida's expression.

Danyel called forth a fiery, blue ball. He outstretched his arms to the sides and then swung them forward, hurling it at Denida.

Lucifer lifted his hand, and clenched his fist, extinguishing the ball. "No magic from you, Danyel."

Denida's hand glowed with magic, and he charged at Danyel, plunging his fingers through the Dark Angel's ribs. He grasped the Dark Angel's frantically pulsating heart. "Judgment day is here!" His eyes, now crimson, glared at Danyel's panicked gaze, as he tore out the Dark Angel's heart and bit into it.

Danyel's eyes glazed over, and he crumpled to the ground.

Lucifer grinned. "Good work, Denny!" Lucifer sauntered over to Denida.

"Am I interrupting something?" a kind voice asked.

"Gabriel!" Lucifer exclaimed ecstatically. "Look who's back. The prodigal son has returned."

"So, I see, and back to his dark ways." Gabriel glanced at the body, then at Denida's bloody hand. "Denny, nice to see you again."

Denida frowned. "Do I know you?"

"Do you know him?" Lucifer ran over to Denida and slung his arm over Denida's shoulders, laughing. "Of course, you know him. He visits often. This is our old friend from Heaven, Archangel Gabriel."

An archangel in Hell? "I guess I'll remember him in time," Denida said as Gabriel watched his every move. Denida shifted on his feet and spat the Dark Angel's blood out of his mouth, dropping the heart on the floor. "Why don't you remove the seal you put on my memories, Lucifer?"

"No." A shadow of fear passed over Lucifer's face. "I can't! The Darkness wanted me to create it. You'll have to break the seal yourself!"

Denida wrinkled his nose. "Aren't you the Prince of Darkness?"

"The Darkness is too strong for even me to fight; it has a will of its own!" Lucifer explained. "You'll understand in time."

Denida was starting to hate that phrase. *This is bad.* Seeing Gabriel and Lucifer together was strange but didn't feel wrong. In fact, Gabriel's presence felt... comfortable, here. Once Lucifer mentioned it, Denida wondered how he'd missed the malicious Darkness watching his every move. *I can feel its satisfaction with Danyel's death.*

Denida knew he'd have to continue to show Lucifer and the Darkness that he was evil, just to buy time until he and his son had an opportunity to escape.

"So, you're back to torturing souls. Are you enjoying yourself?" Gabriel frowned.

"Yes!" Denida forced himself to a smile. "Hello, Gabriel. What brings you here?" He'd stain his soul with evil for Daniel's sake, but he didn't like it. Despite his disgust with himself, Denida was unexpectedly good at submitting to evil urges.

"I wondered why you returned." Gabriel strained a smile, appearing disappointed.

Denida furrowed his brow. "Why?"

"You really don't remember anything?" Gabriel asked.

"I remember who I am!" Resentment filled Denida, chilling his soul. "And I know who you are. Do I really need anything else?"

"Yes." Gabriel stared into Denida's eyes. "You need to remember. There's so much you need to know. You may know who you are, but not what you are."

"I see, and you, Archangel Gabriel, the almighty good archangel, who seems very cozy with the Devil, will tell me everything I need to know?"

"I am the archangel of war," Gabriel corrected him.

"Yes, you do so well fighting evil." Black despair drowned Denida's anger. *Gabriel can't help me.*

As Denida strolled back to Lucifer's mansion, the demons avoided him, making it easier to play the evil apprentice. *At least they'll stay out of my way if they think I'm a monster.* He found Lucifer sitting in a trance with a cloud that resembled frosted glass hovering around him. *Is that the Darkness that controls Hell?*

"Yes," Lucifer spoke into his mind.

"How do you know Gabriel?" Denida stepped closer.

"We go way back, to a time before you can imagine, an era before Heaven, and Hell." Lucifer projected the thought into Denida's mind. "When God and I had our falling out, Gabriel helped me escape from Heaven."

Interesting. Perhaps I'm wrong about Gabriel. Maybe he can help me remember, after all. Denida bit his lip.

"Only you can make yourself remember," Lucifer spoke into Denida's thoughts once more.

Denida tensed. "I will leave you in peace." Denida nodded and strode out. He didn't want to remember right now. He needed to get Daniel and get home. Given what he'd already seen, the flashes of memories he'd started to recover, he feared that remembering could be detrimental to his psyche. *I'm not an evil person, am I?* He closed his eyes tightly, shaking his head.

With a sigh, Denida began searching for Gabriel, all the while wincing at the screams of tormented souls echoing all around him. *At least Daniel is free of this.* Finding no trace of the archangel, Denida gave up. *I'll have to wait for my chance to get away.*

"Hello again, Denny," Lucifer said, appearing out of nowhere with Gabriel beside him.

"How did you find me?"

"I always know where you are," Lucifer jested. "I know everything that goes on in Hell."

Denida frowned. "The Darkness tells you?"

"Good, it's coming back to you." Lucifer grinned. "Come; we want to test how strong you are." He teleported the three of them to a large room, where the second Gate stood.

"I have been in this room before," Denida mumbled.

"I should hope so!" Lucifer chuckled. "You learned dark magic in this very room."

He led Denida into the middle of the largest pentagram he'd ever seen. The magic hung so thickly that even someone without magical aptitude would shudder with discomfort.

"What is it that you want?" Denida knew Lucifer wouldn't harm his body, but his soul was another matter.

"You will be fine." Gabriel smiled reassuringly.

Memories flooded Denida's mind, as the Darkness thickened around him. He'd always wondered about his early days but now, he wished he couldn't remember any of it.

Reficul. The name to summon Lucifer appeared in Denida's mind, but he didn't need him.

The Darkness vanished.

"So, you aren't ready." Lucifer sighed. "The Darkness is not convinced that it's time for you to remember." Lucifer meandered up to Denida and patted him on the back. "On the plus side, you've grown stronger." Lucifer vanished like the Cheshire Cat, leaving his smile burnt into Denida's mind.

Suddenly, a force teleported Denida and Gabriel outside.

"Lucifer has business to attend to," Gabriel explained.

"And you? Why are you even here? Do you have business here, too?" Denida crossed his arms. "An archangel that supports Reficul... does God know?"

Gabriel almost laughed at that, but he stopped himself. "You remember his name, good." Then, he sighed. "Don't use it, unless you want him to overhear you." Gabriel chastised Denida in his thoughts, obviously so that Lucifer couldn't hear him. "But, yes, God knows. I serve them both."

Both. Denida's heart pounded as if to tell him that he should know something important about that. *Damn these bits and pieces of memories.*

"Should I trust you?" Denida's eyes narrowed. "I feel like I should."

A light aura appeared around Gabriel, as if to reveal his intentions.

"How are you light when you're betting on them both?" Denida gawked at the aura in disbelief.

Gabriel chuckled quietly. "That's not why I am here. I am here for Lucifer. I might explain someday, but for now, all you need to know is that my reason is personal."

"Someday Gabriel... someday, you'll tell me what this is all about!" Denida stomped away from him. *Gabriel isn't the answer.* He'd need to find Daniel himself, but Hell was expansive and filled with the Darkness. *I need a hint.*

"Reficul, Reficul, Reficul!" Denida yelled, and Lucifer manifested out of thin air.

"You know my name, good. Everything's proceeding according to plan." Lucifer winked.

"What is your so-called plan? Why am I so important to it? Why was I chosen to be your apprentice?" The questions poured out, despite Denida's determination not to ask.

Lucifer tilted his head at Denida. "You are strong. Therefore, you were chosen."

"By whom?" Denida asked skeptically.

"Destiny!" Lucifer grinned. "The same entity that brought you back to me."

"No, you're wrong! I came for Daniel. We're just trying to get home. Where is he, anyway?"

"Destiny, as I said," Lucifer mused.

Gabriel sauntered up to them.

"I'll take Denny out of your hair." Gabriel dragged Denida away from Lucifer. He didn't stop until he was out of Lucifer's line of sight and away from all the demons in the vicinity. He stopped and turned to Denida, and a cone of light surrounded them, shielding them from the Darkness.

"The Darkness cannot hear us now," Gabriel stated. "When I helped you escape before, I hoped you would never come back here."

"So, you helped me get away," Denida raised his eyebrows. "But I can't leave without Daniel!"

"Your son?" Gabriel raised an eyebrow. "I'll help you." The cone of light magic dissipated, and Gabriel set off. "I will be right back."

Smart, the cone shielded us from the Darkness for a while. Denida returned to the mansion and meditated to strengthen his soul.

Gabriel returned after a short while. "I just spoke to Lucifer."

"What did he say?" Denida pleaded, sensing the angel's presence just behind him.

"Lucifer has Daniel in a safe place."

"He didn't say where?" Denida opened his eyes, a little annoyed at this news.

"He can only be reached by teleportation, so he's safe from dark magic. There is only one place in Hell that matches that description."

Denida rose. "Let's go, then!"

"You must be ready." Gabriel warned him. "As soon as we take Daniel, Lucifer will know that you betrayed him again. You'll have to leave… *permanently.*"

"You think I really want to stay here? I can't wait to leave."

Gabriel nodded and led Denida to the portal in Lucifer's mansion, through which they'd be able to find Daniel. "Lucifer kept him in a place only accessible through this portal. I will show you how to open it. I can't help you more than that, as Lucifer would feel it."

"I'll do it!" Denida clenched his fists.

"Lucifer taught you most of the dark arts because he wanted you on his side. Now is the time to use that magic." Gabriel deployed a cone of light over the area.

Denida glanced at Gabriel.

The archangel knew more than he was letting on.

Denida turned to the door and destroyed the seal on it, then blasted the door to dust, revealing Daniel sitting at a table, staring at the destroyed door with wide eyes.

Before Daniel could speak, Gabriel waved his hand. "Come!" He led them to an abandoned facility in Hell.

"Where are we?" Denida asked. *This place feels familiar.*

"The Dark Angels' hideout," Gabriel replied. "You two wait here. I need to check with Lucifer to make sure we're still safe."

A strange sense of comfort warmed Denida as he stood in the rooms he'd once walked through, surrounded by allies, despite not being able to remember those days.

Daniel gritted his teeth against every tormented scream that rang through the air.

"That man is an archangel; he'll help us get away from here." Denida sighed softly, gently touching his son's shoulder. "Perhaps I could use a spell that would let you nap until we're-"

Daniel shook his head. Despite his trembling, his eyes remained determined. "No, I'm fine."

When Gabriel finally returned, he bore a concerned expression. "I'm back," Gabriel uttered in a low voice.

Denida nodded. "Is the Gate ready?"

Gabriel shook his head sadly. "Lucifer is beside himself because of your escape. The room with the Gate is full of demons and heavy Darkness." Gabriel paced in the room. "It will be only a matter of time before he finds you. He even yelled at me, and he never does that."

"Wait!" Denida almost hissed but kept his voice down on purpose and peered back at Daniel's sleeping form. "We're stuck here?"

Gabriel sighed. "There is only one other way out of here."

Denida shifted nervously on his feet. "How?"

"I'm an Archangel."

Denida raised his eyebrows. "So?"

Gabriel sighed heavily. "I can bring you to Heaven, but then, God will know you're there."

Denida shook his head, trying to put the pieces together.

"It's how you escaped before." Gabriel met Denida's gaze. "Back then, you left Heaven, too. Yet, if you wish, I will take both of you there, now."

I won't be welcome. Denida bit his lip.

"You will." Gabriel replied aloud to Denida's concern. "Just remember that you left Heaven, too." Gabriel seemed to be trying to warn Denida about something without saying it outright.

Denida didn't care. He needed to get Daniel out of Hell. *Nothing can be worse than this.*

"So how do we get out of here, if not through the Gate?" Denida squeezed his son's hand reassuringly.

Gabriel smiled, as he glowed with a brilliant light. Spectacular wings appeared behind him. "With these. I told you; no one will notice me leaving. I have done this for millennia."

Denida watched Gabriel skeptically but had no other choice. He nodded at Daniel, and they stepped into the warm, soothing light around him.

Gabriel enfolded them in his wings and ascended in a flash.

As the Darkness fell away below them, Denida relaxed. *I'm never going there again.*

Chapter 23- Claus's Worry

Nina's gut still twisted at the idea that the young Claus seemed to know something about Denida, but the general didn't want anything to do with it. His desire to punish the young Claus for seventy years of oppression overrode all of Nina's and the Colonel's attempts to convince him.

On the monitor, Nina watched as young Claus was bound, still unable to use or be impacted by magical attacks, but physical strikes could still hurt him.

Their own adult Claus left soon after the young Claus was tied to a post in the square.

Nina couldn't blame him.

Even the Colonel paced around the lab, swearing quietly, clearly upset that one of his soul forms would stoop to these measures.

"General, may we have a word in private?" Nina approached the monitor.

The general led the way back to the dining hall, letting the cheers and shouts of adults getting their revenge on the child fade into the background.

"Colonel?" Nina gawked at him and gestured to the monitor.

The Colonel strode over to the monitor. "What the hell are you doing? Are you not a general, a man of authority and righteousness?" The Colonel clenched his fists.

The general stepped away from the robot, squinting. "They need closure." He sounded defensive. "And Claus is just bluffing."

"I don't care if he's bluffing," the Colonel broke in, his face redder than Nina had ever seen it. "Whether he knows anything or not, this is wrong. You're better than this. Do you want to be just like Claus?" He slammed his fist on the table and stepped away from the monitor, shaking with anger.

Nina shifted in her seat, worried. She'd never seen the Colonel so upset. When she peeked back to the monitor, the general had stepped away.

"Where'd he go?" the Colonel growled.

Dan sent the robot outside and turned the camera around, searching for the general.

The general had stepped between the adults and Claus, who was now bloody and bruised. The general knelt beside the boy. "You want out? Tell me what you know about Denida. What is this 'legend' of yours?"

Claus stared at the general, hope returning to his eyes. "It's not mine. The legend predates all of us," he explained. "I only know about it because, when Denida was born, everything changed for God and the Dark Master."

The General rose and spun around. "Denida was born with some sort of innate destiny, but only God and Lucifer know the so-called legend," he announced.

A dark expression flashed across Claus's face.

"Take him back to his cell!" the general hissed.

The guards untied Claus and helped him to his feet.

"Just so you know, I was going to let you live, even without the story, which is pointless anyway." The general smiled viciously at Claus before gesturing for the guards to take him away.

Dan drove the robot up to the general, who turned to face it.

"You are like me, after all." The Colonel nodded, condoning his counterpart.

"Yes, I guess so," the general conceded. "But I still don't like it." He ran his hand over his face. "You wanted the second Gate, no? Come, I'll take you."

At the Gate, the general nodded to the guards, who stepped away. The general attached the main unit to the Gate. "We don't leave it in. We've learned that strong magic can be extracted from it to achieve horrible things. We're thinking of dismantling the first Gate, too."

"What will happen to Claus, now?" Nina watched the general handle the main unit.

The general shrugged. "I don't know. We need to keep him alive and learn from what happened. We'll figure it out."

Nina nodded.

Once the device was securely in place, Dan used the robot's controller to turn the Gate on.

The general's eyes lit up. "Impressive!"

Nina saw Dan smile brightly at the compliment. Nina wondered if there was something she could do to show appreciation for Dan's work, too.

The Colonel and the general said their goodbyes, then Dan drove the robot through the Gate.

Nina prepared herself for the blank feed.

When the image returned, it revealed a world with advanced technology surrounding them.

Maybe we're done with magic. Nina leaned closer to the monitor, fascinated at the sight of robots carrying grocery bags down the sidewalk and supervising children on walks. She winced several times as cars nearly crashed into pedestrians and other vehicles. A fight broke out on the edge of the screen, and people merely fanned out to walk around it, as if it were an everyday occurrence.

"There!" the Colonel pointed to a face on the screen. "Dan, follow him!"

Dan guided the robot through the crowd and into what appeared to be a restaurant.

"Hello." An android stepped forward to serve the robot. "May I take your order?"

Dan stopped to stare at the android with a fascinated gleam in his expression.

The Colonel yanked the controls out of Dan's limp hand and drove the robot to the counter.

"Colonel?" the Colonel asked his other self. With an annoyed expression, the man peeked up from the counter.

"I'm not a colonel… oh my god." He stepped out from behind the counter and knelt, gawking at the monitor. "How?"

"We're in another Underworld." The Colonel grinned at this new version of himself. The shocked expression on his counterparts' faces was always the same.

"Enough of this!" Nina interrupted. "Did you happen to meet Denida and Daniel?"

"Ah…" the man kneeling by the robot mused. "Come with me." He guided them into the back of the restaurant and sat down at a table. "They thought I was a colonel or a general, too."

"You're not?" The Colonel sounded shocked.

"No." The man smiled and waved, gesturing at the room they sat in. "Just a restaurateur. If you want a meal, you've come to the right place."

"They passed through there?" the Colonel asked.

"Yes, they wanted directions to the second Gate, the dark Gate," the proprietor explained.

"So do we!" The Colonel leaned closer to the screen. "Where is it?"

The proprietor shook his head. "I knew you would ask; Denida insisted, too. It's on the dark side of this world, but no one has ever returned from there, so I must urge you not to go!"

"The dark side?" Nina asked.

"Yes, our world is divided into two halves, one light, one dark. Dark magic reigns there, creating even more lawlessness, than you've seen here."

Nina sat up. Everyone in the room focused on her. She heard the doubt in their thoughts about going to a place with such a foreboding reputation. "Yes, we're going. That's why we're here, isn't it?" Nina glared around the room, and one by one, people dropped their gazes and returned to work, mentally preparing to drive the robot to the other side of the world.

Following Dan's instructions, the proprietor uploaded a map and directions into the robot, then connected an additional power source to the robot, knowing solar power wouldn't keep it running on the dark side of the world. When the robot was ready, Dan drove it away.

The robot trundled through the landscape. Most people ignored it altogether. As the robot's journey progressed, the world became darker, and nonhumans started appearing in the shadows. Eventually, absolute darkness surrounded them, so Dan switched to the camera's infrared mode, but they still struggled to make out anything around them.

The Colonel spotted some demons and pointed them out to Dan. "Be careful."

"This would be easier to navigate if I could see." Dan caught a glimpse of a cottage without any demons around it, so he steered the robot in its direction, eventually driving inside through an open door.

Inside, a man sat at a table, smiling at them. "Hi, I've been expecting you. My name is Luci."

The Colonel eyed him a bit suspiciously. "This is wrong; we should leave, Dan!"

"But there aren't any demons, here?" Luci grinned.

"There must be a reason for that, and we can't risk finding it out." The Colonel yanked the controls away from Dan and drove back out of the little house, leaving Luci watching them.

"We need to find Denida, and if he's anywhere in this godforsaken world, it'll be at the dark Gate. Try to stay out of the demons' way." The Colonel yawned and passed the controls back to Dan.

Nina could tell he was becoming exhausted. "When was the last time you slept?"

"I'm not sure." The Colonel shook his head, but still stretched.

"Go find a bed and lie down. I'll wake you up if we find anything worth reporting."

The Colonel took a deep breath and stood up, before marching out of the room.

"This world is dangerous." Dan peered at the monitor, trying to see farther than a few feet in front of the robot. The demons all appeared to be walking in one direction. *They're approaching something.* After following them for a short while, they arrived at a prominent building, but demons were packed so closely around it that the robot couldn't get close enough to investigate it.

Luci stood off to the side, watching the robot circle the demons.

"Go talk to him." Nina leaned over Dan's shoulder and pointed to Luci.

"But the Colonel said…"

"What other choice do we have?"

Dan sighed but drove the robot up to Luci.

"Hello, Mr. Luci?" Nina greeted Luci cautiously.

Luci smiled kindly. "A woman, this time?"

"How did you know who was operating the robot before?" Nina asked. "Never mind, I was just wondering if you could help us, please?"

Luci's smile grew wider. "Of course," he knelt in front of the robot. "How can I help, my sweet girl?"

Nina ignored Dan's concerned look. "I'm searching for my son Daniel, and my husband, Denny. You might know him as Denida?"

Lucifer stood up. "Interesting… yes, I know Denny and Daniel. They passed through here not too long ago. Come with me, and I'll help you." Luci led them back to the cottage that the Colonel had insisted they vacate.

"You must be really worried about your son?" Luci asked when they arrived at his cottage. "I met them here, and helped them get an audience with Claus, who controlled access to the dark Gate."

Nina and Dan exchanged a glance. "We have to deal with another Claus?" Nina groaned.

Luci's eyes lit up. "Actually, Denida killed him, ripped his heart out, and let his assistant take over."

Nina's stomach clenched at the ease with which Luci described the grotesque turn of events. "He must have had his reasons," Nina spoke softly to convince herself.

"Did I say something wrong?" Luci blinked rapidly.

"No." Nina raised her arms. "I'm just shocked that Denny would do something so… gruesome."

"Why?" Luci raised an eyebrow. "Denida came from Hell, after all. He wouldn't be malicious in your world, but he was, here. Daniel ran away from him, too."

"Denida can't have been from Hell," Nina protested, yet again feeling her heart sink.

"Oh really?" Luci replied. "Denida mentioned that he had a memory gap in his life. He apparently spent it in Hell."

***

Susan's stomach ached as Doc read a text on his phone and laughed delightedly.

"I can't imagine what would make the infamous Doc laugh. Did someone buy you a kitten?" Susan wrinkled her nose.

Doc stopped smiling as if someone had thrown a switch. "Claus is robbing the Underworld blind. I will get it all!"

"You think no one will notice? And here I thought you were smart."

Doc frowned at her, then started working on his computer.

"Denida had a good team, people with real intelligence," Susan continued speaking, hoping to get under Doc's skin.

Doc slammed his fist on the desk and glared at Susan.

Susan bit the inside of her cheek, realizing that pushing him was dangerous. She might have gone too far this time.

Doc rose and stomped around the table. Susan steeled herself in anticipation of a blow, but Doc stormed past her, as if her chair was empty. He pulled out the device and sat down again, studying it closely.

Susan had watched him scratch it, burn it with acid, heat it, and chill it. If it weren't so dangerous, she'd have enjoyed his frustration.

Doc shoved it under a microscope and peered at it, adjusting the focus for the best view.

Damn, I wish I could see what's got him so interested.

"Fascinating," Doc mumbled. "I've seen this before. That idiot, Claus, has no idea what he's got here," Doc muttered to himself.

Susan barely dared breathe and remind him that she was there.

"…Dark Angels… communicate with Master." Doc picked up his phone and sent a message to Claus. "See how he likes that." He dropped the phone. "… even Denida is trivial… summon the Dark Lord."

Susan put together the fragments she'd heard, and her blood ran cold.

***

After Claus had left the lab, he had continued embezzling the Underworld's funds for the mercenaries. He shuddered, then focused on moving money out of the treasury.

"Beep." A text from Doc came through on his secret phone, prompting Claus to close the program, before viewing the text. The odious Dark Angel sympathizer wanted an absurd amount of hush money to keep Susan from revealing what she knew about their efforts. Attached was a video file, which made Claus sick. It was a security video, showing his trip to Dynasty with Susan, including a timestamp. *Damn him.*

Claus sent back a text that he'd get Doc his money. Keeping Doc and Donaldson's mercenaries sated was becoming a balancing act that felt like trying to walk across a tightrope above a pit of spikes.

Claus flew north, heading to several mines, which Denida still had shares in. One had been active during the Dark Angels' reign, but now stood abandoned, due to resource depletion.

Claus rented a car and drove up to the mines, discovering that they were still active, despite HQ's paperwork to the contrary. *That sly devil.* Up ahead, he discovered that two mines had been closed, after all. Claus knew one of those mines was his target destination. An electric fence barred his entry. Claus grinned and fetched bolt cutters from the car to cut the nonelectrified chains holding the gate closed.

Claus drove through the gate and grabbed a flashlight from the car's trunk. His eyes lit up as he entered the first mine. His heart pounded painfully in his chest. Stacks of cash filled the front entrance of the mine. Claus had never seen so much money in one place. He tore open a clear plastic bag protecting the money and thumbed through the stack of bills. *I'll never need to risk stealing from the government again.*

The only challenge he could imagine would be transporting that much cash. Claus could fill the trunk of his car and barely put a dent in the stash, and there were two mines full of cash. Hiring help to move it would be trouble, as he'd have to split the wealth, and possibly explain how he discovered it. Claus returned to where he'd rented the car and returned it before checking out an eighteen-wheeler and a forklift. Back at the mine, he worked all night to load all the money from both mines into the truck. Once Claus returned to town, he'd hire someone to drive the truck south for him, and he'd find an ample hiding place for it.

Claus had always scoffed at the rumors that Denida had a fantastic treasure hidden away in the Underworld. Who would have thought that it was true, and that Claus had found it? As he drove the truck back to town, the Colonel called.

"I need to talk to you; come back to the lab. Immediately."

Claus groaned. He arranged for a driver to take the truck the rest of the way, then flew home, catching a little bit of rest on the way. He needed to keep up appearances, after all. As much as he liked the money he'd found, he wanted the power of being president even more.

***

The Colonel paced in the lab, trying to keep his anger in check. *Where's Claus? How long can it possibly take to get here from headquarters?*

Claus meandered in, appearing tired and dishevelled. "Sorry, I was in the middle of something important."

"So, everyone is here." The Colonel raked his gaze over them.

Nina wrinkled her nose at Claus.

The Colonel didn't have time for that, now.

"I wanted all of you here for a very specific reason." He fought to keep himself from shouting, but he was dealing with insubordination. *It has to end.* "You went back to that Luci fellow. Something about him is very unsettling. Even without magic, I can tell he's bad news."

Everyone in the lab stirred, but their gazes stayed low.

"It was my call." Nina stepped forward. "He knows how to get us through the Gate."

"Nina!" This was the second time she'd defied the Colonel's direct orders.

"No, we need the Gate. I don't care if Luci thinks Denida is from Hell. Nothing will stop me from getting to Daniel." Nina glared at the Colonel, daring him to challenge her, but something else she had said made him forget his anger.

"Wait… Hell?"

"He's just talking out of his-"

"No." The Colonel raised his hand. "I don't think so; Denida has powerful abilities that we never even knew about."

Chapter 24- Heaven

When Gabriel landed, Denida stepped away from the archangel. Heaven stood on a cloud, just like it did in the stories, and though they were outside of Heaven itself, Denida felt the difference in the atmosphere immediately. Heaven's air smelled crisp and clean.

"Gabriel," a voice boomed from the gate surrounding Heaven.

"Saint Peter." Gabriel waved.

"No, not him!" Peter stormed up to Gabriel, casting Denida a fierce glare. "Not again." He shook his head violently.

"I know you?" Denida asked, but Peter had already returned to Heaven's Pearly Gates. Denida turned to Gabriel.

"Yes, you knew him. Get ready; God will be here, soon."

God? I'm not sure I'm up for this but I've met the Prince of Darkness, so why not God? "I'm ready," Denida replied with a smile.

"Denida, long time, no see!" A man appeared, and everyone's eyes shot to him, as if drawn by a magnetic force.

Denida frowned. "God, I presume?"

Gabriel opened his mouth, but God held up a hand.

"Yes, I am who you call God." He nodded. "Gabriel has brought you back to us, but I'm left to wonder why you've returned."

Denida gestured down to his son, whose gaze darted this way and that. "My son and I are trying to get home."

"Come; let's all enter Heaven and figure this out." God waved Denida toward the Pearly Gates.

"Are you sure?" Peter's jaw dropped. "You know what happened last time."

"Open the gates, Peter." God gestured with his hand.

With a slight frown, Peter opened the gates so that Denida and Daniel could enter Heaven.

Where the darkness had oppressed Hell like a suffocating haze, Heaven shone with a clear, warm light, making Daniel's eyes sparkle.

Denida's heart thumped. *I know this place.*

"You do," Gabriel affirmed into Denida's thoughts.

"Denny!" a voice called out before Denida could acknowledge Gabriel. A man hurried over to them. "You don't remember me, do you?"

Denida stared at the man, trying to figure how to explain everything.

Gabriel directed Denida's attention to the stranger. "This is Archangel Michael. You met him when you were here before." Gabriel squeezed Daniel's hand. "This is Denny's son, Daniel. Why don't you show him around Heaven?"

Denida opened his mouth to object but unlike in Hell, Daniel seemed eager to explore Heaven. Denida closed his mouth and nodded reluctantly.

Michael exchanged greetings with Daniel and began leading him away, pointing out buildings and sights as they meandered across the cloud.

"Why did you do that?"

Gabriel winked. "Would you like me to restore your memories? If I do, I presume it is best that Daniel doesn't know about it."

"You can restore them?" Denida's heart raced, but his mind's hesitance gave him a small pang of fear in his gut.

"Of course, the Darkness is no match for Heaven's light!"

Denida stood still. *I can remember everything, but those memories might be bad.* He changed his mind several times before answering. "No, maybe it is best to let bygones be bygones."

Denida trailed after Daniel and Michael.

A tall tower caught Denida's attention. *There's something special about that building.*

"Don't worry about that tower." Michael waved his hand dismissively as he approached with Daniel.

"What is it?" Denida craned his neck.

"Only God knows what's up there." Michael shrugged. "It's nice to see you back again; I've missed you!"

Denida's eyes remained locked on the tower, as if it called to him. "Can you watch Daniel a little while longer?"

Michael glanced at Daniel, who nodded enthusiastically.

Denida hurried back to Gabriel. "I know something about that tower, don't I? I can feel it!"

"Yes, you knew a lot of things, Denny, more than you realize."

"Alright, then remind me!" Denida fixed his mind on it. He'd not change it again.

"I will prepare for it." Gabriel peered at him intently. "It will take a great deal of power, even here."

Gabriel escorted Denida back to Michael, who led him and Daniel to God.

Another boy stood talking to God, but when he saw Denida, he scurried over and hugged him. "Amazing, you're back."

"I… I…" Denida furrowed his brow.

"Jesus missed you too, Denida," Michael said.

Jesus Christ, of course. "It's nice to see you, too!" *How many people and angels do I know here?* Denida arched his neck at God. "Maybe you can show me the second Gate?"

"Don't you worry about that," God replied quickly. "Enjoy your stay, for now."

Denida licked his lips. *Something's weird, here.* "Okay."

"Hey, you must be Daniel." Jesus turned to Denida's son.

Denida approached God, leaving Daniel to talk to Jesus. "We're just passing through." He peeked at Daniel. "Won't you please show me the Gate?"

God smiled back at Denida. "I'm sorry Denny, but we no longer have the Gate."

"The tower, then?" Denida pointed upwards.

"That doesn't concern you," God replied.

"Dad." Daniel approached and tugged Denida's hand. "Can I go fishing with Jesus?"

Michael nodded at Denida, so he ruffled his son's hair.

"Sure, go have fun." *Maybe I'm just imagining it; this is Heaven, after all.* Denida wandered aimlessly through Heaven but found himself back in front of the tower. He stepped forward to explore the tower, but a spell locked its entrance. That seal was the strongest Denida had ever seen.

"So, you were drawn here, weren't you?" Gabriel spoke from behind Denida. "Few are actually allowed in." Gabriel sauntered up to the door. "And I am one of them." He opened the seal and led Denida inside.

Within the tower, Gabriel pointed to a staircase that hugged the building's wall, snaking upwards. Denida ascended the steps. He'd expected to climb for ages, but after a short flight of stairs, Denida reached an open door.

A woman sat in a chair at the top of the tower with a young man beside her. The woman peered up, her face brightening as if she knew Denida.

"This is Saint Heavani," Gabriel introduced her. "And her son, Daniel."

A lot of Daniels.

Gabriel nodded. "Lucifer is his father."

"You're serious?"

"Yes." Gabriel raised his hands and sighed.

"Why is she here, in Heaven, then?" Denida's chest burned at the thought. *Lucifer must miss them.*

Heavani strolled over to them and grabbed Denida's hand. "I knew Luci before he became the Lucifer you know. We met here, in Heaven."

"Heavani's the only one who can lift the curse on you." Gabriel inhaled deeply. "She is as pure as they come, as she is God's sacred daughter."

Denida gasped. "That's why God locked you up?"

"I am happy enough. Gabriel takes care of me, and I can see everything that happens in Heaven below. That's how I know about you!"

Denida sighed. This was not what he had expected, but it wasn't something he could change.

"I have a Darkness-infused seal on my memories," Denida whispered.

"I see," Heavani mused. "Do you have a mark anywhere on your body?"

"Like my scar?" Denida lifted his shirt to reveal the big scar on his side.

"Yes, definitely that!" Heavani examined the scar. "This is old," she mumbled. "I am sorry, but I will need your help, Gabriel."

Everyone helped Denida to the floor.

Denida shuddered. "But God-"

Heavani held finger to Denida's lips. "No one can sense the magic we use up here, not even God! We aren't supposed to have any, after all."

A strong, white light surrounded Denida, and Heavani rested her hand on his scar. Her hand glowed so brightly that Denida had to squint. The Darkness within the scar shattered with an even brighter light, which filled Denida with so much peace that his eyes closed, and he fell into a slumber.

Daniel, Lucifer's son, was watching Denida when he woke up.

"Hello," Denida yawned.

The boy turned and ran away with a shout. "He's awake!"

Denida sat up on the bed and buried his head in his hands. "God…"

"You remember?" Gabriel asked as he and Heavani approached him.

"Yes, Gabriel," Denida muttered from underneath his hands. "I really do…"

"It will come back to you slowly. Instead of just experiencing vague moments of familiarity, you should now remember exact memories." Heavani knelt and lifted Denida's hand away from his face.

"I do remember one thing." Denida raised his head. "The second Gate is here!"

"I know." Gabriel helped Denida to his feet.

Gabriel followed Denida, who walked to go to see God, finding him in his throne room. *Just like Lucifer.*

"My Lord." Denida stepped up close as God gazed curiously at him.

"The tower has a magic seal on it to keep people out!" Denida's fiery eye pierced God. "Gabriel won't tell me why it's there; he told me to ask you."

God shifted on his throne.

Denida frowned. *What about that tower makes God so uncomfortable?*

"The tower is Gabriel's responsibility, not mine." God turned his head to the side.

"Yes, Gabriel figured you would say that." Denida's sharp gaze intensified. "So, he brought me inside the tower." He recognized the Darkness in God's eyes from his time in Hell.

Jesus entered the room, and the Darkness vacated God's face. "Hey, Denny, do you have time to talk?"

"Always." Denida needed a break from the tension in the throne room, so he followed Jesus outside.

Jesus chattered happily as he walked with Denida.

Denida's returning memories reminded Denida of just how sheltered and innocent Jesus was. God had regularly dismissed him during arguments and conflicts, ensuring that Jesus only saw the wonderous side of Heaven.

"I want to show you something!" Denida grabbed Jesus' arm, unintentionally interrupting whatever Jesus had been prattling on about. "You have to see the tower."

They strode to the tower.

"There is a shield on its door; we can't enter." Jesus waved his hand. "Father has sealed it off to protect us all."

Denida glanced around their vicinity to be sure they were alone. "Jesus, trust me; there's no Darkness in that tower."

"I trust you, but it's sealed. No one can get in."

Denida's eye gleamed. "Oh yes, I can!" He chanted a white spell to remove the seal.

"You remembered that?" Jesus' eyes widened.

"Yes." Denida let Jesus enter the tower and followed behind him, waiting for Jesus to discover the tower's secret for himself.

"Jesus, won't you join me?" Heavani waved him to a chair at the table on the tower's top floor.

How did she know he'd be coming? I've only just decided to bring him here.

"Free will is overrated, Denny," Heavani said into Denida's thoughts.

Denida and Jesus joined her for tea.

"I am Saint Heavani. You must be Jesus, the Christ."

Jesus frowned. "I don't understand. Father said this place was full of Darkness!"

The door behind them opened, and they all turned to it.

Gabriel marched into the room. "Jesus? Denny, you didn't!"

"Gabriel, you're here, too?" Jesus stared in amazement.

"You'd better tell him. He should know," Denida insisted.

"God wouldn't like that!" Gabriel shook his head violently.

"Then allow me." Heavani poured Gabriel a cup of tea. "Like you Jesus, I am a child of God." She smiled at Jesus reassuringly. "I am his special child. God locked me up here, and Gabriel was the only one who was allowed to see me." Heavani's smile stayed locked in place as she explained her circumstances to Jesus.

The goodness in these people astonished Denida.

"Who's the boy, then?" Jesus nodded at Heavani's son.

"My son, Daniel." Heavani gestured for him to approach. "God locked us up here after Lucifer and I were discovered together."

"What? You and Lucifer?" Jesus' gaze wandered throughout the room. "The Devil? Does he know about Daniel?"

"Yes, that's why Luci hates God so much," Heavani said.

Denida turned to Jesus. "God is your dad; I understand that, but you must know where he's hiding the second Gate. God says it's gone!"

"I know where it is." Jesus sighed, raising his head.

Denida and Jesus walked together to collect Denida's son Daniel, who was still with Michael, who now knew even less about Heaven than Jesus. Denida would have to be careful not to say too much to him.

Jesus stopped before they reached Daniel and Michael. "You need Michael to take you to the Gate. It is outside of Heaven's Pearly Gates, where Father doesn't want me to go."

Denida nodded.

"I understand what you told me." Jesus sighed heavily. "But do understand that we have a responsibility. And I do, too." With that, he turned back to Michael and Daniel. "Michael!"

Michael rushed over with Daniel behind him. "My Lord."

Jesus returned Michael's smile. "I need you to take Denida and Daniel to the second Gate outside of Heaven, as a favor to me."

Michael nodded.

"I hope you get home soon, Denny. Until next time!" Jesus ruffled Daniel's hair.

"I'm not planning on coming back," Denida replied.

"Maybe not, but I know we'll meet again, Denny; I can feel it!" Jesus smiled and turned to leave.

Denida turned Jesus' words over in his mind. "We have a responsibility..." Maybe Jesus wasn't as naïve as Denida thought. There was something in those words that just felt like he meant it, and he might be right.

Denida turned to Michael. "Shall we?"

"It's out here," Michael said in a low voice. "But if you are leaving Heaven, I think you should know something I regret not telling you earlier."

"What is it?"

"The legend," Michael began. "I am not supposed to know it; only God and Lucifer are supposed to know, but I do, too! And I think you need to know, too."

Denida glanced at Daniel, who was running around on the clouds, enjoying himself. "I feel like I'll regret this but go ahead."

"The legend is old, older than Heaven. It was prophesized by God's own goddess, on her deathbed."

God had a goddess? Interesting. "Really? Go on, then." Denida lit up, intrigued.

"The legend foretells the birth of a child," Michael paused. "During his childhood, he will supposedly bring an end to all the injustices in the world for both good and bad alike." Michael stared deep into Denida's eyes. "Lucifer and God believe that you are that child. Because of that prophecy, God originally wanted to kill you, but Lucifer stole your soul from your body, severing your connection. He brought your soul to Hell before God could act."

Denida's heart sank. "That's why I was in Hell?"

Michael nodded.

Denida furrowed his brow. "But I'm not a child anymore, and God can still kill me!"

"No, they believe that if you die physically, your true powers would be unleashed, but that is all I know." Michael tilted his head.

Denida sighed heavily and peered at the Gate. "I don't have the device to turn it on, anymore."

"Don't worry; I can power it up for you." Michael snapped his fingers, casting white magic on the Gate, powering it up. "Thank you," Denida said with a smile.

Daniel rushed up to his dad, and they thanked Michael for his help getting them closer to home. Then, once more, Denida and Daniel stepped through the Gate, hoping to see home.

Chapter 25- Luci

Nina couldn't tell if Lucifer had been lying or not, but he was the answer to advance to reach Denny and her sweet Daniel, so she had to follow him.

"Why so tense this morning?" Luci entered the cottage and approached the robot.

Nina and the Colonel exchanged a glance.

"Shall we go, then?" The Colonel peeked at Nina.

Luci smiled at them. "I have prepared a welcome wagon for you at the Gate."

Luci led them to the dark Gate.

Dan drove the robot behind him. As before, the trek didn't take long, but unlike before, Dan drove it right into the crowd of demons. They stepped aside to create a path straight to the building.

Nina's eyes widened. *What? Why are they clearing the way for us?*

"He's expecting me!" Lucifer announced to the guards in front of the building, and they led him to an interior door.

"Luci!" A man ran through the crowd.

Luci held up a hand to stop the man. "I'm only here because you might want to help these people out."

"Hello, I am the Gatekeeper." The man knelt to face the robot. He tried to smile, but it was clearly forced.

"Can you get us to Denny and Daniel?" Nina asked, despite the fake smile and her doubts surrounding Luci's motives, which had only grown after seeing how easily he had passed the demons.

The Gatekeeper's eyes trailed over to Luci then back to the robot. "Of course, I can." He continued inside.

Luci followed him, so Dan drove the robot after them, too. It grew increasingly darker in the halls as they traversed the building to the Gate.

"Who is your master?" Nina rested her hands on her hips. "You succeeded Claus, right? For whom?"

The Gatekeeper stopped and turned around. "My master has forbidden me from answering that question."

"You will find out, soon. Let's continue." Luci quickened his pace.

This feels wrong. Nina couldn't understand why she felt as uncomfortable as she did. It was just a normal, dark room, nothing ominous. "Denida passed through here, too?"

The Gatekeeper nodded.

"Just a second." The Colonel maneuvered the robot to take out its controller.

The Gatekeeper yanked the controller out of the robot's grasp and smashed it on the floor, causing everyone in the lab to flinch. "You don't need that, anymore. Denida didn't, either!"

"What do you mean by that?" Nina bared her teeth at the sight of the smashed controller.

"The next world's Gate won't work with the controller's frequency. Denny's wouldn't have worked either," Luci assured her. "I'll come with you." Luci stepped forward and tilted his head at the Gatekeeper. "Well?"

The Gatekeeper nervously fiddled with the Gate. "It's ready!"

For some reason, Nina couldn't read any of their minds. *Maybe this building has a magic seal on it, too.*

The Gatekeeper's fidgety actions all but proved that something was off, but Luci leered at the monitor with his unwavering confidence. "Ready, Lady Nina?"

Unlike everyone else they'd met, Luci didn't seem to peer curiously at the robot, regarding it as strange. Rather, it felt like he saw her in the lab, not just her image on the screen.

Creepy, but we need his help to get closer to Denny!

***

Claus strolled into his office, fully rested and financially secure. *Denida's in a dark world, filled with demons. How can it get any better than this? He might already be dead.*

The secretary stopped Claus as he passed by, wiping the broad smile from his face. "You've got a visitor. He says he's Denida's master!"

At least it isn't Doc or Nina. Claus nodded and pushed open his office's doors, preparing reassuring words for whoever was there. "Hello, I assure you that we're doing everything we can to bring Denida back safely." Claus hung his jacket on a hook next to his desk and sat in his chair.

"Are you really, Claus? In the flesh?" the visitor asked.

Claus eyed him. *Luci, the man from the other world, here?*

"You like being in Denida's place, don't you? You seem awfully tired, though. It must've taken a lot of work for you to steal all the money in his secret stash." Luci smirked.

How does he know about that? "What do you want?"

Luci's smile broadened as he sauntered up to Claus. "You don't want Denida back." He gazed into Claus's soul. "I know Denny; he'll be back, but I can help you to make sure he gets taken back to my world when he returns, President Claus!"

"And why would I do that?" Claus shoved his hands in his pocket.

"Because you want to. I want him back home where he belongs, and you want him gone, so this works for us both." Luci approached the door. "I'll even sweeten the deal for you." With that, Luci stepped out of the office.

"How?" Claus yelled after him, sighing and his eyes fell on the desk, spotting a photograph. Claus picked it up in disbelief. It showed Doc carrying Susan into a building. He turned the picture over to reveal an address on the back. *Got you!* Claus stormed out of the office.

"Where did that man, the visitor, go?"

"I don't know; I didn't see him leave. Is something wrong?" The secretary picked up her phone. "Shall I notify security?"

"No, it's nothing." Claus stumbled into his office and stared at the picture. *How did he do that?*

Claus called the mercenaries and met them several blocks away from the address on the photograph.

"Don't kill him; I want to do it myself!" Claus withdrew a tablet. "This is the house's layout." They examined the live satellite with infrared to verify Doc's exact position on the premises and decide how best to complete their mission.

"What about the girl?" one of the soldiers asked Claus.

"Keep her alive. If Denida returns, we might need her." Claus chuckled. "If not, he can just watch her die when he returns."

***

Susan was thinking about how to escape while Doc tinkered and muttered over the pile of parts on his table. None of her attempts had successfully caught him off guard. *Who could've guessed he's that agile?*

There's movement! Susan glanced to the door without turning her head. Maybe she imagined it. No, the light flicked under the door again, and she knew someone was outside. *They've come to save me! I need to distract Doc.* "Has Claus double-crossed you, yet? Or do you still think he can remove you from the wanted list?"

"I'm a scientist; do you really think I'm stupid enough to fall for your pathetic tricks, or do you still think you can overpower me?" Doc rounded the table, fists clenched.

"Oh, I'm trembling in fear." Susan rolled her eyes.

Doc rushed at her, but the door blew open and men poured into the room. Two of them tackled Doc while the others surrounded him with their guns drawn.

"At last! I told you Denida's people were better than either yours or Claus's."

"Wrong." Claus strolled through the door.

Doc's dark shades hid his eyes from Susan, but his fists unclenched, revealing his calm disposition.

He's up to something.

"Sorry to disappoint you, Susan, but it's just foolish, old Claus." Claus smirked and raised a gun, which he'd acquired from one of the mercenaries. "No one is going to save you, Susan. And as for you…" Claus held the gun to Doc's head. "- you didn't see this coming, did you? Any last words?"

No, it can't be. Susan's heart plummeted, and she dropped her head in despair.

"You haven't won, yet." Doc smirked. "I still have an ace up my sleeve."

"What could that possibly be?" Claus sneered down at Doc, his finger caressing the trigger.

"Lucifer, the Dark Lord."

Claus's smile started to fade.

"The unit from the Gate holds more power than you can even fathom." Even with soldiers holding him on his knees and Claus's gun to his head, Doc sounded like he had the situation under control. Doc smirked. "The device from the Gate can be used to summon Lucifer."

"Please, that's your ace?" Claus's sarcasm faltered when he lowered the gun and faced the mercenaries. "Find it!"

Doc tilted his head to the side. "Sorry, it isn't here anymore. I was already expecting you."

Claus glared at the mercenaries, who were tearing the house apart. He dropped the gun on the table and rubbed his head.

"So, do you want to kill me or get the unit back?" Doc stared Claus down.

Claus's face paled. "Let him go."

The soldiers halted their destruction. The ones holding Doc released him.

"You can have Susan; she's served her purpose. My price for the unit has doubled." Doc rose and dusted himself off.

"Naturally." Claus gritted his teeth as Doc strolled out the door. Claus peered back at Susan. "Bring her."

The soldiers hoisted Susan up, chains and all. All too soon, they arrived back at the cottage, which Susan had hoped she'd never see again.

"You can't win." Susan struggled against her chains. "Denida is better than you!"

"Is he?" A face appeared in the air. Its smile made Susan's skin crawl.

"Who the hell are you?"

"Hello, Susan. I plan to take Denida back to Hell. He won't save you." Luci turned to Claus.

"Claus, why didn't you kill Doc? I gave him to you on a silver platter."

"He still has the device from the Gate and knows it has magical capabilities."

Luci studied Claus for a moment. "Interesting… so, it's still here."

"I will buy it back from him with Denida's money." Claus tried to reassure him.

Luci chuckled. "Will you, now?"

***

At the lab, Nina puzzled over the circumstances as they continued without Claus. The feed had resumed, but Luci was nowhere to be seen. Instead, a stranger greeted them as if he knew exactly who they were.

"I've been expecting you. Follow me."

Nina watched the stranger with hawklike focus. She could feel the Colonel's discomfort as he lost more and more control of the situation.

The world they were in now was pitch black, but they could see somehow, as if the darkness itself was a light source.

They didn't have to follow the stranger very far before they arrived at a mansion. *It feels enchanted. And where's Luci?*

"Wait here," the man commanded as they arrived. He then left them to head inside the mansion.

"Something's wrong!" The Colonel slammed his fist on the table and jumped up to pace about. "This world has no light whatsoever. And your so-called savior, Luci, is nowhere to be seen."

"Oh, but I am here." Luci's voice emanated from the darkness, as a shadowy shape revealed the smiling man. "Don't worry, my dear Colonel; I'm here."

"Where are Denida and Daniel?" Nina jumped straight to the most concerning topic.

"They're not here, Lady Nina," Luci said. "They have ventured out of my domain."

"Your domain? What do you mean?" Nina leaned forward.

"Smart girl." Luci beamed. "Denida was my pupil, here. He escaped then, as he did again… with Daniel, this time."

Confusion boiled inside Nina's head, making it hard to think.

"Why would he escape from there?" In her gut, she knew the answer; she could feel it radiating from Luci himself.

Luci's smile grew broader. The darkness swirling around them cleared, leaving them in a large room with Luci sprawled out on a throne.

"Because…" Lucifer assumed his true form, the classic depiction of Satan. "Who wouldn't run from the Devil?"

"I knew something was up with you!" The Colonel pointed at Luci.

"You're the Devil?" Nina asked sarcastically, though part of her told her that it wasn't wise to irritate him, or anyone in his role, for that matter.

Luci returned to his smiling, human form. "Yes, I am. Lucifer's the name."

"So, let me try to understand. We're in Hell, you mentored Denida, and he's escaped from you twice, now?"

Lucifer's eyes glowed a fiery, red hue as he glared at the robot. A ball of fire flew at the robot but instead of destroying the machine, it shot straight through the monitor and manifested into Lucifer, appearing in the lab with them. "Do you even know what Denny is? He is mine!"

"He is the father of my son, so no, he's mine!" Nina waved the armed soldiers, who'd come during the Colonel's nap and decided to stay after his return.

Lucifer ignored them.

"He was yours… before he returned to my world."

"What is it that you want to say so badly?" The Colonel stepped up to Nina.

"I thought you would never ask." Lucifer paced around the room. "There is an old legend, which you might have heard about, but only God and I know its full contents."

Nina stopped herself from interrupting again. She didn't trust him but wanted to hear what he had to say.

"Shall I continue?" Lucifer asked, staring at Nina as if he had read her mind.

"Yes," Nina replied cautiously.

"Denida is our legend. He has unrivaled magical aptitude, unlike any other. He's even surpassed me!"

"Really?" Nina shrugged doubtfully. "What are you not telling us?"

"I don't like you; don't make me angry again." Lucifer spoke into her thoughts. He then smiled at everyone. "Nothing really, I just wanted you to know who he is."

Nina stared at him. What he'd said into her mind made her trust him even less. His smile annoyed her, but while she supposed she should be afraid of the Devil, she wasn't.

"Denny is mine; he will never return to you!" Lucifer vanished, leaving his voice echoing in Nina's head.

Nina's stomach ached with concern. She'd been so sure that Denny would bring Daniel home, but that faith escaped her, now, all because of the Devil's vow.

Chapter 26- A Sheriff from the Past

"I remember this place," Denida muttered.

Daniel curiously peeked up at his dad. "How can you remember this place?"

Denida met his son's gaze. *Maybe it's for the best that he doesn't know, yet.* "That doesn't matter."

"I thought you said that you'd never been to the other underworlds before?"

A thundering sound roared from over the hill, a welcome distraction. Denida dashed in the direction of the noise, stopping at the top of the hill. A herd of wild horses galloped over the fields with their manes flying in the wind.

Daniel's eyes widened. "Wow, where did all of those horses come from?"

"They're wild. They run free in this world."

"So, you really do know this place? Do you know where the Gate is, then?" Daniel tugged Denida's arm.

"No, but I know who does. Come on!" Denida descended the hill, heading away from the horses. He led Daniel along a dirt road, walking so fast that his son was forced to jog to keep up.

Denida marched through the town, which had wild horses galloping through the streets. *It still feels just as fantastical as it did the first time I was here.*

Daniel's eyes darted around the town. "Is this like an old Western movie?"

Denida ascended several steps and pushed through a saloon's swinging doors. The people inside turned to scrutinize them. *Must be the clothes.*

"Sheriff, you're back?"

Denida turned to the man who'd spoken as he stepped out of the shadows to greet them. "Sure am, Mick."

"Wait! Sheriff?" Daniel glanced around the room, bouncing in excitement.

Denida reached out and shook Mick's hand, while they sized each other up.

"Hey!" Daniel wrinkled his nose, glancing between them. "Who's a sheriff?

"Denida, of course!" Mick pointed at Denida. "No one was as good as he was at catching pesky outlaws, right up until he disappeared."

Denida blushed. "I need to talk to my deputy, Jacob."

Mick's face fell. "He's not here anymore, I'm afraid. I'm sorry to have to tell you this, but he was killed a while back."

Denida stared at Mick, disbelievingly, but the grief embedded in Mick's frown told Denida that it was true. His heart ached; Jacob had been a good friend.

"Who did it?" Anger burned away Denida's sadness.

"After you left…" Mick let out a big sigh. "- their leader, the one you fought, had followers who created unrest."

"They're still here?" Denida cracked his knuckles.

Mick nodded, his head dropping even more.

"You took Jacob's place and didn't avenge him?" Denida shook with exertion, trying to stop himself from hitting Mick.

"We tried," the sheriff replied. "But they're too strong, too quick on the draw. Jacob wasn't the only good man they murdered." Mick finally lifted his head. "No one can beat them."

Denida's eyes glowed red. "Really? I promise you that I will!"

"Wait! You'll need a gun." Mick removed his gun holster and handed it to Denida.

Denida buckled it while staring at Daniel. "Will you watch my son while I'm gone?" he asked, sparing Mick a brief glance.

"Yes, of course."

"You're leaving me again? And for what? Shouldn't we be getting home?" Daniel gasped.

"I need to do this, first." Denida examined his borrowed gun.

Mick handed him his badge. "You'll need this; you're the law, again."

Denida reluctantly took the badge and put it on. *I'm not the same person I was last time I was here, but he's right.* He made a sour face at the weight of the star pinned to his shirt. "Where are they?"

"Look here." Mick grabbed a piece of paper and a pencil to draw a map. "This should help you find their hideout."

That route looks extremely familiar. "I remember the place." Denida stormed out of the saloon.

People stopped on the street to watch him. His clothes didn't fit in the town's style, but he wore a sheriff's badge. Some folks smiled and nodded like they recognized him, but Denida didn't slow down. He mounted Mick's horse and rode it to the hideout.

The sun had started dropping in the sky when Denida arrived. Just as he remembered, the hideout was fortified and well-guarded. *I'm done letting walls slow me down.* Denida dismounted the horse and strode up the door. "Let me in. They're expecting me," he ordered the armed men guarding the door.

They drew their guns.

"I don't think so! We don't allow the law in here." One of the guards nudged Denida.

Denida frowned. "You'll regret this."

The guards lifted their guns higher.

Denida's hand flicked up, and he shot them both before they could've seen his hand move.

Silence hung heavily in the hideout.

Denida exhaled a breath he didn't realize he'd been holding and stepped over the guards' bodies and pushed through the door. "Let's get this over with."

Two more men spotted Denida, but he dropped them like the first two.

Denida reloaded the four shots he'd used as he marched past their corpses.

Men sprang out of the doorway in front of him, guns blazing, followed by several shots ringing out from a side door.

Denida ducked out of the way. *Good thing they're lousy shots.*

Some men tried to ambush him from behind.

Denida's magic gave him an edge. No matter where they came from, the outlaws' shots missed, while Denida's landed. He drew his gun, fired, and reloaded, as he trekked forward with his hands flashing as fast as they had when he'd first drawn a gun all those years ago.

The outlaws became more organized, but barriers of tables and chairs couldn't hinder Denida. His fury blazed in his red eye, and everyone who stood between Denida and his target died.

His gun was getting hot from continual use, so he had to slow down to reload.

A guard with a bullwhip wrapped the whip around Denida's hand in his momentary distraction and yanked the gun away. Guards jumped up and aimed their guns at Denida's head.

Stupid, I shouldn't have let my anger blind me!

"Sheriff Denida, I take it?" The man with the whip asked.

Denida rubbed his hand and glared around the room. His frown deepened.

"My boss is expecting you. Why don't we go see him?" The man with the whip grinned at Denida.

The other outlaws nudged him with their guns, now joined by more men with rifles and shotguns.

I might as well go with them; I want to see their leader anyway.

Their boss sneered at Denida as the group shoved him into his room.

Denida remembered the boss, not just from this world, but from Hell itself. He peered more closely at the outlaws, now realizing that they were all demons. If he'd been thinking straight, he would have spotted that with ease. *Don't show them that you're surprised; play ignorant... keep your ace.* "You killed Jacob!"

"You're here to make me pay?" The boss smirked and waved his hand around the room. "This world is not what you left behind, Denida."

"No, but then, I've changed, too." Denida stepped closer to the boss.

The man with the whip raised his arm in preparation.

"Back off, Whipboy." The boss gestured with his hand.

Denida glared at him, then turned to the boss. "You remember what I am?"

"Of course." The boss leaned back in his chair and chuckled. "You're a sheriff."

"Lars, let's just get rid of him!" Whipboy cracked his whip.

"Not yet," Lars replied while scoping out Denida. "We'll make a proper example of him."

"Your boss won't like that." Denida sneered at them.

"My boss? Who would that be? I'm the man in charge, here. I don't have a boss!" Lars grinned.

"Luci." Denida let a smile twist his lips. "You might want to ask Whipboy if he's ready to face your boss."

Denida watched the seed of doubt he'd planted grow and flower, as Lars and Whipboy bit their lips and faced each other. Demons were all about causing fear, but Lucifer still terrified them.

"Did I strike a nerve?" Denida sneered.

Whipboy wrapped the bullwhip around Denida's neck and yanked him to the side. "You really think you're something, do you?"

Lars raised his hand, stopping Whipboy, fear clearly fighting with his desire to inflict pain. Fear won. "Take him to the dungeon! I'll check with the master."

Whipboy reluctantly led Denida to the cells, where other prisoners moaned from the pain of torture.

They shoved Denida into the cell.

"I know what you're up to, but it won't work. I'll be back as soon as Lars is done speaking to the master." Whipboy cracked the bullwhip, facing the demons. "Watch him!"

***

Lars wasn't happy about summoning Lucifer, just because a former sheriff namedropped him, but he had to. Not checking it out would be worse. He stomped to a room decorated with a massive pentagram, where he often spoke with his master.

A familiar dark presence manifested almost as soon as Lars started chanting, making him even more nervous. Usually, the master liked to keep his minions waiting.

"Master!" Lars bowed. "I'm sorry for summoning you for such an insignificant cause."

The dark presence intensified as Lars's fear grew. "What cause?"

Lars drew in a deep, cautious breath. "Denida…" Before he'd finished speaking the name, the dark cloud took the shape of Lucifer frowning down at him.

"He's there?" Lucifer's eyes glowed, but he was frowning.

Lars stuttered a little. "Yes, he told me to ask you how you felt about us destroying him. Denida was the sheriff here years ago but he disappeared. He's back, now. We were going to have a little fun with him."

Lucifer rested a burning finger on Lars's lips. "Where is he?" Lucifer's eyes grew redder, and Lars writhed in pain.

"Locked up in the dungeon, until I heard from you," Lars squealed. "Is he really important to you?"

Lucifer pushed Lars to the floor. "Denida is important to everyone! He was trained in advanced dark arts. You should fear him as much as you fear me." Lucifer lifted Lars off the floor with magic and smiled, his eyes flaming. "Take me to him, now!"

Lars scrambled to lead Lucifer to the cells.

Whipboy stepped through a doorway. "So, can we torture him, now?"

Lars made a "shush" sign with a finger to his lips.

"The master doesn't know some godforsaken sheriff; Denida's bluffing." Whipboy swung his whip and licked his lips.

Lucifer whirled around and slammed Whipboy up against the wall. "You think you can torture Denida?"

"He's just some sheriff. The master doesn't know him."

Lucifer tightened his grip, and the red hue reappeared in his eyes. "Who do you think I am? Your master does know him, very well, in fact."

"Right." Whipboy's eyes trailed over to Lars, as if expecting help. "Who is this nutjob?" Whipboy readied his whip.

"The master," Lars croaked.

Whipboy's eyes widened, and Lucifer's smile broadened.

"You wanted to see Denida." Lars tried to distract the master.

"Yes." Lucifer dropped Whipboy, leaving the imprint of his hand burned into the demon's neck.

Lars threw the door to the cells open and stepped back in shock. All the prisoners had left, but the demon guards lay in their place, each with their heart torn from their chest. *Gone.*

"Oh, Denny, that's my boy!" Lucifer laughed in delight, clapping his hands in glee.

Whipboy stared at Lars, his eyes blank with fear.

Lars ignored him. Their only hope was to please the master. "Why did he let the prisoners go? They'll slow him down."

Lucifer turned his attention to Lars. "He believes he's good."

"He's not?" Lars frowned.

"No, he can't hide from who he truly is!"

"A sheriff?" Whipboy asked.

Lucifer's entire body glowed crimson. "A demon with magic aptitude that rivals my own."

Lucifer's glare chilled Lars to his soul. Maybe they should have spotted the magic and stowed him in a sealed cell.

Lars looked at the devastation that had impressed the master. He didn't think it would help.

"I'm thirsty," Lucifer turned away from the cells. "Saddle up; we're going to town to get a drink."

***

Daniel paced around town. *There's no magic here… does that mean we're finally away from it?* He accrued many suspicious glances, so he decided to return to the saloon. "So, you knew my dad when he was a sheriff here?"

"Yes, I was one of the officers under Jacob, your dad's deputy." Mick wore a tight expression as he spoke about it.

"How did he leave?"

"I don't know; I only know that the outlaws always wanted him gone, and one day, they got what they wanted."

His dad rushed into the saloon.

"Well, did you actually manage to do it?" Mick ran to Denida, who was covered in blood.

"No, but Daniel and I need to leave… now!" Daniel's dad had sweat all over his forehead.

Did something scare him?

"Do you know anything about a second Gate?" Denida demanded of Mick.

Mick wiped the sweat from Denida's forehead. "No, but I know who does."

Mick rushed to the window with Daniel following him. "Crap, your new friends are coming. Some strange man is with them, too." Mick ripped his eyes away from the window.

"He came sooner than I thought he would. It's time to go!" Denida hissed.

"You know him?" Mick turned to Denida.

"You could say that." Denida replied. "He's the reason I left this world way back when."

"Is that Luci?" Daniel pointed out the window. "He's the one who lied to me about you. I wish I hadn't taken his word for it."

Chapter 27- The Second Gate

Lars rode into town with Lucifer and the others following him.

"I thought we had an agreement?" Mick marched up to Lars.

Lars poked the sheriff in the chest. *I need to impress the master.* "Turn Denida over to us or all of you will suffer!"

Mick glared at them.

"You're stalling." Lucifer pointed at the town. "Search it all; leave no stone unturned!"

The outlaws stormed all the buildings like ants searching for food.

Lucifer smiled and sauntered up to the sheriff. "We won't find him here, will we?" He ran a burning finger down the sheriff's face. "But you know where he is, don't you? The outlaws are looking forward to torturing Denida, but maybe the townsfolk will suffice, instead?" Lucifer smirked at some children behind Mick.

Mick's hand shifted to his gun, but Lucifer's henchmen grabbed him from behind.

"Aw, Sheriff, too slow!" Lucifer raised his arms. "You can save everyone here or let them all die. It's your choice, really. Just ask yourself, is Denida really worth it?"

Mick tried to wrest free, while his forehead developed a slick layer of sweat as he watched the outlaws destroy his town. "Alright! You win."

Lucifer turned to him with a feral smile. "Yes?"

"He's on his way to the second Gate." Mick lowered his head.

"As expected." Lucifer leaned close to Mick's face. "But where is the Gate?"

"I don't know." Mick lifted his head, biting his lip.

Lucifer's eyes glowed red and he grabbed Mick's chin.

"I know where it is." Lars stepped forward.

"Do you, now?" Lucifer grinned and dropped Mick. "In that case, kill them all. Burn the town to a crisp!" Lucifer vanished.

"You can't!" Mick yelled. "I know this world. I can get you to Denida even faster!"

Lars shook his head.

"You might know exactly where he is, but the master wants all of you dead." Lars drew his gun in one swift motion and shot Mick in the eye. A small glow flowed out of his eye, floating to the clouds, as his soul vacated his body. *Lucifer won't have to see him in Hell, now.* "Burn it all!" Lars commanded the outlaws.

***

Flames and smoke climbed in the distance behind Denida and Daniel. Denida's heart sank. He should have left sooner. He cast a spell between Daniel and the fire to prevent his son from realizing that all his new friends were now dead.

Daniel grunted at his dad. "You didn't need to do that; I know they're dead."

Maybe, this experience is making him grow up... Denida sighed, but instead of responding, he scoured his memories, remembering more and more, but it didn't help the people around him. *I wonder if Robert will remember me.*

They strode across a desolate plain, coming to a small farm.

"It's like you can see the horizon from every direction." Daniel tilted his head.

"Halt!" A man stepped out onto a farmhouse's wraparound porch with a rifle at the ready.

"Robert, wait!" Denida waved both his hands. "It's me, Denida... Denny?"

Robert aimed the rifle at Denida and cocked it.

Daniel stood with his hands up beside him.

Damn, I don't want to scare him even more. "I'm Sheriff Denida, see the badge?" Denida nodded down at his shirt.

Robert's eyes fell to the badge, but he held his gun steadily. "Sheriff…" Robert slowly lowered the rifle. "Alright, come in."

Denida smiled reassuringly at Daniel, then followed Robert into the farmyard. "It's going to be alright; he's an old friend."

Daniel nodded then turned his head in the direction of a dog that had run out of the barn. "Can I go play with him?"

Robert lifted his hand lazily. "Knock yourself out."

Daniel approached the dog and began scratching behind its ears.

Denida eyed Robert, trying to find something to say.

"You've grown up, Denny. You're not the little boy I remember." Robert led Denida into the house and sat down at a table in the kitchen. "What brings you here? I'm guessing you're not here by choice?"

Denida frowned, peering through the window at Daniel laughing as the dog licked his face. "I need to know where the second Gate is. Sheriff Mick said you'd know?"

Robert chuckled to himself. "Yes, you're leaving the same way you did last time, huh? Then, you should remember it needs energy, first."

"And how would I get that?" Denida dug for a memory but couldn't find one.

"It will take time, but we can produce it. I'll get it set up for you right away." Robert pushed himself to his feet.

Maybe that's why I don't remember. He did it for me last time, too. While he stood, deep in thought, Robert left for the Gate to start powering it up.

Daniel waltzed inside. "Are we going through the Gate, soon?"

"I certainly hope so!" *This journey must be hard on him.*

Denida met Robert outside as he returned to the farm. "How much longer will it take? Someone is hunting us." He scoped the horizon.

"It shouldn't take long, but I can see folks coming from long ways off."

Denida's heartstrings ached, so he turned to check on Daniel, just in case.

"Who's after you?" Robert asked as Denida sauntered back over to his son.

"The same man who forced me to leave town the first time."

"Thought so." Robert trailed Denida back to the house. "I always figured you'd be back someday, and I feared that that man would return, too. The boy with you, is he yours?" Robert asked as they stopped by Daniel, who had started running with the dog again.

Denida nodded. "He's my son. He accidentally walked through a Gate, so I caught up to him, and we've been travelling, through the Gates to get back home. I'm sure his mom's waiting for us, and she's not the type to sit around doing nothing."

"I see. You miss her too, don't you?" Robert cocked an eyebrow at Denida.

Denida sighed deeply. "You can tell? I can't let that distract me. We aren't safe, yet." Denida glanced after Daniel. *Will Daniel ever trust me again after seeing me use so much dark magic? Will Nina?* "A lot has changed." Denida smiled weakly at Robert.

In the following days, Denida and Daniel stayed with Robert. Denida paced around the farmyard, willing the Gate to draw power faster. A lone windmill near the Gate worked slowly but steadily.

"Daniel needs some stimulus... poor kid must be bored out of his skull. How about I teach him to shoot?" Robert turned to Denida.

Denida nodded. "He'd enjoy that."

Robert picked up his pistol, then sent Daniel out into the field to stand some empty bottles on barrels.

"Those are for later." Robert lined bottles up on the fence. "We'll start with something closer." He rolled another barrel over and had Daniel crouch behind it, pistol trained on the first barrel.

"You're too inexperienced to practice fancy quickdraw techniques like your dad, but that doesn't mean you can't shoot. Just keep in mind that a gun isn't a toy and you'll be fine."

Daniel lined up the pistol and cocked it. When he pulled the trigger, his hands jerked upwards.

"Lean into it more and relax. Aiming true is more important than speed, right now."

After several reloads, Daniel blew one of the bottles to smithereens. He remembered to lower the gun before dancing in delight at his success.

"I take it you still have your fast reflexes." Robert winked at Denida.

"Of course." *I wonder if I can attribute them to my dark magic.* Denida grinned, drew his gun, and shattered a bottle on each barrel in the distance. "I always will."

"I taught your father well." Robert ruffled Daniel's hair, and they resumed their target practice.

"Are you worried about Daniel?" Gabriel's voice spoke from behind Denida.

Denida whirled around to face the archangel. "How are you here? And how did you know where I was?"

"I'm an archangel; I always know where you are, and I am always watching you." Gabriel glanced at Daniel. "Why are you still here? Waiting for the Gate to turn on? You remember magic, don't you?"

Denida struck his forehead with his palm. "You're right; I'm still not used to this magic thing." He hurried over to Daniel, forgetting Gabriel was even there.

"We don't need to wait for the Gate." Denida interrupted their shooting session.

"What're you talking about?" Robert shook his head.

"This." Denida fired a beam of energy from his hand and destroyed the barrels in the field. Denida eyed Daniel. "Get ready to go."

Daniel nodded and scurried into the house.

"You do realize that whoever is after you will certainly have laid a trap near the Gate." Robert rested his hand on Denida's shoulder.

"I'm counting on that. Thanks for everything!" Denida shook Robert's hand before joining Daniel inside.

At nightfall, Denida led Daniel to the plain around the Gate. *There sure are a lot of demons here!* "I will cast a cloaking spell on you, Daniel. They won't be able to see you."

Daniel followed his dad as they ventured closer to the Gate. They passed boulders strewn across a gravel field. The night's crescent moon shed a faint light, which allowed Denida to make out a narrow path weaving around the huge rocks.

They had only been advancing for several minutes when demons jumped out from behind the rocks.

Denida felt their evil presences more clearly than he could see them in the moonlight. He drew his gun in an instant and shot both guards, silencing the shots with dark magic.

Daniel recoiled.

"We have to use magic, or the gunshots would be too loud." Denida crouched behind a boulder.

"Yeah, but that's dark magic," Daniel whispered.

Denida sighed. "Is blocking my memories inherently evil, Daniel?" he asked rhetorically. "Or putting someone to sleep instead of killing them?"

Daniel bit his lip, staring at the ground.

Denida rested his hands on his son's shoulders. "Dark magic isn't evil, unless you use it for evil. And we need it, right now, because it's the strongest magic I know."

Daniel stared at the ground for a moment longer, before nodding.

Denida watched him, waiting for another protest. When his son didn't say anything more, Denida peered out at the Gate. "There are too many demons here; we need to find another way." He surveyed their surroundings. "Come with me."

Daniel followed his father to a small cluster of trees off the path, away from the Gate.

Denida drew in a deep breath. *The demons won't check for him, here.* "Stay here; I'll be back."

"You're leaving me, again?" Daniel clenched his fists.

"I have to, but I'll be back." Denida hurried back in the direction of the Gate.

***

Dad can't be serious! Daniel stood alone in the darkness. *I'm invisible, so why wouldn't he let me follow him?* Daniel meandered toward the Gate. *Wait... they can't see me; this is going to be fun.*

"Whipboy!" a man yelled in front of him.

"What, Lars?" Whipboy turned to face Lars.

"You need to keep watch. Denida should be coming this way any time now."

"Why is he so important, anyway?" Whipboy cracked his whip. "I hate him!"

"I don't know, but the master wants him back!"

Whipboy gazed into the darkness, drawing his eyebrows together.

"What?"

"Somebody's there!" Whipboy gripped his whip more tightly.

Lars's eyes narrowed.

Daniel froze, too afraid to move a muscle. He stayed still for what felt like an eternity, even if it only lasted a few minutes, but Whipboy stood still. *I've gotta get out of here.* Daniel took a careful step backward, while still watching the demons. When they didn't react, Daniel took another step, and a branch cracked under his shoe.

"Gotcha!" Whipboy grabbed Daniel around the waist, and the cloaking spell dissipated.

Darkness surrounded Daniel.

"It's that boy." Lars glared at them.

Whipboy turned to the demons around them. "Hold on to him."

Demons snatched Daniel from Whipboy.

"Denida must be here, too. I'll tell the master." Lars tilted his chin. "Keep an eye on that kid. If he's anything like his father, he'll be sneaky." Lars strode to the Gate.

***

This might just work. Denida enshrouded himself in a cloaking spell, then walked through a crowd of demons. One house stood out here, with Lucifer's heavy presence emanating from it. Denida slipped past the demons patrolling the house as they held the door open for someone else.

Lucifer stood inside, staring out the window. "Leave me!" he commanded the demons. He chuckled nastily as he turned away from the window.

Denida had a hard time believing he'd ever trusted this twisted being.

Lucifer smiled right at him. "Denny, I cleared the room."

Denida dropped his cloaking spell and appeared in front of Lucifer.

Lucifer grinned. "How I've missed you."

"Sorry, but that's not why I came."

"You've piqued my interest." Lucifer smiled deviously. "You must be visiting the Prince of Darkness for a reason."

Denida's eye glowed. "You taught me well, Luci." Denida circled Lucifer. "And you might be disappointed, but I do remember everything."

Their red, glowing eyes met. "I remember the man I dealt a humiliating defeat in this very world for all to see." Denida smirked.

"Enough of this. You'll return to Hell, whether you like it or not!" Lucifer grabbed Denida's arm.

"There's a tiny detail you're forgetting."

"And what's that?" Lucifer stared at him with cold eyes.

"This!" Before Lucifer could respond, Denida drew his gun and shot Lucifer in the chest, muffling the gunshot with a spell.

Lucifer fell to the floor.

Denida immediately enshrouded Lucifer with another spell.

"You missed!" Lucifer grinned, clutching his chest.

"You think so?" Denida bound Lucifer with a rag he found on the floor. "Maybe I remembered something. You can't return if you never leave this world. And you can't use magic if I put a magic shield on you." A red flicker flashed in Denida's eye. "Who's better, now?"

"Lars will come for me!"

"Really?" Denida stood up, leering down at him. "Maybe he will just settle for me!"

Denida's body changed and became identical to Lucifer's human form. "Take care, Luci." Denida almost left the building when he froze in place. "Dad!" Daniel's thoughts reached Denida. *What?*

"Whipboy and Lars caught me!" Daniel's thoughts reached Denida's mind.

"Wait there!" Denida shouted into his son's thoughts and grabbed the door handle, stomping outside.

"Lars, bring Denida's son, Daniel, to the Gate."

"You know we caught him?"

"I know everything. Question me again and I'll show you suffering beyond compare!"

Lars nodded and scurried off.

It's nice that I remember how Lucifer operates, now. When Denida, still identical to Lucifer, reached the Gate, he used a beam of magic to power it up.

Lars appeared with a very terrified Daniel. "This kid had a cloaking spell on him."

"I know; bring him closer to the Gate." Denida pointed at the Gate.

"Why is the Gate on? Isn't that risky with Denida wanting to use it?" Lars frowned.

Denida stopped and turned around, mimicking Lucifer's scowl. "You're questioning me?"

Lars shook his head violently. "No, Master!"

"Good." Denida turned back to the Gate.

"Stop!" Whipboy yelled.

Denida turned with everyone else to see where the shout had come from.

Whipboy dashed out of Lucifer's house. "That's Denida, not Lucifer!" Whipboy charged up to them.

Lars and the huge crowd of demons surged at Denida, but he grabbed Daniel's hand and expelled a stream of dark magic, blowing Lars and the demons back into the night. Denida grinned as Lucifer's house collapsed under the force of the spell.

"Let's go, Daniel." Denida hurried through the Gate, leaving Whipboy, Lucifer, and the rest of the demons behind him.

Chapter 28- Gone Bad

At the lab, Nina was out of sorts. No one seemed to share her concern. The Colonel had ignored her distrust of Claus. No matter what she did to prove it, he dismissed her concerns, but at least he didn't seem to trust Luci, now. *That's a start.* It was time she had a chat with the Colonel, so that she could figure out what he really felt.

"Colonel?" Nina sauntered up to him.

"Nina, are you going to try to talk to me about Claus, again?" The Colonel wrinkled his forehead.

Nina shook her head. "I want to talk about Luci, not Claus."

The Colonel scratched his nose. "When we first saw him, I told you to avoid him. You didn't listen. So, it's too late to do anything about that, now. We can't go back!" The Colonel returned to his paperwork.

I must push him. "Luci said something into my head that nobody else heard."

The Colonel slammed his fist on the desk. "Jesus, Nina, you are not about to tell me another conspiracy theory about Claus, are you?"

Nina raised her hands in surrender.

"We need to get Denida and Daniel back, and the fact that I distrust Luci does not mean I'll tolerate your nonsense." The Colonel exhaled heavily. "You need to accept that Denida is missing, and you have to learn to follow orders if you want us to bring him back safely!"

"Sorry." Nina backed away. *He won't listen to me anymore.* She'd lost him as an ally.

***

Claus visited his stash of cash and packed some into a bag. *I might need this soon.*

"Big stash!" Luci remarked from behind Claus.

Claus was getting used to Lucifer appearing, so he merely shrugged and cocked his head. "You again?"

"Yes, I need to fix your latest screw up."

Claus continued shoving money in the bag.

"You won't need any of that. I will fix it for you." Lucifer sauntered up to Claus. "The Scientist doesn't deserve a cent."

"He goes by Doc, now." Claus glanced at Lucifer. "And why do you care, anyway?"

"That cretin threatened to use the device to summon me. No one treats me like some lackey." Lucifer turned, disappearing immediately.

Claus peered down at the half-filled bag. He sighed and finished filling it. Right as he finished, his phone rang.

"Get back here; it's important." The Colonel hung up.

Claus eyed the money, then his phone. He carried the bag outside and tossed it in the trunk of his car before heading to the lab.

When Claus strode into the lab, everyone was staring at the screen, which depicted an empty room. "Um… hello?"

"Good, you're here!" The Colonel led him away from the crowd of techs.

"What the hell is going on? The screen? The crowd?" Claus gazed with wide eyes.

"We are locked in a strange world." The Colonel shrugged. "Allegedly, the Devil's keeping us here."

The Devil.

"Crunch, crunch," sounded from the monitor.

Claus and the Colonel turned to watch the feed.

"You're both so excited to see me… isn't that nice?" Lucifer smirked.

So, Luci really is the Devil? Claus tilted his head at the Colonel, who nodded.

"You won't like what I am about to say." Lucifer imitated a sad face. "I'll recover Denida, soon. I no longer need you. Goodbye."

"Wait!" Nina screamed.

Lucifer turned back to the monitor.

"Yes, Lady Nina?"

Everyone in the room peered at her. too.

"Are you really planning to keep us here?"

Lucifer winked at her. "Destroy their machine!" Lucifer gestured at the robot and disappeared.

The feed turned black. Static flickered on all the screens in the lab.

The Colonel whipped around to Dan. "Get it back!"

Dan pressed buttons all over the controller, but the static continued to crackle. "The robot's gone." He hung his head.

The Colonel's eyes met Nina's. "I'm so sorry, Lady Nina. Inform me if anything changes."

Devil or not, Claus knew Denida, and he wasn't taking any chances.

The Colonel stopped next to Nina on his way out of the room. "Let me know if you restore the feed!" He stormed out of the lab.

***

Doc hated things he couldn't explain. He'd brought the unit to a lab that Claus didn't even know about. Now that he knew what the device could do, he just needed to make it work.

"Hello." Lucifer appeared in a dark corner of the room.

"Who's there?" Doc snatched up a gun, pointing it at the shadows.

"It's been a long time, Jack, hasn't it?" Lucifer stepped out of the shadows.

Jack lowered his gun. "Master! Yes, it has. What brings you here?"

"Claus! You need to act as if I killed you, and I need that device back."

"But…" Jack ran his fingers across the main unit.

"No, it is too strong of a material for you or him to use to its full potential."

Jack sighed and handed it to Lucifer. "Will you bring the Dark Angels back to this world?"

"And who would lead them? Claus?" Lucifer scoffed at the idea. "All the versions of Claus across the Underworlds have been nothing more than mere puppets. All he has ever been good for is bringing me Denida and he can't even do that right!"

Jack laughed. I'd love to see his face when he learns he's just a pawn here, too."

"I need something more from you." Lucifer smiled. "You will like it; it involves Claus."

***

Claus sat in his office, feeling good about the future. With Lucifer on his side, he'd be unstoppable. With his increased confidence, he had hired more mercenaries for the Gate, just in case.

"Hello." Lucifer appeared with a face so stoic that it startled Claus.

Claus tilted his head to the side but grinned. "Denida escaped, I presume?"

Lucifer's eyes glowed red and Darkness spread throughout the room. "Make sure you catch him when he returns."

"Can't you get him in the next world?" Claus stood up, sweat appearing on his forehead.

Lucifer's smile returned. "I can't reach him in the next world, thanks to God." Lucifer towered over Claus. "And after that world, he'll be back here! Expect him."

Claus sat back down. "Doc?"

Lucifer extended his hands, and the device materialized in his palms. "You were searching for this, weren't you?"

"Yes." Claus's heart raced as he took the device from Lucifer. "Doc is gone?"

Lucifer nodded and continued out the door.

Claus set the main unit down, but he was not finished with Lucifer, so he darted after him, catching up to him in the parking lot. "I have the device; Denida can't return!"

Lucifer smiled. "He couldn't escape from the world in which I had him surrounded either, yet he did. Just remember that, Claus." He turned and smiled at someone, as if amused by them. "Don't forget to check with the Colonel." Lucifer winked at Claus before he vanished.

Claus spun, trying to spot whomever Lucifer had smirked at, but he was the only one around.

***

The lab techs checked and rechecked their connection to the robot, refusing to believe that it had been destroyed after all this time. The Colonel entered the room, stepped up to Dan, pulling him out of the lab with him.

Where's he taking Dan? Nina followed them.

"I have another job for you alone. It's strictly confidential." The Colonel shifted nervously on his feet.

"Sure," Dan whispered.

"Claus has met with Lucifer. I couldn't hear what they were talking about." The Colonel glanced around him again "I need someone who can follow Claus, and I can't, 'cause Lucifer might have seen me eavesdropping. You are the only person I can trust." The Colonel pinched the bridge of his nose. "Nina has already made up her mind about Claus, so she's too biased for this." The Colonel cleared his throat. "You'll have to be careful though, given his connection to the Devil."

"I knew it!" Nina yelled, making Dan and the Colonel jump. "You thought you could drag Dan away without me noticing?"

"Crap." The Colonel nodded to Dan to signal the start of his mission.

"Dan is following Claus. What other measures should we take?" Nina crossed her arms.

"Why don't we wait and see what he comes back with." The Colonel tried to placate her. "We still don't know why Claus-"

"No!" Nina stomped up to the Colonel. "You saw him with the Devil and you're still not convinced that he's up to something? What do you want, Denida's death? Or Daniel's, too?"

The Colonel arched his neck.

"Well?" Nina glared at the Colonel.

"I'm being careful, just as Denida taught me…" The Colonel sighed. "- and if Susan is missing, it's still not a certainty that he has her!"

Nina had read Claus's mind, and she knew that now was the time to act, but the Colonel didn't have that same level of clarity. At least he had started to check up on the weasel, but even she never expected Claus to be colluding with the Devil.

***

Dan drove to the HQ and parked where he could see Claus if he left the building. He hated stakeouts. *Maybe I should just go talk to him.* Dan sauntered to the doors and pulled them open but jumped back as Lucifer appeared in front of him. "L-Lucifer?" Dan stuttered.

Lucifer smiled innocently. "Yes, does that scare you?"

Dan shook his head. "Excuse me." He turned and sprinted back to his car.

Lucifer appeared in front of him, sitting on the hood of his car. "I really need to talk to you, Dan. Won't you spare a little time?"

Dan's heart raced. *If I get back in my car, will he follow me?* Dan nodded.

Lucifer patted the hood of the car beside him. "Good! Sit, won't you? You're Denny's old friend. You helped him fight against the Dark Angels, didn't you?"

Dan bit his lip. "I only convinced him that we had to fight them. The Colonel helped more with the rebellion itself." Dan didn't like the way Lucifer twisted the facts.

Claus waltzed out of the headquarters and sauntered up to his car.

"Oh, I guess you need to go. What a shame." Lucifer stood. "I guess we'll have to continue this another time!" Lucifer winked and vanished in a split second.

Claus drove away in his car.

Dan jumped into his own car, hands shaking. His trembling hand made him fumble with the key in the ignition, taking a moment to start the car, before following Claus.

Claus headed in the direction of the second Gate. Soldiers met Claus at a checkpoint on an old road, which weaved through the woods.

Dan turned his car off. *Who's that? They are more heavily armed than our military.* He hurried to turn his key in the ignition again and tailed Claus and the soldiers.

What's going on here? Dan drove past the soldiers without sparing them a glance, then parked out of sight around the bend. *Time to do some sleuthing.* He clenched his fists and sighed. *I'd rather be in the lab.* He followed the road up to a clearing where he saw even more soldiers on patrol.

Claus strolled into a cottage with some of his soldiers. Dan crept as close to the building as he could. He needed to peek inside; he didn't trust Claus or these soldiers.

One of the soldiers stepped into the woods and faced a tree.

I need a gun. Dan tiptoed up to the soldier. "Hello," he said behind the soldier, who spun around in shock, giving Dan the perfect angle to punch the man's temple. The soldier dropped without a sound.

Dan had come to find out what Claus was up to, and he was going to do just that. He picked up the gun and slipped on the soldier's uniform, tying the man up with his shoelaces, and gagging him with a sock.

Dan marched out of the woods, acting like a soldier. Guards stood by the front door and probably inside the building, too. Dan sauntered up to the side of the cabin and peeked in through the window as he passed it. Susan sat, chained to a chair, with Claus in front of her.

"You got the device back!" Susan hissed.

"Of course, I did!" Claus chuckled. "The Morning Star brought it to me."

"Morning Star?"

"Lucifer!" Claus gloated. "He wants Denida and will do anything to get him."

Dan drew nearer, smiling as nobody paid him any attention. He peered inside, hoping he could hear more of Claus's plans.

Claus sauntered up to a table with a piece from a Gate on it.

Where did he get that? Dan's heart sank.

Claus leaned over to a soldier and whispered something, pointing at Susan. He stepped back in front of Susan. "I'm about to reveal something of vital importance."

"Freeze!" somebody shouted from behind Dan.

"Your friends sent a lab rat to rescue you." Claus smirked at Susan, then sneered at Dan.

Dan turned to see the crowd of men with their guns trained on him. He threw his own gun on the ground and raised his hands.

A soldier stepped forward and hit him with the butt of his rifle, and Dan fell to the ground.

Chapter 29- Everything Gone

Dan came to slowly, seeing Claus gloating as the soldiers chained him up next to Susan.

"This is what you get for listening to Nina!" Claus laughed.

That brought a smile to Dan's face. "Actually, I'm following the Colonel's orders."

The soldiers in the room shuffled about and muttered to one another at the mention of the Colonel.

"Really?" Susan's head shot up.

Dan nodded. "He saw Claus chatting with Lucifer at headquarters!"

Dan enjoyed watching Claus try to reassure his soldiers, but some had already run out screaming.

"The Colonel knows we're here." The chatter between the soldiers outside spread.

"Things with the mercenaries aren't going so well. I hope you haven't paid them, yet."

"This isn't over!" Claus rushed outside to soothe his soldiers.

"Is it really true that the Colonel knows?" Susan asked when they were left alone in the cottage.

"He sent me to follow Claus but all he knows is that Claus met with Lucifer."

Claus sauntered back into the cottage, followed by several soldiers.

"So much for your pathetic attempt to scare my mercenaries. I'm off to discover what the Colonel really knows. Don't go anywhere." Claus winked and stomped out of the room, leaving Dan and Susan alone with several soldiers.

"Hey." One of the soldiers smiled. "Thanks guys! He just doubled our pay."

Susan swallowed, but Dan smirked. "You do realize that when Denida does return, no amount of extra pay will keep you safe, right?"

"He can't make it back." A soldier pointed at the device on the table. "The Gate won't work without it."

"Then why is Claus so worried? He shouldn't need an entire army to hold two people hostages." Dan shifted his position, making himself as comfortable as he could in the chains. "Not to mention the fact that he's made a deal with the Devil, which he can only keep if Denida returns."

"The Devil will deal with Denida, then." The soldier rolled his eyes.

"Right." Dan made a show of shaking his head. "How much do you trust the Devil, or Claus, for that matter?"

***

Claus ambled into the lab, and the Colonel prepared himself for a battle of wits, though a fight such as that would hardly be a challenge with an opponent like Claus.

"Hello, I wanted to know if you had any updates?" Claus asked.

"Sorry." The Colonel shrugged. "We have every lab tech here trying to reconnect the robot's feed, but haven't had any results, yet!"

Claus raked his eyes over the techs. "Why isn't Dan helping them?"

"He's busy making a new robot, in the event that we fail to reestablish a connection."

Claus nodded, but the movement seemed forced.

"Unless you have reason to believe a new robot wouldn't get past that Lucifer fellow?" The Colonel raised an eyebrow.

"How would I know?" Claus shrugged. "But if you have nothing, I'll get back to my office." Claus smiled and sauntered out of the lab.

Nina stepped out from her hiding spot in the corner. "He knows that you saw him with Lucifer and came here to find out what we know."

"In that case, maybe he needs another push." The Colonel strode out after Claus, who was showing his ID to the guard outside the lab when the Colonel caught up to him.

"Colonel?" Claus pocketed his ID. "Have you reestablished connection to the robot?"

"No." The Colonel scowled. "Why didn't you tell me that you met with Lucifer?"

Claus gaped at the question, then Nina stepped up behind the Colonel, and Claus frowned at her. "That doesn't concern you!" Claus turned to leave.

"I oversee Denida's security detail!" The Colonel raised his voice.

"You are forgetting that Denida is gone, and I am running this underworld in his absence!"

Claus sat in his car. "Open the gate," he commanded the guard. As the gate slid open, he smiled proudly at the Colonel. "You're answering to me until Denida returns. Don't you forget it." With that, he sped off, tires screeching.

"Are you sure you know what you're doing?" Nina stared at the dust cloud from Claus's tires.

The Colonel nodded slowly. "The more confident he is, the more vulnerable, and he's out in the open, now."

***

Claus raced off. He'd finally put the Colonel in his place. No need to pretend to be worried. He had neutralized the last threat to his authority.

As Claus walked into his office, he encountered Lucifer, sitting in Claus's chair. "Lucifer, to what do I owe the pleasure?"

"You were reckless to take Dan, but I suppose that's your choice." Lucifer smiled as he rose from the chair and circled Claus. "But then, you proceeded to tell the Colonel that you're in charge! I do not need to tell you how foolish that ploy was, do I?"

"I… don't… care!" Claus sat down in his chair.

Lucifer appeared behind him. "You do remember who I am, right? I never accept failure!"

Claus turned around, but Lucifer had already vanished. Claus's blood pounded in his ears, and his hands shook. He had no choice but to deliver Denida to Lucifer.

Claus left his office and headed to where he'd left Denida's money. He needed more to pay the mercenaries. *Blast that Dan, and those cowardly soldiers. At least I've got the money to keep paying them.*

He sauntered into the warehouse where he'd stowed the money, and his heart almost stopped. All the money had vanished, every single bill. The questions piled up and gave him a headache.

Wait, Dan! He'd been following Claus; he must have stolen the cash before confronting him. Time for another chat with his prisoner. *Maybe Susan can finally be of some use as leverage.*

***

Lucifer appeared next to Jack, who grinned as he watched Claus drive off. "Nice work, Jack."

Jack turned his head to Lucifer and nodded. "Where do you want his money?"

"Keep it; I don't care!" Lucifer disappeared.

***

Claus rushed across the grounds, heading straight into the cabin.

"Out," Claus hissed at his guards.

"Claus?" Donaldson asked. "Got our pay raise ready?"

Claus drew his gun and pointed it at Donaldson's head. "I said out!" He locked the door behind them, then stormed over to the prisoners and held the gun to Susan's head.

"They won't interrupt us, now." Claus glared at Dan. "You followed me to my hideout."

Dan shook his head violently. "I followed you here. Isn't this your hideout?"

Claus wanted to hurt them both. *They're conspiring against me.* "Tell me what you did with my money, or Susan dies!"

"Wait!" Dan yelled. "What money? I don't know anything about any money."

Claus wavered, uncertain how to proceed, now. *Who else could have taken it?*

"Isn't this sweet? You think a lab rat took the money you stole from Denny." Lucifer appeared with a smirk.

"No, not you!" Claus swung around to face Lucifer, then put his gun on the table to ward off his temptation to use it.

"Anger, I love it! Embrace that." Lucifer beamed at Claus.

"I need that money to pay the soldiers." Claus peeked at Dan, still suspicious of him.

"Wrong." Lucifer chuckled. "You have what you've siphoned." Lucifer smiled as he disassembled Claus's gun. "You will, of course, get it all back, when you give me Denny."

"That's your plan? You want me to return him to you when I won't even have any allies to help me?" Claus bared his teeth.

"I knew you'd understand. Congratulations!" Lucifer patted Claus on the shoulder.

"I see why Denida wanted to get away from you," Claus muttered.

Lucifer stopped in his tracks. "You don't want to say that to me! In all the Underworlds, you were nothing but a pawn. This one is no different," Lucifer whispered into Claus's ear. "Denida, on the other hand…" His eyes lit up. "-what a powerhouse! You are nothing by comparison. He only left me because he's the only one who was ever strong enough to escape Hell."

"Twice!" Dan mocked.

Lucifer turned to Dan and smiled, before vanishing.

Damn him! The soldiers I still have better be strong enough.

***

The Colonel had left Nina in the lab with the technicians, but there was nothing for her to do. Dan hadn't returned, and the robot was never going to work again. She stepped outside to smoke and get away from the stress.

A commotion at the front gate made her drop her cigarette and tread over to investigate.

A group of soldiers in heavy tactical gear stormed through the front gate.

Nina had never seen them before, not even with Denida. "What do you want?" She stepped forward.

A man, who was clearly in charge, stepped forward and saluted her. A number of medals decorated his chest. "Lady Nina! It's an honor to be here."

"I called them; let them in!" a voice called from behind Nina.

Nina whirled around to see the Colonel standing there in full camouflage. "Colonel? Um… Dan hasn't returned, yet."

The Colonel nodded. "I didn't expect him to. Claus probably has him, but I know where, now." He turned to his soldiers and started disseminating orders.

"Wait!" Nina sprinted to catch up to them. "Who are these people?"

The Colonel cleared his throat, and his face reddened. "After the Dark Angels fell, Denida felt like we needed a safeguard, an extra layer of security, so we formed a military unit just for secret operations. I'm the only one with command over that unit, and only Denida and I know about it." He half-smiled at that. "This is my team." He gestured at the soldiers. "They're the best of the best in the Underworld!"

That level of foresight sounds like Denny alright. "But how do you know where Dan is?" Nina asked.

The Colonel chuckled and winked at his team. "I expected things to go awry, so I put a tracker on Dan, and these fine soldiers have been following his every move."

Nina's heart lightened for the first time in a long time. "Couldn't Claus see an expense in the budget for this unit?"

"Denida paid for it himself, using untraceable accounts."

Nina rolled her eyes with a smile on her face. "That sounds like him, too."

The Colonel nodded. He slung his arms around Nina. "Don't worry; we'll get Dan back, safe and sound. It's time for Claus to face his reckoning. Denida's secret task force will make it happen."

Chapter 30- The Real World

Denida took two steps in the new world before stopping dead in his tracks, turning as white as a ghost.

Daniel continued past Denida, then spun around. "What's wrong?" He returned to Denida and poked him. "Dad?"

After several nudges, reality set in, and Denida peered down at his son, observing a mixture of concern and annoyance on his face. "I can't believe it!" Denida still glanced about, trying to absorb his surroundings.

Daniel lightly pushed Denida. "What?" Now his face tightened, like his frustration was stronger than his concern.

Denida shook himself and ruffled Daniel's hair. "I know this world; I've been here before."

"Just like the last world," Daniel muttered.

"No, not like that at all." Denida turned in a circle, still hardly believing his eyes. "This is the first underworld, where souls can interact with their human counterpart. We're on Earth!"

Daniel's eyes widened with excitement. "Do you know how to get home from here, then?"

Daniel's question struck Denida like a lightning bolt. Of course, he knew how to get home. "Yes, follow me!" He sprinted off with Daniel running after him.

Denida stopped at two expansive lakes.

"I don't see a Gate, here." Daniel's eyes darted about, confused.

"When our souls come here to visit our human forms, we arrive here!"

"How?" Daniel shifted on his feet.

Denida shrugged. "We use a form of telepathy. It's called astral projection, but maybe…"

"What a ridiculous idea!" Daniel laughed with a snort.

"No, it's not." Denida's temper flared. He sauntered a little farther down the path to calm his frustration. "It's here, Daniel!"

Daniel rushed after his dad, who stood still, not far from him, right in front of a Gate, concealed among the trees. The Gate stood majestically on a bluff, overlooking the twin lakes, which were covered in bushes and vines. The gorgeous blue sky and sunlight reflected off the water.

Denida concentrated and used magical energy to activate the Gate. It powered up with a familiar buzz.

Daniel reached out to grab Denida's hand. "Finally!"

The portal within the active Gate showed their own world for a brief second, but as Denida stepped forward, the Gate shut back down.

"What?" Daniel kicked the Gate. "We want to go home!"

Denida tried again several times, using more energy, but the connection never lasted more than a fraction of a second.

"Why isn't it working?" Daniel sat by the Gate with his head in his hands.

Denida stared at the Gate, stumped. He'd been so sure that it would be easy to get home from here. Dropping beside Daniel, Denida tried to come up with something to say to his son. *It's over.*

"Dad!" Daniel yelled, snapping Denida out of his thoughts. "We could try hanging around your human form. Maybe other souls from our world will visit their human forms and find us."

Denida smiled at that proposal. "I like that idea." He pulled Daniel to his feet. "Follow me."

Denida took Daniel by the hand and ran. He sprinted straight toward a wall, and Daniel squeaked, only to gasp as they passed right through it, like ghosts.

They passed other souls wandering about, but Denida didn't stop to talk to them. Daniel went from squeaking to giggling as they phased through walls, trees, and people.

Denida slowed in front of a school with children, who were leaving class.

"A school?" Daniel asked.

"I may have an old soul, but my body is young."

Daniel watched the crowd of children, then turned back to his father.

"There I am." Denida pointed at an eleven-year-old blond boy playing ball with another child.

Daniel gaped in disbelief. "But… but… but…" Daniel stuttered. "You have brown hair!"

"My hair will darken as I get older. It's what happened to my soul, after all." Denida chuckled.

Daniel pointed at a girl. "Is that mom?" He lowered his hand. "She looks just like the version of Mom we saw in the world with the time machine."

"Yes." Denida's heart ached at how much he missed his Nina. "I met your mom here, in the real world."

"So, it really is all connected?" Daniel asked.

Denida nodded with a longing smile, reminiscing on the day he first approached Nina on Earth.

"What about me? You and Mom are only children, here, so where did I come from?"

Denida winced. The answer to Daniel's question would hurt him, but he deserved to know the truth.

"You aren't from Earth. You're a soul created in the Underworlds." Denida rested his hand on his son's shoulder.

"Are there any others in our world who aren't in the real world?" Daniel peeked up at Denida.

"Claus and the Colonel," Denida mused. "They were created in the Underworlds, too."

"How is that possible? We met different versions of them across the Underworlds!" Daniel insisted.

"Yes." Denida glanced at his human self again. "Their souls were split throughout several worlds, as most are, so that their soul energy wouldn't become too powerful."

"But we haven't met another version of you and your magic is super strong." Daniel tugged Denida's arm.

"Maybe that has something to do with the legend Michael mentioned..."

"Something's wrong, here!" Nina stared straight in their direction.

"Can she see us?" Daniel whispered to Denida.

"Impossible." Denida kept his eyes locked on her.

"You don't know that for sure, do you?" Daniel dropped Denida's hand and strode in a circle around Nina.

Nina's friend approached her and dragged her away.

Denida stared into the distance.

"What are you thinking about?" Daniel nudged his dad's arm.

"None of our friend's souls have appeared, yet. Maybe we should try the astral route."

"To go home?" Daniel smiled.

"It's worth a shot." Denida closed his eyes and started chanting.

Daniel licked his lips.

This isn't going to work. Denida opened his eyes after a moment, frowning at his son. *Probably because Daniel doesn't have a human form.*

"Now what?"

"I don't know, but I have a feeling..." Denida peered in the direction that Nina had gone, followed by his human form.

"That won't get us back," Daniel muttered.

"We should follow Nina!" Denida jogged after the children, catching up to them.

Daniel followed close behind him.

Nina stopped and spun around.

"You feel something, again?" Nina's friend asked.

Nina nodded and peered around, then sighed. "Being special is so irritating." She turned and led her friend away.

"She's always been very sensitive." Gabriel appeared beside them.

"Gabriel! What brings you here?" Denida barely managed to get the question out before Daniel pushed him aside to greet the archangel.

"It is pretty here, but it's not where you belong, is it?" Gabriel smiled.

Now faced with Gabriel's apparent omniscience, Denida chuckled, smiling down at Daniel. *Is this how my son feels every time I say something that doesn't make sense to him?*

"Isn't there somewhere here, where you feel at home… where somebody might have left something just for you to find?" Gabriel locked eyes with Denida, his tone cryptic.

Denida drew his eyebrows together, understanding that to be a hint, however vague. He decided to take it and pondered what he might have missed. *A place where I feel at home? A place someone would think to leave something for me? Who would have done that, anyway?*

"Wasn't there someone on your travels throughout the Underworlds who said that he would leave something for you?" Gabriel's voice jittered right along with his fidgety movements.

The mysterious guy from the past! But where?

"A place that is important to your human side, perhaps?" Gabriel poked Denida's chest, right over his heart. The action released one of Denida's memories, and he smacked his forehead.

"Thanks, Gabriel!" Denida dashed off.

Daniel sighed and scurried to catch up with his father.

When Denida stopped beside the Gate, Daniel sat on the ground and huffed for air. "We already tried the Gate."

"We're not here for the Gate!" Now that he was here, Denida couldn't be sure where exactly the secret hiding spot would be. *Everything in these woodlands looks the same. Just trees and bushes.* He gazed out over the lakes.

"It's pretty here. What's this spot called?"

"The Paradise Lakes." Denida turned to Daniel. A tree with a split trunk stood behind Daniel.

"Come on," Denida stepped up to the tree and ran his finger along it, tracing it with his eyes, until he spotted a white rock. They approached the rock, and Denida climbed up on top of it, searching for a noticeable gap between the trees. They sauntered out of the woods into a tiny clearing, which overlooked the lakes. Denida had never brought another person here, not even Nina. He knelt in the grass. "A special place, where somebody left something for me." The ground glowed under his hand, and light shimmered up between his fingers. Denida dug through the earth until he uncovered the top an old, wooden box. The box had the Underworld symbol and his initials carved into it. *How is this possible?*

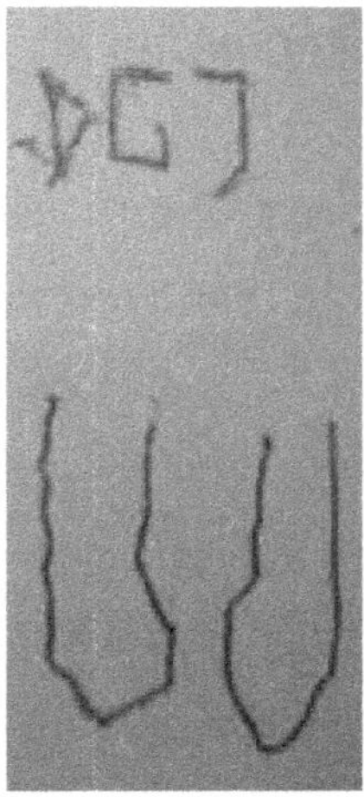

Denida's hand trembled as he lifted the box up out of the hole. He cautiously placed it on the ground and filled the hole with dirt.

Daniel grabbed the box and tried to open it, but the top wouldn't budge, even as he yanked it as hard as he could.

Denida extended his hand, and Daniel turned his eyes down, handing him the box. A spirit appeared above the box, almost startling Denida enough to make him drop it again, while Daniel scuttled back.

"You came, Denny." The spirit of the mysterious man, the president over all the Underworlds, smiled at him. "I've long awaited your arrival. The time has come for you to take your place."

My place?

The spirit nodded at Denida. "I left it here, in the real world. I ensured that it was in a place that only you would be able to find, and only when you were ready. Your soul needed to mature before you could handle the object in this box."

Denida blinked, very intrigued.

"I ruled over all the Underworlds until your arrival; everything changed the day you were born. God wanted you dead, and the Devil wanted your soul, but I had bigger plans for you. I wanted to give you something stronger than them both combined: access to the power of the soul of the Underworlds themselves."

Is that really true?

"You saw the smallest sample of what I could do with that power when we met briefly in the past. In this box, which only you can open, the ring awaits you."

The spirit started to fade away. "You're the only one who can wield this power. Good luck."

As the spirit vanished, Denida peeked at the box. He drew in a deep breath and willed it to open. The box glowed brighter and brighter until Denida couldn't look at it without squinting. When the light had vanished, a ring lay in his palm where the box had been.

The ring felt like it was made of the same material as the Gate, and it had the UW symbol engraved into it.

"Put it on, Dad." Daniel grinned.

Denida slowly slid the ring onto his finger. Like a key in a lock, it revealed all his memories and what he had to do next. "It's finally time to go home, Daniel." Denida's heart pounded quickly in anticipation of Nina's smile.

"How? The Gate still doesn't work."

Denida laughed, the sound echoing back from across the lake.

"We don't need the Gate." He held out his hand, and the ring flickered, creating a silvery portal in front of him.

"Wow, cool!" Daniel jumped up to stand beside Denida, grabbing his hand.

Denida felt Daniel's confidence empowering him, giving him a warm, larger-than-life sort of sensation, resembling their new bond.

Gabriel stood in the forest, now beside them. "So, the time has finally come, Denny."

Denida nodded to the archangel, then stepped through the portal to head back home with Daniel.

Chapter 31- Back Home

Denida exited the portal, only to encounter a dozen soldiers, pointing automatic weapons at him. He used magic to create an invisible shield around himself and Daniel.

"Freeze!" a soldier in sergeant's stripes commanded.

"You work for Claus, I presume?" Denida rested his hand on Daniel's shoulders to keep him close.

"We have Susan; surrender, now." The men stepped closer.

Denida glanced down at Daniel. "What do you say?"

Daniel clenched a fist and punched his open palm. "Show 'em what you've got!"

Denida smirked. "Stay close." Denida glared at the soldiers. "We've decided not to surrender. You'll just have to shoot us."

The sergeant's eyes bugged out, but he shrugged. "It's your funeral. Fire!"

All the soldiers opened fire, and in a few seconds, their magazines clicked, empty.

Denida grinned at them. "You want to reload and try again, or shall we move on?"

A soldier peeked at the sergeant, who reloaded his weapon.

"We've got all day." The sergeant drew in a deep breath to yell a command, but Denida rubbed the ring with his thumb.

"Sadly, we don't." Denida waved his hand, as he remembered the mysterious man doing so long ago. The guards flew backwards, smashing into some rocks, their guns bending and shattering. Denida sauntered over to the sergeant, who scrambled for a knife, but Denida reached down and flipped it away from him, followed by anything else even vaguely resembling a weapon.

All around them, the soldiers groaned as their gear was ripped away from them, as though stolen by a magnet. Their gear formed a pile behind Denida.

Denida knelt beside the sergeant. "You mentioned Susan. Where is she?"

"I won't tell you that."

"You'll regret that decision."

"You can't…"

Denida rested his finger on the sergeant's forehead and let his eye flicker red. "I suggest you tell me. I've heard that having information ripped from your mind is quite unpleasant."

"The cabin!" the sergeant chirped. "Claus took her to the cabin."

"All of you, sleep until I can deal with you properly." With a flick of his hand, the sergeant and his soldiers fell into a deep slumber. *That Donaldson is still rotten…*

Denida and Daniel left the snoring soldiers to head to the cabin. Denida heaved in a sigh, knowing that his friend and political ally had committed treason.

When they arrived at the cottage, Denida chanted a spell, which he enforced with the ring, putting the soldiers patrolling outside to sleep as well. He used magic to drag their weapons out of reach. "Want to have some fun?" He raised an eyebrow at Daniel. "Go knock on the door; I'll take care of everything."

Daniel gleefully rubbed his hands together.

Denida positioned himself near a window so he could see everything inside the cabin.

Daniel knocked on the door and one of the soldiers answered it. "What?" He glared down at Daniel.

"I'm here for Susan." Daniel waved his hand, just like Denida had at the Gate.

Denida waved the ring, flinging all the guards in the cabin into a wall, knocking them out.

Daniel strolled into the cabin and pointed his finger at the chains, so Denida made them shatter.

The expressions on Susan's and Dan's faces made Daniel laugh harder than he had since the whole adventure began.

Denida teleported into the cabin. "Hi, miss me?"

Dan stared at Denida, then at Daniel. "How?"

"Magic." Denida grinned, trying not to burst out laughing like his son had.

Susan ran up to Denida, embracing him tightly. "I'm so glad you're alright. We were worried about you!"

Denida hugged her back, then hugged Dan too, elated to have made it home.

When the three of them exited the cabin, a row of military trucks drove to the roadside, surrounding them and the cabin. Just as before, several soldiers came out, circling them, prepared to raise their weapons.

Susan and Dan raised two guns, which they had snatched from the soldiers.

Denida raised his hand, stopping his friends. "It's alright."

A soldier lowered his gun. "Denida? Colonel, you'll definitely want to see this!"

The Colonel stepped out of the truck. He ran up to Denida and stopped in front of him. "It's you! You're back… and alive!" He glanced around at Claus's mercenaries, seeing them fast asleep. "You didn't leave much for us to do, did you?"

"There are mercenaries at the Gate, and inside, who could stand to be arrested."

The Colonel's troops saluted and marched forward, now capturing the mercenaries.

"Come." The Colonel led Denida, Dan, and Susan to one of the military vehicles.

As they walked, Denida clapped the Colonel on the back. "So, bring me up to date on everything that's happened in my absence."

The Colonel talked about the lab, the robots, Nina's distrust of Claus, and his own decision to send Dan after Claus after discovering his collusion with Lucifer.

At Dynasty, Denida handed Dan a car key and instructed him to go get Nina before Claus did anything to her.

***

Nina paced outside the lab, smoking. The Colonel had gone to rescue Dan, and she hoped they'd discover Susan with him. The techs were still busy, flitting about the lab. Claus had been MIA for a while, making Nina tremble with anxiety.

One of the cars from Dynasty pulled up to the curb, and Dan leaned out the window.

"Dan!" Nina tossed her cigarette on the pavement and ran up to him. "You're safe and unhar-"

Dan laid his finger on her lips to stop her, and Nina took a deep breath. "The Colonel sent me to bring you to Dynasty." Dan smiled.

Nina sprinted around the car and climbed in. No matter what she asked, Dan wouldn't divulge anything. He bore a huge grin and hummed a merry, little tune, but his lack of information was starting to bother Nina.

Just as she frowned, Dan spoke up. "We got Susan back, too."

"Won't Claus find us at Dynasty?" Nina asked, but while Dan's face twitched, he waved his hand and insisted that Claus wasn't a concern anymore. That distracted Nina until they pulled up to Dynasty's front gate. *A lot of activity, here.*

The Colonel's secret unit was setting up a temporary base out front with Susan among their ranks, at least for now.

Nina stepped out of the car, gasping. *The Colonel clearly meant business.*

"Mom!" A cry came from behind her.

Nina's heart stopped, and she spun so fast that she dropped to her knees, as Daniel threw himself into her arms. She embraced her son as tightly as she could, praying that this wasn't just some cruel illusion. The sensation of his warm body released a floodgate, and Nina let everything around her fade as her heart leapt with joy while a tear trickled down her cheek. When she finally released Daniel to look him over, Daniel reached out and wiped her tears away.

"It's okay, Mom. Everything's alright now." Daniel smiled, bearing a powerful, wonderful resemblance to his father.

"I told you I'd bring him back." Denida stood beside Nina, smiling broadly.

"You did!" Nina wiped her tears away on her sleeve. Without letting go of Daniel, she stood up, facing Denida, pulling Daniel along with her. "You did!" Nina repeated with tears of joy causing her voice to shake. *Thank you.*

The couple shared a deep gaze, which contained a thousand words.

The Colonel cleared his throat. "We still have to deal with Claus!"

Denida faced the Colonel. "Not just Claus. We have Lucifer, too!"

Denida led Nina and Daniel to the secret room under Dynasty. The door swung open as he approached it. "This is more than a secure area; it is also the best place in the Underworld to keep someone safe."

Inside, Nina could see screens showing images from all over the Underworld. A computer sat on the desk, connected to the Underworld's server.

"Nina, Daniel, you'll stay here with Susan and Dan. They'll keep you safe. The Colonel and I need to deal with my dear vice president."

***

Claus waltzed into the cottage, and a smile fell from his face. *Where is everyone?*

Claus hurried back out to the Gate. *Nobody's here, either. Lucifer must've crossed me again!* Claus's gut twisted. He ran back to his car and turned on the ignition.

"Going somewhere?" Lucifer sat in the passenger seat, leering at him. "You failed to capture Denida, I see."

Claus was about to utter his defense, but Lucifer interrupted him before he could.

"Don't worry; you don't need to justify this little slip up, seeing as I never expected you to succeed!" Lucifer grinned. "But you do have to bring him to me if you treasure your freedom!"

"I will," Claus vowed.

"Denida's demonic side has returned; I can sense it!" Lucifer tossed back his head as if bathing in a wonderful sensation. With a smirk, he disappeared into thin air.

Claus sighed. *How am I supposed to get him, now?* But he had to, or Lucifer would take him, instead. Denida had weaseled his way through his trap, so Claus had nothing left to catch him. He didn't have any demons to manipulate for a contingency plan, not since the fall of the Dark Angels, anyway. He had the Scientist up until a few days ago, but he was dead, now.

***

Lucifer appeared beside Jack.

"Master." Jack nodded to him.

"I need you to do something for me. Claus is unlikely to succeed on his own. Make sure he does. If he fails, send me his soul." Lucifer's eyes reddened. "I will not permit you to have any personal contact with Denida. If Claus fails, I will take Denida back myself!"

"I will keep an eye on him, but why is Denida so important to you? Why not just kill him and take his soul the old-fashioned way?" Jack suddenly recoiled as Lucifer glared at him.

"God wanted to kill him. He didn't realize how strong Denida could be. The power within him, the potential he holds. I want that. I want his soul, and his power, to be mine!" Lucifer leaned in close. "That's all you need to know."

Chapter 32- End of Claus

Claus sat at his desk, trying to think of new ways to embezzle the government's money. Two heavily armed mercenaries replaced his secretary. They made him feel safe, but they didn't take calls or make coffee for him, even at his request. Eventually, Claus added the mercenaries to the government payroll to enable himself to hire more of them. There was no shortage of veterans-turned-civilians dying for a change of pace, so Claus easily built up his force again, using money he had syphoned. *It probably won't help with Denida; he's slippery, but it's me or Lucifer.* Claus shuddered. He eyed his computer screen, which locked up in the middle of use.

"Ready for the endgame, Claus?" A message scrolled across his screen.

"Who are you?" Claus typed, fearing the answer he was expecting.

"Who do you think? I'm back. Have you already forgotten about me?" The message appeared.

"So what? I still have all the Underworld's resources at my fingertips."

"That won't stop me. Get ready; I'm coming for you."

Claus peered around the room suspiciously. Just how many people were watching him? He opened a drawer and withdrew his gun.

One of his guards shot him a puzzled glance.

"Follow me." Claus meandered through headquarters and down to his car. Once next to it, he slapped his head. *Denida's given away his location; he can only access the server from one location.* Claus grinned. *Let's see how you react to my forces capturing you in your own home.* Claus picked up his phone while his guards drove him away.

The rest of his mercenaries joined him at Dynasty's front gate. Claus drove past the unmanned security check, followed by his little army. Denida wouldn't expect a full-scale attack.

***

Jack followed the convoy to Dynasty but when he tried to enter the estate, a magic shield burned him, and he recoiled.

A trap. Jack raked his eyes over the green lawns a few feet away. The shield inhibiting dark magic was beyond his aptitude.

"Reficul, Reficul, Reficul!" Jack chanted.

Lucifer appeared right next to Jack.

"Claus entered. I cannot follow!" Jack gritted his teeth.

Lucifer frowned. "If you want anything done right, you have to do it yourself!" Lucifer sauntered forward, until the shield burned him, throwing him back. He disappeared, then reappeared, smoking slightly, his eyes flaming red. "That's not dark magic... he has the ring! Where did he find it?" The fire surrounded Lucifer before he vanished, leaving behind a circle of charred dirt.

***

"I don't like this." Claus's commanding officer surveyed their surroundings as they drove closer to the mansion. "We should have seen them by now."

"We can't stop; it's now or never!"

Claus ordered the lead vehicle to crash through Dynasty's front doors. Before the dust even settled, men poured out of their vehicles to follow the vehicle into Dynasty.

Claus caught a glimpse of the butler in the foyer. He was holding a rocket launcher.

"No way." Claus turned to the commander. "Fall back!"

The commander was already relaying the order into a radio, but the vehicle exploded before the men could move. Injured mercenaries crawled away from the flames, as soldiers poured out from around the house's corners. The remaining mercenaries turned to engage them, but their commander ordered them to retreat.

"Morons!" Claus shouted at the commanding officer. "We're not retreating. It's now or never; attack!"

Claus's commander shook his head. "We can't win; they're too well prepared..."

Claus grabbed his gun and pistol-whipped his commander before shoving him out of the vehicle. He turned the vehicle around, but artillery had lined up behind him, blocking his escape. He saw a familiar figure directing the battle, *the Colonel*... and drove straight at him.

Shells struck Claus's vehicle, flipping it over, and filling its interior with dust and shrapnel. Claus ran through the thick cloud of debris, listening to the Colonel yelling orders to triangulate his position, but the Colonel pointed his handgun at Claus as he drew near.

Claus yanked one of the Colonel's soldiers over to him and held his gun to the soldier's head.

"What are you doing, Claus?" The Colonel gritted his teeth.

"Getting out of here!" Claus shouted. "I'll kill him if you don't let me out."

The Colonel signaled for his troops to let him pass. "I'll let you go; just release him. Claus, if you do this, your reputation will never recover!"

"I passed the point of no return a long time ago," Claus hissed.

Claus dragged the soldier into the forest with the Colonel tracking him. He'd trade the soldier for Denida. *Maybe this wasn't a complete disaster, after all.*

"Call Denida! Tell him I'll release this soldier if he comes with me."

"I don't think so." The Colonel crossed his arms.

Claus's face scrunched up with anger. "I'll shoot you." Claus aimed his gun at the Colonel's leg.

The soldier grabbed the gun and twisted it away, before Claus escaped into the woods.

"Is that what you wanted?" The soldier asked the Colonel.

The Colonel nodded.

Claus ran deep into the forest. He couldn't hear anyone following him, so he knew he must have made a clean getaway, even though he'd lost his best chance to capture Denida. *Time to get out of the forest and figure out how to wrap things up.* He stopped, whipping his head back and forth. *Which way's out?*

A feeling compelled Claus forward. He wrestled through thick brush and climbed in and out of ravines. His cold feet were soaked, and painful scratches covered his hands. Just as daylight was fading, he emerged into a clearing with a cottage in it. A faint light burned in the window.

Claus circled the edge of the clearing, but his stomach rumbled, and his gut told him it was safe. *A nice, old couple can invite me in for tea and a late supper. They'll let me dry off. It should be safe for a while, since it seems the Colonel lost my trail.*

He knocked on the door. No one answered, but the door swung open. Inside, a fire burned and offered Claus a chance to warm up. He stepped inside to stand in front of the fire. Then, as if someone had removed a blindfold, he peeked around. *It's a trap.* As he turned to flee, the door slammed shut.

"Hello, Claus," a cold voice greeted him.

Denida! Claus drew his gun as he spun to face his old friend. His gun slipped from his hand and soared across the room as if he'd thrown it.

"Why don't we sit down? We wouldn't want to be hit by any more flying objects." Denida sat down, crossing his legs.

Claus didn't want to join him, but somehow, he was no longer in control of his body. His legs bent, forcing him to sit in front of the fireplace.

Denida poured Claus a cup of tea. "I understand you've been busy."

If only I could summon Lucifer. Claus's hands automatically grasped the teacup.

"You can't!" Denida smiled at him.

"Oh!" Claus's face fell, understanding that Denida had read his mind, just like Nina.

Denida sipped his tea. "That must be some deal you made with Lucifer but you should really know that he never keeps his word."

"Never?" Claus's hands trembled, rattling the teacup on its saucer.

Denida shook his head.

Claus wanted to throw the tea into the fire, but his hands wouldn't cooperate. *So, either Lucifer was playing me, or Denida is trying to do that, now.*

"Naturally, he played you." Denida smiled.

"Enough!" Claus yelled. "I am so fed up with you and Nina always reading my mind. What about giving me some privacy?"

Denida set his teacup aside and stood, facing Claus. His eyes appeared more sad than angry. "I wanted to see you to see if you really were as rotten as all the versions of you in the other worlds."

Warm hope rose inside of Claus. "Yes? Then, you see that I am still the same person I've always been!"

"I know." Denida knelt next to him. "I see that you were always corrupt, just like your counterparts in the other worlds, taking advantage of any opportunity, any means, to seize power, no matter the cost."

Claus wanted to object to that but unlike himself, he could see that Denida had changed.

"I feel responsible for not seeing it from the start, so for that, I apologize!" Denida frowned.

Behind them, the door opened, and someone entered the cottage.

"Ah, Susan!" Denida smiled over Claus's shoulder.

"I need to go settle things with Lucifer. I'll leave you with Susan." Denida patted Claus on the shoulder. "I understand that you two became very close." He approached the door. "Goodbye, Claus." The door closed behind Denida.

Claus tried to turn to see Susan, but his body still wouldn't cooperate. "Is anybody there?" He tried to stand, but his legs refused to move.

Susan paced in front of him. "Hello, Claus."

The hairs on his neck stood on end.

"So, the shoe is on the other foot, now. How's it feel?" Susan smirked at him.

Claus's gut clenched. *What can she do to me?* Did Denida care if Claus lived or died? He shuddered to think that his fate could come down to Denida's compassion.

Susan sat in Denida's chair and poured herself a cup of tea. "Relax; unfortunately, Denida wants you alive, but we get to spend some quality time together while he deals with Lucifer." Susan sipped her tea and stared into the fire.

"So, he really knows the Devil?"

Susan chuckled, then turned to Claus. "Lucifer taught him a lot. Apparently, Denida spent a long time in Hell. He's escaped twice but hasn't forgotten what it was like. Or what he learned."

That explains why Lucifer wants Denida, but not what's going to happen to me. Crap. "You don't have permission to kill me, so what exactly are you planning to do to me?" Claus asked shakily.

"I wanted to kill you, but Denida believes you should face a longer punishment than the mercy death would grant you." Susan smirked at Claus. "You won't die unless someone kills you, so get ready to be locked up for eternity."

"I'll escape." Claus glared at her.

"You think so? You don't even know what prison you'll be in!"

Someone knocked on the door.

"They're here for you." Susan's eyes reflected the flames from the fire, reminding Claus of Lucifer.

Claus clenched his fists, finding it to be the only movement he could muster.

Susan smiled sweetly. "I'll sleep so much better knowing that you're locked away. I wish I could say that it was nice knowing you."

Soldiers in Underworld uniforms marched into the cottage and restrained Claus with chains.

"Shall we?" Claus almost laughed in relief. *Denida is going to help me escape from Lucifer's deal.*

***

Denida meandered into his office in headquarters. *The place reeks of Claus. I'll have to get Nina to redecorate it for me.*

"Reficul… Reficul… Reficul!" Denida chanted. Just as he had anticipated, Lucifer appeared in front of him. "Hello again, Lucifer."

"Hello, Denny. Are you ready to come home with me?" Lucifer grinned as if he believed he'd already won.

"No, and I never will!" Denida scoffed. "I've called you here to demand that you stop trying to get me to return."

"Never." Lucifer's eyes flared red. "You belong in Hell."

"Really? You don't have anyone left here. The Dark Angels were yours, but my friends and I defeated them. They're all gone!"

Lucifer paced throughout the office. "Nice office you've got, here. I visited Claus in this room many times." He turned to Denida "How is Claus, by the way?"

"Apprehended!" Denida waved dismissively. "Just like the rest of his holdouts. It's over!"

Lucifer smiled, and his red eyes glowed. "Is it, now? Even after visiting all those worlds, you still haven't learned that I don't lose?"

Denida rose and peered into Lucifer's eyes. "Are you saying that I didn't beat you the first time you came to the Wild West World? I never escaped Hell, not once, but twice? Every time we've gone toe-to-toe, you've lost."

Lucifer's eyes burned bright red, and his clothes began to smoke.

"And yes, I did all that before I had this." Denida removed a glove on his left hand and waved the ring on his finger in front of Lucifer. "It's over." Denida clenched his fist. "You're just going to embarrass yourself."

Lucifer burst into flames as Darkness filled the room. Dark magic twisted and tore open a portal to Hell. Denida found himself standing in Lucifer's throne room. He saw Nina and Daniel in chains, staring at him, shaking in horror.

"Don't leave me here, Dad," Daniel pleaded.

Tears ran down Nina's cheeks. The sight of them wrenched Denida's heart.

"Stay with me, and they'll return to your world." The flames around Lucifer vanished.

"Nice try." Denida waved his hand, and the visage of Nina and Daniel transformed into reality, now revealing two restrained demons. With another wave of his hand, Denida swept Lucifer back to his office. "You're forgetting my memories are back; I remember your tricks."

"The ring." Lucifer's shoulders slumped for just a moment. "I have more demons here, and on Earth."

"If you weren't the Devil, I'd admire your tenacity." Denida sat down and steepled his fingers. "Did Gabriel tell you that I met Heavani?"

Lucifer became very still, and pain flitted through his eyes.

"She is your Achilles heel, isn't she? I understand why you want me but you're not getting me. Stop embarrassing yourself. The pain you suffered when you lost Heavani is what made you turn to the Darkness. I don't want Nina and Daniel to hurt like that, just like you don't want Heavani and your Daniel to suffer, either."

"What do you have in mind?" Lucifer slumped into a chair.

"Claus failed you, so he's yours. Take him, and we're even."

Lucifer stared at Denida for a long time, then straightened up.

Gotcha. "Do we have a deal?" Denida extended his hand and waited. He could see the gears turning in Lucifer's head. It gave Lucifer an out and ensured Heavani's safety.

Lucifer stood and took Denida's hand. "Deal."

***

In Claus's transport van, soldiers kept their weapons trained on Claus, even though he could hardly move in his chains.

A cellphone rang up front. The commander answered, said "yes," and hung up.

"We have the go-ahead." He tapped on the driver's shoulder, and they took the next turn.

Claus's heart sank. *For what?* "Aren't you taking me to the prison?"

"We're taking you back to the cottage!" the commander replied.

Claus's stomach ached as he tried to process this turn of events. *If you lock me up there, it'll be extremely easy to escape!*

"We're here!" the soldier sitting opposite him announced.

The soldiers climbed out and surrounded Claus, loosening the chains to allow him to walk. His stomach sank as they approached the second Gate.

Two people waited for him. They turned with identical smiles.

"Hello." Lucifer waved.

"Claus." Denida smirked.

Claus tried to break free but fell flat on his face.

"God will be disappointed that he didn't kill you," Lucifer said to Denida, then approached Claus and pulled him to his feet.

"Wait! What's happening, here?" Claus demanded. "Why are you two together?"

"I told you that you'd pay if you failed me!" Lucifer yanked Claus forward as his eyes met Denida's. "Selling his soul to save your own hide... oh, how impressed I am, Denida."

Claus tried to pull away, but Lucifer's grip was as tight as a vice. Darkness filled the air, and the black storm devoured Claus, causing his scream of terror to ring in the air.

"Always a pleasure, Denida." Lucifer grinned. "Until next time!"

"There won't be a next time," Denida asserted, but Lucifer just smiled.

"Wait!" Claus attempted to wrest free of the chains and the Darkness around him. "There's a way I can-"

Lucifer wrapped his hands around Claus's neck, and, with crimson eyes, he dug his nails into Claus's skin.

Claus emitted an agonized scream, just before disappearing with Lucifer.

Epilogue

Spring freshened the air again. Green had returned to the trees, giving them a more graceful appearance. Birds sang in the distance. Denida sat, enjoying the sights, finally enjoying the forest that he always loved.

It had been a long trip, after all, and a lot had changed over the course of it. He started wearing a patch over his bad eye, so that nobody would be able to see its red glow when his darker side took control.

Denida had only one thing left to do; he needed to tell Daniel about his memories, what he'd been trained for, and how he had escaped Hell… in short, everything.

"Dad?" Daniel left Nina's side and waltzed through the woods to meet him. "Mom said you wanted to talk."

Denida nodded. "Sit." Denida drew in a deep breath. "I wanted you here so that I could finally tell you something. I guess I should start at the beginning."

Denida glanced around the forest, before he began. "God had a goddess, once upon a time. On her deathbed, she prophesized that a child would be born. He would hold the power required to set all wrongs right. On Christmas, when I was born, God and the Devil believed that the time had come…"

Thank you for reading *No Way Back- The Underworlds*. If you enjoyed this book (or even if you didn't) Please write a brief review.

Your feedback is important to me and will help other readers decide whether to read the book too.

Sneak peek on the sequel, *Taken With a Dark Desire: The Underworlds.*

Prologue

Screams of terror sounded in all directions, but Claus was not concerned, as he had his own terror to deal with. Time in Hell felt eternal for each soul. Claus might have been suffering torment for decades as time passed differently here than in the Underworld, as it did between the Underworld and Earth.

Claus held onto his sanity by nursing his hatred for Denida who'd handed him over to Lucifer.

"Enjoying yourself?" Lucifer appeared and gave a devious grin.

Lucifer never paid the slightest attention to the torture surrounding him, somehow making the suffering worse, Claus had noticed.

Fear and anger warring in Claus's soul, he glared at Lucifer.

"What do you expect? I'm in Hell, not on vacation," Claus spat out discontent.

Lucifer just smiled back at him. "What would you say, if I had a way for you to buy back your freedom, a way to get back at Denida?"

The same damn smug look on Lucifer's face he remembered from the Underworld, but painful hope blossomed in Claus.

"How?"

Lucifer's smile broadened and suddenly they were inside his throne room.

I know this place. The lack of torment made Claus dizzy. Denida was here, this is Lucifer's throne, where the Gate is!

"Denida has two weaknesses. Nina and Daniel," Lucifer said. "Nina is too headstrong… Daniel on the other hand…" Lucifer chuckled.

Am I hearing right? "You want me to kidnap Daniel? Why?"

Lucifer chuckled. "Denida with his ring is too strong even for me. Bring me the ring, you have your freedom!"

Claus's mouth twisted into a smile. *My freedom!* And a way to make Denida suffer too. Anything was bound to be better than being tortured in hell, after all.

Claus's hatred and hope burned in his soul. "I like that idea."

"We have a deal then?" Lucifer held out his hand.

Claus had a small glint of red within his eyes as he grabbed Lucifer's hand and shook it. "We do!"